BRICK

CONRAD JONES

Copyright © 2016 Conrad Jones
All rights reserved.
ISBN:153473306X
ISBN-13:978-1534733060

PROLOGUE

'Let's take a selfie with your phone, upload it to your Facebook page and see how many likes, shares and comments you get before you bleed to death,' Tucker said with a twisted smile. The man who was strapped to a chair in front of him was semiconscious. His eyes rolled backwards into his head and blood-filled saliva dribbled through his broken teeth and onto his chin before trickling onto his chest, dangling like a gooey stalactite. Tucker switched the Samsung to camera mode and held it above the injured man. He adjusted the phone so that the image would have maximum impact, his swollen face, twisted fingers and the bullet holes in his kneecaps, all included. 'You had better hope that someone you know wants to save your life, David, or you'll die here.' He squeezed Johnson's shattered knee with one hand and took the photo with his other. The injured man's body convulsed with pain. 'Or you could stop all this by telling me where my container is.'

David Johnson whimpered; the sound was like a mewing cat. His bloodshot eyes pleaded for mercy, but none was forthcoming. Tucker typed a message above the photo, pressed the share button and posted the image onto Johnson's Facebook account. He grinned as the seconds ticked by; shocked responses appeared on the timeline almost immediately.

'Last chance saloon, David,' Tucker said holding up the phone to his face so that he could read the responses. 'I don't understand why you're protecting them. Either your brother or one of your retarded cousins stole it didn't they?' the injured man shook his head in the negative and mumbled incoherently. Blood dripped onto a plastic sheet that had been spread beneath the chair, sounding like the ticking of a clock, each drop a precious moment of his life, gone forever. 'Just tell me where it is.' A garbled moan. Another drop of his lifeblood hit the plastic.

'Nine times out of ten, if a container goes missing from the docks, you tossers have stolen it; this time you've stolen the wrong one.' He poked his index finger into the bullet hole on the left knee, one eye on the phone. Johnson jerked violently, the blood flow faster now. 'I want my property back, that's all. You understand that this isn't personal, don't you?' Johnson whimpered again and blood and saliva dribbled from the corner of his mouth. The phone began to beep as dozens of notifications came through. The reaction to the image was both quick and overwhelming, friends and family unsure if it was a twisted joke or something dreadful was happening before their eyes. Tucker read them as they appeared and smiled. 'Wow, that has caused a stir, hasn't it?' he said almost conversationally. Johnson moaned, weaker now. 'Oh, your mother has got a nasty mouth on her hasn't she, little wonder that you're a turd is it?' Tucker seemed genuinely offended. 'She's rude, can you read that?' Despite the serious swelling around his eyes, he held the phone up for Johnson to see. 'Look at that, thirty comments and rising fast. I'm impressed.' Tucker nodded like a man watching a rival team scoring a brilliant goal. 'There are some very concerned comments here, David. Some think it's a sick joke, which I suppose you would, wouldn't you?' Tucker nudged Johnson as if they were old mates sharing a joke. 'Oh, now some people are being very aggressive and making nasty threats. That's understandable.' Tucker shrugged. 'Some have actually liked and shared it. Now that's a bit weird isn't it?' he nudged Johnson again, causing more goo to dribble from his chin. His eyes rolled to the back of his head. 'Mind you when you look at the names of the people who liked it, they're the people who don't really like your family aren't they?' Tucker looked at Johnson for a response and kicked the chair leg when none came. 'This is for your benefit, are you listening?' David Johnson started to shake violently, his body twitching. His eyes all but disappeared into his head, only the whites visible now.

'He's going to bleed to death,' Joseph Tucker's younger brother, Tommy, said nonchalantly. His white decorators' overalls were heavily stained with blood. 'We need to stop those bullet wounds bleeding.' Joe nodded in agreement looking unconcerned, if not a little disappointed. His expression changed when Johnson's mobile rang. The word 'Bro' flashed on the screen.

'You took your time, Mathew,' Tucker said chirpily. 'Poor old David is in a bit of state here but I'm glad you saw his selfie. He's not looking his best, is he?' His tone changed completely. 'Where is my fucking container?'

'Who is this? How have you got Dave's phone?' Mathew Johnson asked angrily. 'Is this some kind of sick joke?'

'It doesn't matter who it is, you've got my container.'

'And you've just posted a photograph of my brother bleeding to death, who is this?'

'Tucker,' he answered with a throaty growl, referring to himself as he was known across the underworld. The silence at the other end of the phone indicated the fear that his name instilled in others. 'Where is my container?'

'Fucking hell, we didn't know it was yours, Joe.'

'You do now. David is struggling here, where's my container?'

'Don't hurt him anymore. It's an empty container for fuck's sake. We took it to sell on quickly,' Mathew Johnson said in a panic. 'We wouldn't have taken it if we had known it was yours.'

'I'll ask you again.' Tucker kicked out David's ruined knee and put the phone next to him. He cried out in pain, an agonised gurgling sound. 'Where is my container?'

'Don't, don't, don't; stop it now, please!' Mathew snapped. 'Don't hurt Dave anymore, please, Joe. Not over an empty container,' Mathew pleaded, his voice as calm as he could keep it. 'Dave doesn't know where it is.'

'I figured that out for myself,' Tucker said with a shrug. 'So, for the last time, where is it?'

'It's been stashed but he doesn't know where it is, honestly!'

'Honestly?' Tucker scoffed. 'Do you even know how to spell that word?'

'Look, I'm really sorry,' Johnson said. He was racking his brains for the next words. 'We didn't know. There's no way that we would have taken it if we had known it was yours.'

'You've said that already,' Tucker said dismissively. 'Your brother is bleeding to death…where is it?'

'That's the thing, Joe,' Mathew said, his voice breaking. 'We steal the empty ones to order.'

'What are you talking about?' Tucker's voice was menacing.

'I've moved it on, but I'll get it back.' he tried to sound convincing. 'It will be tricky, but I'll speak to the buyer and I'll get it back. I'll put it on a lorry myself and bring it to you.' Silence on the line; he wasn't sure if Tucker was still there. 'Don't hurt him anymore, Joe, please. I'll bring the container to you myself just tell me where and when.'

'You had better be quick, Mathew.' Tucker sounded aloof. 'He'll bleed to death otherwise.'

'Get someone to take him to a hospital and I'll bring you the container. You have my word on it.'

'Your word?' Tucker laughed.

'Give me an hour and I'll meet you wherever you want me to. Get Dave to casualty.'

'I don't think so, Mathew. Bring me the container and you can take your brother to hospital yourself.'

Mathew thought about his options for a second. He had none. 'Where?'

'Do you know the old B&Q on Edge Lane?'

'Yeah.'

'There's a car park behind it, used to belong to the bowling alley before they shut down.'

'I know it.'

'You have an hour.' Tucker waited for a response. 'Did you hear me?'

'I heard you. How do I know you'll let him go?'

'You don't, Mathew.' The line went almost silent, only Tucker's breathing could be heard. His voice was cold, full of malice. 'You can't be sure that I won't skin you both alive but one thing you can be sure of is that David will die unless I get my container back, understand?'

'Yes. I'll be there.'

Tucker ended the call and looked at the screen for a while. He removed the back of the Samsung and flicked out the battery and the SIM card so the GPS couldn't be tracked.

'Are we going to let them go, Joe?' Tommy frowned.

'Don't be ridiculous.' Tucker dropped the phone onto the floor and stamped on it. 'Stop his bleeding. I need him alive for the time being. Put him in the van and make sure you bring the petrol.'

CHAPTER 1

Bryn popped his head into the living room where his elderly parents were slowly rotting away inside a cloud of cigarette smoke. The oversized television droned in the corner, the only source of light in the room. It flickered across the heavy drapes that blocked out the daylight while they watched daytime television. A bitter stench drifted from an overflowing ashtray that sat on a low coffee table between their armchairs. It mingled with the greasy aroma of bacon and sausages that had hung in the air since breakfast and that would still be there until teatime. They ate the same thing every morning, relishing their cholesterol-soaked breakfast, washed down with a mug of tea and a Marlboro. His older brothers called them 'Mum's artery hardening butties'. Bryn knew that their chronic ill health was the result of their lifestyle and he worried continually that he would be left an orphan before finishing his education. They smoked as much as they liked, ate whatever they wanted without thinking about the nutritional value and drank every night until the bottle was empty, never moving from their armchairs except to go to the toilet. Their idea of five-a-day was the number of cans of extra strong lager they drank between meals.

It hadn't always been like that. Barbara and Robert Evans met when they were ambitious young managers at a tour operator chain. They spent their best years working for them, travelling the world to review new destinations and maintain communications with existing ones. As holidays moved online the company struggled and then eventually crashed. Knowing nothing else, their lives spiralled out of control. Following the collapse, neither of them managed to hold down a job for more than a few years and their health began to deteriorate. They defaulted on the mortgage and lost their marital home, forcing the family to move into social housing. The bailiffs took the car on the back of a low loader.

On benefits, their life was very different, no more foreign holidays, no treats for the kids. They fell into a mutual depression, anaesthetised by alcohol, and rarely ventured out onto the estate.

Simon and Mark were their oldest boys and coped better with their addictions. Bryn was born late in their lives and had grown up watching them sitting in their armchairs, losing the will to live. The television was their only window into the world, and they spent their waking hours glued to it.

Bryn glanced at the widescreen television; one of their favourites was on. Jeremy Kyle, spouting his usual pompous shite at a succession of intellectually challenged benefit leaches. They couldn't work because of numerous disabilities but could manage to have sex and churn out children at the same rate as a small African nation. His parents being on disability allowance was a major embarrassment to Bryn at school, but at least they didn't flaunt the fact, not like the spongers who lined up to go on Kyle. He wondered if having no front teeth was a prerequisite to being invited onto the show. His teenage imagination was baffled by the concept of the programme and why people wanted to go on it. Surely the stigma would stop most people, especially the liars. What about their poor kids at school? As if it wasn't hard enough to get on in the inner-city schools without your mum going on Jeremy Kyle to find out who your dad actually is, rather than, who she thought it could be. What on earth were they thinking?

'I'm lying to my girlfriend about shagging her best mate, so the best thing to do is phone Jeremy Kyle and ask him to conduct a lie detector test so that rather than just her knowing that I'm a lying bastard, half the country will know?'

It didn't make sense to Bryn's young mind. He wondered how the interviews to appear on the show were conducted.

'Have you decided how many men could be the father of your third child?'

'Not for sure. I slept with two or three but definitely no more than that.'

'Are any of them your current husband?'

'Oh, I forgot about him. That would be four if we include him.'

'Smile into the camera, please. No front teeth, perfect. She's on. Make sure she doesn't wash her hair before the show and give her some leggings a few sizes too small from wardrobe, perfect. That's Tuesday's show sorted.'

Leaning against the doorframe, Bryn shook his head and smiled at the scenario while Kyle lectured another dentally challenged muppet about using a condom.

'Next time put something on the end of it…' Bryn shook his head. He wondered how the interviewee had managed to find a woman to have sex with once never mind a second time. Bryn had had a few girlfriends but not even a sniff at sex. He had felt Casey Welling's tit through her jumper but then her brother had come home and glared at him. That was as far as his sexual journey had progressed thus far. His friend Leon reckoned he had fingered his girlfriend Suzie, who was a year above them, after she'd drunk three Bacardi Breezers, but she hadn't let him touch her since. Leon reckoned that they were waiting until her parents were away at their caravan in Towyn so that they could actually do it.

Bryn could understand that but how the cretin on Kyle had had numerous sexual partners, multiple times was beyond him. It didn't add up. In school you had to have the latest hairstyle, like the best music, wear the best brands, the newest trainers, smell of the right fragrance and it still wasn't happening for anyone that he knew. It seemed obvious to Bryn that the Kyle creatures didn't care who they shagged. His English teacher had set the class a four-hundred-word essay to be completed before the end of the week. It had to revolve around family values. He didn't think that she watched Kyle, or she would know that there were no family values left in the world. Unless your name is Jeremy of course, then not only do you have values, but you can preach them daily and introduce a stream of fatherless children to their creators for the amusement of the nation. A nation fascinated by the sexual exploits of their lesser intelligent but genetically related fellow humans. Adults were weird.

'I'm taking Alice for a walk,' Bryn said loudly. Neither parent responded, glued to the Kyle programme. He stepped into the room and talked to the mirror sarcastically. 'Are you taking the dog out, Bryn?' he said in his father's voice. 'That will be nice. You be careful in that park,' he said pointing to his reflection with his index finger, warning himself of the possible dangers. 'Don't talk to any of the dirty old perverts that hang around the toilets.' He paused for a reaction, looking at both their faces; none was forthcoming. 'Unless your uncle John is with them, he's a nonce but he's our nonce. You can talk to him.'

'Stop being such a knob and don't talk about your uncle John like that,' his mum said without taking her eyes from the screen. 'He's not a nonce. That was a misunderstanding.'

'The judge and jury didn't think so,' Bryn countered but they didn't look away from the screen. 'Anyway, I'm off to be a knob in the park with the dog.'

'What have I told you about giving your smartarse backchat?' his dad mumbled with a shake of the head.

'I don't think you ever mentioned it, Dad.' Even his sarcasm couldn't break their concentration. To be fair, it looked like a paternity result was about to be revealed by Kyle so he could almost understand their anticipation. 'See you later.' He sighed. Their response was the same, numbed concentration.

He grabbed his bubble jacket from beneath the pile of coats that was permanently on the newel post at the bottom of the banister. Every three months or so, his mother would kick off and hang them all up in the cupboard beneath the stairs. She would threaten terrible things upon any who dared to dump their coats there ever again. The ban would last a few weeks before coats appeared there sporadically, earning the culprits an ear bashing. She would soon become exhausted by the constant monitoring and the pile would slowly begin to grow again. Eventually they would drive her insane and the cycle would repeat itself.

'Come on, girl,' Bryn said to the excited staffie who was circling his feet, wiggling her backside and wagging her tail at a hundred wags a minute. 'Let's go to the park and find me a girlfriend who looks exactly like Jourdan Dunn. You never know who will be walking their dog.' He checked his appearance in the mirror. His closely cropped hair was no more than a dark shadow on his scalp and despite his years, his nose was already slightly misshaped by his hours at the boxing club. He was capable but not a future champion. The girls at school swooned at his blue eyes and broad shoulders but he lacked the confidence to exploit his assets. Alice looked up at him; her staffie smile wrinkled her face. 'Don't look at me like that. A boy can dream.' She had no idea what he was saying but she loved him anyway. Bryn clicked the lead to her collar and headed for the front door.

As he opened the door, the shadow of a large male loomed, approaching quickly. The figure was dressed head to toe in Adidas, the hood pulled over his head covering the top half of his face. Alice reared up onto her back legs and barked excitedly. The man stopped still and swore under his breath as he removed his earphones.

'All right, Squirt,' he said rubbing Alice's head and punching Bryn in the shoulder playfully. 'You made me jump.'

'Try taking your earphones out sometime.'

'What did you say?'

'Funny.'

'Where are you off to, Squirt?'

Bryn held up the lead and shrugged, 'Take a wild guess. I've got the dog on her lead so am I…going shopping, to the snooker hall, swimming, popping down to the gym or none of the above?'

'You're a dick,' his older brother, Mark, punched his shoulder again, harder this time. They trained at the same gym. Mark was six inches taller and two stones heavier than Bryn. His most recent fight was at light heavyweight, a three-round war, which he won on points. Mark was shaping into a successful amateur with the professional ranks in his sights. 'Your smartarse mouth will get you into trouble one day.'

'You sound like the old man.'

'Are they okay?'

'Yep.'

'What are they doing?'

'Watching shite on telly, eating crap and smoking fags.'

'Same routine?'

'Not exactly the same.'

'How come?'

'Well, they got out of bed and cooked a packet of low-fat sausages.' Mark raised his eyebrows in surprise and made an impressed whistling noise. 'Then they added a packet of bacon, placed them between a loaf of bread slathered in butter and ketchup and wolfed the lot in front of the telly.'

'Yes, but low-fat sausages?' Mark cooed. 'That's a step in the right direction. Where are they?'

'In front of the telly.' He smirked sadly. 'And that's where they'll stay until second breakfast.' Mark raised his eyebrows in question. 'It's their snack between breakfast and lunch. Mum's buying low-fat stuff, but they eat more of it.'

'That's one of the reasons I left.' Mark shook his head. 'It's frustrating watching it every day. Good to know that they're following the doctor's orders.'

'They've given up, Mark,' Bryn said walking down the path with his head down. Alice was pulling, eager to go to the park. 'They're just doing whatever they like and waiting to die.'

'They might have the right idea, Squirt.' Mark winked but Bryn noticed that his eyes were touched with sadness. 'You had better get her to the park before she pulls your arm off. I'm going to sit with Mum and Dad for a while. I'll see you when you get back.'

'Okay.' Bryn smiled. Mark was his best friend as well as his brother. 'Are you training later?'

'Of course. I'll give you a few rounds if you like.'

'I don't want to tire you out.'

'Cheeky bugger.'

'See you in a bit. Put the kettle on.'

Mark nodded, waved and closed the door. Bryn waved back and walked down the path. Their garden was a mess in contrast to the neat and tidy ones on either side. His parents rented from a housing association while their next-door neighbours had purchased their homes. It was a similar story across the estate. The privately-owned properties stood out a mile, well maintained, freshly painted with tidy gardens. The rest of the estate ranged from average condition to shit-holes.

'Hello, Bryn,' the elderly neighbour from next door shouted over the fence.

'Hello, Mr Dale,' Bryn said without slowing down. He didn't want to get drawn into a long-winded conversation again. Mr Dale had a habit of wasting thirty minutes of his life every time he walked by.

'Taking the dog for a walk, I see?'

'Yes. We're off to the park for a run.'

'They never used to walk their dogs around here you know,' Mr Dale said with a nod of his head. 'They used to open the front door and let them out on their own!'

'Yes, you've said, Mr Dale.' Bryn nodded, a half-smile on his face. 'Wouldn't get away with that nowadays, Mr Dale,' Bryn said trying to get away.

'You know thirty years ago; the estate was a dump.'

'Yes, you've said that before.'

'A lot of the houses were boarded up, gardens strewn with burnt out cars and discarded sofas,' Mr Dale said putting his pipe into the corner of his mouth. He gazed down the street as if seeing the memories in his mind. 'People dumped stuff anywhere, broken washing machines and fridges became dens and climbing frames for the local kids. It was like a tip in places.' Mr Dale lowered his voice. 'The council moved too many bad apples into this barrel,' he said in a conspiratorial tone, hushed with a knowing wink. 'It was rough back then, I'll tell you, no one walked their dogs on a lead; packs of mongrels roamed the streets, crapping everywhere. You didn't see people walking dogs on a lead back then.'

'It sounds terrible, Mr Dale,' Bryn said edging away slowly, Alice yanking at the lead.

'And imagine if you were seen picking up dog crap in a bag!' he grinned displaying tobacco stained teeth. 'They would have thought that you were completely mad. You would have been arrested and sent to the looney bin!'

'Funny, Mr Dale, anyway I'll have to get going,' Bryn said walking away quickly.

'You don't see white dog shit anymore either,' Mr Dale looked up, happy with his realisation but not aware that Bryn was gone. 'You used to see it everywhere back then,' he said, calling after him. An elderly neighbour was passing by and had only heard half of the conversation. She looked at him with alarm. 'I was just saying to young Bryn, you don't see white dog poo anymore,' he explained, tempering his language for the old lady. 'You'll be old enough to remember white dog poo.'

'Bloody idiot!' the woman snapped and walked on quickly, her head down and shoulder stooped with age.

Mr Dale sighed and looked disappointed, turning back to his garden, any chance of a conversation about the old days gone. When he was a safe distance away, Bryn slowed down. He couldn't imagine those days gone by. Now, the council estates of old had become middle class suburbia. The 'right to buy' schemes had allowed families with nothing to get a foot on the property ladder and the working class became the middle class. But it had also bred resentment between the haves and have-nots. There was no doubt that some of the more unkempt properties were dragging the value of their privately-owned neighbours' houses down. Obviously, the tower blocks in the middle of the estate were different. Three buildings with twenty floors of urban misery packed into them. It was a lottery which neighbours lived above and below, on either side, opposite or indeed, behind. Unlucky occupants could be bombarded with reggae, hard rock, dance, deafening video shoot-em-up games and domestic violence simultaneously and then there were the drug dealers. Their homes were easy to spot, fortified to the maximum with electronic gates and sporting top of the range security cameras. Bryn knew who was dealing, the police knew who was dealing; everyone knew yet it still went on.

Alice bolted along the path. Her claws scrabbled at the pavement, desperate to reach the open fields of the park. Bryn held the lead tight as he closed the gate behind him. The sun was trying hard to break through slate-grey clouds but was failing miserably. There was little warmth in its rays. A sharp wind grasped at his clothes, pulling at his tracksuit bottoms and its icy fingers tickled his scalp. He pulled woolly gloves and a beanie hat from his inside pocket and put them on as they walked briskly through the estate. The pavements were empty, mid-sized saloon cars lined the kerbs, some new, some old and some not far from the scrap yard. An even number of Liverpool and Everton stickers adorned the rear windows of most. Bryn was red but he secretly wanted the blues to do well too as long as they were below Liverpool, although he could never share his thoughts with anyone. The bitter rivalry between the two halves of the city had fallen into insignificance when compared to the hatred between Liverpool and Manchester United fans and no one dare mention the Chelsea rent-boys at school. Asking how they played could earn you a fat lip.

Bryn loved football but money was tight at home. His eldest brother, Simon, had access to a couple of season tickets so he often went to watch his heroes play. Simon was technically his stepbrother, a product of his father's first marriage. He idolised Simon, who was in his thirties, even though he didn't see him very often. Simon spoiled him whenever they went out. Nothing was too expensive; they ate in trendy restaurants where everyone knew his brother and Bryn usually went home with some new jeans or trainers. Simon had done well escaping the estate, escaping the mundane routine of marriage, mortgage and kids, escaping Mum and Dad; Bryn would give anything to escape.

As Bryn approached the local shops, an old copy of the Liverpool Echo unravelled from a litter bin. The front pages hovered in the air for a moment and then blew by on the wind. The headline was familiar.

'Two Russian men gunned down in broad daylight as drug war escalates'

Bryn read the headline but it hardly registered. It was news from a different world, a parallel universe where drugs and money made the planets turn. He didn't know much about the city's criminal underworld apart from the facts that those who ventured into it died violently or spent most of their lives in jail. All the gangsters nowadays were foreign, their names all ended in 'ski' or 'ov'; it was hard for a schoolboy to empathise with foreign criminals. His parents weren't perfect by any stretch of the imagination, but they'd worked hard at stressing the downsides of drugs. Between them and his teachers, he had absolutely no illusions of how dangerous taking or selling drugs could be. The newspaper pages flapped as they tumbled by, their importance as insignificant as the headlines they carried. It was old news and the sad deaths meant nothing to anyone outside of the families involved and they were in Russia. Nobody else cared. Not really. Bryn heard people say that they cared about drugs but unless its effects touched their life directly, then it was just lip service. Why would they care? Their own lives were far more important than those of the people who chose to deal narcotics. Ultimately, it was their choice. As for the dealers, they made a lot of money and either retired abroad, rotted in jail or died young. Why would anyone care about them? Bryn didn't care and he couldn't see why anybody else would. He was going to continue studying hard at school, go to university and leave the estate behind him. Just like Simon had.

Bryn turned the corner and headed past the shops. Bargain Booze, Betfred, the chip shop, Domino's Pizza and the Co-op. The latter attracted the kids from the estate, especially at night. Walking by them could be like running the gauntlet sometimes. Bryn could hold his own in the gym, but he was average size for fourteen. When the older kids were out, he kept his head down and his mouth shut. His older brothers were well known and well respected, so he didn't attract too much abuse. He was thick skinned and could cope with the odd comment or insult. It wasn't worth the hassle to answer back. If you made enemies on the estate, then they usually remained enemies for life. Family feuds lasted from generation to generation. Bryn had no interest in them. He had no intention of sticking around.

As he neared the chip shop, the smell of vinegar drifted to him making his mouth water. They weren't open but the doors were ajar while they heated up the vats and precooked their pies and sausages. The shutters were down on Bargain Booze. No doubt his parents would send him back there later to stock up for the evening's session. Despite being underage, he was often sent on resupply runs. Mark had lent him some ID months ago and never asked for it back. It was easier to let Bryn buy their alcohol. Eight cans of super strength, four each and a bottle of cheap vodka. He dreaded asking for super strength. All his friends at school took the piss out of anyone who drank it.

'Nine per cent proof! Who would drink that fucking stuff? Its tramp juice, that's what it is!'

Tramp juice! His mother and father drank tramp juice every night. That was a detail he kept to himself. Simon knew they'd fallen into a damaging routine, but he was removed from it; Mark knew all about it but pretended it wasn't happening. Bryn had to watch them deteriorate every day. They never mentioned it. Not ever. Three brothers knew that their parents were killing themselves, yet they did nothing to stop them. For as long as Bryn could remember his parents had drunk and probably always would. They drank tramp juice not for enjoyment but for the oblivion it brought. It blotted out everything that they'd lost, for a while at least. He sometimes listened to them reminiscing about places they'd been, tropical beaches and fragrant marketplaces that Bryn could only relate to from the travel programmes they watched religiously. Their happy memories made him sad.

He turned the corner into an alleyway that led towards the park; the wind bit through his clothes and made him shiver. Bryn stopped in his tracks. A small crowd was gathered, blocking his path. Yellow crime scene tape flapped in the breeze and uniformed officers manned the cordon. He nudged his way through to a better vantage point. White clad figures crouched over the bodies of two youths and a forensic tent was being constructed to restrict the public view. Bryn listened to the onlookers gossiping.

'The one nearest is the youngest Johnson boy.'

'Bad bunch, the Johnsons.'

'Mary from the Co-op found them. She was putting rubbish into the skips at the back and said she could smell something funny.'

'I heard they've been shot.'

'Did she see them up close?'

'She said they'd been set on fire. Smelled sickly sweet and made her vomit, she said.'

'Poor Mary.'

'She said they've been battered to a pulp. She couldn't recognise them.'

'How does she know it's one of the Johnsons then?'

'Tattoo on his neck, apparently.'

'Oh, yes. He does have a tattoo. Under his ear it is.'

'Which one is the youngest Johnson?'

'David, I think. Nineteen he is, I think.'

'Was.'

'Drug related, I bet you.'

'Well, you don't have to be Inspector Morse to work that out, Beryl.'

'I'm just saying. Drugs I bet.'

'Wonder who the other lad is? Poor buggers. They don't deserve that, no one does.'

'Drugs. It happens all the time with drugs.'

'You at the bingo later?'

'Double jackpot today.'

'I'll be there. Our Sarah is coming with me.' The tone of the woman's voice became secretive. 'Her fella has pissed off with another woman. She needs a trip to the bingo to cheer her up, bloody shame it is.'

'Ooh, what a bastard. Do her good a trip to the bingo.'

As the conversation changed to the mundane, Bryn made his way out of the alleyway. He took an alternative route, which would take a little longer but would skirt the incident. He weaved his way through the estate until they reached the last row of houses before a zebra crossing that would take them into the park. Alice stopped to sniff a gatepost. Bryn laughed at her and waited while she sniffed the layers of scent built up over years by hundreds of animals who had walked by that way. He looked around while she decoded the doggy messages. It had been a long time since he had ventured to this part of the estate. The gate post belonged to a house that was surrounded with ornate metal railings fixed to a new brick wall. There were cameras on every corner of the building.

'That dog had better not be taking a shit on my pavement!' A voice growled from beyond the high fence. Bryn turned around and saw a morbidly obese man waddling out of his house. He was six feet four at least and Bryn guessed he weighed somewhere between twenty-five and thirty stones. His facial features were almost lost in the fat that surrounded them. He had no cheeks or chin or neck, just rolls of flab that joined his head to his shoulders. Bryn had never seen anyone that huge. 'I'll kick it up the arse! What are you staring at, you gormless scrote?'

Bryn realised that he was staring at the man with his mouth open. 'What?' he mumbled, embarrassed. His face reddened. He looked behind him in case the man was talking to someone else. He noticed that the paving slabs around him were a different colour to the rest of the pavement. The slabs directly in front of the man's property were spotless, not a single blob of chewing gum to be seen. Bryn couldn't compute how a man couldn't care less about his appearance but had new fences and the pavement steam cleaned.

'I said your dog had better not be taking a shit on my pavement! I'll kick it up the arse!'

Bryn was gobsmacked. A mixture of anger and amusement fought inside him for control. He looked down at Alice, who had finished sniffing and sat waiting patiently. 'She's sniffing the gatepost, that's all.'

'Good job or I'll kick it up the arse.'

That was the third time that the threat to kick Alice was made. Bryn had heard enough. He was normally polite, but he hated rudeness and aggression. 'You couldn't kick a football, mate, never mind my dog,' Bryn quipped as he walked away. 'You couldn't lift your foot high enough. Fat bastard,' he added quietly under his breath.

'What did you say?'

'You heard me.'

'No one talks to me like that, you little scumbag!'

'You want to calm down or you'll give yourself a heart attack.' Bryn said walking away. 'Go back inside and have a couple of Mars bars,' he added a little louder.

'I'll have you!' The man looked towards a red mobility scooter that was parked on the driveway next to a new Range Rover.

'What are you going to do, chase me on your fat scooter?'

'It's a mobility scooter,' the man growled.

'You're not disabled, you're just fat. So, it's a fat scooter. You're a disgrace, mate. You look like you've eaten your parents.'

'You cheeky little scrote,' the fat man growled. 'I'll have you when I get my hands on you!'

'You won't get your hands on me. Fat pervert.'

'I'm warning you,' the man's breath was becoming forced. His face reddened. 'I'm sick of you scummy kids from that estate.'

'Whatever. I was just walking my dog.'

'Scum! That park is full of dog shit because you lowlife kids from the estate don't pick it up. You're scumbags the lot of you!' Alice sensed that Bryn was angry and under attack. She snarled and bared her teeth. 'That thing should be muzzled!'

'She doesn't need a muzzle. You obviously do. It might stop you eating the contents of your fridge before lunchtime,' Bryn called over his shoulder.

'Scum that's what you are!'

'Whatever, Jabba.' Bryn walked on faster much to Alice's delight. She could see the grassy expanses across the road.

'I'm going to phone the police!'

'Phone them,' Bryn called back to him. 'Picking up the phone will do you good. It'll be the most exercise you've had for a decade, fat knacker.'

'Just you wait, little shit! I'll have you and your dog!'

Bryn waited for a gap in the traffic and crossed the road. The fat man had made it to his fence. He waved a podgy fist in the air between the railings and shouted abuse that Bryn could no longer hear; his words were carried off in the wind.

He spent the next twenty minutes watching Alice run around like a lunatic. She didn't chase a ball or a stick. She ran in ever increasing circles, changing direction every now and again. When she ran a little too far away for Bryn to be comfortable, he whistled and she would come back and sit at his feet panting, tongue lolling from the side of her mouth until he said that she could run again. 'Go on, girl,' he said and off she went like a greyhound chasing a hare.

Alice was tiring when Bryn spotted a fat scooter heading in his direction. It was red. His heart thumped in his chest when he recognised the huge bulk of the man he had argued with. A much younger man was striding alongside the scooter; their faces were dark with anger. The fat man had a twisted scowl, his accomplice a half smile half snarl, menace oozed from him. Bryn called Alice to him and secured the lead to her collar. The men were a hundred yards away and closing fast. He wished that he hadn't been quite so insulting to the fat man now.

'Your smartarse mouth will get you into trouble, Squirt!' rattled around his mind. 'How many times have I told you about your smartarse answers? You think you're funny, Bryn but one day you'll get yourself into trouble!'

The men parted making it harder for Bryn to escape. His eyes darted left and right looking for a way out. He wasn't particularly afraid of them, but he was worried about Alice; he needed to avoid physical confrontation at all costs. Had he been alone, he would take his chances running away. He jogged every day and he was quick too but with the staffie on her lead, he wasn't sure that he could change direction quickly enough to outrun the younger male. He looked lean and fit, older and stronger than himself. Bryn chose to walk to his left, plotting a path fifty yards in front of the fat scooter. He could only hope that they would shout some abuse, threaten him and let him walk home.

The men anticipated his manoeuvre and altered course to intercept him. 'Come on girl,' Bryn broke into a jog. Alice wagged her tail and kept pace with him. He waited a few seconds and darted to his right, accelerating quickly. The staffie broke into a canter much faster than his, threatening to pull him over. It completely wrong footed his pursuers. Bryn put his head down and sprinted as fast as he could, arms and legs pumping in rhythm.

'Come here, you little bastard.' The fat man cursed and tried to change direction, but the path wasn't wide enough to accommodate his machine's turning circle. 'I told you I would have you and your mutt!'

Bryn heard his foul curses on the wind, but he didn't slow to look back. He maintained his speed, Alice dragging him to his limit, enjoying the game. Dog walkers and joggers began to watch what unfolded, alerted by the abuse being shouted across the park. Bryn ducked beneath a branch and darted across the park towards the lake, but the men changed their angles, always looking to intercept him at some point. Bryn realised that the younger man was gaining quickly, and he completely changed direction, running deeper into the trees but he couldn't shake him off. He fell over a tree root, losing more ground, scrambled to his feet and bolted out of the trees and across a stretch of grass. A number of people were now looking on with concern, but the man was running like a demon, gaining all the time. He was hissing threats and abuse with every breath.

'I'm going to fucking do you!' Bryn dug deep and pushed as hard as he could, but the footsteps neared and neared, coming dangerously close, every metre narrowed the gap. 'You've had this coming, cheeky little bastard. Stop there, you little prick!'

Bryn heard the words from close behind him. Too close. He heard the rhythmical padding of training shoes on the grass growing nearer still, close by and gaining ground. The man was quick and fit, quicker than Bryn and Alice while they were joined by the lead. He tried to increase his pace once more, adrenalin and fear coursing through his veins but he simply couldn't run any faster. The options raced through his mind. He couldn't outrun the man over a distance. If he carried on running at full tilt, he would be exhausted when the man caught up and that would hinder his ability to protect himself and Alice. He made the decision to stop, unclip the staffie and face his pursuer. She would be more able to avoid the men if she was free.

Glancing over his shoulder, he gauged that he had enough time to stop, let Alice off the lead and ready himself. He spotted a park bench and ran behind it. Alice stopped and sat panting while Bryn unfastened her. The fast approaching footsteps didn't slow down. Bryn thought the bench would act as an obstacle to hinder the man's progress, but it hadn't. As he turned to face him, the man leaped onto the bench using it as a launch pad and hurled himself headlong at Bryn.

When the impact came, it was brutal. The man tackled him, and Bryn felt the breath knocked from his lungs. He landed heavily on his right shoulder with a sickening thud. His head bounced off the ground sending white hot bolts of pain through his brain. He struggled to catch his breath as the man turned him onto his back and straddled him, his knees pinning Bryn's arms to the floor. A flurry of heavy punches rained down. Bryn felt his front teeth piercing his lip and the coppery taste of blood filled his senses. His nose burst and he twisted and bucked beneath his attacker, but he couldn't throw him off. The blows continued to hammer down.

'Leave him alone!' a woman shouted. A couple of passers-by had stopped. A teenager took out her phone and began filming. 'I'll call the police!'

'Get off him, he's just a kid.'

'You're a fucking bully, get off him!'

'You'll mind your fucking business if you have any sense.' The man shouted in reply, but he didn't relent from his attack. Many witnesses watched and shouted for it to stop but none dared to intervene. The sickening blows rained down, drawing blood, breaking bone and causing the brain to reverberate against the skull. Bryn thought he was going to die, right there in the grass. He wondered what would happen to the staffie, would she run off and be lost, captured by the dog wardens and destroyed? The thought of Alice not getting home spurred something in him. Bryn cried out for help, his shout made thick and guttural by the blood.

'Get off me! Help me!' he wailed. 'Someone get him off me, please!'

Alice heard the panic in her master's voice, and she attacked. Her teeth sank into the man's ankle, ripping and tearing the flesh, her powerful jaw crushing the bone beneath. A fang pierced the fibula with an audible crack as Alice bit down harder. The man screamed and shifted his weight. He lashed out at the angry staffie, but she wouldn't release him. Bryn twisted beneath him and freed his right arm. He looked around, desperately searching for a weapon. His eyes fell on a perforated house brick. He reached out, fingers groping, touching the mud and moss that covered it. Finally, his fingers found the perforations and gripped the brick.

Alice redoubled her attack and Bryn saw the man reach inside his leather jacket. He saw the flash of steel as he pulled out a hunting knife and Bryn knew that he had seconds to act. The jagged blade arced through the air towards Alice. Bryn aimed the brick at his attacker's head and brought it up as hard as he could. The corner of the brick impacted with the temple, splintering the sphenoid bone and driving a fragment of the skull into the brain. A soft squelching thud echoed across the park. The man was silenced instantly, and he slumped onto the wet grass, a surprised expression on his face. Bryn watched his pupils narrow as his life was extinguished. He had never seen a dead person before, but he knew that this man was dead, and he knew that he had killed him.

Bryn felt tears stinging his eyes. He spat blood onto the grass and climbed out from beneath his attacker. Alice had to be persuaded to release her grip on his leg and she growled at the lifeless body as Bryn put her back on the lead. He stumbled over to the bench and sat down. Onlookers spoke to him, asked him questions, dabbed his bloody nose with a tissue and offered soothing words but he was barely aware of them. Shock was shutting his brain down. As the first police car arrived on the scene, Bryn noticed the red mobility scooter in the distance. The traffic stopped as the fat man steered it onto the zebra crossing and made his way back to his house. The policemen approached slowly, carefully.

'Put that down, lad.' One of them said softly. 'Put it down and walk towards me slowly.'

Bryn was confused. He looked down at his right hand and realised that he was still holding the bloodstained brick. His eyes fixed on a flap of skin and hair that was fixed to the brick. That was once attached to that man's head, his brain processed. For some bizarre reason he held the brick up in front of his eyes and inspected it. An ambulance squealed to a halt. The crowd of faces looked at him, their mouths moving but their words garbled. The police officer pointed to the brick and shouted instructions, but they didn't mean anything to him, he looked back at them, eyes glazed.

'I didn't mean to kill him,' Bryn said, voice cracking. Blood flowed freely from both nostrils. Alice sat as close to his leg as she could, still protecting Bryn; her tail wagged at the approaching strangers, but she sensed something bad had happened.

'Okay, son,' the officer said with a raised hand. 'We believe you, but you need to put the brick down.'

'I didn't mean to hurt him,' Bryn tried to explain but his lips were numb, brain confused, and the power of speech disabled. His top lip quivered as he spoke. Hot tears fell from his eyes as he put it down on the grass and walked towards the policemen. Alice trotted alongside him excited to meet new people but oblivious to how dire the situation was.

CHAPTER 2

'I'm DI Braddick,' Marcus introduced himself as he entered the forensic tent. His blue forensic suit distinguished him from the CSI team, who donned white. 'You must be Kathy Brooks?'

'That's me.' She paused to make a split-second assessment of the new DI. Thirties, black, lean, designer stubble flecked with grey; so far, a significant improvement on the last DI she'd worked with. He had been a fat ignoramus from Manchester, who smelled of cheap aftershave and stale sweat.

'I don't think we've worked together before.'

'No, we haven't, nice to meet you.'

'I'm told you're running forensics here.'

'I'm senior SOCO on this one unfortunately. You may want to use some of this,' she said handing him a small jar of tiger balm. 'It's much stronger than the usual stuff. Don't get it in your eyes and wash your hands before you use the toilet.'

Braddick smiled and nodded knowingly, inside his stomach was churning. The smell of burnt flesh knocked him sick, brought back memories, memories that he fought with daily.

'Will do,' he said smearing some of the gel across his top lip. The corpse at his feet was broken and burned. He wrestled with similar images in his mind, images from the past. Images of her. Pushing them back into the dark reaches where they belonged, he focused his mind. 'What have we got so far?' Kathy identified his accent as outside the city but not far away, somewhere between there and Manchester. She'd heard rumours about Braddick. He had been on secondment with the National Crime Agency for three years, with a spell as an observer with both Europol and Interpol, being groomed for the fast-track up the ranks. Rumour had it that his progress had been derailed by some indiscretion, but the details were sketchy. The tent rattled as DS Adrian Burns entered. His big frame filled the doorway. 'You know my DS?'

'Ade and I have worked together more times than I wish to remember.' Kathy joked. Ade blushed and grinned. 'Sorry. That sounded wrong didn't it.'

'Not for the first time,' Ade grunted. He shuffled inside his paper suit; his size not designed for the disposable garment.

'Or the last,' Kathy said as she stepped back from the body at her feet and put her hands on her hips. 'Okay, if you're comfortable, I'll tell you where I'm up to.'

'Please, carry on.' Braddick nodded.

'We have two males, brothers.' She smiled thinly. The thought that someone would have to tell their mother that her sons had died in such terrible circumstances was not missed by her. 'They're David and Mathew Johnson, age nineteen and twenty-three respectively.' Braddick raised his eyebrows at the details. Kathy noticed his reaction. 'I'm not psychic, both had their ID on them, debit and credit cards are still in their pockets and a few hundred pounds in cash was stuffed into Mathew Johnson's mouth,' she explained. 'Tells me they ripped someone off?'

'The wrong someone by the looks of things,' Braddick said gruffly under his breath.

'The level of violence is way over the top,' she added. 'It was systematic and sustained over several hours.'

'Any defence wounds?' Braddick asked.

'No,' she shook her head. 'They didn't fight back. They were restrained and beaten.'

'I agree with you, Kathy.' Braddick said kneeling down to get a better view of the facial injuries. 'The level of violence is excessive. They left their belongings in their pockets so that we would identify them quickly and their identity would leak out sooner rather than later. The level of violence and the dumpsite are done for effect, to shock the locals. They ripped off the wrong people...' He shook his head as he analysed the level of destruction inflicted on the bodies, bloated faces deep purple in colour, congealed blood blocked every orifice; their suffering had been intense and prolonged. Their expressions were twisted in agony and frozen in time, just like Karin's had been. Onlookers could be under no illusions as to the pain they'd endured before death finally took them. It was etched into their faces, just like hers. Her death mask haunted him, drifted to him day and night, the same question on her lips. '*Where were you?*' Braddick felt Kathy's eyes on him, waiting for him to finish. He refocused his mind, banishing the memories but knowing they would return soon. He looked at her and rubbed the bristles on his chin, the rubber gloves snagged on them. 'Over a dozen emergency calls were made last night about an image posted on *Facebook*. You're aware of it?'

'Yes.'

'Have you been shown the post?'

'No, but I've seen the picture.'

'And this is definitely the man in the photo?'

'Yes. It's him without a doubt,' she said confidently.

'Sorry to interrupt you, please carry on.'

'They've been badly beaten and suffered severe burns below the waist. The smell would indicate that an accelerant was poured over their legs and feet and then ignited. To top it all, David Johnson was shot twice, once in each knee.'

'Before the picture was posted to Facebook,' Braddick said for his own benefit. Ade and Kathy nodded.

'I would say so,' she agreed. 'His injuries are significantly older than the ones inflicted on his brother. Some of his facial injuries have scabbed. I don't have the cause of death yet, but you can take your pick for now; exsanguination is my guess,' she finished with a sad smile. 'Posting it online for the family to see was cruel. I believe his mother saw it.'

'She left several comments before the post was removed. You can only imagine what she's going through.'

'They wanted a reaction from someone on his friends list,' Ade said.

'What exactly did the caption say?' Braddick asked him.

"*One of you has stolen something you shouldn't have. Give it back or I'm dead.*" Ade read from his Blackberry. 'There were hundreds of comments posted before Facebook removed the post. I've got Google and his team working on recovering whatever they can,' Ade said, referring to one of the team by his nickname. 'They're compiling a list of people who responded, starting with their relatives.'

'I think he might be a likely candidate for someone who responded,' Kathy said pointing to Mathew Johnson's body. 'His injuries tell me that he arrived at the party late. He may have been prompted to help his brother by the photograph.'

'He walked into an ambush.'

'He had no choice. If he saw his brother on Facebook then he would have reacted, no doubt,' Ade agreed.

'If we find out what the post was about, what exactly was stolen and by whom, we'll know who to look at,' Braddick agreed. 'This happened last night sometime?'

'Definitely.'

'Somewhere else obviously,' Braddick thought aloud. 'This is the dump site.'

'Yes. There are tyre tracks leading from the road, but we'll need to check them against any delivery vans from the last twenty-four hours.' Kathy reached for an evidence bag and handed it to the DI. Through the clear plastic he could see a badly burned leather wallet. The owner's bank cards and driving license were relatively intact. 'They live a mile away on the estate behind the shops.'

'They brought them home to dump them,' Braddick said calmly, 'it's a message for anyone connected to them.' Kathy nodded her agreement. 'I think we have enough to get things moving, thanks, Kathy.'

'No problem.'

'Here is my direct dial number,' he said handing her a business card. 'Could you call me as soon as you have anything more?'

'Of course.'

'Thanks,' Braddick smiled before turning to leave. As he lifted the tent flap, he paused. 'Are you working on the murder in the park too? It came in about fifteen minutes ago.'

Kathy nodded, 'It's literally around the corner. I'll be a while here yet though. We've sent a team to preserve the scene. Once we have finished here, we'll be over.'

'Another long day for you I'm sure. It's not worth taking this off,' he said with a thin smile holding the lapel of his paper suit. Braddick couldn't wait to get away from the nauseous stench of burnt flesh. 'We'll talk later, thanks again.'

The detectives left the tent and looked around the alleyway. Braddick took a deep breath through his nose, trying to clear the stink from his nostrils. The CSI team and uniformed officers were running a fingertip search of the bins. Refuse was piled in the doorways, clinging to the bricks and mortar. Fish and chip wrappers, empty Coke tins and discarded betting slips mingled with cardboard boxes and used hypodermic needles.

'There're a lot of drugs on the Stockbridge estate, most of it purchased in or around the park,' Ade said as he kicked at a used needle. 'I did a two-year stint with Matrix. We ran a few ops on that estate. There are three or four main gangs in competition with each other but they're mostly small time.'

'Did you ever come across the Johnson family?'

'Nope but looking at the state of those two, I'm not surprised that I haven't.'

'What do you mean?'

'It is rare to see that type of attack on senior hierarchy isn't it?'

'I've seen a few in my time,' Braddick mused. 'Mostly in London though.'

'But it doesn't usually happen to anyone high up,' Ade pushed his point. 'This is disrespectful. The way they have been dumped, it's undignified.' He pointed to the bins. 'When the big boys come to blows, we never find their bodies. They're never humiliated like this.'

'I'm with you so far.' Braddick knew Ade had a good point.

'This is a punishment beating. They're low level members or rivals in my opinion.' Ade continued. Braddick suspected he was right and let him carry on. As the new DI, he needed to build a rapport with his new team, especially his DS. 'And it's a message to others. They're stamping their authority on the estate. Whoever the Johnsons crossed is making it clear that they won't tolerate any arsing about on their patch.'

'Agreed,' Braddick said. His time with the NCA had given him an in-depth view of Britain's organised crime families and their mechanics. Their businesses were worth billions, well managed, brutally disciplined and incredibly influential. The Johnsons were at the wrong end of the scale and suffered the ultimate punishment, minnows devoured by sharks. Braddick took another look around. 'Let's go to the other scene, take a look while we wait to see what Google comes up with.'

'He's about as thorough as it gets,' Ade grinned, 'he's a geek but a brilliant one. He'll build a decent list of people to talk to.' His face was still tanned from a fortnight in the Canaries, his stubble a few days too old. He pointed towards his car. 'I'm parked there.'

'Okay, we'll wait and see what he comes up with,' Braddick said, stopping next to Ade's car. 'Someone knows what that post was about, and the Johnson's friends and family should be queuing up to talk to us.'

'No one queues up to talk to us, Guv.'

'I'll see you at the park,' Braddick waved a hand and headed towards his black Evoque. A gust of wind caught the door as he opened it, threatening to rip it from his hands. He climbed onto the beige leather interior and started the engine. Rubbing his hands together, he blew into them to stimulate his circulation. Slowly, the heater kicked in, chasing the chill away. He flicked on the radio and the group, Passenger was strumming Karin's song; he hadn't heard it for days, the haunting melody stayed with him hours after it had finished playing.

'Only know you've been high when you're feeling low. Only miss the road when you're missing home. Only miss the sun when it starts to snow…Only know you love her when you let her go, and you let her go…'

The words cut into him like an axe to the heart. He changed channels quickly and tried to put thoughts of her from his mind. It was too soon, too raw, too fucking painful to try to make sense of her death. The truth was that there was no sense to it. As far as the authorities were concerned it remained unexplained, no motive, no suspects. For him, there was no justice, no peace of mind and no grieving process. He turned up the volume as Adele was saying hello from the other side and tried desperately to focus on the now.

The drive to the park was quick and uneventful. He could see marked police cars and crime scene tape at the northern edge of the park. The park was a green space surrounded by concrete and asphalt; a peaceful airy space with colourful borders and a lake at the centre. The crime scene was a carbuncle on the face of a beauty. It was an ugly scene in a natural oasis. Braddick knew only too well that murder was ugly, and he was tiring of looking at it, each encounter sucked some of his soul from him, leaving only a dark vacuum in its place.

He steered the Range Rover onto a grass verge and formed his first impressions. Four small groups of people were talking with uniformed officers, witnesses, each one worth their weight in gold. Mentally, he sighed with relief. Guessing what had happened to a victim was every detective's nightmare. Eyewitnesses could help to wrap up a case before the suspect had been processed at the station. He hoped that this would be one of those cases. The public believed every murder was made a priority but in truth, some were more a priority than others. Some murders were brushed under the carpet, unsolved, unwanted, embarrassing crimes that no one wanted to investigate. From the details he had been given, this one would be put to bed quickly. Turning off the engine, he reluctantly opened the door and stepped out into the cold. A uniformed officer spotted him coming and broke away from a group of witnesses. Ade was approaching from the opposite direction, heading straight for the forensic tent.

'This will be a messy one, Guv,' the sergeant said sternly. It wasn't what Braddick wanted to hear. He lifted the yellow tape and ducked beneath it.

'Walk me through what you have so far,' Braddick said with a frown. He always frowned when he was thinking. Karin used to chastise him for it. *'You'll end up being a wrinkly old man if you keep frowning...'* her voice echoed in his mind. He wanted to grow old and wrinkly with her. He had wanted the wedding, the kids, the grandkids, the company of his Karin long into their twilight years but someone stole that from him. They'd stolen her. He walked to the tent and stepped inside.

'This is the victim, Anthony Farrell, aged twenty-six from the Childwall area.' The sergeant handed Farrell's driving license to Ade, who raised his eyebrows in response.

'Anthony Farrell?' Ade asked thoughtfully. 'That could spell trouble.'

'That's what I thought,' the uniformed officer shook his head and carried on. 'Witnesses say that he chased a youth, Bryn Evans, across the park and attacked him. He leapt over the bench there and brought him down here. Witnesses say that he pinned his arms down with his knees and began punching him in the face and head. Evans is very badly bruised around the eyes, nose and mouth. Farrell pulled a knife, nasty looking weapon—' he pointed to the hunting knife which had been bagged '—at some point Evans's dog attacked Farrell. Evans got an arm free and struck him with a house brick.'

'A brick?'

'Looks like someone built a campfire using bricks and rocks there,' the officer explained. 'This park is as busy at night as it is through the daytime. The kids from the estate camp out, play music, smoke drugs, you know the score.' Braddick nodded. 'The brick is covered in mud and moss. Evans cracked him across the head with it and killed him instantly. He's in shock, just sat on that bench until we arrived, poor kid didn't know what day it is.'

'How old is Evans?'

'Fourteen, Guv.'

'Bloody hell, fourteen?'

'Do we know him?'

'No, Guv.'

'Doesn't make sense, grown man chasing a kid.'

'It doesn't. Any of the witnesses got any idea why Farrell was chasing him?'

'No, Guv but a couple of witnesses have indicated that he was with a fat man who was on a red mobility scooter,' the sergeant checked his notes. 'One said that she saw him leaving the park across the zebra crossing to the south of the park when the altercation turned nasty.'

'Have we followed that up yet?'

'Not yet.'

'What has Evans said?'

'He didn't know who the man was or why he attacked him and that he didn't mean to kill him. I daren't press him any further because of his age, Guv. He's been escorted to the Royal to have a doctor look at him. I think his nose was broken. He seemed like a nice kid, more worried about getting his dog home than being arrested.'

'Have his parents been informed?'

'I sent two officers to his home with his dog. They'll inform them and take them to the hospital.'

'Good. We need to find this fat man. If he was with Farrell, he'll know what this was all about. Anything else?' Braddick asked.

'What about the Farrells, Guv?'

'We'll arrange for them to be brought in. They'll need to identify him formally.'

'That's what I mean about it being messy. I don't fancy delivering that message.'

The lines on Braddick's forehead deepened. 'I don't follow.'

'The Farrells from Childwall are a tasty outfit, Guv,' Ade said handing him the driving licence. 'Eddie Farrell has been on our radar for a long time, drugs, prostitution, extortion, you name it, he's involved in it.'

'Eddie Farrell…Farrell…Farrell…' Braddick nodded and rubbed the bristles on his chin. 'Jesus, I know the family. The name didn't register at first,' he said shaking his head. 'They were implicated in the Karpov trial before it collapsed last year.'

'That's them,' Ade nodded. 'I don't know if this bloke is related or not, but I know Farrell has a couple of sons about his age. I think we had better find out before we go knocking on his door.'

'Were the sons involved with their father's business?'

'Both of them as far as I can remember, Guv. There could be more to this than meets the eye.'

'Definitely, make some calls and find out.' The sergeant spoke into his radio to chase up the information. 'What were you doing over here?' Braddick asked the corpse. 'How far is it to Childwall from here?'

'Twelve miles at least,' Ade shrugged. He twigged what the DI was thinking. 'He didn't come here on a bus, did he?' Ade said as he took out his mobile and made a call.

'No. My guess is his vehicle is parked nearby and if I had to make an educated guess, it will be at the fat man's house on that estate.' Braddick nodded towards the Evoque. 'Let's have a drive around and see if we can't find him.' He made towards the vehicle. 'When your men have finished taking statements, have them canvass the estate. See if anyone knows who the fat man is and what Farrell was doing in this part of the city.'

'Yes, Guv.'

Ade ended his phone call. 'Farrell drives a new Range Rover, silver sports model.'

'Can you circulate that please, sergeant, I want it found before we notify anyone of his death.'

'Yes, Guv,' the uniformed officer said, 'I'll get on it immediately.'

'We'll take my car,' Braddick said to Ade. They climbed out of their forensic suits and dumped them in the boot. The Evoque rocked as Ade climbed into the passenger seat; his years of playing rugby and drinking lager had piled on slabs of muscle that were covered in an ample layer of fat. 'How far does a mobility scooter go on one charge?'

'How long does a smartphone work?' Ade scoffed. 'My old Nokia would last a week but this Blackberry needs charging every day. The witnesses said the man was fat, very fat. That would sap the energy and limit the range. It's nearby.'

'That's what I think,' Braddick nodded and steered the Evoque through the park towards the estate. He spotted the zebra crossing and slowed down. 'You know the estate well?' he asked pointing through the window. 'Is that the only entrance into it?'

'On this side, yes.' Ade nodded. 'It's essentially rectangular with an entrance on each side. The next entrance is about two miles around the park.' Braddick indicated and turned onto the estate. He had hardly straightened the steering wheel when Ade pointed across the road. 'Look there, Guv. The corner house, a red mobility scooter and a silver Range Rover sport model.'

'I'm guessing that our fat man lives there,' Braddick said, peering through the window. 'Let's go and see what he has to say.'

CHAPTER 3

Big Paulie stared at the phone. He had punched in the number but couldn't bring himself to press dial. He didn't want to have the conversation, not now, not ever. The boss would go ballistic and that was never pretty. Paulie had wanted out for years but they wouldn't let him go. He offered to sell them the house, but they refused. They needed the house and they needed him in it. He glanced at the CCTV screens. The police were all over the park. That would ruin business for the rest of the day and night probably, but that was the least of his problems. He had to find some way of explaining what had just happened, but words failed him. Lying had always come naturally to him but not today. He had eaten his way to thirty stones, and no one could do that without lying, but his talent had deserted him momentarily. It dawned on him that the longer he waited, the more likely Farrell was to find out that his son was dead from another source. Plucking up the courage to call, he pressed dial.

'Paulie,' Nicolai Karpov answered almost immediately in a bored tone. As Eddie Farrell's sidekick and the linchpin between him and the Karpov syndicate, Paulie knew he was both powerful and dangerous. He was also an arsehole. 'What can I do for you?'

'Is Eddie there?'

'He's abroad, Paulie. What's up?'

'Anthony came over this morning.' Paulie swallowed hard.

'I know I sent him, so what?'

'Look, there's been an accident, well more of an incident really.' He sat heavily onto a leather armchair and glanced at the screens as he spoke. Police officers were arriving every few minutes.

It was the position of the house that had dragged him into this mess in the first place. Its cameras gave an almost panoramic view of the park to the rear of the house and the entrance to the estate at the front. At first, he had been reluctant to get involved but the money was too good to resist. Paulie was naturally lazy and he used his obesity as an excuse to claim benefits and avoid working for a living, but he had a taste for gadgets and fine food that was beyond what benefits could buy; his debts mounted quickly to a point where they were insurmountable. The opportunity to earn money by staying at home was too good to refuse. And then there were the freebies from the working girls that used his house to service their punters. They trawled the park at night under the watchful eye of the cameras, using the backdoor of his house to access the toilet and a hot drink when they needed them. Farrell had told him some of them would stay at his house from time to time. None of them wanted to but they were ordered to sort out Paulie whenever he had the urge. In return, Paulie took the Farrells' share of the takings from the girls and the dealers who sold their drugs and stashed it until Farrell sent someone to collect it.

He was a big man and if the young dealers got lippy, he brought them back into line. He managed the Farrells' interests in the park area. He had been wary about getting involved but the Farrells coaxed him at first, never revealing their true personalities; once he was involved the mask slipped and it was too late. He was guilty by association and nobody walked away from that life.

'You're not making sense, Paulie,' Nicolai moaned. 'What are you talking about?'

'It was a freak accident; well it wasn't really an accident. But it was a total freak, really it was, I'm not even sure how it happened to be honest…'

'Paulie!' Nicolai snapped. 'For fuck's sake!'

'What?'

'What are you talking about?'

'Okay, I'm rambling. I'm nervous.' He took a deep breath. 'This morning Anthony came over to collect the laundry and drop off some powder.' Paulie put his podgy hand to his head and closed his eyes. 'He got into a fight in the park…perhaps fight is too strong a word…well, it was a scuffle that went wrong,' Paulie stammered. Nicolai's silence made him more nervous. 'He was hit with a brick. Hard,' he paused, still unable to say the words.

'Anthony was hit with a brick?'

'Yes, across the head.'

'Who hit him with a brick?'

'A local kid from the estate.'

'A dealer?'

'I'm not sure,' Paulie stammered. 'Well I think so. Probably,' he lied. It sounded better than the truth.

'Is he okay?'

'No.'

'What do you mean, no, Paulie?' Nicolai snapped. 'I'm beginning to lose my temper here!'

'Sorry.'

'Is he in hospital?'

'No.'

'No? What are you telling me, Paulie?'

'He's dead, Nicolai.'

'Dead?' Nicolai went quiet while he absorbed the news. 'Are you kidding me?'

'No.'

'You're sure?'

'Yes. There's police all over the park.'

'Who was this kid he was fighting?'

'I'm not sure,' Paulie mumbled. 'I've seen him walk from the estate before. That's all I know.'

'But he's a dealer, right?'

'I think so,' Paulie lied again.

'Not one of ours?'

'Oh no, definitely not.'

'Who does he work for?'

'I don't know, Nicolai.'

'Did he get away?'

'No. The police took him away.'

'You saw them arrest him?'

'Yes,' Paulie answered, but he didn't tell him that he'd watched it on the cameras from his armchair.

'We need to know exactly who he is, understand?'

'The kid, why?'

'Why?' Nicolai asked incredulously. 'Have you lost your fucking marbles?' Paulie didn't think that he had but he kept quiet anyway. 'He killed the boss's son by hitting him over the head with a brick. How do you think he's going to take that?'

'When you say it like that…'

'How else can you say it?'

'I'll ask around about him.'

'You'll do better than that. Find out who he works for.'

'Okay, okay,' Paulie wished he hadn't lied but he had to deflect the blame.

'Have the police been to the house?'

'No.'

'Where's his car?'

'On the drive.'

'So, it's only a matter of time before they knock on your door, Paulie,' Nicolai said flatly. 'Where's the powder?'

'I'll hide it.'

'Okay, do whatever you need to do,' Nicolai paused. He was suspicious. 'Did you actually see what happened to Anthony?'

'Yes, of course. I was there.'

'But you don't know why they were fighting?'

'No. I was too far away to hear what was said...' Paulie stuttered.

'I'll let Eddie know what you've told me.' There was menace in his voice. 'You had better get your story straight, fat man because I don't think you're telling me the truth and if you're lying to me your life won't be worth living, understand?'

'Yes.'

'Yes what?'

'Yes, I understand.'

'You'd better.'

'What shall I do if the police come?'

'Sit tight and wait for us. We'll be in touch,' the Russian said, 'Oh and, Paulie...'

'Yes.'

'If the police do come before we get there, you say nothing. Act dumb, shouldn't be too difficult for you.'

'Got it,' Paulie said in a whisper. The call ended but he kept the phone to his ear as if waiting for inspiration to speak to him. He thought about leaving the house, getting on his scooter and driving away until the police had gone. He thought about going and never going back. It seemed like a solid plan until he heard a loud knock on the front door.

CHAPTER 4

Joe Tucker washed the blood from his hands; red streaks clung to the porcelain. He looked in the mirror and bared his teeth. They were unnaturally white, a three-hundred-pound treatment worth every penny. His face was weathered and brown, his fifty years mapped into the skin around his eyes, his salt and pepper hair styled shoulder length and parted in the middle. He was more rough than handsome, but he tried to make the most of what Mother Nature had given to him. Things could have been worse, a lot worse; he could have been Tommy. His brother was born with a misshaped jaw and a nose that belonged to someone of Aboriginal decent. He had lost his hair in his early twenties, needed glasses and had no social skills. All in all, Joe had the better deal. He splashed his face with warm water and ran his fingers through his hair, dabbing himself dry with a damp towel.

It had been a long twenty-four hours, long and traumatic. When he'd realised that the container had been stolen from the docks, his heart had nearly punched through his chest. The container carried their future. Everything that they'd been working towards was in that metal box. It was the deal that they'd been waiting for, the one big payoff that would set them apart from the other crews in the city. It would establish them as an outfit to contend with. This was also the biggest gamble of his life. All or nothing. Not only had he invested everything that they owned into it, he had also borrowed heavily from a well-respected financier that was happy to take repayment in the form of product. Losing the container meant losing everything and that's why he had been so brutal with the Johnsons. They'd taken liberties and almost cost them everything, possibly even their lives. Not repaying their debt would turn everyone in the city against them. They would be forced to run abroad or be hunted down and killed along with their families, friends and associates. Running might save himself and Tommy in the short term but those that they left behind would be bullied, harassed, assaulted, raped and worse until payment was received, or they were dead. It was not a debt one could default on and arrange a repayment plan.

The noise from the workshop was irritating, the persistent grating sound of grinders on metal. Joe took two paracetamol and swallowed them dry. He opened the door into the workshop and the noise became deafening. His brother Tommy looked up and nodded. A welding mask covered his face. The grinder in his hand sent a shower of sparks skyward as it crept slowly through the metal sills of the container. The red shipping container had been jacked up, the doors removed, and the roof and side panels cut away so that they could access the flatbed and the sills. Tommy and two other men worked relentlessly to cut the metal and expose the void spaces. Joe watched them for a while and then headed to the office which overlooked the workspace. Once a factory unit producing caravans and trailers it made an ideal hideaway to organise their operation from. The Tuckers had been importing amphetamine and crystal meth for fifteen years, some by air, some by sea but this was the biggest gamble, the biggest risk with the biggest rewards. Lately they'd been using the migrant chaos at Calais to smuggle product from the continent, but they had to vary their entry points. His mobile rang and he checked the screen before answering.

'Hello,' Tucker answered.

'How did your trip to Amsterdam go?'

'Sweet, we picked up a lot of zombie and I mean a lot.'

'That's the new stuff that the kids are doing flips for?'

'Ketamine based hallucinogenic,' Tucker explained. 'It's bringing top dollar in the clubs.'

'I heard the Latvian crew are the only importers,' the voice said cautiously. 'I hope you're not crossing swords with them. Trouble like that, I don't need.'

'The Latvians are all behind bars,' Tucker scoffed, 'They're banged up. The opportunity came up to fill the gap and we obliged. Zombie is coming to the UK one way or the other, someone will bring it in and it might as well be us.'

'As long as it's trouble free and the price is right, I'll take whatever you've got.'

'There's a long queue,' Tucker said flippantly. It felt good to be in control. 'This is the big league. Over a mil…think you can raise that?' the caller remained quiet. 'I want one buyer, two at the outside. If you're still interested call me back tomorrow.'

'Don't get too carried away with yourself, Tucker,' the voice warned. Tucker felt a bolt of fear shoot through him. This was a man that he didn't want to cross, and his tone of voice told him that he had crossed the line. 'I was putting million-pound deals together when you were still shitting yellow.' He left the comment to hang. 'I'll be in touch.'

Joe looked at the phone, sat on the edge of the desk, wiped a coffee mug with his sleeve and poured himself a whisky. He took a long slug, the liquid burning pleasantly. He felt it sliding down, an alcoholic warmth spreading through his body, the soothing effect almost instant. A second slug emptied the cup, he refilled it and watched the men working. Tommy stopped his grinder and lifted his mask. He wiped his brow and spoke to one of the other men. Joe couldn't hear them, but their demeanour wasn't right. He felt the nerves on the back of his neck tingling, not in a good way. Sipping the whisky, he walked to the door. The sills were exposed from end to end and the flatbed was peeled back like the lid of a sardine tin. He looked Tommy in the eye and Tommy shook his head, almost imperceptibly.

'There's no drugs in this container, Joe,' he said apologetically.

'We watched them putting them in, Tommy.' Tucker pushed his fingers through his hair, the strands sticking out in an unintentional Bob Geldof style. 'We watched them sealing it up!'

'I know all that, but they're not here now. How can this happen then?'

The Tuckers stared at the twisted chassis and searched for explanations. Joe paced up and down, trying to think clearly. It wasn't easy, his mind close to absolute panic. There was too much at stake. 'There's only one way this could happen. This is not the crate we saw in Amsterdam,' Joe raised his hands, his fists clenched. 'It's been switched somewhere.'

'How though?'

'Think about it,' Joe said, trying to maintain his cool. 'I posted that image of Johnson online. Mathew sees it, phones me, arranges to make an exchange but knows that he can't deliver. Mathew Johnson brought us the wrong crate to get his brother back.' Joe scowled. 'It looks exactly like our crate, but it isn't.'

'It's a shipping container, Joe, they all look the same. I don't know how the fuck this has happened,' Tommy said kicking the container. A metallic clang echoed around the unit. 'One thing I do know is we can't ask the Johnsons, can we?' he looked at his older brother. 'We're fucked, Joe!'

Joe shook his head. 'Calm down.' He pointed to the office. 'Go and check the serial number on the chassis. I'll get the shipping document. Let's check if this is our crate for certain.'

'We should have done that last night.'

'We weren't thinking straight last night.'

'This is a major fuck up.'

'Losing it now won't help.'

'The Johnsons double fucked us!' Tommy shouted as he walked towards the container.

'And that's why we set them on fire,' Joe shrugged. 'They're stinking in an alleyway for what they did. Get a grip, we'll sort this out.'

'What are we going to do if we lose those drugs, Joe?' Tommy knew how much they were in debt on the deal. Joe hadn't told him everything, but he knew enough to be concerned, very concerned. 'They'll crucify us if we don't pay up.'

'We'll find them.' Joe rubbed his chin and pointed to the sills. 'We saw those drugs being put into the crate, didn't we?'

'Yes.'

'If the drugs had been removed in transit, the sills would be damaged, right?'

'Yes, what's your point?'

'Johnson said he had already sold the container on to his buyer,' Joe said emptying the mug. 'Let's assume he did, and he couldn't get it back. We had his brother, so he brings us a double.'

'So, our crate is still out there?'

'Exactly. Whoever has our container has no idea that they're sitting on a million quid's worth of zombie. All we have to do is find out who Johnson sold our container to and take it back.'

'Where do we start?' Tommy asked, calming down slightly.

'We start with their cousins, Ray and Liam,' Joe said knowingly. 'That family are all joined at the hip. Ray and Liam will know who they were stealing containers for and I've got a pretty good idea that they'll know where it is too.'

Tommy picked up a sawn-off shotgun. 'Let's go and ask the Johnsons shall we.'

CHAPTER 5

Braddick knocked on the door again, harder this time. He gave it ten seconds and increased the force. Ade inspected the red mobility scooter, took his hands from his dark overcoat pockets and touched the battery housing.

'Battery's still warm and there's mud on the tyres.'

'He's in,' Braddick said banging with the heel of his fist. 'I saw movement when we arrived.'

'Maybe he doesn't want to talk to us,' Ade said sarcastically.

'Nobody wants to talk to us,' Braddick said, banging harder still.

'Fair enough.' Ade wandered over to the Range Rover and peered inside. It was upholstered in leather and fully loaded with extras. 'That's two years' salary parked there. Drug dealing wanker,' he muttered as he turned away.

'Dead drug dealing wanker,' Braddick corrected him. He banged harder still, the door rattled in its frame. He heard the lock being turned and the door opened a few inches. He shoved his ID through the gap and pushed the door open a few inches with his shoulder. 'DI Braddick and this is DS Burns.' The fat man behind the door nodded silently. His face blushed red. 'You are?'

'Paul Williams. Everyone calls me Paulie,' he said, eyes moving nervously from one detective to the other. 'What do you want?'

'Are you deaf, Paulie?' Braddick noticed Paulie's clothes. Baggy tracksuit pants and a hoodie, part of the ever-growing army of fat sportswear wearing clones, most of whom had never seen the inside of a gym.

Paulie looked nervous and confused. 'What do you mean?'

'It's a simple question. Are you hard of hearing?'

'No.' He shook his head, his fat jowls wobbled.

'Is there a reason that you didn't open the door to us?'

'I was busy.'

'Busy?'

'Yes, busy.'

'Doing what?'

'None of your business.'

'You see when someone doesn't open the door when we knock, we get to thinking that they don't want to talk to us or they're doing something that they shouldn't be, don't we, sergeant?'

'We do,' Ade agreed. 'Makes us very suspicious.'

'Very suspicious indeed,' Braddick stared at Paulie. His bottom lip was quivering slightly, worried, guilty.

Paulie looked from one to the other, his embarrassment deepening. 'I was just busy.' He coughed and cleared his throat nervously. 'What do you want?'

'Is this your Range Rover?' Braddick asked, stepping away from the door so that Paulie could squeeze out but he didn't take the bait. He remained in the house and didn't even look at the vehicle. He shook his head nervously that it wasn't his vehicle. 'Whose is it then?'

'It belongs to a friend of mine.'

'What's his name?'

'Who?'

'The owner of the vehicle.'

'Anthony something,' Paulie mumbled. Braddick could see the cogs in his brain whirring. He was nervous and lying, beads of sweat formed at his temples.

'Anthony what?'

'I can't remember his second name.'

'Well I find that hard to believe, don't you, sergeant?' Braddick turned towards Ade. 'We're running the plates, so we'll know shortly,' he added, offering Paulie the chance to come clean. He didn't.

'It's slipped my mind.'

'Someone parks their Range Rover on my drive, I would know their name.' Ade sniffed loudly. 'I can smell bullshit, Guv.'

'Me too.'

'Could it be Farrell?' Ade prompted. 'Anthony Farrell?'

'I think so. It might be,' Paulie mumbled. 'I can't remember for certain, all right. I have a bad memory,' Paulie snapped. 'Now what exactly do you want? I'm very busy.'

'Did you see your friend getting into an altercation in the park?' Braddick pushed.

'Erm...' Paulie squirmed.

'Before you tell us another lie, we have several witnesses who said that you were there,' Ade added before he could answer. Paulie looked like a rabbit in the headlights. 'They have told us that you were in the park…on your scooter.'

'That scooter there.' Braddick pointed to it. 'The red scooter,' Braddick added. Each question sapped Paulie of the energy to respond with anything worth saying. Lying seemed to be pointless. 'They have told us that you were chasing a teenager across the park on that red scooter. The one that's on your driveway right there.'

'It is yours, isn't it?' Ade followed up quickly. 'The scooter…'

'Erm…' Paulie was tongue tied and frightened.

'Yes…is the word that you're looking for,' Braddick prodded.

'Yes. The scooter is mine.' Paulie caved in with a sigh.

'That's better. And you were with Anthony Farrell on your scooter in the park?'

'Yes.'

'Excellent,' he nodded, thin lipped. 'So, you saw your friend, Anthony getting into an altercation?' Braddick kept on.

'I wouldn't say that I saw it,' Paulie stumbled. 'I saw something happen, but I was quite far away.'

'He died at the scene, Mr Williams,' Braddick said flatly. 'But then you know that already, don't you?'

'Yes.'

'Good, now you can stop pissing us around and tell us the truth.'

'Sorry, detective.' Paulie sighed. He was sweating profusely. 'I don't like violence. I saw them fighting, panicked and came home.'

'So, you know he's dead, how?' Braddick asked.

'I saw the police and the ambulance. When they didn't take him away, I guessed he was dead.'

'You have no idea what the fight was about?' Paulie shook his head and blushed deeper.

'You have a lot of cameras on your house, don't you?' Ade changed tack with a smile.

'Which is good for us,' Braddick said leaning on the door. Paulie put his foot behind it. 'Hopefully your cameras will have recorded you going towards the park with your friend, Anthony, won't they? They might even show us what happened over there.'

'I don't think they're on at the moment,' Paulie blustered.

'The lights are on,' Ade said pointing a finger. 'That means they're on.'

'They're on all right.' Braddick sighed. 'I can't see why someone with nothing to hide would leave their friend dead in the park and then lie about knowing their second name. Why would anyone do that?'

'Can't see it myself,' Ade said shaking his head. 'Unless that person has something to hide.'

'Can't imagine what though.' Braddick frowned. Sweat was running in beads down Paulie's forehead. 'Do you know what your friend did for a living?'

'No,' Paulie said in a fluster. 'I don't really know him that well.'

'Really?' Braddick said with a shake of his head. 'He is Eddie Farrell's son. Does that ring any bells?'

Paulie shook his head.

'Do you know Eddie Farrell?' Ade asked innocently.

'He never mentioned any family.'

'You see, Eddie Farrell is a well-known drug dealer.'

Another shake of the head. The colour drained from Paulie's face.

'That might explain why you're shitting your pants,' Braddick said tilting his head. 'If you're working for the Farrells, I mean?'

'I'm not. I'm on benefits.'

'It would also explain the cameras,' Ade added.

'I'll bet the rear of the house looks out over the park, don't you?'

'Without a doubt,' Ade agreed.'

'I think you monitor what's happening in the park.' Paulie started shaking. 'You rushed back here to hide the gear, didn't you?'

'I didn't!' Paulie's knees bent a little. His eyes widened. 'I don't know what you're talking about.'

Braddick shrugged and turned to Ade. 'We have enough for a warrant?'

'Definitely. I'll phone and have one arranged.'

'Wait,' Paulie snapped; his voice hoarse with panic. 'You can't come in here!'

'Not without a warrant but we'll have one within the hour,' Ade said with a sarcastic grin.

'There's been a murder and you're up to your eyes in it,' Braddick barked. 'This will be very bad for you, Paulie!' Braddick pointed his index finger in Paulie's face. 'You do know that possession with intent carries a very long jail term?' he paused for effect. 'The burden of responsibility tends to be placed where the product is found. In this case, your house.'

'Are you arresting me?'

'Not yet.' Braddick frowned.

'In that case, get off my property.' Paulie slammed the door and leaned against it. He wiped sweat from his forehead, his eyes stinging where it had run down his face. His knees buckled and he allowed himself to slide down the door until he landed on the floor with a thump. Tears filled his eyes as he thought about what was going to happen next. He balled his fists and pounded them against his thighs.

'The Farrells will have their people over here rapidly,' Ade said with a shrug.

'There's a very good chance they will. Get a warrant. He's a key witness to a murder. That will open the door for us.' Braddick buried his hands deep into his pockets and walked to the window. He could see the fat man sitting on the floor his head in his hands. 'That man is at breaking point. He has something to hide and I want to know what it is. If we put pressure on him, he'll crack.'

'Once he pulls himself together, he'll be flushing the evidence down the lav,' Ade said, eyebrows raised.

'I reckon he already has,' Braddick shrugged, 'but they're not his drugs to throw away. Make sure that the warrant includes the drains.'

CHAPTER 6

Bryn Evans was sitting up in a hospital bed, the sickening smells of antiseptic and urine drifted into his anteroom from the ward. The x-ray results had come back and the doctor was holding them up to the light. He was a skinny Indian man, his black hair deserting him fast, leaving a tiny fringe island at the front of his shiny brown scalp. He tutted and removed his glasses, turning towards his patient.

'They confirm my suspicions that your nose and cheekbone are broken.' Bryn remained silent. Apart from the pain, he was reeling with shock. The entire episode seemed surreal, as if it was happening to someone else, like the men found murdered in the alleyway that morning. He had seen the bodies, charred dead bodies, tendrils of smoke still rising from them yet the horror of it didn't register. For the women around him, it was nothing but gossip for the bingo. For him, it was a curious thing to see. Gangsters smouldering in the alleyway, deleted from the planet by bigger, more frightening gangsters, who could themselves be eliminated at any time. It was an existence that balanced on a razor's edge, terrifying, but belonging to strangers, of no consequence to Bryn. Yet he had heard their names before, somewhere in a distant memory, shadows of older kids at school talking about aspirations to be like so and so, drive a Porsche like so and so, have a gun and a Rolex like so and so. Did the women say they were called, Johnson? He couldn't remember. Their first names eluded him too. It seemed like a year ago.

'I want to take some advice on the cheekbone before we prescribe treatment, okay, you understand all that?' the doctor asked with a toothy grin. 'Your brother, Mark and your dad are in the corridor waiting to see you, but the police won't allow them in until they have taken a formal statement from you.'

'Is my mum here?'

'She's at home, I believe,' he adopted a serious tone, 'her doctor was called. The shock was a little much for her.'

'She has heart problems,' Bryn said. 'Doesn't stop her smoking like a chimney though.' He half smiled. 'She'll be worried, really worried. I hate it when she's stressed; drinks more, smokes more, eats more and it's all my fault this time.'

'Don't worry, once the police have spoken to you and straightened things out, she'll be fine. It is rarely as bad as it seems, believe me.'

'When will they do that?' Bryn asked quietly. 'I've told them what happened. He attacked me. He was going to stab Alice. I didn't mean to…'

'Take it easy,' the doctor raised his hand to stop him. 'It makes no difference to me what happened. I believe you so save all the explanations for the police. I'm here to fix your face.'

'Sorry.'

'Don't be sorry.' He smiled. 'Oh, before I forget, your brother, Mark asked me to tell you that he contacted your older brother, Simon is it?'

'Yes.'

'He has told the police that you're not to say a word until his solicitor has arrived.'

'Oh, I see,' Bryn said. His spirits were lifted a little by the news. Simon would know what to do. He looked after everything for his parents, their bills, their rent, their medical insurance and his school expenses, uniforms, dinners and trips. All their benefits were theirs to spend on the crap that they shovelled into their mouths, food, cigarettes and alcohol. He daren't think about what a mess life would be if Simon didn't support them. 'He's good like that. I hope he isn't pissed off with me.'

'I'm sure he isn't. I told the detectives what your brother had said and they were a bit miffed that a solicitor was on the way,' he lowered his voice and leaned over, 'between me and you, they were double miffed when they were told who he was.' He winked. 'He must be a good one, eh?'

Bryn nodded. Smiling was too painful. He had no idea what distinguished a good lawyer from a bad one but if he worked for Simon then he was probably very good. The door opened and a uniformed officer poked his head around the door. 'There's a solicitor here, doctor. Can he come in?'

'Yes, of course!' He winked at Bryn. 'The cavalry has arrived. Now, I think that we might need to keep you in for a few days at least. As I said before, I want a second opinion on your cheekbone. It might need an operation, but we can talk more about that later on.' He turned to meet the tall man, who had entered while he was talking. 'Come in, come in,' he said gesturing with his hand. The solicitor was silver haired and immaculately dressed in a dark three-piece suit and a lambs' wool Crombie overcoat. 'Do you need anything?' he asked. The lawyer shook his head with a polite smile. 'I'll leave you to it then.'

'You must be Bryn Evans,' the solicitor said approaching the bed, hand extended. Bryn went to shake it, but the handcuffs rattled and bit into his wrist painfully.

'Sorry.' Bryn gestured to the handcuffs.

'Not at all,' his apology was accepted with a narrow smile. 'My name is Jacob Graff and your brother, Simon, has directed me to act on your behalf. You may call me Jacob.' Bryn nodded silently. His accent was educated, not posh, not localised. Jacob oozed intellect and authority and it both intimidated him slightly and gave him confidence. 'Before we say anything to the police, I need to hear from you exactly what happened.' He held up his finger in warning. 'Remember that I'm on your side and it is fine to tell me the truth, no matter how distasteful. Once we're straight on your story, we'll decide which bits we will tell the police, understand?'

'Yes,' Bryn nodded. He took a deep breath and exhaled it slowly. 'Where do I start?'

'Funnily enough, I want you to start at the end,' Jacob smiled thinly. 'Did you kill Anthony Farrell?'

'If that was the man's name, yes.'

'Yes,' Jacob said sternly. 'It is very important that you call the victim by his name, Anthony Farrell. Try it for size…'

'Anthony Farrell.' Bryn shifted uncomfortably. Anthony Farrell was a victim, a murder victim, his victim.

'Very good, Bryn. Identifying that your victim was a human being with a name, a family and a life will go a long way to showing remorse.' Jacob sensed Bryn's discomfort. He spoke slowly, calming him. 'You killed a man, Bryn. You took his life, parted him from his loved ones and you will go through a range of emotions, none of them pleasant.' Bryn's eyes became watery. 'What we must do is demonstrate that there was no malice or preplanning to the murder, that it was the result of a series of events over which you had no control.' He paused to allow Bryn to compose himself. 'Are you okay to continue?'

'Yes,' Bryn's voice was no more than a whisper. The severity of what he had done was soaking through his being. He had killed someone's son. Anxious guilt began seeping through his body making him numb.

'You hit Anthony Farrell across the head with a house brick, I believe.'

'Yes…' it felt like there was a 'but'. Bryn chose not to say it. There was no but; he had hit the man with a brick, simple.

'That's a good start,' Jacob said sitting down in the chair opposite Bryn, 'because that's the bit that we can't refute so I know you're telling me the truth.'

'I see.'

'Why did you hit him with a brick?'

'He attacked me, beat me up, pulled a knife,' Bryn thought back. 'Alice bit him and I wriggled free. He was going to stab Alice…'

'Slowly, Bryn, one step at a time.'

'Sorry.'

'You were walking the dog, Alice?' Jacob said in a calm voice. 'And then Anthony Farrell started chasing you, yes?'

'Yes. He chased me for ages, and I couldn't get away,' Bryn began, his voice weak, breaking in places. 'I stopped to let Alice off the lead, and he tackled me to the floor. He was punching me in the face over and over. Alice bit him and he pulled a knife. He was going to stab her. I grabbed the brick and hit him across the head, but I didn't mean to kill him.'

'Where were you when you hit him?'

'Where?'

'What position was your body?'

'On my back,' his voice cracked slightly. 'On the floor.'

'Farrell was where?'

'Sitting on top of me, pinning me down. I couldn't move my arms and he kept punching me. I could hardly breathe because of his weight squashing my chest and then when my nose started bleeding, I thought I would choke…'

'Then what happened?'

'Alice attacked him, bit his leg.' Bryn half smiled at the memory, but pain shot through his face and it faded as quickly as it appeared. 'He shifted his weight and I managed to pull my arm free. I reached out into the grass and touched the brick…and hit him across the head.' A tear rolled free.

'In summary, you were attacked by a total stranger, much older and more powerful than you are. He quickly overcame you, injured you and pulled a knife to stab your dog.' He paused for a breath. 'You hit him once from beneath him with the first thing that your fingers grasped?' Jacob ignored Bryn's tears and steepled his fingers beneath his chin. 'Which just happened to be a house brick, correct?'

'Yes.'

'Very good, Bryn,' Jacob said encouragingly. 'We have established that you're not a murderer.' Bryn wasn't as pleased with that fact as he should have been. He didn't think that he was a murderer in the first place, and it frightened him that anybody else might do. 'Now I need to know exactly what led up to this unprovoked attack.'

Bryn thought about lying but didn't see the point. Jacob Graff had the kind of deep brown eyes that could burrow into his soul. He would spot an untruth before it left his lips. 'I might have provoked it,' he said meekly.

'Okay, how so?'

'I had an argument with a man…I called him a fat bastard…'

'Oh dear,' Jacob looked slightly amused and mildly disappointed, 'and you see this verbal insult as grounds to be attacked, beaten and stabbed with a knife?'

'No,' Bryn shook his head. 'Of course not.'

'Good, because it is not,' Jacob thought for a moment. 'Is the man you insulted Anthony Farrell?'

'No.'

'But they came into the park together?'

'Yes. It must be because of what I said. I can't see any other reason why that man attacked me.'

'Okay, you think that you may have provoked the situation. Let's see how you've arrived at this assumption, shall we?' Jacob closed his eyes for a moment. 'Who was the man that you insulted?'

Bryn looked at his fingernails and thought about where to start. 'We were walking towards the park. Alice stopped to sniff at a gatepost and the man from the house said, 'if your dog shits on my pavement, I'll kick it up the arse,' and he threatened to kick her three times!' Bryn said with a shake of his head. 'I lost my temper with him and said he was too fat to kick her, he kept calling me scum from the estate and I called him a fat bastard as we walked away.'

'Then what?'

'I was playing with Alice when they came after me in the park.'

'Was anything further said in the park?'

'No.'

'So, Anthony Farrell spotted you in the park and immediately began to chase you?'

'Yes.'

'And you had never seen him before and as far as you know, he has never seen you?'

'Yes, I guess.'

'You didn't taunt them, swear at them or exchange insults?'

'No, nothing like that.'

'So, the fat man must have pointed you out to Anthony Farrell.'

'I don't know, I suppose so.'

'That wasn't a question, Bryn,' Jacob said with a tilt of his head. 'We can safely assume that he did.' Jacob mulled over the facts for a moment. 'Did the fat man threaten you at all?'

'At the house,' Bryn said. 'He said he would have me and my dog, a couple of times.'

'That sounds like a threat to me,' Jacob said with a knowing nod. 'It might explain why Anthony Farrell attacked you.'

'You think so?'

'Maybe the fat man exaggerated what had happened. We need to provide evidence of a threat and it certainly constitutes one, but it hardly matters what I think, Bryn. It is what we can make the police and the Crown Prosecution Service believe that counts,' Jacob stood up and walked to the window. They were on the first floor and the wigwam shaped form of the Catholic cathedral dominated the view. The university buildings to his right were shrouded in mist from the river and the car park below him was full. 'I want you to tell the police everything that you told me. Don't change anything, okay?'

'Okay.' Bryn nodded. 'Will they let me go home?'

'I wouldn't think so.' Jacob shook his head. 'A man has been killed and they must investigate it thoroughly. It is only because of your injuries that you're not in a police station. They'll take a statement formally and keep you under arrest while they seek advice from the

CPS. I think that they'll bail you within the next few days although there's no guarantee. You understand that, don't you?'

'Yes.'

Jacob Graff looked down at the car park and watched a man staring up at the hospital through binoculars. He scanned left and right along the windows until he was looking right at him. Jacob could see that he was smartly dressed, dark leather coat over a grey suit. His hair was shaven at the sides with cropped dark fuzz on top, military style. He had seen enough mobsters in his time in courtrooms to be able to spot one when he saw one. Concern gripped him. The man waved a gloved hand and lowered the binoculars; he reached for something and an icy grin crossed his face. Instinctively, Jacob stepped backwards as the window exploded into a maelstrom of fractured glass. Bryn closed his eyes as his face was sprayed with a bloody gloop that was once inside Jacob Graff.

CHAPTER 7

Barbara Evans lit another cigarette, her tenth since the police arrived. She was sitting on the arm of the settee, staring out of the window, one eye on the road, the other on the phone. Her husband, Robert, had promised to call as soon as there was news. The police had taken him and Mark to the hospital. He said that he would get a taxi home later on and let her know if there were any problems in the meantime. Since then, an hour or so had ticked by, feeling more like six. She wanted Robert to call and say it was all a big mistake that it wasn't Bryn but the longer it went on, the less likely that was. At least her heartbeat had settled down, the doctor satisfied that she wasn't having an arrest; although he left her with a flea in her ear about not cutting down on her smoking. It was times like this when the stress and pressure of life peaked, that she smoked more than ever.

'Have you ever had any problems with, Bryn, Mrs Evans?' a family liaison officer called Ying asked. Her genetic mixture of east and west made her pleasing on the eye. 'You know what I mean, problems with schoolwork or homework and the like?'

'No. Nothing like that.' Barbara wiped her nose with a tissue, sniffled loudly and turned towards her. 'Never a minute's trouble.' She shook her head and turned back to the window. Ying's pen was poised over a blank page of her notebook.

'What about his friends, any bad apples that he hangs around with?'

'No.'

'Any single mums, broken homes or troubled childhoods that you know about?' Ying asked scraping the barrel.

'Have you done a psychology degree?' Barbara scoffed. She took a deep drag on her cigarette. 'If that's the best that you can do, you want to get your money back.' Ying looked offended. 'He's fourteen for God's sake, single mums? He doesn't know what a woman is yet,' she chuckled dryly. 'My Bryn doesn't hang around with anyone,' Barbara said blowing her nose. Her eyes were red from crying. She stubbed out her cigarette and immediately reached for another one.

Lighting it, she stood up and then lowered herself awkwardly into an armchair. 'He's never been an ounce of trouble since he was born. He goes to school, very clever he is too, and he spends his evenings at the boxing gym with Mark. He goes to the football with his elder brother, Simon whenever they're playing at home. He doesn't have many friends outside of that, good or bad.' Ying waggled her pen over her pad, the page still blank. 'Did you write that down or do you only write down the bad stuff?'

Ying made a few notes, embarrassed but not defeated. 'Did you hear about the two men found dead near the shops this morning?' Ying changed tack.

'I heard something about it on the news.'

'They were local men from the estate,' Ying said nonchalantly. Her sergeant had warned her to be subtle. 'Did you recognise their names?'

'I mustn't have because I don't remember them.'

'David and Mathew Johnson, does that ring any bells?'

'No. Why are you asking about them,' Barbara frowned behind a cloud of swirling blue smoke.

'In case there's a connection,' Ying bit her bottom lip, knowing she'd put her foot in it. 'Between the cases,' she added with a shrug.

'A connection my arse, young lady,' Barbara said angrily, 'No. I don't know them and neither does Bryn,' Barbara snapped. 'I don't know why you're digging for dirt, young lady because you won't find any.' She took another deep pull on her cigarette. 'Whatever happened in that alleyway had nothing to do with him. He was in the wrong place at the wrong time. I suggest you put your pen away and leave it at that.' She glared at the police officer long enough to allow the tension to dissipate a little and then looked out of the window again.

'I'm not insinuating anything, Barbara,' Ying said. 'Can I call you Barbara?' she added with a patronising smile. Barbara nodded that she could. 'Someone saw him in the alleyway this morning where they were found,' Ying probed, 'he was walking Alice so he must have been on his way to the park.' Alice recognised her name and wagged her tail. 'Is that the way he would normally go to the park?'

'Behind the shops? Probably, I wouldn't know.' Barbara rolled her eyes skyward and struggled to stand up. 'I can't move about as much as I used to.' She sighed, ignoring the question for now. She ambled towards the kitchen using the walls for support. 'Do you want tea?'

'Yes please,' Ying said deflated. Her questioning was going nowhere. It seemed that the Evans family was about as normal and law abiding as a family could be. She folded her notebook into her pocket and slipped her pen inside it. As she buttoned the flap, she noticed a van pulling up in the street outside. She didn't recognise the logo on the side, but it advertised a local fruit and veg and flower shop. The phone number was in a suburb nearby, the same dialling code as the estate. 'Do you have any green tea, Barbara?'

'Only when the milk is off.'

'Pardon?'

'Do I look like I drink green tea?'

'Black, no sugar then, please,' Ying replied diplomatically avoiding the question. 'Are you expecting a delivery?' she asked as the driver got out and began searching in the back of the van. He glanced at his delivery notes and then at the house.

'Delivery?' Barbara called from the kitchen. 'No…At least I don't think so why?'

'There's a delivery van outside.' Ying stood up as the man opened the gate and walked up the path. She looked at what he was carrying but it didn't register immediately. When its significance struck her, she rushed into the hallway.

'I'll go and see what it is, wrong address probably,' Barbara moaned.

'No!' Ying replied a little too loud. 'I'll go. You make the tea,' Ying cut her off before she left the kitchen. 'Leave it to me,' she said to a confused Barbara. 'Nothing to worry about.' Ying opened the front door and pulled it closed behind her. She met the deliveryman on the path.

'Hello, officer. I have a delivery for Mrs Evans,' he said very quietly. 'Never nice delivering these things; is she in?'

'I'll take it,' Ying said taking the wreath. 'And I'll need the details of who sent it.' The open card attached read: RIP Bryn Evans.

CHAPTER 8

Ray and Liam Johnson watched nervously as the service doors opened to reveal several shiny Mercedes saloons in various states of being resprayed. Ray whistled through his teeth as he totted up the sum total of their worth in his head, but his brain couldn't work with so many noughts. Liam steered the lorry inside the cavernous garage, guided by three men in overalls. The atmosphere in the cab was tense, both men soaked in sweat. It had been a long emotional night; news of their cousin's demise had terrified them. They knew they were in above their heads, but it was too late to stop the ride and get off. As the doors closed behind them shutting out the sunlight, Liam felt sick to the core.

'I really don't want to be here,' Liam said turning the engine off. 'We never should have listened to Mathew.'

'If I had known it was anything to do with this lunatic, I would have told Mathew to fuck off. Always full of big ideas, wasn't he?' Ray agreed. 'Well this one was a fucking cracker, best of the lot. Look where they are now.'

'What's in this crate that makes it worth all this shit?'

'I don't know, but I would love to know if Dave and Mathew did.'

'We'll never know, and I don't care. We're going to have to wing it,' Liam said opening the door. 'Whatever this prick says, we agree, right.'

Ray nodded and followed suit, jumping down from the cab. He half smiled at one of the men but was greeted with a cold stare.

'Put your hands against the van and spread your legs.'

'Just like the telly, eh?' Ray joked nervously but no one shared it.

'Shut up. Search them,' the man said. They were patted down roughly from head to toe. When they were deemed to be unarmed, he gestured to an open metal staircase that hugged the garage wall. 'The boss is up there. He wants to talk to you.'

Liam looked up at the office that was built on a mezzanine floor. A man stood in the window; his hands pushed into the pockets of his Italian suit. His expression was one of curious caution, scrutinising the new arrivals. The Johnsons exchanged glances, both recognising the man instantly.

'Whatever shit we're in, just got deeper,' Ray muttered.

'Leave the talking to me,' Liam whispered nervously. Reluctantly, Liam and Ray climbed the steps to the office, every move they made watched by many eyes, no chance of escape. As they reached the landing, the door was opened by a man built like a truck. He ushered them in with a nod of his head and closed the door behind them.

'Take a seat,' Nicolai Karpov said without looking at them. He continued to watch through the window. 'We need to check the container for a few things, then you can leave.'

'We wanted to have a word about that,' Ray said nervously. Nicolai turned to face them; a frown creased his face. 'Whatever is in that crate got our cousins killed.'

'So, I heard,' the Russian said calmly. 'They knew that there was a risk involved, there's always a risk.'

'Some people might be inclined to offer a little compensation payment.'

'We had a deal. It is what it is. When things don't go my way, nobody offers me compensation. If you want compensation, get a proper job and join a union.'

'We understand how things work, like you said, it is what it is.' Liam stepped in. He nudged Ray with his elbow and gave him his best 'shut-the-fuck-up' glare. 'Obviously, it's been a bit of a shock for us. We work containers month in month out and nothing like this has ever happened.'

'Losing family is never good, obviously.' The sound of grinders cutting into metal drifted to them. 'I offered them twenty thousand pounds to steal a container. A very specific container granted, but for that kind of money they knew the risks involved.' he paused and stared at Ray. Ray looked away nervously. 'And so do you, don't you?'

'Yes, we do,' Liam said. 'A deal is a deal. It is what it is.'

'Good, twenty thousand is a lot of money.'

'I don't think it's enough for what happened to them,' Ray mumbled. 'Whatever is in that van is worth a shit load more than twenty grand.'

'Of course, it is, but business is business,' Nicolai shrugged.

Ray wanted to ask what the cargo was, but he also wanted to live. 'Did you hear what the Tuckers did to them? I'm surprised you're going to let the Tuckers get away with that.' Ray was nervous and upset, rambling. He didn't know when to shut up. 'Did you see what they did?'

'I did see it, yes.' Nicolai sat on the edge of the desk. He picked up a gold-plated Parker pen and tapped his teeth with it. 'Tucker is getting…how do you say…too big for his boots.'

'You're not kidding,' Ray agreed. 'His outfit is becoming a nuisance. He'll be knocking on your door if you're not careful. You should do something about him before it's too late.'

Nicolai sighed. Ray Johnson was clever enough to spot a rising threat but not clever enough to see the solution in front of his nose. 'Why do you think we've gone to all this trouble, taking his container from him?'

Ray shrugged and looked at Liam. 'I wish you would shut up,' Liam hissed.

'Your brother is right in what he says,' Nicolai said raising his hand to quieten them. 'Tucker has grown too big and become unpredictable.' He paused and put his pen down as if he had made a decision. 'And that is my dilemma; you see they'll do the same to you as they did to your cousins to find that container.' Liam and Ray looked at each other. Fear snatched any further arguments from them. 'I can't take the risk that Joseph Tucker and his brother will find out who has their container. It would lead to a war and that would be bad for business.' Liam's blood turned to ice. His hands trembled and beads of sweat trickled down his spine. 'I'm sure that you can understand that, can't you?' the Russian asked as if talking to a child.

'We've fulfilled our part of the deal,' Liam said as assertively as he could. 'We're not the type of men who grass, no matter what happens. We'll take our chances out there.'

'I'm sure that you can hold your own, family connections and the like but do you think that you could hold your tongue while someone set fire to your feet?' Nicolai scoffed and shook his head. 'Tucker's younger brother has a talent for inflicting pain. No one could withstand that man questioning him for any length of time.'

'Mathew and David didn't grass,' Ray said quietly. 'And neither would we.'

'Your cousins didn't tell Tucker where the container was because they didn't know. Had they known, you would be dead, and the truck would be in Tucker's hands.'

'How do you work that one out?' Ray asked, offended.

'You always do the same thing. They take it from the docks, you hide it in a different location every time,' he said with a thin smile. 'You've never used the same place twice, have you?' The Johnsons shook their heads, part proud, part surprised that he knew so much. 'So, they could never spill the beans because they didn't know where the container was. Only you and I did. We made sure of that.'

'What? How could you do that?' Ray was staggered.

'Simple, by hiring you to steal it from Tucker,' Nicolai said. 'We have tracked that container from Amsterdam. It never left our sight. The safest way to smuggle drugs into this country is to get someone else to do it.'

'Why not just take it from Tucker yourself?' Ray asked, baffled by the process.

'Because we never know who else is tracking a shipment. If customs or the drug squad were following it, they would have pounced when you took it. You follow a different routine every time.' The door opened and one of the mechanics peered in. He put his thumb up and spoke in Russian. Nicolai nodded and turned back to the Johnsons. 'Everything is as it should be, gentlemen.' The clicking sound of bullets being chambered came from behind them. 'My men will escort you out. Our deal is completed, permanently.'

'What about our money?'

Liam felt a barrel above his ear, its metal cold and hard. They'd stayed away from guns, choosing not to work with the outfits that used them. He felt helpless and angry. 'Stand up and put your hands behind your back,' a guttural voice growled from behind them. He heard Ray swearing as they fastened Plasticuffs tightly around his wrists. Liam knew that once they were on, it was game over.

'You, double-crossing bastards!' Ray shouted. A heavy blow to the back of the head silenced him, dropping him to the floor with a thump. Liam knew that they were as good as dead. Karpov couldn't risk the Tuckers finding out who had set them up. If he was going to kill them then he needed to do it right there and then because Liam wasn't going to wait; being made to dig his own grave, in the woods, at gunpoint wasn't how it was going to end. He knew that there was no time left. In a split second, he decided that he wasn't going to die without putting up a fight. He took a deep breath, closed his eyes and ran full pelt at the window.

CHAPTER 9

Ward five had descended into chaos. The wind and rain were blowing into the room unchecked, curtains flailing almost horizontally. Bryn was whisked out of his room, the bed pushed down the corridor and into another anteroom that had no windows. A nurse dabbed at superficial cuts on his face caused by flying glass. Most of the blood on his skin belonged to Jacob Graff. His father and brother were ushered into the room, normal protocol broken for their own protection. Uniformed backup and an armed response unit had been summoned; their sirens audible in the distance.

'Are you okay, son?' Robert Evans asked, while thinking that he had never seen Bryn looking worse. He hugged his son and held him tightly for the first time in a long time. The bruises from the beating were blackening, the swellings deforming his handsome features. He resembled a car crash victim.

'I'm okay,' Bryn said, recoiling slightly from the smell of stale smoke but enjoying the rare show of affection. Sometimes he felt older than his years but now he felt like a child again, vulnerable and in need of a parent's protection. 'How is Jacob?'

'We don't know anything,' his dad said running a hand over his son's scalp. 'This is a nightmare, son. What the hell have you got yourself into?'

'I honestly don't know, Dad.' Bryn sighed. 'I wish I'd never gone to the park.'

'How can things get so out of hand walking the dog to the park?'

'Someone is dead, Dad. Take it easy on him,' Mark said.

'I didn't mean to do it,' Bryn said defensively. His face reddened and his eyes became moist again. He was frightened and confused by what had happened. Remorse was pulling at his soul. 'The bloke attacked me for nothing. He was going to stab Alice.'

'Better if he had done than all this,' Robert said shaking his head. 'What did you think would happen if you hit someone on the head with a house brick?'

'I didn't think at all,' Bryn protested. 'He was going to stab Alice!'

'Leave him, Dad,' Mark said calmly. 'Whatever is going on, it is hardly his fault is it? He's hardly to blame, is he? Look at the state of his face!'

'I'm not blaming him,' Robert said reaching out to touch his son's hand. The nurse carried on with her delicate task. 'I'm not blaming you, Bryn. I'm asking you if you know what's going on. What happened in your room?'

'I don't know,' Bryn said again. He was as confused as the rest. 'How the fucking hell would I know?'

'Don't swear at me,' Robert stuttered. His face was purple, and his hands were trembling, his body craving nicotine. 'I'm asking a question, that's all.'

The door opened and a uniformed sergeant stepped into the room. 'Just to let you know that everything is under control for now,' he said with a reassuring nod. He looked at Robert and gestured him out of the room. Mark followed and closed the door behind them, leaving Bryn to his treatment. 'I need to let you know what happened. I'm sure you're concerned.'

'That would be good,' Robert said, looking at a trolley being pushed along the corridor. 'Bloody hell!' he said with a sharp intake of breath. 'Is that Jacob Graff?'

'Yes,' the sergeant replied in a hushed tone. The bloodied face was swollen and bruised, the silver hair stained deep red. 'Someone threw a brick through the window, caught Mr Graff square in the face.'

'Did you catch them?' Robert asked weakly.

'No. I'm afraid not. Nobody saw it happen.'

'Was it aimed at Mr Graff or Bryn?' Mark asked.

'We're not absolutely certain but we have to assume that it was for your brother's benefit,' the sergeant confirmed his worst fears with a nod. 'Has anyone spoken to you about the victim's family?' Mark and Robert exchanged glances, neither finding the words to answer. A shake of their heads was enough. 'Anthony Farrell is from a very bad family. This is exactly the kind of reaction that we should expect but let me assure you that they will be spoken to. We won't tolerate this kind of intimidation.'

'Spoken to?' Mark said sarcastically. 'They need more than a talking to!'

'They'll get the message, don't worry.'

'You said they were a bad family. What do you mean 'bad family'?' Robert asked.

'They're career criminals, part of a wider criminal organisation,' the sergeant tried to play down the situation. 'But you mustn't worry.'

'Do you mean they're gangsters?'

'Yes.'

'You said they're bad, how bad?' Robert asked. His shoulders had slumped as if the life was being sucked from his body.

'They're angry. As far as they're concerned, one of their family has been murdered. We will protect you, but I wanted to tell you so that you can look out for each other,' the sergeant said touching his arm. 'That's all I can say for now. Please stay in there with your son and we'll keep you updated.' His mobile rang and he turned his back and took the call, walking further down the corridor as he spoke. He looked angered as he turned back to them. 'Mr Evans, we're having your wife brought here. She'll be here shortly.'

'I don't want her to see Bryn like this,' Robert complained. 'She's not well enough to come here. That's why we left her at home.'

'We have no choice I'm afraid.' The sergeant sighed. He looked tired of the case suddenly, his enthusiasm and confidence sapped from him. 'There's been an incident at your house. She'll be safer here.'

'What kind of incident?' Mark asked, disturbed. Anger flashed in his eyes, his muscles tensed and the tendons in his neck protruded like wires. 'Is she okay?'

'She's fine. It's a precaution.'

'What happened?' Mark wouldn't be fobbed off.

'Someone sent a wreath to the house,' the sergeant replied. 'Please wait with Bryn and try not to alarm him. He's been through a lot.'

Mark took his father by the arm and guided him into the anteroom, noticing how much the muscles in his flabby arm had atrophied. His face was deathly pale, and his breath was coming in shallow gasps. Bryn looked on, strain and concern etched onto his young face. Mark saw a frightened boy not a murderer. He put on a false smile for his younger brother but behind it, he knew that a storm was brewing; one that he wasn't sure that their family could weather.

CHAPTER 10

Six thousand miles away, Eddie Farrell was sitting on a barstool watching the sun go down into the Andaman Sea. The island of Koh Lanta was a tropical paradise, white sands, turquoise seas, and thatched beach-bars baked in sunshine all year round. He loved the local food, the beer and more importantly, the virtually nonexistent police force. It was the perfect place to conduct business with his Russian partners. They could talk openly, play golf, drink, and plan the next shipment or the removal of their enemies with impunity. However, it was not the place to be when the news of his oldest son being murdered arrived.

'One more Chang,' he said pushing an empty bottle across the bar to a local woman whose smile never faded. He kept the Koozie, a sleeve that keeps bottled beer cool. He slid the new bottle into it before taking a deep slug, emptying half the contents. The sun was still hot, making sweat run down his shaven head. His Adidas vest was sticking to him and his shorts were uncomfortably moist. He looked at the screen of his phone, desperate for more information, willing it to ring. He shared idle chitchat with the other patrons, hardly focusing on what they were saying, their words a blur. By the time it finally rang, he was on his third bottle.

'Eddie, I'm glad that you have a signal at last, I've been calling for an hour, but your phone goes straight to voicemail. It was terrible news today, my condolences to you and your family.' The voice was familiar. 'How are you?' Nicolai Karpov sounded preoccupied, slightly insincere.

'How do you think I am?' he slipped his feet out of his flip-flops and dug his toes into the soft sand. Normally it relaxed him but not today.

'Sorry, that was a stupid question,' Nicolai conceded. 'I know that you don't want to make small talk, so I'll give you the itinerary briefly and then I'll text your travel plans to your phone later.'

'Thanks, Nicolai. I need to get home, when do I leave here?'

'There will be a taxi with you in one hour, seven o'clock your time, that will take you to the harbour where the fast boat to Krabi leaves at eight,' he paused. 'Your flight to Bangkok from there, leaves at nine-thirty and then you're booked on the first flight out of Bangkok tomorrow morning with Emirates.'

'Thank you,' Eddie said swallowing his Chang. He gestured to the barmaid for another. 'Tell me what you have found out about Anthony. Who killed my son?'

'He went to see Big Paulie and got into a fight in the park,' Nicolai told him. 'The kid he was fighting with cracked him across the head with a brick. He died instantly. I'm very sorry for you, Eddie.'

'Who is he?' Eddie felt his fingers gripping the bottle painfully tightly. Anger rose in his throat, threatening to blow the top of his skull clean off. Even the beauty of the glowing orange orb sinking into the blue sea couldn't quell the pain, the anger or the burning desire for revenge. Eddie had recently lost his wife, the mother of his sons, to cancer following a long drawn out battle. His sons were his life. The thought of not seeing Anthony alive again was like a red-hot spike through his guts. He clawed at the warm sand with his toes, desperate for some comfort but not finding any.

'His name is Bryn Evans,' Nicolai said. He thought about adding more detail to it but wasn't sure what was apt, so he resisted. The silence was deafening.

'Is that it?' Eddie asked astounded. 'My son has been murdered and all you give me is a name!'

'What more do you need at this stage?' Nicolai asked. Anthony's death was nothing to him. He had never liked Eddie's sons. He found them arrogant and thought they were a liability. They strutted around the city like peacocks, attracting unwanted attention in their flash cars and brash clothes. He was pandering to Eddie because his Uncle Victor had ordered him to.

'What do you know about him, who is he?' Eddie asked biting his lip. 'I want to know who killed my son, Nicolai!'

'Calm down, Eddie,' Nicolai quipped impatiently. 'He is a local kid from the Stockbridge Village housing estate across the road from the park.' Nicolai was offended but he bit his tongue. 'Do you know it?'

'Yes.'

'We have done some digging. We have his address, family names, everything that we will need when you arrive home.' He waited for Eddie to comment but he didn't. 'We have already sent a message to him.'

'Like what?'

'I've sent a wreath to his parents. They'll know what's coming.'

'Good. I want this fucker dead!' Eddie slapped the bar with his hand, not realising that the other customers were watching him. 'I want him to suffer and I want him dead.' Eddie looked around him suddenly aware that he was swearing, his voice, raised and angry. A couple stood up and moved away, taking their drinks onto the beach. He lowered his voice. 'I want his entire family dead!'

'All in good time, Eddie, the police are all over this,' Nicolai cautioned. 'It is a murder investigation.'

'I know what it is.'

'Then you know that we need to let the dust settle for now, but we'll do what you want when you get home. We must not overreact yet.'

'Which prison is he in?' something niggled at Eddie about how blasé Nicolai was about the death of his son. *Overreact? How could he overreact?*

'He isn't in prison yet.'

'Why not?'

'He's at the hospital.'

'Hospital?'

'Anthony hurt him badly.'

'Good,' Eddie grunted. 'He'll be remanded once they've treated him?'

'I'm not so sure about that but we'll see.'

'Why aren't you sure?' Eddie paused. Something was missing. 'What are they playing at?'

'I don't think they'll remand him to a prison because of his age, maybe he'll go to a young offenders' unit or something.'

'What?'

'He is fourteen.'

'Fourteen?'

'Yes.' Nicolai sighed.

'Anthony was killed by a fourteen-year-old kid?'

'Yes.'

'What the hell happened?'

'All we know is that Anthony attacked him in the park, chased him for a while and then beat him up,' Nicolai explained. 'The kid fought back and hit him with a brick. Our sources at Canning Place think that it is a case of self-defence.'

'I don't believe this,' Eddie hissed angrily.

'He is a young boy and because Anthony is your son.' Nicolai sighed. 'You're not a favourite with the police. I don't need to spell it out for you, but there are doubts about what Anthony was doing. We're not sure ourselves.'

'Surely it's obvious?' Eddie said trying to keep calm. 'He was looking after business.'

'How do you figure that out?'

'I thought he was a dealer from the estate?'

'That's what Paulie told me but I'm not so sure.'

'Sure, about what?'

'He might not be.'

'What are you talking about?' Eddie was beginning to lose his cool. 'If he was in that park, he's either a dealer or a junkie, either way someone must know him.'

'What if he's just a school kid walking his dog?'

'Why would my son be fighting with a school kid?'

'We don't know. That's not clear at all.'

'But I thought you had asked Paulie all about this.' There was an edge creeping into his voice, almost accusing; hints of disbelief.

'I've spoken to him on the telephone, Eddie however I don't trust what Big Paulie is saying,' Nicolai said defensively. 'I don't trust that fat fuck as far as I could throw him. I think he has more to do with this than he's letting on.'

'We need to find out quickly. When can you speak to him properly?' Eddie asked confused, 'I mean face to face?'

'We can't do anything right now. The police are all over the park, the house and Anthony's vehicle, Eddie,' Nicolai explained. 'We'll have to wait for them to finish what they are doing.' He was becoming irritated. 'Look, I'm doing everything that I can. Once you're home, we can decide what to do next.'

Eddie thought for a second, the distance from home frustrating him. 'Can't you get a message to him or something?'

'Like what?'

'Are you sending Boyce to represent Paulie?'

'He's on his way.'

'Good. Then ask him to find out exactly what happened,' Eddie said taking a swig of beer, 'And send someone to search the kid's house too,' he added. 'I want to know everything about his family, jobs, bank accounts, siblings, partners, hobbies, phone numbers, what is in their bins, everything…I want to know everything.'

'That's all in hand,' Nicolai said calmly. His tone became icy. 'I know you're upset but please remember that we know what we're doing.'

'Okay, okay, sorry. I know you do,' Eddie agreed, resigned to his position. His hands were tied until he got home. 'Don't let the little bastard that killed my son out of your sight.'

'Do not worry, we won't. Have a safe journey.'

The line went dead and Eddie felt a surge of anger rushing through his veins. Nicolai was a patronising bastard at the best of times. He had been a willing partner over the years; working with the Karpovs was better than working against them, plus the fact that they were backed by the Russians made them a potent force in the city and beyond. The agreement was to be equals, equal share of profits and equal share of decision making. Sometimes Eddie realised that he wasn't Victor Karpov' equal whether he liked it or not. That was about to stop. The balance of power needed to change. 'One more Chang and a SangSom,' he said turning to the bar. He wanted the Thai whisky to take the edge off his nerves for a while.

'We need to talk,' Yuri Karpov appeared on the stool next to him. The heavy scent of Aramis arrived with him. He twisted the Rolex on his thick wrist, the hairs on his arm bleached blond by the sun. Eddie looked at him and smiled sourly at his garish flower-patterned shirt, the buttons straining to bursting point across his gut. 'I've been speaking to Mikel about what has happened.' He paused and called the barmaid over. 'Two more Chang, please.'

'Where is Mikel?' Eddie asked looking towards the path that led to the rooms. Yuri and Mikel were cousins to the Pakhan, Victor Karpov. Their role was spreading the Karpov 'franchise' and developing outfits, like the Farrells, to control operations on the ground.

'He's still in his room talking to Victor on the phone,' Yuri paused to take the beers and took a long slug from his. 'Victor is very concerned.'

'About what?'

'Anthony, of course,' Yuri drained half his beer and raised it up. 'Another Chang. It is so hot, I'm thirsty!' He turned back to Eddie. 'He sends his condolences by the way. Your loss is our loss. We will pay for the funeral, of course.'

'Tell Yuri that I'm grateful for the offer but I can bury my own son.' Eddie studied the Russian and watched his face darken, angered by the rejection. He waited to see what he would say next, sensing that something unpleasant was coming.

'Victor is concerned about the timing of this tragic death, it's attracting unwanted attention from the police at a very sensitive time,' Yuri tried to look concerned, his voice softer now. 'You know that the container of zombie has arrived into the country and we've taken it from Tucker?'

'Of course, I do.'

'This is a very sensitive operation. You know this.'

'Of course, I know,' Eddie was keeping his cool despite the anger rising in his belly. 'I don't see what the problem is. We have the container and Tucker hasn't got a fucking clue where it is,' he hissed. 'My son's death and the timing of it are not something that he, nor I, could control. I'm sorry if his death is an inconvenience but it couldn't be helped, for fuck's sake!'

Yuri looked at him and shook his head. He clinked his beer bottle against Eddie's but the gesture went unappreciated. 'You're taking what I'm saying the wrong way, my friend.' His smile became lizard-like. Eddie wanted to punch him in the face. 'I'm devastated that Anthony is dead, truly I am.'

'Are you?' Eddie raised his eyebrows.

'We have watched your children grow up over the years,' he emphasised his words by tapping his forefinger on the bar. 'And we will go to whatever lengths are necessary to take your revenge.'

'When?'

'When the timing is right and that is not now.'

'Let's not beat around the bush. What exactly are you saying?' Eddie asked, gulping his beer down, 'Just so that I'm clear and we all know where we stand.'

Yuri sighed and shifted on his stool; his belly threatened to pop out of his shirt. 'Look, you have our sympathy, of course you do but Anthony's death has brought the police to Paulie's house. The operation there was a profitable one and we have no idea how much damage has been done. We don't know how much Paulie has told the police. We know that the women got out of the house before the search but that's all we know.' He paused to drink, 'The police found money in Anthony's vehicle too, our money.'

Eddie thought about breaking his beer bottle in Yuri's throat but resisted the urge. 'You can tell Victor that I'll repay anything he has lost.'

'He wouldn't hear of that. The money is not an issue for us,' Yuri shook his head, 'but the police are. We must not attract any more attention at this time. The zombie is in pure form, it needs to be cut and packaged and that takes time. The shipment is vulnerable until it is distributed.'

'I don't see what difference it makes,' Eddie said angrily. 'The fact that Anthony was murdered will attract attention anyway. There's no getting away from that. We've dealt with worse pressure from the law.'

'You're missing the point,' Yuri placed his hand on Eddie's arm. 'The police are a major concern of course but the real problem is, if the police start digging and find the container, then Tucker will find out who took it from him and then we'll have trouble, big, big trouble.' He smiled like a bad actor. 'There would be a war and we can't allow that, Eddie. Bodies on the streets will set us back years. We don't operate like that.' He pointed his finger at Eddie as he spoke. 'And neither do you, understand me?' Eddie swallowed hard and thought about what was being said. His son had been murdered and he was being told to shut up about it. He didn't answer; his blood reaching boiling point. 'We must process the shipment and distribute it without interference, or we stand to lose millions. Keeping Tucker and his crew down is our focus for now and to do that we must keep everything quiet.'

'Joseph Tucker?' Eddie scoffed loudly and laughed harshly. The other customers glanced uncomfortably in their direction. 'I think that you should revaluate the priorities here. My son is lying on a slab and you think that I give a fuck about Joe Tucker and his retard brother?'

'Keep your voice down,' Yuri shifted uncomfortably. He pulled at the collar of his shirt and wiped sweat from his brow. 'It's still so hot even at this time of night isn't it?' he said to onlookers while he thought about his next words, but no one replied. No one wanted to make eye contact, several drifting onto the beach. 'Two more Chang,' he waved at the barmaid. She scurried over, wary of the bad atmosphere. Replacing the empties with full ones, she made a quick retreat to the other side of the bar. After a few minutes of prickly silence, he spoke again. 'Eddie, do you know what Vorovskoy Zakon is?'

Eddie rolled his eyes and shook his head. 'You know, whenever things become tense, you Russians have to come up with some historical horseshit.'

'It is what we call, The Thieves' Code and we have used it as a guide for hundreds of years,' Yuri said, ignoring Eddie's comment. 'Rule number one is that in times of need we have to forsake our relatives for the better good of our family of thieves. You can understand this, yes?' Eddie drained his beer and listened, staring at the sea. 'The business must take priority over any personal issues that we have until the time is right. You must put your revenge on hold for now, my friend.'

'Because of the Tuckers?' Eddie said shaking his head. 'I don't see it that way.'

'The Tuckers have been a threat for too long now and they're clever. Whenever we have tried to take them out, they are one step ahead. Victor thinks that taking this shipment from them will break them and make them someone else's problem. It is a way of getting rid of them without attracting attention to ourselves. It makes sense, Eddie. Surely you can see that?'

Eddie thought about it. He looked out to sea; the bright lights of the night trawlers lined the horizon as the night sky began to creep upwards from the horizon. It was a magical time of day when the sky was still blue, but darkness tinted the farthest perspective. He couldn't shift the feeling of despair from his stomach. 'I just don't see why you can't see things from my point of view.'

'Come on, Eddie.' Yuri sighed. 'A container load of zombie is worth how much?' he said with a shrug. 'A few million, three maybe even five or more, yes?'

'Probably.'

'Tucker doesn't have that kind of money sitting around.' Yuri tapped his nose with his finger. 'Victor knows that they have borrowed heavily to finance this deal. If they lose this shipment they're finished for good and they'll owe people a lot of money.' He laughed dryly. 'They'll owe very bad people a lot of money and when they can't pay it back those people will take them out of the game completely, leaving us to mop up their assets without breaking a sweat.' Yuri shrugged; a wide grin on his face. 'This is a golden opportunity to be rid of them without having a war. Those days are gone, Eddie. We must use our brains before our guns. Victor has been planning this shakedown for a long time. So, you can see why there must be no reprisals right now?' his face pleaded for agreement although his voice had taken on a darker tone. 'Nothing must happen that will attract police attention, understand?'

'It is all a matter of priorities, Yuri,' Eddie said standing up. He tilted his head, finishing his beer. 'Your priority is Tucker. Mine is squaring things up for my son and I can't see past that.'

Yuri took a deep breath and shook his head with a sigh. 'How long have we known each other, Eddie?'

'A long time. What does that matter?'

'It matters because we want you to do the right thing at the right time and now is not the right time,' Yuri urged him again his palms facing skyward. 'Victor was very clear in his orders. There are to be no reprisals until the Tuckers are out of the picture and that is final.'

'Victor is clear with his orders?' Eddie chuckled sourly. 'Victor gives me orders now does he?'

'You know what I'm saying.'

'No one gives me orders, Yuri.'

'Look, you have to do whatever you have to do, Eddie but we will have to react to protect our business. We will forsake all relatives for the business.' He patted his shoulder, but Eddie shrugged his hand off. 'Vorovskoy Zakon, Eddie. We will forsake anyone, even our closest friends for the business.' He paused. 'You're grieving and you're not thinking straight. I'm urging you to think about it rationally. You're understandably upset but please be sensible and follow Victor's wishes,' he said, playing down his words. 'This is business.'

Eddie nodded slowly. He pushed all thoughts of burying his child into the shadows, but they kept creeping back, taunting him, haunting him. In his mind he thought about how much Bryn Evans would suffer watching his family slaughtered before he died. 'You tell Victor that I won't do anything that he wouldn't do himself if he were in my shoes. That's the best that I can do.' He picked up his flip-flops, tossed some crumpled Baht onto the bar and walked away from the Russian, barefoot in the sand. On the beach, a line of long tail boats was waiting to take tourists back to their hotels, a floating taxi rank. He checked his watch, his mind made up. There was half an hour until his taxi arrived and there was someone he needed to speak to urgently.

CHAPTER 11

Braddick watched the Range Rover being loaded onto a flatbed truck. Their cursory inspection had revealed three bags of money stashed in a lock box under the passenger seat, all used tens and twenties, banded into bundles of a thousand. A uniformed officer counted sixty bundles into an evidence bag and watched it being sealed and taken away.

'It looks like your friend Anthony was on a collection run, Paulie.'

'No comment,' Paulie mumbled as they led him from his house.

'This is not an interview,' Braddick tutted. 'This is me thinking aloud.'

'No comment,' Paulie mumbled, ignoring Braddick.

'He was picking up the takings, wasn't he?'

'No comment.'

Big Paulie was being put into the back of a police car, his weight making the suspension tilt. He looked around at the onlooking neighbours and blushed. Braddick bent towards the door.

'There's a lot of money in that vehicle, Paulie and when it comes to sentencing, I've seen people get years for much less than that.'

'It isn't my money,' Paulie said, confused.

'It's on your drive so it's your problem,' Braddick shook his head as if he felt sorry for Paulie. He pointed his finger at him. 'On your way to the station, you need to have a long hard think about what you're going to say to me, or you won't be coming home for a long time…understand?' Paulie nodded, his face dark and sulky like a chastised child.

'I'm not saying anything. No comment.'

'Where are the drugs, Paulie?'

'What drugs?' Paulie frowned, feigning offence.

'Eddie Farrell's drugs.'

'No comment.'

'Get him out of here,' Braddick snapped. The vehicle pulled away and he watched it turn the corner towards the park, wandering what had happened to cause Farrell's death.

'What have you locked him up for?' a female voice asked from behind him. Braddick turned to face her. She was attractive but thin, very thin. Her suit looked like she'd borrowed it from a larger friend and her shiny black hair hung down her back in a long ponytail. 'I'm DI Cain, Drug Squad.' She held out her hand. 'You must be DI Braddick?'

'I am,' Braddick said with a thin smile. Her hand felt as skeletal as she looked; no engagement or wedding rings. 'What brings you here?'

'A soon as we got the call that you had a warrant, I rushed over.'

'Thanks for coming so quickly,' he said insincerely, wandering which idiot had called the Drug Squad. As the new kid in the playground, he needed to identify where old allegiances lay. Someone in his team had tipped her off and he didn't like that one bit. 'Sorry, I didn't catch your first name.'

'Steff, but most people call me Cain, to my face anyway. I've heard a lot worse behind my back,' she answered. 'I've not come to trample on your toes…I know this is to do with the Farrell murder, but we've been watching Big Paulie for a long time. He's a bit of a celebrity around here.'

'He's certainly difficult to miss.'

'We certainly couldn't lose track of him.'

'The search has started but you're welcome to tag along.'

'Thank you very much, it's appreciated,' Cain smiled, 'I wouldn't miss this.'

'How long has the place been under surveillance?' Braddick tried to scratch beneath the surface. Cain was holding her cards close to her chest and a glint in her eyes said she was holding an ace. He didn't want a previous investigation trumping his.

'We haven't had full obs on the house as such,' she said looking towards the park, 'but we've had a Matrix officer in the park area for nearly six months. She's been trying to infiltrate one of the local crews that operate there in a joint operation with Vice.' Braddick nodded but showed no emotion, disappointed that another department was now linked to the property, Vice as well as Drug Squad. 'Our operative fingered this house as a base for the Farrells, one of three on the estate.'

'Three?'

'Yes,' Cain nodded. 'They seem to be well established in this part of town,' she said, skirting the full truth. Braddick could sense that they had a lot more than she was letting on. He wondered why they'd been holding back on searching the place. 'We've been building up enough information to get inside, but you beat us to it.'

'Six months' worth of obs and you couldn't get a warrant?'

'Yes, we weren't ready to move,' Cain ignored the barb, 'You've done us a big favour getting a warrant. It's been a priority for a while, but we didn't want to blow our Matrix cover.' She looked at Braddick to gauge his reaction. His black skin was wrinkled at the corner of his eyes, but he gave nothing away. 'What have you charged Big Paulie with?'

'Obstruction for now,' Braddick replied, boring of the game. 'We need to talk to him about Anthony Farrell's death first; whatever else we find is a bonus.'

'Anthony Farrell,' she said with a quiet intake of breath that made a whistling sound. 'I've only just heard he's dead.'

'Are you familiar with him?'

'Oh, yes. I can't believe someone has whacked Anthony Farrell in broad daylight.'

'It's an odd one,' Braddick agreed, 'A fourteen-year-old kid with a house brick.'

'With a brick?' Steff said with raised eyebrows. 'I thought that if he was going to go, he would go with a little more finesse, you know, taken out by a machinegun in a hail of bullets outside a casino or something.' She shook her head with a thin smile on her lips. 'He was hit across the head with a brick by a teenager in Stockbridge Park. I didn't see that one coming.'

'Neither did he,' Braddick said thoughtlessly. 'Have you ever had eyes on Anthony over the years?'

'Oh, yes.' Steff nodded and bit her lip. 'Both him and his brother are their father's right-hand men. They're a real pair of arseholes.'

'Well there's one less now.'

'Anthony was our main focus for a number of hits last year but there was never enough evidence to charge him. Our witnesses had a habit of disappearing; we could never get near them.'

'I'll put it down to karma. What goes around, eh?'

'They say karma is a bitch.'

'Oh, she is.'

'You know that this is not going away without a backlash,' she warned. Braddick nodded that he understood. 'The Farrells are a nasty bunch.'

'So I've heard.'

'And they're in bed with the Russians, the Karpov family.'

'I know all about the Karpov family,' Braddick said looking away. A needle of hate pricked him. Karin's blistered face appeared; her eyes blackened pits. She vanished as quickly as she'd appeared, banished to the darkness at the edge of his mind, waiting, watching and reminding him constantly that he was to blame. He left her alone. 'The Karpovs have business interests everywhere. Liverpool is merely one of their outposts.'

'Of course, you would know all about them, wouldn't you?' Cain said fishing for information.

'They survive on their reputation,' Braddick explained. 'They move into an area, identify a local outfit to use as muscle and then move on leaving a few key members to oversee things. They can run a city with just a few people because the threat of them coming en-masse is enough to make them untouchable. If they do have to get heavy with another crew, it's like Armageddon for a week and then they're gone.'

'Sounds like they're running a franchise.'

'The principle is the same.'

'Your secondment with the NCA would have brought you into contact with the likes of them?'

'Them and too many others.'

'They're at the top of the tree though?'

'Yes. I came across them two years ago in London,' Braddick explained. 'Victor Karpov is an especially interesting psychopath. I believe his nephew runs things in the North-West, Nicolai?'

'He does. He fronts things for the family using the Farrells as muscle. You're going to have your hands full there.'

'We'll have to manage them, won't we?'

'We will,' she agreed. 'You're back from your secondment early, aren't you?'

'Yes.'

An awkward silence followed, and she knew that it was of her own creating. Braddick wasn't playing her game. She changed tack. 'Was there anything in Farrell's vehicle?'

'No. The dogs reacted but we didn't find anything but money,' Braddick gestured to the house. 'Something was carried in it recently but it's clean now. Let's hope forensics find something solid.'

'Like the blood of an unsolved murder victim in the boot?'

'Be nice but unlikely, eh?' His mobile rang, the screen showing an extension at Canning Place. He apologised for the interruption with a wave of the hand and turned away to answer the call, 'Braddick.'

'It's me, Guv.'

'Google, just the man,' Braddick said. 'I was about to call you.'

'What about?'

'Have you had any joy with the Facebook post?' he asked looking around. Cain was mooching near the back door, peering into the windows.

'Depends what you call joy,' Google moaned. 'We've got plenty of names and addresses but so far, no one wants to talk to us officially.'

'All those comments and no one will talk?'

'No, Guv. There's plenty of 'off the record' info but nothing solid.'

'I'm surprised,' Braddick said disappointed. 'There was venom in some of the posts that I read. I thought they would be queuing up to talk to us.'

'No one queues up to talk to us, Guv.'

'So I've been told.'

'They're keyboard warriors, Guv, full of fire and brimstone when they're online but in the cold light of day, it's all piss and wind,' Google said sourly.

'I suppose so.'

'The news pictures of the Johnson brothers, dead in an alleyway, doesn't help one bit.'

'No, not one bit.'

'People are terrified, family or not. No one wants to talk to us.'

'And no one is pointing a finger at anyone?'

'Nope, we've had a few random theories but nothing of substance.'

'Keep digging, someone will come forward. All we need is a name and someone knows it.'

'We will, Guv. On a brighter note, the Crime Stoppers line has had a number of anonymous calls, all saying that the Johnsons made a living stealing containers and articulated lorries from the docks, truck stops and airports.'

'Stealing containers would fit with the caption on the photograph,' Braddick mused. 'A container load of anything could be worth killing for but if it is drugs, well there are a few million reasons.'

'Without a doubt. We're running checks on everything that was reported stolen in the last seven days; shipping containers, trucks, lorries, large vans and the like,' he paused, 'obviously there's a good chance that it was never reported stolen.'

'Good work,' Braddick said. 'What else did you want me for?'

'Oh yes, that's why I called in the first place. I've had a couple of calls from the uniform looking after your suspect, Bryn Evans, at the Royal.'

'What's the problem?'

'There have been reprisals, Guv,' Google explained. 'A wreath was sent to the family home, frightened the life out of the mother.'

'What?' Braddick shook his head. Bullying, tormenting and instilling fear into people sounded like something the Farrells would enjoy. 'So, they're scaring old ladies, very tough. Is she all right?'

'She's a bit shaken up, so they've taken her to the hospital. She's not in the best of health anyway,' he paused. 'There's more, I'm afraid, Guv.'

'Go on.' Braddick kicked at the floor with his boot while he listened.

'Someone has traced Bryn Evans to the hospital. They threw a house brick through the window of his room.'

'They couldn't have traced him, Google,' Braddick said with a sigh. He rubbed his eyes with the back of his free hand. 'Someone told them he was there.'

'That's what I thought.'

'Was anyone hurt?'

'Yes, Guv, it hit his brief square in the face; he's in a right state.'

'Who is he?'

'Erm, hold on a second I have his name written down somewhere, Jacob Graff,' Google read from his notes.

'Jacob Graff?' Braddick asked, surprised. 'I know of him. He's a very big hitter in these parts.'

'Maybe the Evans family have money, Guv.'

'They'll need it if they're employing Jacob Graff's services,' Braddick said. 'The thing is, Jacob Graff bats for the opposition. His client list is like a who's who of local villains.'

'I can look into who's paying the bills, Guv.'

'Yes, do that. Were there any witnesses?'

'No, Guv. The wreath was ordered locally, and the buyer paid with cash, no CCTV in the shop. We've got a couple of grainy images of the hospital car park, but nothing we can use to identify whoever threw the brick.'

'So, the Farrells are on the warpath,' Braddick shook his head and continued to kick at the floor with the toe of his boot. 'Have we managed to track down Eddie Farrell?'

'He's travelling abroad, somewhere in South-East Asia apparently.'

'So, he's out of the country and we still have a backlash?'

'They're a big family, Guv.'

'Doesn't bode well, does it?'

'No, Guv. We've got the Evans family together in a secure area and armed response is there. There's an older brother not accounted for but he's on his way apparently.'

'Okay, good work thanks, Google. Let them know that we'll be there shortly.'

'No problem.'

Braddick mulled things over. A reaction from the Farrells had been anticipated but this had happened quicker than he expected. If Eddie Farrell was away, then someone else was orchestrating it. 'Sorry,' Braddick turned back to Cain. 'It appears that the Farrells are already on the warpath.'

'Really?' She frowned. 'What's happened?'

'Someone threw a brick through Bryn's room window at the hospital,' Braddick explained. 'The fact that it was a house brick can't be a coincidence.'

'Oh dear,' Cain said with a shake of her head. 'I feel sorry for that kid.'

'Have you ever come across the Johnson family?' Braddick asked.

'The men found in the alley?' she shook he head again. 'They're new to me. I don't think they're connected to the Farrells.'

'You need to see this, Guv,' Ade called from behind a garden gate, just his eyes and forehead showing above the wood. He struggled with the bolt and the gate rattled open. Braddick and Cain walked towards him. Ade looked surprised when he saw her, and they acknowledged each other with the slightest of nods. 'You okay, Guv?' he asked Braddick.

'We've got mither at the hospital,' Braddick told him. 'I've just had a call from Google. Someone is after Evans already. They chucked a brick through the window and hit his brief in the face.'

'That will be the Farrells, eh?'

'Good work, detective,' Cain quipped. Ade looked at her, his eyes narrowed slightly. There appeared to be no love lost between them. 'Nothing gets past Ade.' She joked, but Adrian Burns didn't see the funny side.

'They also sent a wreath to his mother,' Braddick added as an afterthought. 'She's been taken to the hospital.'

'Bloody hell, subtle if nothing else,' Ade grunted. 'Are you thinking of putting them into protective custody?'

'That's the problem,' Braddick frowned. 'Evans is a murder suspect, not a witness. We can't put his family into protection and if we put him in custody, he's a sitting duck.'

'He would be.'

'It would take the Farrells five minutes to get to him inside.'

'What can we do?'

'Nothing much,' replied Braddick. 'Ultimately, it will be down to the Crown Prosecution Service and Social Services.' His confidence in both agencies was low. They were short staffed, swamped with cases and he had lost touch with all his contacts there. There would be no favours coming his way. He sighed and pulled his leather jacket together tightly against the wind. 'I'll going to the Royal when we have finished up here to speak to Evans myself; what have you found?'

'You were right about the drains, but it's not what I expected. You'll be surprised.'

'Not Shergar is it?' Braddick mumbled. He stepped through the gate and peered into an inspection hatch; the cover removed by the CSI's. Paulie or his associates had fitted a wire mesh trap across the pipe to catch anything that they had to flush down the toilet. Lumps of tissue paper and excrement clung to the wire, the stench eye-watering. 'Didn't he think that we would check if they had a trap?'

84

'It's a bit of a giveaway that you're up to no good, unless you're in the habit of flushing your valuables down the lavvy.' Cain agreed with a grin. Her face became serious again. 'No sign of any drugs?'

'No.'

'Money?'

'Not quite.' Ade held up a clear evidence bag. Inside was a bundle of passports, dark green in colour with gold writing embossed on the front. 'There are eighteen in total, all Russian, all female.'

'Good. Paulie Williams is up shit creek,' Braddick said. He looked around the garden area frustrated. 'Where are the drugs?' he asked no one in particular.

'They were moved recently. The dogs reacted all over the house but there's nothing there, Guv,' Ade shrugged. 'Maybe he unwrapped it all and flushed the powder down the drains?'

'Would you flush Eddie Farrell's drugs down the toilet?' Cain scoffed. 'They would cut his legs off and feed them to him.'

'The search team have combed the house.' Ade shrugged.

'Let's have another look,' Braddick said. He turned and headed into the house through the back door. The kitchen was immaculate, floors and worktops gleaming, cupboards tidy and organised. He opened the lid on a pedal bin, a large empty bottle of Fanta its only content. A single unwashed glass in the sink was the only blemish on perfection. 'Do you think this bloke has got OCD, a cleaning obsession?'

'Maybe, Guv,' Ade nodded opening the tin cupboard. 'Anyone who lines up their beans and peas has either got issues or too much time on their hands, or both.'

They moved through the hallway into the living room, the same story faced them. His books were colour coordinated, surfaces dusted, carpets and rugs vacuumed. There wasn't a thing out of place. The search team was busy moving things and putting them back where they belonged. Braddick left the room and walked upstairs. A small bathroom tiled and converted with a walk-in shower and oversized toilet, showed no signs of drug dealing. A small cabinet had a mascara stick and a box of tampons, the only trace of a female. It had been adapted for the morbidly obese. The main bedroom smelled of stale sweat and despite Paulie's obsessive cleaning, he couldn't remove his own odour. Braddick wrinkled his nose and moved on to the spare rooms.

'There have been women up here,' Cain commented.

'Yes. The first thing they noticed were the mortice locks fitted to these two rooms.' Braddick pointed to the doors.

Cain nodded. 'They can only be unlocked from the landing?'

'Yep. The windows are sealed units, so unless they're smashed, the occupants are trapped. I think they let them out to work then lock them up.'

'Poor buggers can't run,' Ade said holding up the passports. 'Their families in Russia would be punished; makes me puke.'

They looked inside the bedroom. 'It looks like something from a sixties porn film,' Cain commented, looking at the leopard print covers and satin sheets.

'Sixties porn,' Braddick said sarcastically. 'If you were eighteen in the sixties, you would be over sixty.' He looked at Cain. 'You're not over sixty.' She grinned and carried on looking. Braddick opened a wardrobe and flicked through a number of 'costumes', nurse, policewoman, naughty maid and a selection of tight Lycra dresses. Ade walked in and stood in the doorway. 'Either Paulie rents out fancy dress costumes or he lets them bring punters back here.'

'It would explain the passports, Guv,' Ade said.

'Definitely.' Braddick nodded. 'The house is in the ideal position for a brothel. It's a corner plot so it's easy to drive to and the park at the rear offers great cover for punters on foot.'

'Plus, the owner of the house is huge. If there is trouble Paulie would sort it out and he takes all the risks,' Cain added. 'Punters could come and go through the backdoor without alerting the neighbours. Then if you hired a few young villains from the estate to sell smack in the park at night it would be a little goldmine.'

'You know that Paulie is selling smack?' Braddick asked surprised.

'Our Matrix officer says that it's the Farrells' product of choice,' Cain said matter of factly. 'The Russians import it from Afghanistan and ship it across Europe. No one else in the area sells smack and the Farrells don't sell coke. That keeps a fragile peace.'

'That's what I don't get,' Braddick said scratching the bristles on his chin. 'Why attack the Evans kid and attract attention?'

'You wouldn't, unless he owed money or was a threat.'

'Maybe this kid isn't as innocent as we're being led to believe.' Ade shrugged.

'Big Paulie Williams is going to give us the answer to that,' Braddick walked to the window. 'He knows why Farrell attacked Bryn Evans.'

'And if we lean on him, he might give up that he's fronting for the Farrells.'

'There are a couple of things missing there, Guv,' Ade frowned, 'women and drugs.'

'He had plenty of time to pack the women off through the back door, give them some money and an address to get to and then…'

'And then stash the drugs.'

'Yes, but where?'

Braddick closed the wardrobe door. He looked up at the loft access hatch in the ceiling. It had been painted with white gloss paint years ago and never opened since. He could see the paint still formed a seal around the lid. They headed down the stairs to the hallway. To the left was a sitting-room, which was an elongated L-shape. He walked behind a patterned settee into a dining room. The walls were magnolia, black and white prints of the mountains of Snowdonia hung next to prints of the Lake District. The condition and decoration of the house was not compatible with a single male of Paulie's profile. It was tasteful and subtle, not what Braddick expected from a thirty stone pimp. He glanced over the room once more, his eyes settling on a mark on the oak dining table. It was the only thing that looked out of place. He walked over to it and bent down to see it in the light, which was filtering in through beige vertical blinds, two sticky circles, one bigger than the other.

'Look at this,' Braddick turned to Ade. Ade bent to look at the marks. 'There was an unwashed glass in the sink.'

'You've lost me, Guv.'

'Look at this place. It's bloody spotless.' Braddick waved his hand. He looked around the room and found what he was looking for. 'He wouldn't leave a glass in the sink unwashed and he wouldn't leave sticky marks like this on his table unless he was in a rush.'

'He would have used a coaster or something,' Cain said catching up with them.

'There look, next to you on the windowsill.'

Ade picked up a set of six coasters. 'Am I missing something?'

'He didn't use a coaster,' Braddick pointed to the sticky marks. 'That's a glass mark and that's a bottle mark. The empty bottle is in the kitchen bin. It was a two-litre bottle of Fanta. He didn't use a coaster and he didn't wash his glass because he was in a rush. We were coming.'

'So, he drank a bottle of Fanta in a rush?' Ade asked, confused.

'I think that he was washing something down with a bottle of Fanta,' Braddick pointed his finger to his head. 'I think our fat friend has swallowed his stash.'

'It would make sense,' Cain agreed. She flushed red which Braddick thought was odd. Was she pissed off that she'd missed the collar or was there something else? 'I'd be interested to sit in on that interview.'

'I want to speak to Bryn Evans at the hospital before I speak to Paulie.' Braddick said watching her reaction. There was a twitch at the corner of her mouth when she was annoyed. He patted Ade on the back. 'I want you to go back to the nick and make sure Williams doesn't go to the loo. Why don't you both interview him?' Cain and Ade exchanged glances, neither looked excited by the prospect of working together. 'Put some pressure on him, Ade, see what comes out. You know what I mean.'

Ade nodded, not quite understanding exactly what he did mean, rumours about why the new DI had returned from his secondment early echoed around his mind. 'I will do, Guv. I'll see you back at the station,' he added turning to Cain.

'Great. See you there,' she mumbled to Ade as he left; a forced smile on her lips. 'I'll keep you posted,' she said to Braddick. She half smiled and headed for the door.

'You do that,' Braddick said to himself as she closed the door behind her. Something about Steff Cain didn't sit right with him but keeping her close to the investigation couldn't hurt and might pay dividend.

CHAPTER 12

As he hit the glass, Liam covered his head and face with his arms. The force of the impact shattered the window and his momentum carried him through. He felt glass slice his forearms, hands and legs, stinging pain fizzled through his brain. Suddenly he was falling through the air, his eyes closed, his muscles tensed for impact. Visions of landing impaled on a trolley jack flashed through his mind. Fear gripped him. He heard glass shattering as it hit the garage floor beneath, voices shouting, angry voices, aggressive and threatening but he paid them no heed. His only concern as he fell was when he was going to stop falling. Time seemed to stop as he dropped. The impact came with a thunderous clang and a bone shaking jolt. His head bounced off something hard and metallic. White lights, like a giant camera flash, went off in his brain and he felt the breath knocked from his lungs. Liam opened his eyes and looked up, unsure where he had landed, waiting for the first hand to grab him, the first punch to land but none came.

His vision was filled with the sight of the sloping moulded roof, open girders and bare fluorescent tubes that bathed the unit in a harsh white light. Watery daylight glimmered through skylights far above him. Looking around he realised that he had landed on top of the container. The men below couldn't reach him but the men in the office could follow him if they were brave enough to jump, and they could certainly shoot him. He saw Nicolai and his men staring through the broken window, pointing, shouting and gesturing wildly to the top of the truck. He could hear the men below running around the lorry trying desperately to find a way to reach him. Liam knew that it wouldn't take them long to fathom a way up. Without thinking, he jumped up onto one of the girders that supported the roof and shimmied up towards a skylight in the moulded panels. The men below shouted abuse and a stainless-steel spanner bounced off the girder with a clang, followed by a hail of makeshift missiles. Nuts, bolts and tools whistled past his head as they tried to make him fall.

Liam climbed faster. His foot slipped and kicked a fluorescent light and the bulb exploded, showering those below with tiny shards of glass. The light fitting broke loose and swung like a pendulum from its chain, threatening to drop at any minute. The men below scrambled for cover as its fastening snapped. It dropped, clattering to the floor with a deafening crash. A chorus of expletives echoed through the unit, spurring Liam to climb faster towards the skylight. He shimmied up the girder, his progress slow and painful. As he neared, he realised that the skylight was open. He followed the winding mechanism with his eyes. It could be opened and closed from below with a winding system and he knew someone would realise where he was going and run for the handle, closing the skylight and trapping him. As his eyes followed the winder across the roof and down the wall, he saw one of the men running towards the handle. His heart was in his mouth as he scrambled upwards. Liam reached up and grabbed at another girder, but his blood had made his fingers slippery. He couldn't find purchase and slid backwards a few yards, his back slamming into a metal stanchion. Without daring to look down he tried again. He jumped, reached out and gripped the edge of the skylight; his legs dangled and kicked in thin air. Swinging upwards, the muscles in his shoulders felt as if they would snap. He grunted and gave one massive effort, pulling himself through; within seconds he was crouched on the roof with the breeze on his face. He slammed the skylight closed, sucked clean air into his lungs and sighed with relief. Blood was running freely from several nasty cuts, some deeper than others. He watched as droplets dripped onto the roof forming a sticky crimson puddle. It was at that moment that he thought about his brother. Ray was inside, handcuffed and hurt. His guts twisted with anguish and tears of frustration filled his eyes. How could he leave Ray behind?

The options raced through his mind, stay and die or run and live to fight another day. Being a dead hero wouldn't save Ray. He had to run, hide and recover his composure. If he could summon help, he may be able to mount some kind of rescue attempt although it was a stretch. His last resort was the police. He couldn't leave Ray in the hands of the Karpov family. With his mind made up, Liam began to run along the apex of the roof. The chop shop was part of an estate of long low buildings and moving across the roof, Liam put some distance between himself and his pursuers, who had to go around. Thankfully no one followed him across the rooftops, and he kept on running up and over each one until his muscles burned. Only when he felt that his lungs would burst did he slow down.

He peered over the edge and checked the roads on both sides of the building. Two dark people carriers were careering around the narrow lanes that threaded through the industrial estate. Their progress was slow and pained as they couldn't see the roofs. Liam doubled back and positioned himself at the rear of the industrial estate. He had to drop down as far away from them as he could. Sliding down the roof, he peered left and right. The Manchester Ship Canal ran behind the buildings and in the distance, he could see the River Mersey winding through the marshes beyond. He could hear voices and vehicles driving at speed, squealing tyres and slamming doors but they were on the opposite side of the block to him. Liam knew that it wouldn't take them long to circumnavigate the buildings and reach his side. Dangling his feet over the edge of the roof, he grabbed at the guttering and began to slide down a drainpipe. The blood on his hands made his grip slippery and he lost his hold halfway down, falling ten feet onto the concrete with a sickening thump. He felt his ankle twist in a direction that it should never go, and his right elbow was grazed and bruised, swelling quickly and making it throb.

Liam stood, listened intently and limped painfully towards the canal. Brightly painted barges lined both banks, their flower boxes empty, and windows shuttered for the winter. He reached the edge and sat down on the towpath, icy water flooding his boots and numbing his legs. As the first vehicle turned the corner, he slipped down into the freezing brown water. The temperature took the air from his lungs, his breaths rapid and shallow. He heard the vehicles approaching as he slipped beneath the surface and let himself sink beneath the barges.

CHAPTER 13

When Braddick arrived at the hospital the sun's watery rays were fading fast. He hated the short days and long dark nights that accompanied winter. Concerning messages about the death of Anthony Farrell had filtered through, muddying the waters and making his decisions far more difficult. Nothing was ever black and white, except death. Death had clarity. Clarity was something that he craved.

Braddick parked his car at the rear of the new hospital buildings, turned the engine off and climbed out. Remnants of sunlight glinted from the coloured glass roof of the Catholic Cathedral. The wind was turning icy and he reached inside the glove box and slipped his hands into a pair of fingerless mitts. He locked the door and looked up at the hospital, searching for the broken window. Spotting it, he mentally worked out where the missile was thrown from and how much force a man would need to launch an object that far. He decided that the culprit either was or should be an Olympian. A uniformed officer was positioned at the rear entrance as a deterrent to any further revenge attacks. It was a deterrent that Braddick knew would stop no one determined enough to reach a target inside. As organised crime families became stronger and more powerful, the thin blue line had never been thinner or more vulnerable to corruption. He flashed his ID and nodded hello. The uniformed officer seemed disinterested but polite. It was nearing shift changeover and Braddick didn't blame him for not wanting to be stood in a car park guarding a door.

'What did you do at work today, darling?'

'I guarded a door and then filled out a report about guarding it.'

That's nice, darling how interesting.' Braddick imagined as he took a quick look around the parked vehicles, but he couldn't see anything untoward. The Farrells were out there somewhere, watching and waiting. It was just a matter of time. The wreath and the brick were warnings, portents of what was to come. The Evans family were in imminent danger and Braddick wasn't sure what they could do about it.

A wide staircase that smelled of antiseptic and floor polish took him up to the first floor. Half a dozen staff were going about their business despite the uniformed police presence, nurses walking at a hundred miles an hour fetching medicine, carrying bedpans and assuring the wellbeing of all under their care. Braddick reckoned it would take more than a brick through a window to ruffle their feathers. As he reached the reception desk, the uniformed sergeant in charge spotted him.

'DI Braddick?'

'Sergeant,' Braddick extended his hand. The sergeant was in his twilight years, greying hair and beard. He had the dimpled red nose of a whisky drinker. 'How's the patient?'

'He's battered fairly badly, broken nose and cheekbone,' the sergeant gestured towards the room where Bryn had been moved to, 'he's in shock. I don't think he knows what's going on to be honest. His family are with him. You're aware of what's been happening?'

'Yes,' Braddick nodded. 'I need a few minutes with him, nothing formal, I just need to get a feel for what happened.'

'I can't see them having a problem with that.'

'Are they keeping him in?'

'I believe so. The cheekbone fracture may need an operation.'

'What's been said so far?' Braddick asked.

'How do you mean?'

'You know, what are your first impressions of the family?'

'He seems like a decent kid, Guv. The family are ordinary, polite, no criminal record. I think he was in the wrong place at the wrong time.' The sergeant rolled his eyes and leaned closer. 'This is the Farrells after all, Guv. No one will shed a tear about that arsehole dying.'

'His father might, Sergeant,' Braddick said coldly.

'Of course,' he stuttered a little. 'I didn't mean anything by it, Guv.'

'Just be careful where you express your opinions. The press will be all over this when the story breaks and the last thing we need is a comment like that in the papers,' Braddick lowered his voice, the sergeant nodded embarrassed. 'What are the family's names?'

'Father is Robert, mother Barbara and his brother is Mark.'

'Okay,' Braddick said thoughtfully as he watched two women talking in hushed tones further along the corridor. 'Let's go and have a chat with him. Are they from Social Services?'

'Yes, Guv.'

'I need a quick word with them before we go in,' Braddick walked towards them. 'Excuse me,' he said as he approached. Both women stopped talking their mouths still a little bit ajar as they appraised him for the first time. 'Marcus Braddick, I'm the DI looking after the Bryn Evans case.'

'Sharon Bower, I'm the case worker on this one,' she blushed as they shook hands. Her business suit gave her the look of professionalism. 'This is my colleague, Tina Holden.' Tina grinned like a teenager with a crush. 'I'm glad you've arrived, inspector. How do you think this will play out?'

'From what I've heard so far, he's from a good family with no record.'

'Absolutely,' she agreed. 'This appears to be completely out of character.'

'The CPS will make the final decision, but I think he's looking at manslaughter at the very worst. There's no mens rea or premeditated intent and if his brief is any good, he'll get him off on a self-defence plea. Between now and then we have to go through the motions.'

'Excellent.' She jotted down some notes. 'What is the next step?'

'We can recommend he goes to HMP Altcourse once the doctors are finished. There's a vulnerable prisoner unit there for teenagers.'

'The Reynoldstown Unit?'

'Yes,' Braddick said impressed by her knowledge. 'You've dealt with them before?'

'Often, unfortunately. He should be safe enough there,' she said writing it down. She looked up through her steel rimmed glasses. 'What about the family?'

'We can put their address and phone numbers into the system and put an urgent response marker on them,' he said knowing that it sounded inadequate. 'If anything happens, we can get someone there in minutes. I can't do anything more for them.'

'Oh well, it's better than nothing.' She sighed. 'Thanks.'

'Nice talking to you, I need to get on.' Braddick smiled and turned away before she could ask him any more questions. She wanted a cast iron plan that would protect all involved in the case and he didn't have one. Nobody did.

'Okay, thanks, detective,' she called after him, 'we'll be here until he's moved.'

'Good,' Braddick said over his shoulder. 'This kid is going to need looking after.' The sergeant led the way to the room and knocked before opening the door. Inside, the Evans family stared at Braddick, nervous and frightened. 'Mr and Mrs Evans.' He half smiled at the parents. His first sighting of Bryn and his facial injuries told him a lot of what he needed to know. 'I'm Detective Inspector Braddick,' he said removing his gloves, slipping them into his pockets. He undid the leather jacket and walked to the end of the bed. 'You must be Bryn.' Bryn nodded almost imperceptibly, glancing at his brother for help. Mark winked at him for reassurance. 'How are you feeling?' Bryn shrugged. His shoulders seemed to sag, making him look smaller and more vulnerable. Braddick didn't think this kid would last more than a few seconds against a thug like Anthony Farrell. 'I know this is frightening for you but I'm not here to drag you to jail.' He nodded to his parents to help put them at ease. He could tell from their faces that it would take more than that to settle them. 'I need to talk to you to see if what our witnesses have told us is true.'

'Why wouldn't it be?' Mark asked. He didn't want to come across as overprotective, but his nerves got the better of him. 'Why would they lie?'

'You're Mark, aren't you?' Braddick looked Mark in the eye. He looked like a fighter, something about his physique, his nose and something else in his eyes. 'You do a bit of boxing?'

'Yes,' Mark replied.

'Are you any good?'

'He's turning pro soon,' Bryn spoke for the first time.

'Wow,' Braddick said genuinely impressed. 'Good for you.' He smiled. Mark stood to shake his hand. Braddick returned his handshake and met his gaze. 'Mark, you meet a lot more people who don't want to fight than who do want to, right?'

'Yes. Most of the lads at the gym just want to keep fit. They don't want to fight for real.'

'The majority of people are frightened by conflict.'

'Yes.'

'Then you'll understand me when I tell you that eyewitnesses are unreliable at the best of times but when someone like Anthony Farrell is killed then they can say one thing today and tomorrow they can't remember their names,' Braddick said with a narrow smile. 'Most people avoid physical confrontation because it frightens them. You know what I'm talking about.' Mark nodded that he understood and sat down. Braddick wanted five minutes with the kid alone but it was more than his job was worth. Social Services would crucify him just for talking to him without a responsible adult present, no matter what they talked about. He had to get something straight in his mind before he spoke to Big Paulie. 'I know the sequence of how things happened, but I need to understand why Anthony Farrell attacked you, okay?'

'I don't know why,' Bryn said quietly. 'I argued with the fat man outside his house and the next thing the other guy was chasing me.'

'I've heard that bit, but it doesn't make sense to me, Bryn.'

'That's what happened.'

'I know, but why did he attack you?' Bryn looked confused. 'Why didn't he attack one of the other people in the park?'

'I don't know.'

'Farrell wouldn't just attack someone randomly. He had too much to lose.'

'What are you getting at,' Robert Evans asked. A sheen of sweat covered his face.

'Let me explain, Mr Evans. The big man who you argued with,' Braddick walked around the side of the bed. 'He runs a business from his house. Not the kind of business that you would want to draw attention to.' He looked at the family one at a time. 'It's a very lucrative business but it's also a business that could get you locked up for ten years. Do you follow me?'

'Yes, I think so.'

'So, I don't understand why they would jeopardise their business by attacking you.' The Evans family looked at each other, faces blank and minds numbed by events. 'Why would they do that, Bryn?'

'I don't know.' He shrugged. His eyes became watery once more. 'I've been thinking that it could be mistaken identity.'

'Could be, I suppose, or did you owe them money?' Braddick pushed.

'What for?' Bryn asked innocently.

'He's asking you if you ever bought drugs from them,' Mark intervened.

'You cheeky bugger,' Barbara snapped. 'My boys don't take drugs and you're out of order insinuating that.' She stood up but her knees buckled, and she had to sit down again clutching her hands to her chest. 'What a nerve,' she wheezed.

'Are you all right, luv?' Robert leaned over and touched her hand. 'Don't get yourself worked up now. Do you want a glass of water?'

'I'll need something stronger than that if he keeps asking stupid questions,' she said between breaths. 'What a bloody barefaced cheek.'

'I know you have to ask,' Mark stepped in, 'but my brother and I train at Kelly's gym every day except Sundays. He's never taken so much as an aspirin never mind drugs.' He paused and shook his head, pointing to Bryn. 'I don't know why this guy Farrell attacked my brother, but he doesn't owe anyone any money for drugs. Test him if you don't believe me.'

'Yes, test me.' Bryn shrugged. 'I've never taken anything.'

'Testing my son for drugs,' Barbara said shaking her head. 'Cheeky bugger.' Her face flushed red and beads of sweat trickled from her temples. Robert handed her a glass of water. And she sipped it.

'Okay, I believe you,' Braddick nodded. Bryn looked surprised, as did Mark. His parents looked relieved but confused. 'Something made Farrell attack you and I think the blame lies elsewhere.' He looked at Mark. 'Can I have a word with you outside, please?' Mark stood up and looked at his parents. His father was holding the glass to his mother's lips, her face darkening to purple at the ears. 'We'll speak again once the doctors give us the all clear to do so,' Braddick said to Bryn. 'I'm sorry for the upset Mr and Mrs Evans but a man has been killed and I have a job to do.'

The parents looked up at him. Robert nodded and Barbara, still clutching her chest tutted, 'He's a cheeky bastard!'

'Barbara!' Robert said looking shocked by her language. 'The detective is doing his job. What will happen to Bryn now?'

Braddick sighed. 'He was arrested on suspicion of murder but once he is released from here, he'll probably be charged with manslaughter and remanded to HMP Altcourse.' Mrs Evans looked like she was about to vomit. 'There's a vulnerable prisoner unit there designed specifically for teenagers like Bryn. He'll be safe there until this is all worked out.'

'Worked out how?' Mr Evans asked quietly.

'I think there's a very good case for a self-defence plea. The CPS could well look at the evidence and decide not to prosecute at all but that will be down to your solicitor to prove.' He paused. 'I know of Jacob Graff and he's very good at his job. I think you'll be fine once they fix his nose.'

'Thanks, detective,' Mr Evans said after a few seconds of silence.

'You're welcome, this is a difficult time so look after each other,' Braddick said leaving the room, holding the door open for Mark to follow. He glanced back at Barbara and she glared at him, but he knew that he couldn't win the hearts and minds of all. Taking Mark by the arm, he guided him down the corridor where they could speak unheard by others. 'What do you know about the Farrells?' he asked in a no-nonsense manner.

Mark looked around. 'I've heard of them, mostly through boxing circles. They've sponsored quite a few local title bouts over the years. It goes hand in hand in this city, boxing and gangsters, always has.'

'You don't have to tell me that,' Braddick lowered his voice. 'The last fight I went to see at the Echo Arena, the bar was like a line up for most wanted.' He smiled. His voice turned serious again. 'You're going to have to look out for your family. The Farrells will come after Bryn for certain and they'll probably come after you too, all of you.'

'They've already put the fucking window through in here and sent a wreath to my mum! What more do they want?'

'They were warnings, nothing compared to what is coming, Mark,' Braddick warned. 'I'll do what I can for you, but my hands are tied financially, whatever we do won't be much and it won't be long-term. The onus will be on you to protect them. Is there anywhere else you can go for now?'

'I'll take them to my house tonight,' Mark said concerned. 'It's the best I can do today. We don't have the money to go away.'

'Here is my number,' Braddick handed him a card. 'Text me your address and do not tell anyone else even if they ask. Make sure all your windows are locked and I need you to screw your letter box closed from the inside.' The implication of accelerant being poured through it registered on Mark's face. 'I'm not trying to scare you, but this is the brutal reality.' Mark nodded; his face pale. 'Make sure you have something heavy or something sharp near your bed and have an escape route clear in your mind in case you have to get out of there quickly.' Mark looked worried but listened intently. 'Your mother and father can't jump out of windows so make sure that you can get out of the ground floor.' Mark nodded again. 'I'll make sure we have a uniformed police car there tonight, but I don't know how long we can keep that up. I'll put an urgent response marker on the address so if you make a call, you'll be the priority.' Braddick looked back at the theatre door. 'Bryn will be under armed guard here so don't worry about him.'

'Thanks, detective,' Mark said with a nod. 'I appreciate the advice.'

'If there's any sign of anything dodgy, you ring nine-nine-nine and then you ring me. Keep your eyes and ears open and take care of them,' Braddick patted his shoulder firmly and headed off down the corridor. Mark watched him go, his mind racing and his heart thumping a steady rhythm in his chest. Braddick didn't look back. He needed to get back to the station, but he couldn't help but think that the Evans family were in dire trouble.

CHAPTER 14

Big Paulie was feeling unwell. His clothes were saturated in sweat, a sickly sweet musk pervaded from his body. He knew from experience that within an hour, he would stink. His mind was struggling to compute the amount of shit that he was in and just how deep it was; deeper than he had been before and then some. He had been in custody less than two hours and already his shaky confidence was beginning to crack. The day that he had always dreaded had finally arrived. All the excuses and credible denials that he had planned for years had turned to dust, simply because they all involved pointing the finger at the Farrells. Now the time had come, blaming his employers and claiming he was forced into it was clearly a death sentence. Whenever he had plotted his escape from the law, his excuses seemed so plausible but now they appeared ridiculous. Coercion was not going to fly. The truth was that he was far more frightened of the Farrells than prison and as for the Karpovs, there wasn't a word for how frightened he was of them. He had seen what they were capable of.

The lock on his cell clicked noisily and the door opened with a clang. 'Your brief is here, Williams,' a custody officer snapped. The policeman looked at Paulie as if he was taking the piss by having a lawyer at all. 'Stand up man, stand up!' he shouted. Paulie stood and a wave of nausea hit him. A bald man stood behind the officer looking on angrily, 'DI Cain is waiting to talk to you in the interview suite so if you could be as quick as you can, I'd be grateful,' the officer said sarcastically.

'We'll be as long as it takes, constable,' the bald man in a brown pinstripe suit said, squeezing through the door. The police officer looked like he had been slapped. 'Now fuck off and leave us in peace.' The officer made to reply but thought better of it. Colm Boyce wasn't a man to annoy. He could have an internal investigation started every day of the week and the Police Complaints Committee was on first name terms with his secretary. The brief frowned and waited for the door to be closed before speaking to Paulie. 'My name is Colm Boyce.' He introduced himself with a brief nod of his head. There was no warmth in his eyes. 'I've been instructed by Fenton Holdings to represent you.' He handed Paulie a business card, which listed Nicolai Karpov as the Managing Director of Fenton Holdings and then placed the card back in his pocket quickly. 'It is your choice but I'm recommending that you say nothing except to confirm your name and address,' Boyce said placing a pair of black rimmed glasses onto his nose. He leaned close to Paulie's ear. '*If you say anything at all, Nicolai will have your testicles removed with a hacksaw before your throat is slit and then he will feed you to your parents*,' he whispered so quickly that Paulie wasn't sure if he had really heard it. He stepped away. 'If we stick to a no comment interview, we can bide time until they reveal all their evidence, okay?' he said politely, although his eyes were fixed and threatening. Paulie looked down wringing his hands together nervously. Boyce spoke with acid tinged words. 'I said, is that okay with you?'

Paulie nodded and turned around, feeling uncomfortable and in need of fresh air. He was about to speak when he felt a rush of blood to his brain. His chest felt like he was being squeezed by a giant hand. He had the strange sensation of floating and then nothing. Big Paulie Williams fell like a toppled tree, unconscious before he hit the floor.

* * * *

Liam Johnson had stayed beneath the barges for nearly twenty minutes, surfacing and clinging to the hulls to catch his breath whenever possible. Eventually the cars moved on and the search of the canal bank was abandoned. He could barely climb out of the water. His hands were so cold that the pain in his fingers was unbearable. He slumped onto the far side of the bank and crawled on his hands and knees along the line of moored boats looking for a window with weak spots. His search paid off when he spotted an aluminium framed window, big enough for him to crawl through. The seal was degraded and the edges, spotted with rot. With numb fingers, he pulled the window out and then slipped inside the barge headfirst. He dragged the quilt from a single bunk and wrapped it around his shivering body. He took off his shoes and socks, curling up in a foetal position in an attempt to raise his body temperature. He could feel his ankle swelling and knew that he wouldn't be able to walk far unaided. Exhaustion seeped into every cell in his body. His eyes closed and as he lay shivering, the need to sleep overwhelmed him.

It was dark when he woke up and it took him a while to recall the day's events and where he was. Checking his watch, he realised that he had slept for three hours while his body recovered from the shock and the cold. His mind focused on Ray and spurred him into action and he knew exactly what he was going to do. He kept the quilt wrapped around him tightly while he fumbled his way to the galley and searched in the darkness for the cooker. His fingers found a two-ring hob and he twisted the switches on and off and listened for the sound of gas. There was nothing. He reached down and opened a cupboard door, fumbling inside to find the Calor gas canister. Turning it on, he switched on the cooker which ignited with a blue flame and illuminated the interior of the barge with a weak blue glow.

He reluctantly dropped the quilt and searched through drawers and cupboards, finding a T-shirt and a thick black jumper which he pulled on. A first aid box provided an elastic crepe bandage and he carefully wrapped it around his injured ankle fastening it tightly before pulling his socks and shoes on. The cutlery drawer held a selection of carving knives of which he chose the two longest, sliding them into his belt. He was hoping to find a mobile phone, but his luck was out. Feeling strong enough to move, he turned off the cooker and climbed back through the window onto the muddy towpath, his sense of direction took him left towards home where he knew he would be able to get help for Ray from a very unlikely source.

CHAPTER 15

The traffic was heavy and Braddick flicked through the channels and settled for a local station which, played ballads in the evening; he needed to wind down, his nerves on a knife's edge. The news of Big Paulie Williams keeling over in the custody suite was a blow but not exactly a surprise. He was a heart attack waiting to happen and his chances of dying went through the roof when he ingested three dozen packets of heroin, several of which had dissolved in his stomach. The doctors said that he had no chance of pulling through although he was still technically alive. A death in custody was a nightmare, every step that the police had made would be scrutinised and analysed for signs of culpability. Internal investigations would begin, and it would be for Braddick and his team to prove that they were not at fault or didn't contribute to the circumstances of his collapse. Every link in the chain would be tested. There would be weeks of arse covering and finger pointing until the furore died down and the focus shifted elsewhere. His collapse would increase the workload massively.

They'd missed the chance to interview him for now, which would save a few hours of labour costs but the information that could have been gleaned was lost, not least what provoked Farrell to attack a teenager; the repercussions of which could resound for a long time yet. Bryn Evans, his family and their vulnerability were top of his mind. He had witnessed the cruelty of organised crime families and in his experience, revenge attacks tended to be the most brutal. The murder of Anthony Farrell, intended or not, wouldn't go unpunished. The vulnerability of the family concerned him deeply and shadows of his past whispered warnings in his mind. *'You can't protect them, no one can. You couldn't even protect me, could you?'*

His past was etched into his present and it would be a constant in his future too. It couldn't be left behind, forgotten or rationalised. He had broken the rules by falling in love with Karin and her death was his fault. He crossed the lines by trying to protect her off the books and reaped the rewards for his mistakes by attending her funeral on his own, her only mourner. The only people that knew she was dead were her murderers, the local authorities, who cremated her as a female unknown and Braddick. Her family and the few friends she'd stayed in touch with over the years had never heard from her once she left Essex. They had no clue where she'd gone or why and no idea that she was dead. After a few months of no contact, her parents had reported her as a missing person and her file was sitting online with millions of others and that's where it would stay, unsolved and un-investigated.

Braddick first laid eyes on her behind the bar in the notorious Essex nightclub, Rachel's, which put Basildon on the map when it was linked to the 'Essex Boys' murders in Rettenden in December 1995. Braddick was leading a squad for the NCA, who were focusing on Essex because a brutal war over the territory, which had been simmering for years, had erupted. The body count was rising, and entire families were being targeted, no matter how loose the relationship to gang members was. The targeting of innocent people brought the violent struggle into the spotlight and the NCA were tasked with aiding the local constabularies to bring the situation under control. Essex was an incredibly lucrative territory for drug dealers and its closeness to London made it simple to service and control. The amounts of money involved made it a stronghold that was always vulnerable to attacks from rival gangs from the city. Just a few months in control of Essex could make enough money to exit the game completely.

Parts of the seaside towns of Southend, Clacton and Jaywick, once thriving Victorian holiday resorts had become bedsit land for London's homeless addicts. There were entire estates of addicts trying to feed £100 a day habits, which made rich pickings for the dealers. Jaywick had become the focus of several documentaries about addicts living on benefits. One documentary stated it had a population of four thousand people, at least half drug users. Dealers watching did the maths; two thousand people with a habit, all living within a few square miles of each other meant that Jaywick was worth thirty-five million a year to whoever controlled the drugs. It was a captive audience that needed supplying. Southend and Clacton were bigger still and rival firms tried to muscle in. The documentaries had highlighted the opportunities of supplying the small rundown towns on the coast. Rival suppliers from the city clashed as several of them wanted a piece of the business and the wars began.

During the investigation, Braddick met Karin Range. She was a nineteen-year-old barmaid with the looks of a pop star and the ability to attract men with trouble running through their veins. Her ex-boyfriend had paid for her to have breast implants and then threatened to cut them out when she finished with him for shagging her best friend in the club's disabled toilet. When the threats were ramped up and became more frequent, Karin turned to her employer for help. The ex-boyfriend had his legs broken and still walked with a limp, but he never bothered her again and her employer took her to Paris to get over it. She became involved with him very quickly and the relationship became serious, but it wasn't long before she realised that she'd made a huge mistake. Her lover was a much older jealous narcissist with a violent streak and a cocaine habit. Karin was dragged along to a whirlwind of parties, boozy beach holidays and business dinners with leery strangers, who stunk of cigars and expensive aftershave. She was a trophy on his arm, a slut in his bed and a punch bag when things didn't go his way. As time went by, he became less secretive about his business dealings and it was clear to her that he was mixing with some very dangerous characters. Some of the most notorious names in Essex were his associates, names that she'd only ever heard whispered because talking about them could land you in hospital. It was only later that she realised that they were all in business together and their business was drugs. Some of the conversations that she was party to, especially when they holidayed in Spain, made her feel very frightened indeed. They talked about burying people as if it was a football result. She'd stepped into a world that she didn't belong in, but she couldn't see any way of walking away from him unhurt.

Three months later, she was with her boyfriend and four of his colleagues and their partners, drinking champagne in a nightclub in Southend when two men approached their table. Words were exchanged and then one of the men pulled out a gun. He aimed and fired but the gun jammed. The failed assassins, who turned out to be bitter rivals, were overcome by the group and the security staff from the club. They were beaten senseless, bottled and stabbed before the women were taken away from the club, their men remained behind. Karin knew that they would take the rivals somewhere and murder them. Over the following months, it was an event that was frequently brought up when the group were drunk. They laughed and joked about it as if it was nothing, more gruesome details revealed each time. The men were dismembered with a power saw and disposed of in barrels of acid. One of the limbless men was still screaming when they lowered him into the liquid. The incident terrified her, and she couldn't look at her partner after that. She became an automaton, going through the motions to remain alive.

When the Essex investigation began and the NCA swooped, Karin was secretly relieved when her boyfriend was arrested and charged. She wasn't twenty years old and yet she felt tired of the world. The pressure, the violence and the drugs had taken their toll. She was only too happy to make a statement and was interviewed for hours but she didn't recount the nightclub incident and she refused to go into the witness programme. Karin didn't think that she'd said anything that the police didn't know already, and she didn't believe that her boyfriend would see her as a weak link. It was the biggest mistake of her short life. While the gang was locked up on remand, she tried to make her own way again, but no one wanted to know her. The good people that she knew thought she was damaged goods, a gangster's moll and the bad ones thought she was a grass for cooperating with the investigation. Karin was oblivious to the fact that she was a witness, a loose end that needed to be tied up.

Braddick was tasked with working on her, making sure that she didn't bolt and trying to squeeze her for more information. He fell for her the first time that he saw her, but he resisted his urges because of her age and the job. The more he talked to her, the harder he fell and the harder it became to ignore the fact that he was completely smitten. As they spent time together it became clear that she felt exactly the same. They had a powerful chemistry. The magnetism between them was too strong for either of them to resist and they fell in love. They spent their days walking, eating and laughing, comfortable with each other despite the age gap. Their nights were long and hot and when their lovemaking was over, they would talk until the first tweets of the dawn chorus drifted to them. Karin spilled her heart out about her time with her ex and eventually the story about the murders came out. Although they didn't realise it then, their fate was sealed. Braddick convinced her to make a statement, promising her that the firm would be jailed for years and that he would help her to start over with a new identity and she trusted in him. She loved Braddick but she underestimated how feared her ex and his firm were and how far their reach stretched; so had Braddick.

Within a week, several NCA witnesses disappeared and another was found dead in suspicious circumstances, an apparent overdose despite the victim having no record of drug abuse. The Essex case was disintegrating before their eyes as one witness after another recanted their statements. A tidal wave of fear washed over Essex and left silence in its wake. Braddick knew that they would come for Karin. She was now the key witness who could put some of their senior hierarchy at the scene of two high profile murders. She was taken into witness protection but Braddick knew that there was at least one rat in the team. He didn't trust anyone and as their relationship intensified and the gangsters drew ever nearer, Braddick made her vanish.

They'd hidden their relationship well enough for suspicion not to land on him. He moved her north and put her into an apartment at the edge of Keswick in the Lakes, a friend's holiday home. Convinced that she would be far enough away to be safe, he insisted that she cut all contact with anyone until things settled down. He promised that he would protect her and keep her safe, but they found her. They found her, and they injected her with a lethal speedball, heroin, cocaine and Ketamine in one injection, set her on fire and left her for dead. The killers were clever. They'd arranged candles around the room and made the fire look accidental, a junkie fallen foul of her recklessness. He knew that they'd murdered her, but the Essex case collapsed and there was nothing Braddick could do about it.

When they found her body, there was no way of identifying her and Marcus Braddick left it that way. The guilt crippled him. She was cremated as Jane Doe, another junkie who succumbed to her habit. He didn't know how they'd found her and probably never would and it haunted him daily. His nights were full of dark dreams, images of her struggling in her last lucid moments and his days were laden with the guilt. On more than one occasion he had contemplated going to his boss, coming clean and taking the consequences but he backed out each time. He knew that if he stayed in the job, he would find them one day. It was his overriding motivation to avenge her death. It was what kept him going. The lyrics to her song echoed around his head with painful frequency.

You see her when you close your eyes,
Maybe one day you'll understand why,
Everything you touch surely dies,

His guilt was compounded by the fact that he hadn't taken her calls on the last day of her life. He was working on trying to salvage the case, interviewing potential new witnesses and didn't check his phone until much later, by which time, she was already dead. Did she know they'd found her? Was she calling for help? Her voicemails were vague and increasingly more panicked; her voice more desperate, sobbing. Her sobbing still resonated in his dreams many months after he had deleted the voicemails from his phone. He couldn't delete them from his memory. They would remain there for the rest of his days.

A blaring horn disturbed his thoughts and headlights dazzled him in the rear-view mirror. He looked up and realised that he was stopped at a green light, waving an apology he pulled away and checked the satnav. The property was less than a mile away, a steep climb up Frodsham Hill and he steered the Evoque along the narrow lanes until he reached a set of ornate metal gates set into a high wall. He pulled in front of them and looked around. The lights of the chemical factories along the Mersey twinkled brightly, looking like small cities in the darkness. The Wirral peninsula spread out to the left of the river and beyond that, the dark shadows of the Welsh hills loomed against the night sky, the odd yellow twinkle indicated their height and how sparsely populated they were. It was a nice view and Braddick knew that it came at a price. The house was worth a fortune. He lowered the driver's window and reached out, pressing the intercom button. After a few seconds, it crackled to life.

'What?' an irritated voice snapped.

'I'm Detective Inspector Braddick and I'd like to talk to you about Anthony.'

'Have you got your ID?' the voice snapped.

Braddick flashed his badge at the camera above the gate. The gates whirred and opened slowly, revealing a narrow twisting driveway overhung with trees. As he approached the house, the front door opened and Braddick recognised Edward Farrell Junior, Anthony's younger brother.

Braddick parked up and took his time climbing out and locking it. He glanced around at the landscaped lawns and sculptured hedgerows as he walked towards the door. Eddie Farrell was smart. He laundered his money through his legitimate businesses so the law couldn't touch the proceeds of crime.

As Braddick approached, the security lights above the porch blinded him and silhouetted Farrell. He was squat and muscular beyond what natural bodybuilding could achieve.

'You must be Edward Junior,' he said extending his hand. The distaste in Farrell's eyes told Braddick that he had either a problem with policemen or black men, probably both. 'DI Braddick.'

'Have we met?' Farrell asked abruptly, ignoring the handshake.

'No, but I checked your file before I came over, so I recognised you.'

'Clever boy, what do you want, a medal?'

'No.' Braddick smiled coldly, his hackles rankled. 'That won't be necessary. Have you got a problem with me?'

'You've turned up at my house, on your own, unannounced,' Farrell said suspiciously. He folded his thick tattooed arms. 'What do you want, money?'

'Shall we go inside, and I'll explain,' Braddick said politely trying to keep his cool.

'I hope you're not after money because if you are, you can fuck off back to wherever you came from,' Farrell said pointing his finger angrily. 'We know plenty of bent coppers and we don't need any more.'

Braddick kept calm. Stepping forward, he said, 'I need to ask you some questions about Anthony. I'm trying to understand what happened, that's all.'

'You've got five minutes.' Farrell stepped back and opened the door to allow him in, closing it behind him. The porch opened up into a wide slate tiled hallway divided in the centre by a wooden staircase that was topped with a chrome and glass balustrade. Tall Picasso prints adorned the walls, lit from above by at least a dozen spotlights. From the floor space, Braddick reckoned there were five or six bedrooms upstairs. Farrell folded his arms across his chest and glowered at him. His skin was tattooed from wrist to shoulder. 'Right, now let's not pretend to like each other, what do you want?'

'Did you know that Paul Williams is in intensive care?'

'Of course, I do,' Farrell replied in a bored tone. 'Like I said, we know a lot of bent coppers. What has that sad fuck got to do with anything?'

'He was with your brother when he was killed.'

'So I've been told.'

'Anthony attacked a kid called Bryn Evans and I wondered if you know why?'

'I assume you've asked the little scumbag that hit him across the head with a brick?'

'Yes, of course. He doesn't know why he was attacked,' Braddick nodded and kept eye contact. 'I spoke to Paulie briefly when we arrested him, but he wasn't much help.'

'Then you know about the same as me don't you.'

'Have you ever heard of Bryn Evans before?'

'No.'

Braddick looked around and smiled. 'Nice place, business must be good.' he nodded, a sarcastic grin on his face. 'Your father is in Thailand I believe.'

'Yes, he's on his way back.'

'That would mean that you're in charge of things here then?' Farrell shrugged; a narrow smile on his lips. 'Are you in charge?'

'Let's not fuck about. What exactly do you want?'

Braddick stepped closer, his face a few feet from Farrell's. 'Someone sent Mrs Evans a wreath this afternoon,' he lowered his voice. 'She's old and she's sick and she's very frightened.'

'Who would do something like that?' Farrell snorted. He raised his eyebrows and sneered. 'That's a crying shame.'

Braddick smiled coldly. 'Isn't it,' he said. 'Look, I'm not a hundred per cent sure exactly what happened in that park, but I do know that this kid's family are innocent. I want whoever sent that wreath to make sure that nothing like that happens again and I think that you can ensure that, can't you?'

Farrell inhaled, expanding his considerable frame to its maximum size. He stepped forward, nose to nose with Braddick. 'Your five minutes are up, Sambo.' He stabbed Braddick's chest with his forefinger. 'Now I suggest you fuck off out of my house and you can go and tell the scumbag who killed my brother that he'll wish his mother never opened her legs,' he hissed his face a mask of hatred. He poked Braddick again. 'Get out before you get hurt…'

Braddick grabbed at the outstretched finger and bent it back hard until it snapped, simultaneously reaching down between Farrell's legs with his right hand. He grabbed Farrell's genitals, squeezing and twisting at the same time. Farrell's eyes almost popped out of his head, his mouth was wide open, a mewing sound coming out. Braddick slammed him backwards against the wall, squeezing as hard as he could. 'You've just assaulted a detective inspector. I could nick you right now but you're not worth the hassle.' He squeezed harder. 'Do you know what I hate?' Farrell shook his head, tears streaming from his eyes. He couldn't catch his breath. 'I'll tell you.' Braddick put his head to Farrell's ear and squeezed harder still. 'I fucking hate bullies; can't stand them.' He twisted his hand bringing the pain in his balls to a whole new level. 'Now listen to me,' another twist brought more tears and gasps. 'You're just as vulnerable as that kid and his family and if anything happens to any one of them, I'll come back and rip your bollocks off and stuff them down your throat.' Another twist and Farrell's legs couldn't support his weight. He started to buckle. 'Do you understand me?' Farrell nodded furiously, tears streaming from his eyes. Braddick released his grip and let him fall to the slate tiles. 'And another thing that you need to think about,' Braddick said landing a heavy kick to Farrell's midriff making breathing even more difficult. 'The brick that one of your cronies tossed through the hospital window hit Jacob Graff in the face,' the name registered with Farrell, but he couldn't move, doubled up in agony. 'I don't think he's going to be best pleased and some of his clients make you lot look like boy scouts.' He grabbed a handful of Farrell's hair and lifted his head off the floor. 'Now I know that you're angry and you're not thinking clearly but you've made some silly mistakes today. If you make another one, I'll make sure that it's your last.' He pushed his head against the tiles with a loud crack. 'Leave the Evans family alone.'

Braddick turned around and walked to the door, opening it. 'You're the one who's made a mistake, you fucking pig,' Farrell gasped his words hardly audible. 'You're as good as dead.'

'Listen to me, Eddie. I do things a little differently. Don't make me come back to see you or you'll be seeing your brother sooner than you think,' Braddick pointed two fingers at him, a pretend gun and pulled the trigger. He closed the door and walked back to the Range Rover, thinking that he had bought the Evans family a little bit of time until Eddie senior arrived back in the country. Then the real storm would begin.

CHAPTER 16

The house was in darkness when he arrived. The Evans family were still at the hospital. He looked around the parked cars to check if there were any paparazzi lurking in their vehicles, waiting for a ghoulish snap of the family of a teenage murderer. The press would swing one way or the other on this one. They would either hail Evans as a hero, forced to defend his dog and his life, or he would be just another council estate failure, a product of broken Britain.

He couldn't see anyone else around; the street was quiet. The lights were burning in the house next door and he saw the curtain twitch. He turned off the engine and opened the door just as the heavens opened and hailstones began to bounce off the road; a cacophony of metallic pings came from the parked vehicles. Tiny balls of ice stung his skin and he pulled his coat over his head, locked the door and jogged up the path towards the lights. The front door opened as he reached it.

'Mr Dale,' he said puffing. 'I'm the detective that called earlier. What about this bloody weather, eh?'

'Bad timing…come in for a moment until it goes off,' Mr Dale said trying to keep a Staffordshire Bull Terrier inside with his leg. 'Get in Alice! I'm dog-sitting.'

'You've got your hands full there.'

'She's a good dog, lovely temperament,' Mr Dale digressed. 'They're a very misunderstood breed, you know. I blame the owners…'

'Sorry, Mr Dale but I'm in a bit of a rush. Have you heard from the hospital?' he interrupted him, the hailstones stinging his exposed hands.

'I'm sorry, I do go on sometimes. Young Mark called about an hour ago and asked if I could have Alice for a few days,' Mr Dale said with a shake of the head. 'I don't think they're coming home for a while. It's a terrible business, isn't it?'

'It is. I want to have a good look around the house and make sure it's secure. As I said on the telephone earlier, we're expecting a bit of a backlash and we want to be on the safe side.'

'Of course, you do.' Mr Dale took a set of keys from a hook near the door. 'I said I'll close the curtains at night and move the post from the door in the morning, so it looks like someone is in. You have to help your neighbours out at a time like this don't you.'

'Of course, you do and it's much appreciated, Mr Dale,' he said taking the keys. He turned and ran down the path. 'I'll have these back with you in ten minutes. I'll drop them through the letter box when I'm finished.'

'Right you are,' Mr Dale said, with a wave and a smile, closing the door and heading back to his armchair with the excited staffie getting under his feet.

Next door, he fumbled for the right key, found it and pushed the door open. He paused in the darkness and waited for a sound, a movement, anything that would give away the presence of a member of the family. 'Anyone home?' he called as a double check. The smell of stale cigarette smoke hung heavy in the air, mingled with a pine scented plug-in air freshener that was doing its best to mask the stink but was failing miserably. He switched on the hall light and closed the door behind him, leaning against it, he looked around. He walked into the living room and switched on the lights; the smell of cigarettes became stronger. Everything looked to be where it belonged. There was no sign of any disturbance. He walked through the living room into the kitchen and checked that the windows were secure. The backdoor was locked with the key left in it. He turned the key and unlocked it. Opening the door, he stepped outside and looked around the garden. The recycling bin was next to the door and he lifted the lid and glanced inside. It was full to the brim with lager cans and vodka bottles. He stepped back into the kitchen and closed the door, locking it behind him, removing the key from the lock for safety.

He opened the cupboards and scanned the contents and then moved slowly through the other cupboards. A thorough search of the kitchen drawers gave up bank and credit card statements, utility bills and phone records. He photographed them with his phone and put them back before moving into the living room once more. Some boxing trophies in the sideboard cabinet revealed which gym the sons trained at and Mrs Evans's address book was particularly helpful. He photographed her Christmas card list, the addresses gold dust. Ten minutes later when he slid the keys back through Mr Dale's door he had everything that Eddie Farrell wanted. He checked his watch. It was late and Kelly's Gym was on his route home. He was in no rush to go home so he thought he might call there on the way.

* * * *

Liam Johnson hobbled along the canal bank until he was comfortable that he was far enough away for it to be safe to rejoin the roads. The Karpovs would be out there searching for him somewhere and he couldn't afford to stumble into them by walking along the roads. He needed to find transport quickly. His ankle was twisted, swollen and painful to walk on, although the bandage strapping helped. The canal was raised above the road at that point and when he reached an intersection that he recognised, he decided to climb down. He slid down an embankment on his backside and slipped through some railings onto a main road that joined Warrington to Manchester. There was a phone box nearby and he hobbled over to it, fumbling for change with numb fingers. He picked up the handset and put it to his ear, hearing nothing but static. Calling home was his priority. He slammed the receiver down angrily and kicked the door open. The traffic was light, but every pair of headlights was a threat. As each vehicle approached, he imagined it to be full of Karpov's men. He pulled up his collar to hide his face and waited for a taxi with the 'for hire' light on. He shifted his weight from his injured ankle, the minutes feeling like days. Eventually, he crossed the road to flag down a black cab as it came into view. It stopped and the heavens opened, and hailstones bounced off the cab roof, stinging his face. He struggled inside and sat heavily on the back seat, feeling damp, cold, miserable and frightened. It was a thirty-minute journey to the house he shared with his long-term partner and her son from a previous marriage. The driver tried to engage him in conversation but soon got the message that he wasn't feeling talkative. He had visions of his family being held at knifepoint by men in balaclavas, Ray being shot in the back of the head over a shallow grave. His guts churned with panic and anxiety, fear and regret. He had chosen this life, stealing for a living, always on the edge waiting to be arrested or shot. Thinking back, it was only a matter of time before they stole the wrong lorry and crossed the wrong person. Danger had the ability to highlight the mistakes he had made, the mistakes that his cousins had made, mistakes he was paying for now. The world they lived in was a lucrative one but when things went wrong, it was a lonely place to be and the usual rules didn't apply. He couldn't protect Ray and he couldn't protect Katelyn and her boy and he couldn't ask for help from the state. The police were as much his enemy as the Karpovs. His mind raced as he wished he could make it all go away.

When they arrived at his street, he asked the driver to drop him off at the top of his road, paid him with soggy twenty-pound notes and jogged across the road without collecting his change. He stayed away from oncoming vehicles and the edge of the pavements. Each car was a potential weapon, every van a mobile torture chamber. His thoughts focused on Ray again. He was convinced that as long as he remained beyond their grasp, he could bargain with them. The Karpovs didn't want him to talk to the police and they didn't want him to talk to Tucker either. He could offer their silence in return for Ray. If he could do it right, they would have to let him go. He looked up and down the street and checked for unfamiliar vehicles. The Karpovs would find out where he lived and he didn't think it would take the Tuckers too long to work things out either. Tucker was an arrogant psycho who wouldn't think twice about knocking on his front door and putting a gun in his face. Liam couldn't risk that happening in front of his stepson. As he scoured the parked vehicles, he spotted a dark van a hundred yards down the road on his right-hand side, almost opposite his house, two men sat inside. He could see their cigarettes glowing in the dark. The van didn't belong to any of his neighbours, he was sure of that. Going home was always going to be a gamble. He had taken too long to recover on the barge, and someone had beaten him to it. Time was ticking away for Ray and he needed to get to his family. He needed a mobile phone and some money and to get his family out of the house. He looked around and then crossed the road to a phone box, relieved that it was in full working order. Memorising the registration plate, he picked up the handset and dialled nine-nine-nine.

'Hello emergency, which service do you require?'

'Police.' The connection was made with a clicking sound.

'Police emergency, how can we help?'

'I've just seen a woman dragged into a black Mercedes van by two men, the registration plate is, EX56 JK3,' he said watching the van. 'She was kicking and screaming.'

'Can you confirm where this took place?'

'I'm not from this area,' he lied, 'it was just down the street from this call box,' he added knowing that they would trace it. 'Oh, they're looking straight at me. I'll have to go…one of them has got a gun.' Liam hung up and stepped out of the phone box knowing that armed police would be all over the street in minutes and evacuating the houses in the vicinity would be the first thing that they would do.

* * * *

Yuri and Mikel Karpov dropped into the crystal-clear waters, a forty-minute sail from Kho Lanta. As they floated in the water next to the boat, their Thai pilot, Rut, handed them their masks and snorkels and then broke up a banana and threw the pieces into the water above the coral reef, which was ten metres below the surface. He handed the Russians two more bananas each and then gave them their Sports Cams. They spat in their masks, cleared the lenses and set off to explore the reefs. Rut couldn't stand the Russians; they were rude and arrogant and tipped badly, but Yuri and Mikel were especially unlikeable. They took arrogance to a whole new level. He was introduced to them after taking Eddie Farrell on boat trips whenever he visited the island. Eddie had been a regular visitor for over ten years and whatever Eddie needed while he was there, Rut supplied it.

Rut watched as the Russians swam leisurely along the reef line, occasionally diving beneath the surface to photograph something or other, flippers splashing noisily. Beyond the turquoise sea above the coral, the water was dark blue where the sea floor plummeted to a series of submarine valleys at a depth of 4000metres. Rut had convinced them that it was worth the long sail out to this particular reef because it was visited by the much bigger fish from the depths beyond. He waited patiently until they were a hundred metres away from the long tail boat and then climbed from the bow to the stern along the bulwark to the engine block. From beneath it he pulled out a five-gallon petrol canister and unscrewed the lid, recoiling from the stench of fish guts, heads and blood. He lifted the canister and lowered it into the water on the blind side of the boat. Tilting it, he allowed the sea water to run over and then let it sink slowly beneath the boat, its bloody contents spewing out as it drifted to the bottom. Dozens of small fish began to nibble at the chum. It only took a few minutes for the first shark fins to appear. The Russians were enjoying the multicoloured sea life completely unaware as the sharks began to arrive in numbers. When he spotted some larger fins circling, he started the engine, pulled up the anchor and headed away towards Phi Phi Don, an hour in the opposite direction.

He thought he heard panicked shouting on the breeze, but he didn't look back for a long time. An image of the Russians thrashing about waving their arms in the air as the sharks circled appeared, but he chased it away. When he did look, the wake spoiled his view of the reef. There was no sign of the Russians, but the water appeared to be tinged red, although it might have been a trick of the light. Rut took out his mobile and typed in a text message to Eddie Farrell.

'It's done.'

CHAPTER 17

Jacob Graff looked in the mirror and grimaced at his reflection. A three-inch gash on his nose and a smaller one on his right cheek had been stitched neatly. The ibuprofen had taken the edge off the pain but the throbbing in his face hadn't subsided much. He filled the sink with warm water and cupped his hands, splashing his hair to remove the blood. It was a pointless task, his blood dried and congealed. Without a hot shower and a bottle of shampoo, it wasn't going anywhere. His bloodstained white shirt was open at the collar now, his tie rolled up in his jacket pocket. He dried his face and hands and walked out of the toilets onto the ward. Simon Evans was waiting for him, still in his dark work suit, leaning against the wall, his trench coat folded over his right arm.

'Hello Simon, I'm glad you're here,' Jacob said extending his arm. 'What an interesting afternoon I've had representing your brother.'

'I'm sorry I couldn't get here sooner. I believe there's been some bother.'

'A little, which my bill to you will reflect, no doubt,' Jacob smiled.

'Bloody hell, Jacob,' Simon said shaking his hand. He gripped his wrist, a gesture of the respect that they had for each other. 'You look awful.'

'Thank you so much,' Jacob quipped. 'Have you seen your brother yet?'

'No,' Simon said in a hushed voice. 'I wanted to speak to you first. What do you think the CPS will do?'

'It's hard to say at this stage although young Bryn is very credible. He'll be remanded at some stage of course until they decide what action to take.'

'That's what I'm most worried about. He's just a kid. Prison is no place for him,' Simon said with a sigh. 'I've just found out who Anthony Farrell is. Bryn will be a sitting duck on remand.'

'Not necessarily. I will insist that he's put into a vulnerable juvenile unit, probably HMP Altcourse. He will be safe there until we can get him out.'

'What are the odds on getting him out?'

'Fair to slim, I would say. He has admitted killing Farrell, but it is clearly a case of self-defence. If we can convince the CPS of that then he may be released sooner rather than later. I'm more worried about further reprisals against the family than I am of the judicial system.'

'Me too,' Simon agreed looking at the ugly scar on Jacob's nose. 'What do you think we should do?'

'You must trust that Bryn will be protected by the state and concentrate on keeping the rest of your family safe. Get them out of the city if you can.'

'I will.' Simon nodded and loosened his tie. 'I'm going to go and speak to them now.'

'I'll join you.'

'Are you sure?' Simon asked surprised. 'You're going to be sore in the morning. Shouldn't you go home and get some rest?'

'I'm well enough to put your family at ease if I can. They need to believe that I'll be doing everything that I can to secure Bryn his freedom.' He smiled touching his nose with a finger, 'And then I will go home and have a very large brandy or two. I have the feeling that sleep will evade me tonight. Shall we go and see them?' he asked, pointing towards the ward exit. 'Your brother is in a room along the corridor.' They walked through the doors into a corridor where a cleaning crew were buffing the floor. The lights were subdued so that patients could sleep, giving the hospital an eerie feel, casting shadows where danger could lurk. 'You need to get them out of the city. Do you have somewhere to take them?'

'Not really,' Simon said shaking his head. He pushed his sandy hair back off his forehead, the fringe a month overdue for a cut. 'I'm thinking a hotel in North Wales somewhere for now just to get them out of the city. What do you think?'

Jacob shook his head, his hands pushed deep into his jacket pockets. 'I think that with persistence, someone could easily find you in a hotel. A few hours of phone calls and they could get lucky.' He stopped and rubbed his chin thoughtfully. 'Listen, I have a cottage on Anglesey, in Trearddur Bay, which an aunt left to me. I haven't been there for a few months. It's up for sale but you're welcome to use it for as long as you need to. It will be breezy there this time of year but it's a safe place.' They skirted the woman who was controlling the buffing machine. She smiled and nodded as they went by. 'I have the door keys in my briefcase. Take them and make your family safe for the next few days, Simon. I'll do what I can from here.'

'That's very kind of you, Jacob,' Simon said touching his arm. 'I think we can cope with the wind if it means Mum and Dad are safe.'

'And Mark.'

'He's big enough to look after himself. I'm glad he's on our side though,' he joked. 'Thanks again for the offer.'

'You're welcome. It will take you two hours from here.' Jacob lowered his voice. 'They know Bryn is here and they may be watching who comes and goes. Make sure you're not followed, Simon and if you think you are, call the police and drive to the nearest police station.' Simon nodded thoughtfully. 'In the meantime, I will make some calls and try to put a stop to this nonsense. Some of my clients are familiar with the Farrell family.'

'I appreciate it, Jacob but I can't see Eddie Farrell listening to reason, can you?' Simon grimaced; the name synonymous with violence. 'Bryn is a kid, but he's killed Eddie's son...' his voice trailed off, enough said. As they walked down the corridor, uniformed police officers stopped them and asked for ID. An armed police officer further along gave away which room Bryn was in.

'I'm afraid that you're right,' Jacob said matter of factly. 'I cannot see a happy ending, no matter which way I look at it.' They paused outside the door, Jacob nodding hello to the armed officer. 'But I suggest that we keep our concerns between ourselves. Your parents will be worried enough.'

They opened the door and stepped inside. Bryn's swollen face lit up, a smile from ear to ear. 'Si,' he said excitedly. 'I didn't think that you were going to get here.'

Simon walked over to the bed, shaking Bryn's hand with one hand and hugging him with the other. 'All right, Squirt. You look like you've been hit by a bus,' he said turning his face towards Mark. 'Hiya, bruv,' he said hugging Mark.

'Thanks for coming,' Mark said squeezing him. 'I could do with your help. The police were very good, but I wasn't sure what to do next.'

'We'll sort it out, don't worry,' Simon said. He turned back to Bryn. 'What have the doctors said?'

'They think that I might need an operation on my cheekbone.'

'Well, that's the modelling career out of the window then, eh?' Simon turned to his parents, hugging his father and kissing his mother on the cheek. 'Definitely no modelling career with a mug like that, what do you think, Dad?'

'Modelling career? He's always been an ugly bugger,' Robert joked. 'I blame your mother, she dropped him on his head when I wasn't looking.'

'Bloody cheek,' Barbara growled, half joking, half not. 'Our Bryn isn't an ugly bugger, are you, love.' she looked at Bryn, a concerned smile on her face. 'He's a handsome lad, aren't you?'

'You have to say that,' Robert said seriously. 'You're his mother but my job is to tell the lad the truth and he's an ugly bugger.'

'Well he gets it from your side of the family if he is.'

'Thanks, Mum.' Bryn grinned. As he was laughing, he noticed Jacob Graff had entered the room behind Simon. 'Oh, Mr Graff, how are you?' Bryn asked concerned. The laughing died down and they focused on the ageing solicitor.

'I'll live thank you.' He pointed to the gash on his nose, dark circles starting to spread beneath his eyes. 'It would appear the chance of my modelling career taking off has been ruined too. We're quite a team, aren't we?' Jacob smiled. 'How is everyone holding up?'

'As well as can be expected,' Mark answered first. 'The police have told me to take Mum and Dad to my house tonight but I'm not sure we'll be safe there.'

'You won't be,' Simon said, 'Jacob has a property on Anglesey. We'll drive there tonight and settle them in for a few days while we sort things out for Bryn.' He turned to his youngest brother. 'I think that you'll be here for a few days until they've fixed your cheekbone. There are armed police outside your room, so you don't need to worry, okay?' Bryn nodded his head slowly. He didn't like the idea of being left alone in the hospital, but he didn't want his brothers to think he was scared. Inside he was terrified. 'Jacob is going to make sure that when you're remanded, you'll go to a vulnerable youth unit where you'll be isolated from the other prisoners. You'll be safe there.' The family looked at Bryn. He looked scared and fragile. Barbara started sniffling again, her handkerchief held tightly in her right hand, her left hand in Robert's.

'Don't worry, Mum. We'll get through this.' Everyone nodded but nobody looked convinced. 'It probably isn't as bad as we think it is right now.'

'Quite,' Jacob rescued him. 'Rest assured that I will be working on Bryn's behalf full-time until we have a satisfactory resolution. Now, I need to track down my briefcase. I will give you the keys to the cottage and I suggest that you make tracks. I'll leave you to say your goodbyes for now. I will remain here until we know for certain that Bryn will be here overnight.'

'Thanks,' the family mumbled. The thought of leaving Bryn weighed heavily on their conscience. The atmosphere in the room was emotive, desperation pervaded the air.

'Can't we stay with him until he goes?' Barbara asked.

'The sergeant said that we could stay until Simon arrived,' Mark said. 'He said that once they knew that all the family was safe, we would have to go. We shouldn't be in here at all, Mum.'

'I can't see what the problem is,' Barbara said with a sniffle. 'What harm can it do?' As if prompted to, the door opened, and the uniformed sergeant stepped in. 'Oh. Bloody hell.' Barbara sighed.

'Okay folks,' he said with a serious face. 'It's time to leave. My officers are going to escort you to a service elevator on the far side of this wing. They'll take you through the kitchens and take you to your vehicle. I assume you're leaving in a vehicle?'

'Yes,' Simon said. I'm parked at the rear, near the university exit.'

'Ideal, when you're ready we need to move you.' He looked at Barbara, her distress obvious. 'Don't you worry about Bryn, Mrs Evans. We'll look after him.'

'How can I not worry about him?'

'Behave yourself, Squirt,' Mark said, shaking Bryn's hand. He made fists and held them on his chin. 'We'll see you soon, keep on your toes, chin down and hands up.' Bryn nodded, his eyes filled with tears and his bottom lip quivered.

'Jacob will get you out,' Simon said. He shook Bryn's hand and hugged him. 'Just sit tight and do as you're told until then, okay?'

'Okay,' Bryn nodded his voice a whisper. A tear broke free and ran down his cheek.

'Don't cry, son,' Barbara said, making him worse. She leaned over the bed and hugged her youngest child. The pressure of the day peaked, and Bryn broke down, sobbing on his mother's shoulder like a baby. 'I'm so sorry, Mum! I didn't mean to kill him…' he repeated over and over until his words became a garbled whine. His brothers looked at each other feeling awkward, as if they were intruding on their sibling's grief, glad that their mother was there for him. Their father hugged Bryn and his wife from the opposite side of the bed. Simon signalled to Mark that they should leave them to it, and they slipped through the door into the corridor.

Jacob walked towards them, hand outstretched; a set of keys dangled from his fingers and a metallic Welsh dragon glinted in the lights. 'The address and postcode are written on the tag. Ring me if there are any problems. I'll stay with Bryn until the doctors make a decision and, in the meantime, I'll make some calls.'

Simon took the keys and slid them into his pocket, 'Thanks again, Jacob.'

'Don't thank me until you've seen my bill. Now get your family out of here to safety.'

Mark's phone buzzed and he checked the screen. 'Oh shit,' he gasped.

'What is it?' Simon asked.

'Someone's torched Kelly's Gym.'

Jacob looked confused. 'Mark and Bryn go there for boxing training,' Simon explained.

'I see,' Jacob said, concerned. He knew that it was no accident.

'I've got a fight coming up,' Mark said shaking his head. He hadn't made the connection. 'Can today get any worse?'

Simon and Jacob exchanged glances, which said that there was a possibility that it could indeed get worse, much worse.

CHAPTER 18

Liam Johnson watched as the police set up a cordon at the end of the road and then shepherded the residents from their houses via their back doors along an alleyway. As his neighbours appeared one family at a time, the armed police were readying to move in on the van. When he saw Katelyn and Daryl emerge from the alleyway, he ran to them. 'Are you okay?'

'Yes,' Katelyn said, frightened but angry. 'Where have you been?'

'I'll explain when we get out of here.' He said guiding her along the pavement. 'Are you okay, Daryl?' he said with a half-smile.

'What is going on?' Daryl moaned; his Xbox paused on level six of his favourite game.

'We need to get away from here for a while, mate,' he said ruffling his hair. 'The police are going to arrest someone and there might be trouble.'

'Is this anything to do with you?' Katelyn asked suspiciously. She knew that Liam and his brother made a living stealing lorries, but he had always promised her that no one would ever get hurt. She loved him and his word was good enough for her. He had done more for Daryl than his real father had ever done, and he treated her like a princess, always romancing her with flowers and meals out. No one had treated her like that before, so she turned a blind eye to his activities and had never asked any questions until now. 'What the hell have you been up to?'

'Ray is in trouble. I'll explain later,' Liam said nervously as they got beyond the police cordon. 'Have you got your mobile?' he asked in a panic. She searched through her bag and then handed him her mobile phone. Opening the back, he took out her SIM card, replacing it with his. He could only hope that it would work. The phone came back on and he scrolled through his contacts looking for a number. He found what he was looking for. Once he had his family safe, he would make the call. He guided Katelyn and Daryl along the road until he could flag down a cab. His family away from the house, he had to work on getting

Ray freed before it was too late. As the cab pulled away, he didn't notice the black Nissan that slipped into the traffic behind them.

* * * *

Braddick looked around the office and felt like a stranger. Some of the old faces were still there. The view of the river and the Albert Docks was the same, but he didn't feel at home anymore. To the south, the Anglican Cathedral towered above the city, a gothic monolith that dominated the skyline. Across the road, the mythical Liver Birds sat atop the Three Graces, guarding the city from their stone perches. They were sights that were emblazoned in his heart and mind and would stay there for life. The surroundings were familiar but something inside him had intrinsically changed. The city was a constant; it was Marcus Braddick that was different. He knew that coming back to the city from London would be difficult, but he hadn't anticipated being tossed onto the frontline from day one. There had been no time to readjust. His feet hadn't touched the ground since he walked into the first briefing. The Major Investigation Team's figureheads, Detective Superintendent Ramsay was taking a sabbatical and his DI, Annie Jones was on extended sick leave. The word was that she wouldn't be coming back following an arson attack on her home, her abduction and a near fatal assault and that Ramsay and she had become an item.

Braddick knew of both of them but hadn't worked directly with either. The MIT was in transition, but the criminals seemed to be completely unaware that they needed a breather while they got reorganised. There was no let up, no timeout and no holidays in the criminal underworld; making money from illegal activities was a round the clock business. Braddick felt like he was wading through concrete. There had been no breakthrough on the Johnson murders and the Farrell case was a ticking time bomb that could go off at any time. The fact that the Karpovs were linked to the case was a further complication that he hadn't expected. His blood boiled at the mention of their name.

Ade Burns walked out of the lift, his hair tussled and in need of washing. He waved as he headed in a straight line for the coffee machine, cursing when he realised that someone had put the empty jug back on the hotplate without making a fresh brew.

'There are some lazy bastards in this office,' he moaned. His suit jacket looked like he'd screwed it up, jumped on it and then put it back on. 'Do you want one, Guv?' he asked as he opened a packet of grounds and set up a fresh pot. He looked tired, bags beneath his eyes, his shoulders sagging from fatigue. 'It's been a long day.'

'It has.'

'Did you say you wanted a drink?'

'No. I'm still nursing one here,' Braddick said yawning. 'I need something stronger to be honest.'

'Don't tempt me. If I start drinking, I won't stop. I've only just finished giving my report on Paulie Williams. Fancy nearly dying in the cells before we interviewed him, inconsiderate at best,' Ade tutted and shook his head, a sarcastic grin on his face. 'I'm just glad that I didn't have to pick him up and carry him to the ambulance,' Ade added, his dark humour not lost on Braddick who tried to hide a smile. 'What a fucking pain in the rear end. Fourteen hours and I feel like I've achieved bugger all. It's been a shitty day.'

'It has,' Braddick agreed. 'Did they find out anything from the *Facebook* list?'

'Nothing, Guv. Google went home an hour ago. Nobody is prepared to make a statement. He said he'll be back in at seven to have another crack at them but he's not holding his breath that anyone will come forward.'

'I'm not holding mine either, but someone knows who killed the Johnsons. If we keep shaking the tree, something will fall out.' Braddick sighed. He stood up and picked up his overcoat. It was too late for fresh information to come in and he needed to clear his head. His brain felt like it was turning to sludge. There was a point where staying at work became counterproductive and he had reached it an hour before. 'We're not going to achieve anything tonight. Go home and get some sleep. I'll see you in the morning.'

'Okay thanks, Guv,' Ade put his empty cup down. 'It's good to have you back. See you tomorrow.' He smiled awkwardly and turned towards the lifts. Braddick made a mock salute in response. He looked at Ade's crumpled jacket and wondered if he had tipped off the Drug Squad about the raid. He'd known Adrian Burns for ten years. They were the same rank before Braddick transferred; they were never close friends, but they got on well enough on the odd occasion that they met. There was a mutual respect between them although Braddick knew that time changed people. It had changed him. He didn't figure Ade as a snake but then he didn't know him anymore, time would tell. Whoever tipped off the Drug Squad was trying to make his life difficult and he intended to find out who it was. When he did, he would kick them up the arse.

Braddick put his coat on and walked to the window. The Ferris wheel at the Albert Docks was dormant, the ferries moored up for the night. He thought about walking to one of the bars in the docks, maybe booking into a hotel for the night to save driving home. His tussle with Eddie Farrell Junior had unsettled him and he needed something to help him unwind. He didn't think that he would sleep, knowing that the Evans family were targets. Mark Evans had sent him a text message with an address on Anglesey where his brother was taking them. He made the arrangements with the neighbouring forces to make sure that they would be made a priority if they made an emergency call, but it didn't feel like it was enough. Bar taking them home with him, there was nothing more that he could do.

'I thought you might still be here,' a female voice disturbed his thoughts. 'I'm going for a drink across the road. Do you fancy coming?' Steff Cain said from the doorway of the office. Braddick desperately wanted to say yes. He wanted alcohol and he wanted to discuss the day's events. Female company wouldn't go amiss either. It made sense to socialise with colleagues from the station. It was the best way to catch up and familiarise himself with the force as it stood. The problem was that he knew that she just wanted the gossip on why he had come back. He didn't trust her; not one bit.

'No thanks,' Braddick said glancing around at her. 'I'm going to go home and get some sleep, early start tomorrow.'

'Are you sure?'

'Positive, thanks for the offer though.'

'There are some decent bars over there nowadays if you fancy a late drink. We go quite a lot. I'm going to book into the Holiday Inn Express.' She held up a small rucksack. 'I'm sharing a twin room with one of my DC'S, half the cost.' She shrugged. 'No strings attached, just a drink…'

Braddick smiled and shook his head, confused. 'Nothing like having your arm twisted when your willpower is at an all-time low.'

'I was pretty sure that I wound you up today. I certainly didn't mean to, this time around anyway,' Cain smirked. 'I'm not trying to get into your pants. I'm going for a drink with a few colleagues and I thought it would be nice to invite you.'

'Life's very short and I do want a drink,' Braddick shrugged. 'Sod the early night.'

'So, is that a yes then?'

'Yes. Your round first,' Braddick said, his mind made up. He thought about Anthony Farrell, Bryn Evans, the Johnsons, and Karin. Especially Karin. They'd had no choices; fate forced their arm.

'You're right. Life's short,' she agreed.

The phone on his desk rang. He thought about leaving it and then picked it up. 'DI Braddick.'

'Are you the bloke in charge of the Johnson murders?' a male voice rasped, slightly muffled by a tissue over the mouthpiece, Braddick guessed.

'I am, yes.' He fumbled for a pen and held it poised above his pad. Cain rolled her eyes skyward and frowned, pointing to her watch. 'How can I help you?' Braddick asked.

'It is more a case that I can help you,' the voice said. Braddick could hear traffic in the distance. The caller was using a phone box. 'I know who killed the Johnsons, the ones found in the alley, but I'll only talk to you and I'm not going to court.'

'Okay, where and when?' Braddick thought that it could be a set-up, Eddie Farrell Junior seeking revenge for their spat, trying to lure him somewhere remote.

'Meet me at the McDonald's drive-thru on Edge Lane. I'll be inside,' the voice sounded frightened. Farrell wouldn't have picked such a public place. 'You make sure that you come alone, or I'm gone.'

'I'll be alone, don't worry.'

'What car do you drive?'

'A Range Rover Evoque.'

'How long will you be?'

'I'm on my way.' The line went dead and he replaced the receiver, looking at Cain. 'Sorry.' He shrugged. 'Another time maybe?'

'Maybe,' she said aloofly. She turned and walked through the doors to the landing. He heard her footsteps on the stairs, and he waited until they'd faded before he followed her. He opted to take the lift, feeling slightly relieved that he wasn't going to wake up in the morning a bit hung-over and a little embarrassed. There was no sign of her on the ground floor and he jogged across the secure car park to the Evoque. The drive through the city to Edge Lane took fifteen minutes, the roads virtually empty. When he pulled into the car park, he picked a spot in full view of the restaurant's dining area. He could see four people inside, a couple and two lone diners. None of them took any notice of his arrival. He checked his mobile and turned off the engine, nervously looking into the darker reaches of the rundown trading estate. The yellow light from the lampposts that surrounded the fast food outlet couldn't penetrate the blackness beyond the car park and the shadows seemed to shift and swirl as he stared into the night.

A knock on the passenger window made him jump. He turned to see a crooked smile, most of the teeth missing, the remainder stained. A beanie hat was pulled low to brow level, his ears covered. Braddick wound down the window a few inches.

'Are you going to let me in or what?' the man snapped, looking around nervously. He pulled at the handle. 'Come on I haven't got all night.' Braddick looked at him, assessing the threat level. He unlocked the door and watched him climb in. The odour of stale sweat and mould came in with him. His skin looked pale and grey in the dull light, his time in the sun limited at best. 'I could murder a coffee,' he said closing the door, rubbing his hands together against the cold. He cupped them together and blew onto them, nodding towards the drive-thru. 'A hot drink would work wonders. It's getting cold at night isn't it?'

'It is,' Braddick agreed, realising that the man was one of the city's many homeless people. The smell of living rough hung thick in the air. He started the engine and pulled the vehicle towards the drive-thru lane. A taxi and a van pulled into the line before him. 'Have you eaten?'

The man shook his head and blew into his hands again. 'A cheeseburger wouldn't go amiss,' his toothless grin appeared once more. It wasn't pretty but it was disarming. There was something genuine about his manner. The order post crackled into life.

'Will a quarter pounder with cheese and fries, do you?' Braddick asked with a grin.

'It would be much appreciated.'

Braddick talked into the order post and bought two large coffees, a quarter pounder with cheese and a large fries. They picked up their order at the next window and found a place to park a hundred yards away from the building. Braddick handed him the food and his drink and kept his own coffee. 'What's your name?' he asked as the man shoved a handful of fries into his mouth.

'People call me Cookie,' he said chewing greedily. He bit into the burger and washed it down with a mouthful of coffee. 'Danny Cook is my full name, Cookie for short.' He wiped his greasy hands on a napkin. 'Thanks for this. I didn't realise how hungry I was. You get past it when you haven't eaten for a while, you know what I mean, don't you?' He gulped at his coffee. 'Actually, you probably don't know.'

Braddick shook his head, sipped his coffee and allowed Cookie to finish his food. He had sympathy for him. It didn't take much for life to fall out of kilter. There were plenty of people on the streets who could have been police officers if life had been different for them and there were plenty of police officers who could have ended up destitute if luck hadn't shined on them. There was a fine line between lucky and unlucky. Fate was fragile in the inner cities and many lives once full of hope and promise fell by the wayside. 'What can you tell me about the Johnsons, Cookie?'

'I don't know them personally,' Cookie said wiping his mouth. 'But I know what happened to them. Fucking shocking it was.'

'I'm listening.'

'See where the old B&Q is over there?' He pointed across the car park to a row of unused warehouses. They were rotting hulks silhouetted against the yellowed light pollution from the city beyond them. 'There's an old bowling alley behind it. It's been closed for years now.'

'It used to be the Superbowl.' Braddick nodded, remembering a few boozy nights out as a teenager. 'I remember when this retail park was in its heyday. Do you remember the skateboard park over there on Rathbone Road?'

'I do.' Cookie smiled ear to ear. 'I used to play there from dawn till dusk when I was at school. Loved my board.'

'Me too, although I think I would break my neck on one nowadays.' Braddick laughed.

'You're indestructible at that age though, aren't you?'

'We thought we were, eh?' Braddick sipped his coffee and looked towards the derelict hulks. 'What's the old retail park got to do with the Johnsons' murders?'

'Drive me over there and I'll show you,' Cookie said enthusiastically pointing into the gloom. 'It'll be easier to show you,' he insisted. A car turned the corner, headlights glinting in his eyes. His pupils were tiny pinheads of black against the green irises, heroin a common visitor to his bloodstream.

Braddick hesitated and looked at Cookie sternly. 'That's not happening.' He wanted a breakthrough on the murders, but it was too risky. 'I'm not driving out of sight of the road on the word of a man I've just met, Cookie.' He paused and sipped his coffee. 'You seem like a nice bloke but I'm going to need more than what you have told me so far before I make any decisions.'

Cookie sipped his coffee. 'Fair enough, I understand you have to be careful but I'm on the level.' He shrugged. 'I'm trying to help because what happened to the Johnsons was wrong in so many ways. It was sick…I mean burning their legs like that.'

'Wait a minute.' Braddick stopped him. They hadn't released any details. 'How do you know what happened to them?'

'I saw it, man.' Cookie shook his head and grimaced.

'You saw it happen?'

'Not quite.'

'What are you saying exactly?'

'I've been sleeping in the bowling alley for about a month,' Cookie said pointing at the dark shadows beyond the derelict hardware store. Braddick remembered back to when the bowling alley was open. There were three or four other buildings there, a carpet warehouse, an electrical store and a furniture outlet, all which shared a football pitch sized car park. They were all empty now and it was too dangerous to go alone on a tipoff despite the temptation. 'It's dry in there and more to the point it was safe. Safe is hard to find these days but it was safe in there,' he nodded, a sad look on his face. 'It was the best place I've slept for ages. Not anymore.'

'Tell me what happened?'

'The Tuckers that's what happened.' Cookie frowned and shook his head. 'They broke in last night with some of their goons. The noise woke me up. I was upstairs so they didn't see me. I'd been using, so I hid, but I was listening to them. I heard every word they said and I knew them straight away.'

'By their voices?'

'Yes,' he nodded. 'They were waiting for something. I didn't know what until a lorry turned up with a container on the back. I saw the lights on the car park.'

'Go on.'

'The next thing is I crept to the top of the balcony and looked over. They had two blokes tied to some old chairs. One of them was fucked up, man.'

'What do you mean?'

'They had torches so I could see them,' he grimaced. 'One of them was okay at first but the other one was ruined when they got there. His face was like a balloon, blood everywhere. Then they started torturing them, both of them. It was shocking to listen to, made me sick, the sound of them in pain.' He paused and put his hands over his ears. 'They were screaming for hours but I daren't look. Then they set fire to them. I could smell the petrol and the smell of burning skin, stinks it does. Knocked me sick, I can tell you. I couldn't get out, so I waited until they'd gone. I waited ages in case they were outside watching, I was shitting myself.'

'I'm not surprised. You said that you know their names?'

'Yes. It was the Tuckers.' He nodded. 'Everyone knows the Tuckers, fucking bastards they are.'

'I've been away for a while, Cookie so fill me in, who are the Tuckers?' Braddick asked.

'They're brothers, Joe and Tommy,' Cookie looked around, nervous again as if the darkness could hear him betraying them. 'They grew up in Toxteth. I knew them when we were all teenagers. We used to hang around together back then, you know drinking, a bit of weed here and there and girls.' He laughed sadly. 'There were loads of girls around in those days. I used to take my pick back then.' Braddick nodded but didn't comment. Whatever assets Cookie had as a young man; time had taken them from him. He looked to be in his mid-sixties but Braddick reckoned he was twenty years younger than that. 'The Tuckers started nicking cars and selling them and then they moved into drugs too, made a lot of money before they were twenty.'

'How long ago are we talking about here?'

'Twenty years or so, give or take.' Cookie half-smiled. 'I've probably lost a decade off my tits somewhere.' He joked but there was no mirth in his eyes. 'We were all in our late teens when we met.'

Braddick nodded and smiled. 'Carry on.'

'I did bits and pieces for them. They looked after me in the early days, always had a few bob in my pocket,' he looked at Braddick; his eyes seemed to glaze over, his mind focused on a time gone by. Whatever he could see in his mind were bittersweet memories. His expression was melancholy, but a smile touched the corner of his lips. 'They were bad bastards back then but they're ten times worse nowadays. When they stepped into drugs, I started to deal a bit of smack for them, but I got a taste for my own stock and ended up taking more than I was selling. When I couldn't pay them, I went in to hiding for a few weeks, but they found me. They broke both my arms and threw me in the river, nearly drowned I did. I spent three months in a cast and my arms were never the same again. I never worked after that.' He shrugged as if it explained his predicament. 'I've fucking hated them ever since but what could I do.'

'So, you recognised them and you're sure it was them that you saw?' Braddick could feel excitement building in his gut. 'It was definitely the Tuckers?'

'I didn't say that I saw them.' Cookie raised a finger. 'I recognised their voices. You never forget someone's voice. It was them all right and they're as nuts as they ever were.'

'Okay, Cookie, then what happened?' Braddick said taking out his mobile phone.

'They were there for hours hurting them poor blokes. Eventually they fucked off in their vehicles and took the men with them. I can't go back in there.' Cookie grimaced. 'There's blood everywhere and it stinks. I've moved next door into the old carpet warehouse.'

'You've done the right thing by telling me.'

'I knew what they'd done was really bad but when I heard they were dead and dumped in an alleyway, I knew I would have to tell you; I couldn't say nothing, it isn't right.'

'You've done the right thing,' Braddick repeated. He took out his wallet and pulled out four twenties. 'Here, make sure you use some of it to eat.'

'I will, thanks.'

'You'll be in the carpet warehouse if I need to speak to you?'

'I'll be around here somewhere, it's home now. If you pull behind B&Q and beep your horn, I'll come to you,' Cookie opened the door and jumped out. He held up the notes and smiled, 'Thanks for this. You're a good one.' He shut the door, turned around and pulled up his hood, jogging into the darkness; his dark clothing made him invisible in seconds. 'You're a good one!' his voice echoed across the car park from the blackness.

'So are you,' Braddick said to no one. He put in a call to Canning Place and finished his coffee. An armed unit would come to check the place over to make sure it was safe, and the forensic team would be at the bowling alley in an hour. In the meantime, he needed to find out all about the Tuckers and begin the difficult task of putting together the risk assessments that would be required to plan their arrests. Any chance of sleeping vanished into the darkness with Cookie. He looked towards the derelict retail park and sighed; he was completely unaware of the eyes that watched him from the darkness.

CHAPTER 19

At the hospital, the Evans family had to leave Bryn and were taken through the ward by two armed officers. The lights were low, only the odd murmur from sickly patients could be heard. They walked by the nurses' station and the ward sister looked up from her paperwork for a moment. She smiled at Barbara Evans, a mother empathising with another; the gesture said, 'Good luck. I hope your family survives this unscathed', all in a split second of eye contact. Barbara nodded and returned her smile, the message received and appreciated. They pushed through a set of doors into a brightly lit area that was fitted with comfortable seats and vending machines; its sole occupant sat with his elbows on his knees, a cup of tepid coffee-like liquid in his hands. He didn't notice the strange group appearing as he stared into the cup looking for the answers to a million questions. 'Why couldn't they cure it? Why had it come back? Why had it chosen his daughter in the first place?'

Simon looked at him and felt for him. Anyone that was drinking vending machine coffee at that time of the night while the hospital slept was too scared to go home in case their loved one died. The lonely man's agony was similar to his own; a loved one in life threatening peril, the family helpless to protect them. No amount of money could help the grieving man; all he could do was wait.

Above the door an exit sign pointed to their left, but the officers ignored it and turned right. When they reached the main corridor, they skirted by the public lifts and reached double doors that were covered with plastic dust sheets. The policemen lifted the plastic and opened the doors, allowing the family inside. They headed through a newly constructed wing, as yet unoccupied. The odour of paint and polish mingled with dust and plaster. Thick tape crisscrossed the window glass and electrical cable hung from the ceiling tiles waiting to be fastened to light fittings. Their footsteps sounded louder than they should against the newly laid floors. Simon was nervous as he listened to his parents panting. A hundred yards on, they pushed through some double doors into a dimly lit corridor and made their way silently for fifty yards to the next set of doors. The lights of the city twinkled below, filtering through the dusty glass, casting long shadows inside. Barbara and Robert were struggling with the pace, their breathing heavy, loud, and laboured. Robert kept wiping sweat from his brow with his sleeve, his sons glancing at him each time, worried that he might keel over at any second. Simon and Mark flanked them, patiently guiding them behind the policemen. Mark looked around nervously, agitated at leaving his younger brother behind yet eager to get his elderly parents to safety. Simon appeared cool, a calming influence on them all.

'The service lifts are at the far end of the ward opposite this one,' one of the officers said over his shoulder.

'Thank heavens for that.' Robert sighed. 'I'm knackered. I was going to stop and ask for an iron lung.'

'Better make that two.' Barbara puffed.

'Nearly there,' the officer chuckled dryly. 'Have you got somewhere safe to go tonight?'

'Yes,' Robert began to answer but a nudge in the ribs from Simon silenced him. He looked at his son confused.

'We're heading to the Lakes,' Simon interrupted. 'We've booked a hotel for tonight and we'll see what tomorrow brings.'

'It's the best we could do at such short notice,' Mark added.

'I love the Lakes, Bowness is my favourite,' the officer said as they turned a corner. 'Me and the wife used to go there often. Mind you, it's expensive now. Whereabouts are you staying?'

Simon and Mark exchanged glances.

'Ambleside,' Simon lied. It was difficult to have an innocent conversation even with their protectors without giving something away. Braddick had told Mark to tell no one where they were going, not even the police, even if they asked. Paranoia pricked their minds like red-hot needles, their faceless stalkers hiding behind every door. The clatter of metal rattled from the walls, sounding louder in the empty building.

'Hello!' One of the officers called out. There was no reply but the sound of metal scraping against tile reached them from beyond a bend in the corridor. The group edged forward slowly, the policemen setting the pace. A voice drifted to them, the words garbled, then another voice whispering. Simon couldn't tell if it was English or not, but they were male voices, a distance away. The group waited while the policemen listened, tense, alert and ready for trouble. Footsteps came now, two sets approaching slowly, the whispering voices interspersed with hoarse laughter, closer but still out of sight, hidden by the bend. The policemen gestured for them to move slowly and then stopped dead as two men appeared at the other end of the corridor. They were wearing overalls seemingly oblivious to their presence, lost in conversation, one of them carrying a stepladder, the other a toolbox. Their chatter stopped when they saw the armed officers and they moved over to one side of the corridor to allow them to pass. As they neared, they eyed the family suspiciously as if wondering why an armed escort was required in a hospital.

'No one is supposed to be in this wing, it's not finished yet,' one of them said gruffly. 'Are you lost?'

'We're not lost thanks,' an officer replied curtly. He stopped and looked them up and down. His hand moved towards his Glock. 'We were told that this section would be empty. What are you doing here?'

'Working obviously,' the workman shrugged, nodding to his stepladder.

'In the dark?'

'It isn't dark where we've been working obviously,' the workman grinned. 'We're just heading to the next section. He's a painter and I'm a network fitter.' The officer eyed their tools. One of the men had some paint brushes in his top pocket, the other a toolbox. 'We're on our way through here to another section that needs some cabling and a bit of touching up.' He paused to look at the group. 'What are you lot doing in here anyway?' he asked frowning. 'What would you be doing in here so late? I mean we've got work to do…'

'Then I suggest you get on with it,' the officer replied. 'And mind your own business on the way.'

'No need to be so rude,' the painter grumbled. 'It's bad enough working nights without getting grief from you lot.' The men looked at each other and frowned. They moved away without answering, mumbling as they went. The policemen remained tense and alert until they'd gone.

'They're just doing their job, officer,' Robert said, feeling the policeman was a touch heavy handed. 'They're just trying to earn a living.'

'We were told that this corridor was nearly completed and that we shouldn't encounter anyone at all at this time of night,' he explained. 'They may well be a couple of contractors skiving but we can't take any chances with your safety, Mr Evans. You understand that don't you?' he said to the family as a whole. They nodded silently, the gravity of their situation becoming clearer with each turn. 'Okay, let's go.'

The group moved onwards and turned the corner where the workmen had appeared. Mark noticed spots of dark paint splashed every few yards. The paint spots appeared wet and sticky. It seemed odd but he didn't want to alert the others and scare his parents. He reached around and tapped Simon on the hand, nodding to the random splashes. Simon looked down, his face deadpan. A concerned look crossed his face almost imperceptibly. The group moved on; the officers apparently oblivious to the paint spots. Mark didn't know much about constructing multimillion-pound medical facilities, but he didn't think that any accidental spillages would be left on newly laid floors, especially not in the middle of the night. He wasn't sure why it struck him as strange, but it did. The sound of metal crashing to the floor echoed down the corridor from behind them followed by the sound of running feet thumping on the ground. It seemed to bounce from the walls, engulfing them in noise. Mark couldn't tell if the footsteps were advancing towards them or retreating. His heart was pounding in his chest, his muscles tensed for an attack.

The armed officers turned and pointed torches along the corridor. In the far distance, two figures were running away, and something lay across the floor. Mark thought it might be a set of stepladders, but it was difficult to tell for sure. His hackles were rising, the blood pumping through his veins. The silence was deafening.

'We move on,' the officer said assertively. Their weapons remained holstered, but their hands were never far away from them. 'Stay close and do not stop, no matter what happens, understand?' The family nodded as one. Mark saw the officer eying the paint splashes. His eyes flickered to his colleague who had spotted it too. He knelt and dipped his index finger into the sticky liquid, sniffing it. 'It is paint,' he said, reassuring everyone that it wasn't blood. No one had said it but everyone was thinking it. 'Let's go.'

The officers moved quickly; their strides wide but remarkably quiet. Mark and Simon did their best to guide their parents along at a pace that wouldn't exhaust them completely. With five yards to go to reach the next set of doors, the paint drops became more frequent, thicker and pooled; some were smeared, half footprints leading from the doors. No professional had made the mess. The officers didn't hesitate, their hands closed over their holstered weapons. They pushed the doors open and stepped into a wide stairwell which housed two lifts and was lit by fluorescent lighting. Tall windows ran from one landing to the next, allowing the sun's rays to flood in during daylight hours. A thick layer of building dust covered everything, and the cloying smell of paint was thick in the air.

One of the officers stopped still in his tracks and pushed Mark towards the lifts. 'Get them over there,' he said trying to hide something. 'There's a stairwell to the left of the lifts. Get your parents down them quickly! I'm right behind you.'

Mark steered his mum and dad across the landing, looking over his shoulder as he did so, trying to make sense of what the officer had seen. Someone had painted a morbid mural on the white wall that spanned from one floor to the next. It was more than fifteen feet tall. The crude image of a hanging man, his neck snapped, tongue lolling out had been daubed on the stairwell wall. It looked like it had been painted by a child; the crudeness making it more striking. Painted below the gallows were four headless bodies, the red paint representing their blood. Scrawled below it was...

RIP THE EVANS FAMILY, YOU'RE GOING TO BURN IN HELL

* * * *

Liam Johnson toyed with the mobile phone and stared at the road, his thoughts bouncing around his head. No matter how he played it out, Ray was going to end up badly hurt or worse. Time was ticking away, and he still couldn't come up with the answer. He had gone through each scenario in his head but each one ended as a disaster. The truth was that there was no one that he could turn to and no one that he could trust. He pushed up his sleeves as he pondered, and Katelyn noticed the wounds on his hands and arms for the first time. She drew breath sharply, the air hissed between her teeth.

'What the hell have you done to your arms?'
'I fell through some glass.'
'You fell through some glass?'

'Yes.'

'What glass for God's sake?'

'It happened at work, don't go on.'

'Oh. I'm going on, now am I?' she tutted dramatically. 'Silly me for caring.'

'Don't have a go at me, Katelyn. Not right now.'

'And what are you wearing?' Katelyn nudged him and looked into his eyes. Her son Daryl had his earphones in and seemed oblivious, staring out of the glass as the rain dribbled down the windows. Traffic was light, brake lights blurred through the glass and rain, warping into coloured blobs. Katelyn looked into Liam's eyes, searching for an explanation, part of her dreading the answer, not daring to know the truth in case it destroyed what they had. She'd warned him that the first sign of anything that would endanger her, or Daryl, and she was gone. Daryl's real father had been a small-time dope dealer and despite her warnings, his clients continued to knock on her door until one day one of them became violent with him and made threats against them. She packed her bags and never spoke to him again. 'They're not your clothes. What is going on?'

'I got wet,' Liam shrugged, his face reddening.

'Wet?' she asked calmly. 'You fell through some glass and got wet. Did you fall into a shower or something?'

'It was an accident at work, that's all.'

'Is this the best you can come up with?'

'Please don't go on at me.'

'I'm not going on at you,' she said shaking her head, 'I'm trying to find out what is going on but it is like playing give us a clue with a tree.'

'It is complicated, and I don't want you to worry.'

'Don't worry.' She sighed. 'The police evacuated the entire street and you mysteriously turned up at the same time in someone else's clothes, battered and bruised but you don't want me to worry?'

'Yes. I don't want you to worry.'

'I bet your stupid brother has got something to do with this hasn't he?'

'Ray is not stupid.'

'Where is Ray?'

'He's sorting something out at work.'

'Sorting something out? Is he wearing someone else's clothes too?'

'Don't be ridiculous.'

'Ridiculous?' Katelyn tutted. 'I thought it might be dress down Friday or pay a pound and swap clothes day. Why don't you just tell me what is going on?'

'We really need to sort some stuff out and then I'll explain everything.'

'Stuff?' She sighed. 'You go missing overnight and then come home with someone else's clothes, cuts on your arms, a limp and all you can tell me is that you got wet and you have some stuff to deal with?'

'I know it sounds crap, but it is just work stuff.'

'Work stuff?'

'Yes.'

'Is that all I'm getting?' Katelyn asked angrily. She turned to face him and leaned closer. 'Let's be honest with each other. You don't work, Liam,' she hissed in his ear. Daryl looked at them concerned. 'You steal things.' He looked hurt but didn't answer her. 'You and your brother are thieves and I think you've fucked up.' he looked away. 'Have you fucked up, Liam?'

'Big time,' he said; his voice almost a whisper. 'You have no idea.'

'Tell me the truth,' she said quietly, 'is this something to do with what happened to David and Mathew?' Liam couldn't hold her gaze. Her eyes filled with tears, 'If it is then I need to know because they're dead, Liam.'

'I know they're dead.'

'Who is dead?' Daryl asked removing one ear bud.

'No one,' Katelyn said turning to him. 'Listen to your music while I talk to Liam.'

'Are you having an argument?'

'No. We're discussing something.'

'That's the same as arguing isn't it?'

'Put your headphones in and turn the volume up!' Katelyn snapped. Daryl huffed and turned back to staring out of the window. Katelyn took a deep breath and tried to calm down. She wiped tears of frustration from her eyes. 'You told me that you and Ray had nothing to do with their business. Your cousins were murdered, Liam.'

'I know they were.' He sighed. Images of David and Mathew flashed through his mind and mingled into a picture of his brother's face, younger, smiling and trouble free. His guts wrenched again. He had to do something and quickly.

'Please tell me this is nothing to do with what happened to them?' He turned away and looked out into the rain. 'I'm asking you a perfectly reasonable question, Liam, and you owe me an honest answer.' He looked back at her, his eyes watery and tired. 'Is this anything to do with their murders?'

'Look,' Liam tried to touch her hand, but she snatched it away. 'I can sort this out.'

'Answer the question.'

'I promise you that I can sort this out.'

'Answer the question!'

'Just give me a few days and I'm out of this game all together. I promise that I'm done with it. We'll move away and start again.'

'Move away from what, Liam?' Katelyn asked incredulously. 'My family?'

'Look...'

'Daryl's school?'

'I mean...'

'My job?'

'Let me...'

'This is where I live, why would I want to move away?'

'Just...'

'Just what, Liam?' she snapped. 'Tell me what you have done that's so bad that we need to move away. Go on tell me!'

'I don't know what to say, Katelyn,' Liam said blowing air from his lungs noisily. 'I'm just talking. I'm not thinking straight.'

'What have you got involved in?' Her voice softened. 'Please tell me that it is nothing to do with what happened to your cousins.'

'Okay.' He sighed. 'It is nothing to do with them.'

'You promise?' she said suspiciously.

'Yes,' he lied. 'And when this is over, I'm walking away from it all. I'm done with it.'

She looked into the rain, her heart wishing that he could walk away but her head knew the truth. 'And what will you do, Liam?'

'What do you mean?'

'What would you do.' She shrugged. 'You're a thief. Your cousins were thieves until someone set them on fire and God knows where Ray is because you won't answer the question...' she folded her arms and stared at him. 'I'm going to ask you once more because I don't believe you. Is this anything to do with your cousins?'

'No.'

'You're sure?' She frowned. 'If I find out that you're lying to me, we're finished.'

'I'm not lying.'

'Did the police evacuate us because of something you've done?' she changed tack trying to shake the truth from him. She knew he was lying but she wanted to know why.

'Sort of,' Liam shifted uncomfortably in his seat.

'Sort of?' She sighed. 'What the fuck does that mean, Liam?' He shrugged and shook his head, placing his face into his hands. She didn't swear in front of Daryl, in fact, she didn't swear much at all. 'If you can't give me an honest answer about what you're involved in then just answer me this one question.' She gripped his arm, her nails digging deep into his bicep. 'Are Daryl and I in danger because of something you and your stupid brother and stupid cousins have done?'

'Don't call them stupid.'

'They were set on fire and dumped in an alleyway,' Katelyn snapped. 'How fucking stupid was that?' she glared at him incredulously. 'If you can't see that getting involved in something that could wind up with you being burnt and dumped on the street then you're worse than stupid, Liam, you're an idiot and my son and I can't be anywhere near you.'

'I'm going to fix this.'

'Are you?' She sighed. 'Can you raise the dead now, Liam?'

'That's not what I mean.'

'What do you mean?' Katelyn asked. 'Please explain it to me because I haven't got a fucking clue what you've done and I'm not sure that I want to know.' She put her hand beneath his chin and lifted his face gently, looking into his eyes. 'I love you, Liam,' she said, 'but I need you to answer my question. Are Daryl and I in danger?'

'Yes.' He nodded.

'And is Ray in danger?'

'Yes.'

'You're a stupid bastard!' she said slapping his cheek. The tears flowed heavily now as realisation sank in. Everything had changed for the worse.

'I'm sorry but I'll fix it.'

'Stop the cab,' Katelyn called to the driver. He looked at her in the mirror. 'Stop the cab, please right away!'

'Don't get out.' Liam sighed.

'I'm not getting out,' she said shaking her head. 'You are.'

'What?'

'You've just told me that this was nothing to do with your cousins' murders and you looked me in the eye and lied to me.'

'I'm sorry.'

'Don't be, you've done me a favour. I can't believe that you have put us in danger.' She shrugged as the taxi pulled to a halt. 'Get out.'

'Don't do this, Katelyn,' Liam whined. 'I can fix this, but I need you with me.'

'Get out, Liam,' she said firmly. He tried to touch her, but she recoiled. 'I said get out!'

'I'll call you later.' Liam opened the door and climbed out into the rain, his body sore and bruised.

'Don't bother, Liam. I've had enough.'

He turned and closed the door, Katelyn refusing to make eye contact. They'd been together long enough for him to know that he had just lost the best thing that ever happened to him. She was a strong woman and she wouldn't see anyone in trouble without trying to help them, but her son was her number one priority and he had compromised his safety. The taxi pulled away, the tyres splashing through a deep puddle, leaving Liam alone to ponder his next step. He felt sick to the core, numb and frightened. His options were running out quickly. Liam rolled his head towards the sky and let the rain splash onto his face. His stomach felt tight, his heart heavy. He made his decision and took out the mobile dialling the number for the emergency services for the second time that day. His plan was to turn himself in and pray that the police could rescue his brother. As he did so, a black Nissan pulled alongside him. The side door opened, and he looked into the twin barrels of a sawn-off shotgun and the angry face of Joe Tucker.

'Put the phone down, Liam,' Tucker growled as his men jumped out and dragged him into the Nissan. Katelyn's face came into his mind, sad and accusing. 'Now then, where is my fucking container?'

CHAPTER 20

Uniformed officers sealed off the old Superbowl, more for the benefit of the press photographers that would turn up than to hold back the crowds. It was late, it was cold, and the building couldn't be seen from the road. The car park was buzzing with patrol cars and Forced Entry Team vehicles. Armed officers were milling around, the building searched and declared safe. Braddick leaned on the back of the Evoque and pulled on a forensic suit before heading inside. He searched his memories for any images of how it looked when it was new, a sparkly new facility for the city to be proud of. His memories were old and faded, black and white with no sound, the details warped by age and the alcohol that he had consumed at the time with his friends. There was nothing of any substance in his memory to relate to. This was the same place, but time had changed it. The bowling alley where thousands had fun was long gone, the owners old or dead; what was left was a soulless void surrounded by bricks.

The front of the building was weather beaten, the paint blistered and peeling. The giant letters on the roof were reduced to SUP…the rest long gone but survived by the metal scaffold to which they were once fixed. Braddick briefly wondered where the other letters had gone, blown away one day by high winds; a local pensioner shocked by the appearance of a six feet tall letter 'B' in her hydrangeas. He looked around in the artificial light. Thick heavy tyres had carved a huge semicircle into the degraded asphalt, which would tie in with Cookie's version of a truck arriving. There was no way of knowing how long they'd been there but Braddick was confident that the homeless man had been honest. It would also tie in with the Facebook post. Someone had taken something that they shouldn't have, and the owners wanted it back very badly; badly enough to torture and kill.

He turned and walked up wide curved steps that led to the reception area; the concrete was crumbling and broken, tall weeds protruded through the cracks reaching skyward, thistles, brambles and nettles all competed for space. Litter from the drive-thru was strewn across the entire scene, blown there by the winds for a decade, trapped into corners, nooks and crannies, faded and rotting. He picked his way up the steps and entered the building, feeling the temperature change immediately. Cookie had been right; it was warm and dry although the stench of fire and decay hung heavy in the air. There was no smell of damp, but other familiar odours drifted to him, none of them pleasant.

The interior was illuminated by halogen lights on tripods. It was a scene from an apocalyptic movie. The ceiling had collapsed in places, exposing the balcony and floor above. Braddick could remember that there was a bar upstairs where customers could wait for a lane to become free. To his left, the reception desk was still intact, behind it the pigeonholes that held bowling shoes; a swathe of cobwebs covered them. A lone bowling pin stood on the desk; its red collar faded to pink by the years. Some of the lanes were still intact although the wood was warped and rotten. Metal scavengers had been through the building stealing the copper piping and electrical wiring for scrap, leaving huge dark rents in the walls and ceilings. The floor felt spongy and unsafe and he was careful where he placed his feet. Footprints in the dust had been marked with evidence tags and a CSI was busy photographing them. The foyer opened out in front of him to where the lanes once stood. He headed towards a group of white clad CSI's who seemed to be focusing on an area to his right. Kathy Brooks saw him coming and beckoned him over to an area which had been processed.

'It looks like your source was telling the truth,' she said, pointing to two office chairs that were being dusted and photographed. 'We've found blood splatter, skin, hair, teeth fragments and there are signs of accelerant and charring on the floor. One or two human beings were dismantled right there, and I would say that it matches the way our victims were killed.'

'So, this could be where the Johnsons were killed?'

'Definitely looks that way although I need to match up the DNA.'

'Good. We needed a break on this. No one was talking.'

'Do they ever on a case like this?'

'No, not very often.' He smiled sadly, 'I need to get back to the station, Kathy but I wanted to be sure that this is the place,' Braddick said tiredly. 'I was given the name of who did this and I need to get on with finding them.'

'Anyone that I might know?'

'Probably.' He nodded. If they had been criminals as long as Cookie had said, then the chances were that Kathy had encountered them 'Brothers with the surname Tucker.'

'Joseph and Tommy,' Kathy said with a knowing nod of her head. Braddick raised his eyebrows and smiled. 'I've examined several of their alleged crime scenes over the years, but they have managed to avoid being locked up. Steff Cain has them high on her priority lists.' She looked at the bloodstained chairs. 'This is exactly what I would expect from the Tuckers and we have their DNA on file. Let's hope they have left something behind.'

'I won't hold my breath,' Braddick said turning to leave. 'But if they have, I know you'll find it.'

'I'll be on the phone as soon as I have anything solid.'

'Thanks, Kathy.' Braddick turned away, trying to escape the stench. It wasn't the rot and decay that turned his stomach it was the combination of other odours. Petrol, blood, sweat, tears, burning flesh and death.

CHAPTER 21

In the early hours, Eddie Farrell senior joined the queue at passport control. It zigzagged across the Manchester arrivals hall, tired travellers queuing thirty lines deep, an atmosphere of frustration and simmering anger in the air. Overtired kids whinged and whined while their parents longed for the days when they could tap them on the back of the legs without someone calling *Childline*. He had tried to sleep on the flight but couldn't. Anthony was on his mind, his death burned like a hot metal spike through his guts. Nothing could take his thoughts from the fact that he was going to have to bury his son. His wife, their mother, had lost her battle with cancer three years earlier and burying her had been the hardest thing that he had ever done. He had never known the pain of loss until then and he thought that it would kill him. In the dead of night when his sons slept, he would cry until he thought that he would choke. He consoled himself with the knowledge that he would never have to suffer such grief again. Not once had it occurred to him that he would have to bury one of his sons. They were in a dangerous business, but it had never crossed his mind that they could be killed. Anthony was like his right arm, Eddie Junior his left, neither of them less able than the other or less loved by him. They were the reason that he carried on. Making sure that they were set up for life was the driving force behind him. He wanted to retire soon and live in Thailand full-time and leave his sons to run their businesses but that had been snatched away from him by a worthless shite from a council estate. Revenge was spreading through his body cell by cell, consuming him so that he could think about nothing else. Nothing else mattered. He wanted to be at home, needed to be there so that he could organise the coordinated destruction of Bryn Evans and everyone related to him. Anyone who tried to stand in his way would be annihilated and that included the Karpovs. What had happened to Yuri and Mikel was necessary. No one would tell him how to grieve for his son. They'd insulted him and belittled his grief. They had the affront to tell him that his son's murder was not as important as a container of drugs. It may have crossed their minds that they'd been a touch insensitive as the first shark bit and ripped a chunk from them. They would have had considerably more time to think about it than they would have wanted at that point. As they were being torn apart, they would have been begging for death to come and take them and they would have regretted trying to bully him in an hour of need. He was aggrieved and he would have vengeance. It was his sole focus. His anger was immeasurable, no words could describe it, nothing but the blood of his son's murderer would extinguish it.

As he cleared customs, his suitcase left in Thailand to speed up his journey, Eddie Junior was there to meet him. They embraced for a long time, onlookers glancing and wondering what had happened that could make two men sob openly. It was a release of all their pain and frustration which had been exasperated by the distance between them. As they settled down, Eddie patted Junior on the back of the head.

'Come on, son,' he said hoarsely, his voice thick with mucus. 'We've got a lot of work to do.'

'Where do you want to go first, Dad?'

'I want to go and see that fat fuck Paulie.' Eddie shook his head and rubbed the bristles on his chin. 'He was there, and he should have had his back. He knows what happened to Anthony and I need to know the truth.'

'He's in hospital, he collapsed in the cells.'

'Good, then we shouldn't have a problem getting to him. In my mind, all of this is his fault.'

* * * *

As Simon and his family descended the staircase, one armed officer was ahead of them, one behind, both had their weapons drawn. The Evans family hadn't said a word to each other since seeing the bloody mural; there were no words that would suffice. Simon was becoming increasingly concerned about his parents. They looked shell shocked by what they'd seen. The implications were seeping through their very being, their youngest son alone in a hospital, them running away from it all, helpless to protect him. Their despair was etched into their faces, every step becoming harder and each breath more difficult to take. When they reached the bottom, the officers hurried them through a short corridor to a fire escape.

'Stay here.' One of them pushed open the door and stepped out, crouching and covering all the area in front of him in a wide arc. The doors led into a large yard which was the storage area for the medical waste skips. It was surrounded by a solid black fence with hinged gates opposite them. The group couldn't be seen from the car park. 'Clear, let's move.'

'I can't leave Bryn here,' Barbara said her voice breaking. 'I just can't leave him.'

'We don't have a choice, Mum,' Simon said pushing her gently to keep her moving. 'Bryn is safer where he is for now. It's you and Dad that we need to protect, and we can't do that here.' Barbara looked at her husband and he nodded that their son was right, although he didn't speak. He looked drained, his eyes wide and frightened. 'Once we get you to safety, we'll contact Jacob and make sure that Bryn is okay.'

'I'll never forgive myself if anything happens to him,' she mumbled. 'He's only a child.'

'Keep it down,' one of the officers turned on them. They were tense, fearing an ambush. 'Where is your car?'

'About two hundred yards straight ahead near the university exit,' Simon pointed.

'Okay, get your breath back,' he said to the panting parents.

'Can we smoke?' Robert said already placing a cigarette between his lips. He passed one to Barbara before the officer could answer. 'I'm gasping.'

'Yes, smoke if it helps. Give me the keys, Simon and I'll go get the car and bring it back here.' He looked to his colleague who nodded in agreement. 'It's better than you all being out in the open.'

Robert looked at Simon, his mouth held open in disbelief. He took a deep drag and blew out the smoke as he spoke. 'Surely it's not that bad,' he frowned. 'They're just trying to frighten us, aren't they?'

Simon and Mark exchanged a glance. 'I really hope so, Dad,' Simon said calmly, 'but we can't take any chances. Things will calm down with time but until then, we need to be careful.' The officer opened one of the gates and checked outside. He holstered his weapon and stepped out, crossing the ground between parked vehicles quickly.

They watched as the policeman neared Simon's vehicle. The lights flashed as he unlocked it with the remote. He reached the front wing and then looked around the car, hesitating as he inspected it. The light flashed again, confusing Simon. He had locked it again. Instead of getting into the vehicle he moved quickly away from it calling into his radio as he did so.

'What is he doing?' Barbara asked from behind a plume of smoke.

'He's coming back,' Robert said confused.

'I can see that much,' Barbara moaned. 'Why?'

'Well how do I know?'

'Shush please!' the other officer said in a scolding voice. He waited for his colleague to return, 'what's the matter?'

'The tyres are slashed.'

'All of them?'

'Yes, all four.'

'We need to get you back inside for a few minutes while we wait for plan B.'

'What is plan B?' Simon asked.

'I radioed it in, and the sergeant was talking to your brief upstairs.'

'Jacob Graff?'

'That's him,' the officer nodded as they huddled inside. 'He's given the sergeant the keys to his car. He's bringing it around; said he'd be five minutes. It might be better for you in the long run; they won't be looking for his car.'

'He's a nice fella that's for sure,' Robert said. 'He can't do enough for you, can he? How do you know him?'

'We've done some work together,' Simon said. A black seven series BMW pulled up and the sergeant climbed out. 'Looks like our lift is here,' Simon said opening the back door to let his parents get in. 'Thanks for everything,' he said to the policemen.

'Good luck and stay safe,' the sergeant said patting him on the back. Simon thought that that was easy to say and not so easy to do.

****

Louise Grimes finished buffing the hospital corridor and dragged the heavy machine to the cleaner's cupboard. She punched the access code into the lock and opened the door, wheeling the buffer behind her. It was like Groundhog Day, twelve-hour shift, sleep, eat followed by another twelve-hour shift. The pay was crap, but it was the best job that she could get at the moment. It was supposed to be a temporary fix but three years later she was still polishing the same three corridors every shift, five days a week. The only saving grace was that she didn't have to clean up puke and shit from the toilets in the accident and emergency department. That was a job saved for the new recruits. She'd done her time down there for the first month until a new starter began, and she moved up a floor.

'Hey,' a voice startled her from behind. She turned quickly to face a big man in a long dark overcoat. His hair was slicked back with gel and he smelled of expensive aftershave. He read her name badge. 'Louise isn't it?'

'Yes,' she replied nervously.

'I'm a detective.' He smiled warmly. 'You have probably seen a lot of us around today.'

'Yes, they're everywhere,' she said relaxing a little.

'I couldn't help but notice that you were cleaning the corridor when these two men walked by,' he showed her a picture on his phone. It was Simon Evans and Jacob Graff on their way to see Bryn. 'Do you remember them?'

Louise looked at the picture and smiled. 'Yes, I remember them. He was nice, he smiled and said hello. Most people walk by like I'm invisible.'

'I can imagine, the world is full of rude people.' He smiled again. 'Did you happen to overhear what they were talking about?' Louise frowned. 'It is part of our investigation and you could really help me out here.'

'I'm not sure,' she hesitated.

He held up a fifty-pound note with a gloved hand. 'I would be very grateful.'

She took the money and pushed it into her pocket. 'I heard them talking about a house on Anglesey.'

'You have a brilliant memory because that fits in with what I thought.'

'Does it?' Louise seemed pleased with herself.

'Yes. Can you remember any details?'

'One of them said it was for sale in a place beginning with T—' she paused and put her finger to her lips '—something bay I think.'

'Something bay and it begins with T and it is on Anglesey?'

'Yes.' She nodded. 'And it is for sale.'

'Brilliant.' He smiled. 'You should think about joining the police with a memory like that. Well done.' He turned and walked down the corridor punching numbers into his phone. Louise thought about asking him how she could apply but he was gone before she could get the words out.

CHAPTER 22

The black Nissan Elgrand drove slowly through the night, never stopping, never really aiming to arrive anywhere. Liam Johnson was trussed up, hands behind his back, gagged and blindfolded. He wanted to talk. He wanted to tell Tucker everything because he didn't want to be hurt, and he didn't want to die. He hadn't struggled, he hadn't cursed; he had just remained compliant, but they'd restrained him nonetheless. Tucker had blindfolded and gagged him to disorientate him, to strike terror into his being. Driving him around in silence gave the terror time to fester and spread into his bones. It worked every time. His captives had usually pissed themselves by the time Tucker was ready to ask questions.

'Take the blindfold off,' Tucker growled. Rough hands grabbed at him catching his hair painfully as they pulled it off. Liam found himself sat between two gorillas on a bench seat facing Tucker. A fourth man, who had his back to him, was driving the Nissan. From the layout of the seats, he guessed the vehicle was some kind of people carrier. He also noticed that the windows were covered in reflective plastic making it impossible to see into the back of the vehicle. It was the closest thing to a van without being a van and it accommodated multiple passengers; a great way to transport half a dozen goons into battle without breaking the seat belt laws and attracting attention from the law. 'And the gag,' Tucker ordered. 'If you think about screaming, you'll get hurt.' Liam blinked and nodded. 'Where is my container?'

Liam thought very carefully about his next words as they could be his last. 'What you should be asking me is 'who has my container' because it is more likely to help you get it back without dying.'

The goons looked at each other and grinned. Tucker grinned too and shrugged. He pushed his long hair back from his face. 'Okay, Liam,' he said affably. 'Who has my container?' he tilted his head in question. 'Who might kill me if I go and take it back?'

'Your container is in a Mercedes garage that fronts a chop shop in Warrington,' Liam said his throat dry. 'It's owned by Eddie Farrell.'

'Eddie Farrell?' Tucker sounded surprised.

'Yes. He owns the place.'

'You're sure?'

'I was there a few years back with a stolen Merc. He bought it from me with cash, no questions asked. Eddie runs the legitimate car business, backed by the Karpovs who export all the knock-offs to Eastern Europe.'

'The Karpovs?' Tucker shook his head slowly.

'Yes,' Liam almost smiled at the impact the name had. It took the wind out of Tucker's sails.

'Those scumbag Russians have stolen my shipment?'

'In a nutshell, yes, with Eddie Farrell's help.'

'I heard that he was their puppet, but he's crossed the line stealing from one of his own,' Tucker spat. 'He's turned on his own kind. I'm going to kill him.'

'That's easier said than done,' the driver quipped. Tucker ignored him.

'Was he there when you delivered the container?'

'No, I didn't see Farrell. I drove the truck there and shit myself when I saw Nikolai Karpov. I wasn't expecting to see him there.'

'Nikolai Karpov was there?'

'Yes. He was running the show, no doubt.'

'Farrell is one thing but Karpov is another. Nobody mentioned fucking about with Nikolai Karpov, Joe,' the driver said over his shoulder. 'That's a world that we don't want to step into, bro.'

'Shut up, Tommy,' Tucker snapped at his brother. 'We don't have any choice. We need that container back.'

'Yes but…'

'But nothing, Tommy,' Tucker interrupted angrily. 'This isn't a fucking game.' Tommy looked at him in the mirror, his face reddening. 'We can't go home and tell Mum that the big kids have nicked our football. Everything we have and more again is in that shipment. We lose that and we lose the lot.'

'I know that but…'

'Shut your face, Tommy!' Tucker snapped. 'Do you want to spend the next twenty years hiding from the people we owe money to knowing that we didn't have the bollocks to go and take back what is ours?'

'No.'

'Good. Then we go and take it back and we carve up anyone who thinks that they can fuck with us.' He looked around the faces of his men. 'Anyone not got the stones to go and take back that container needs to say so right now.' No one spoke; no one dared. 'Right, now we have that straight, where is this garage?' Tucker's face seemed to darken in an instant. 'I'll make the Karpovs sorry they messed with us.' Liam felt the goons either side of him tense suddenly at the thought of being on the side opposing the Karpovs. It was a war that no one had won before. They said nothing but their expressions said it all. Mercenaries didn't knowingly take the losing side and Liam knew that all criminals were mercenary. Tucker would be lucky to keep half of his men when they realised who they were going up against.

'On the canal side of an industrial estate called the Riverside. It's the last building on the plot before the canal. You keep going until you can't go any further.'

'And you definitely saw Karpov there?' Tucker frowned.

'Yes,' Liam answered honestly. 'I can take you there.'

'Why would you want to do that?'

'He has my brother, Ray.'

'Karpov has your brother?'

'Yes.'

'That won't end well.'

'It could be worse.'

'How do you work that one out?'

'You could have him.'

'What do you mean by that?' Tucker feigned offence.

'If what happened to my cousins is anything to go by, this won't end well for me either. I think Ray might have the better deal right now.'

Tucker didn't know whether to be insulted or not. He half smiled and nodded to one of his goons. The goon punched Liam in the nose hard. Bright lights exploded in his brain and bolts of pain scythed through his skull, making his eyes water. He tasted the coppery blood before it began to drip from his nostrils. Tucker flicked his hair back again. 'Don't get lippy with me, Liam. I don't like cheeky bastards.'

'Sorry,' Liam said choking back blood. 'I'm nervous and frightened.'

'Fair enough,' Tucker said. 'I can understand that.' He thought about what he had been told, trying to make sense of it. His goons were visibly disturbed by the news of the Karpovs. Liam could see that their arrogance was gone, replaced by concern. The driver kept glancing in the mirror, half listening and half concentrating. 'Why has Karpov got your brother?'

'We delivered the container to the address that we were given…'

'How did you get that?' Tucker interrupted.

'It was texted to a prepaid mobile,' Liam explained. 'We had no idea who we were delivering it to but once we knew then he couldn't let us go…'

'Karpov couldn't let you live in case I found you?'

'Exactly,' Liam nodded. 'They pulled guns on us, but I made a break for it and escaped. Ray was knocked out in the process.'

'How did Karpov find out about the container in the first place?'

'He knew from the beginning.'

'What?'

'They set you up from day one.'

'What do you mean?' Tucker looked annoyed.

'They were tracking it all the way from Amsterdam.'

'That isn't possible.'

'Look, I don't know what is in that container and I don't care but whatever it is, the Karpovs used you to pay for the load and they used you to get it into the country and then they took it from you.'

'Bullshit,' Tucker said beneath his breath.

'They set you up and they set us up to take the container from you. We had no idea who it belonged to.'

'That would mean that they are working with our suppliers in Amsterdam,' Tommy said from the front seat. His face was dark and angry. 'Those bastards set us up and we didn't have a fucking clue that we were being played.'

'I don't believe that,' Tucker said pushing his hair back behind his ears. He frowned and looked at his hands while he thought things over. He looked up into Liam's eyes. 'Tell me how you think this was played out.'

Liam shrugged. 'Someone made a deal with you and told the Karpovs about it. Simple.'

'Simple?' Tommy said banging his fist against the steering wheel. 'It was fucking simple too…'

'Shut up, Tommy!' Tucker turned and slapped his brother hard across the back of the head. 'Why didn't they just take the container themselves?'

'They're clever,' Liam half smiled.

'What do you mean?' Tucker asked quietly; his voice controlled, masking his rising anger.

'They were worried about a double-cross,' Liam shrugged again as if it was easy to understand. Tucker glared in silence. 'They wanted to make sure that the law wasn't tracking the container too. They used us to take it knowing that if they were following it, they would swoop as soon as we took it and we would have been arrested. They watched as it was taken and then switched over to me and Ray. Once it was handed over to us, they knew that they were safe.'

'We have been mugged off,' Tucker nodded, his eyes wide and distant. 'Clever, very clever.'

'It was the perfect plan and you financed it. You took all the risks and paid for it too.' Tucker nodded to the goon and he punched Liam again. His huge fist pulverised the fragile bones in his nose with an audible crack. Liam saw blinding light behind his eyes and his senses blacked out for a second. He rocked back violently in the seat. As his sight cleared, he shook his head. 'I really wasn't taking the piss. It is exactly what Karpov said to us.'

'He actually said that to you?'

'He was going to kill us, make us vanish. What difference would it make to tell us what happened?'

'Why didn't your cousins tell me this?' Tucker asked frustrated. His face was angry; the pulse in head visible.

'They didn't know,' Liam spat blood into his lap. 'None of us knew that container was yours until it was too late. We were set up just as much as you were.'

Tucker nodded as if acknowledging that the Johnsons had been pawns in a much bigger game. 'How long is it since you dropped the container?'

'Nearly six hours ago.'

'You know that your brother is already dead, don't you?'

'Yes,' Liam nodded, his stomach twisting at the thought. He had known that he would never see him again as soon as he climbed onto that roof.

'You know you have really caused me a lot of hassle but I'm actually sorry that you all got roped into this.'

'Thanks,' Liam whispered.

'I really am sorry.' Tucker looked at the goon and winked.

The goon grabbed Liam's forehead forcing it backwards, exposing his throat. Tucker punched him hard in the larynx. Liam began to choke. Tucker punched him again, shattering the larynx and splintering the windpipe, then he held Liam tightly against the seat and looked into his eyes as he struggled for breath; his resistance weakened slowly as he drowned on his own blood. Blood bubbles formed on his lips, grew and then burst to be replaced by another, and then another and then slowly but surely, they stopped.

CHAPTER 23

Simon looked in the rear-view mirror and checked to see if the car was still there. The dark Volvo was close behind them; it had been shadowing them for fifteen minutes. He could see the driver focused on his every turn, watching and waiting for the right time. The atmosphere in the car was tense, the occupants nervous and silent. The tailing car flashed its headlights and the sergeant waved as he put on its blues and twos, bringing all the traffic behind them to a sudden standstill. It was the sergeant's idea to put an unmarked traffic car behind them until they reached the motorway network and then stop everything behind them for a while so that no one could tell which direction they'd taken. Simon knew that it would eliminate the chance of being followed from the hospital. It was a good plan as long as he used the limited time to put as much distance as he could between them and any pursuers.

He put his foot down and Jacob's BMW accelerated at a frightening pace, putting a safe distance between them and trouble. He stayed in the fast lane for twenty minutes until they were approaching the junction of the M56 which would take them onto the A55, the road to North Wales. The motorway networks converged outside Warrington, meaning that there was no way that anyone could know if they'd travelled north or south, east or west.

'We can relax now,' Simon said checking the mirror. 'Are you okay in the back?'

'Fine, son,' Robert answered. 'Nice car isn't it?' Robert said to his wife. She hadn't spoken since they'd left the hospital. Her face was a picture of a mother's concern, wrinkles deeper than usual, mouth turned down at the edges and eyes frightened and watery. Every mile they travelled away from Bryn, her heart broke a little bit more, her anxiousness became more intense. She didn't answer the question because she hadn't heard him. Her mind was still with her youngest son; her thoughts lacerated her brain, torturing her with the worst possible outcomes. Each time she tried to put a positive spin on events, her imagination threw up a bunch of negative alternatives.

She still couldn't get things clear in her mind. Her fourteen-year-old boy, her baby, had killed a man with a brick. If that wasn't bad enough, now people wanted to kill him and the rest of her family. Their simple lives had been turned upside down, shaken and sent spinning. It was as if she'd woken up in a parallel universe. Her family was in peril and separated. It was her personal hell. 'I said, it is a nice car isn't it, Barbara?'

'What are you going on about,' she mumbled, wanting to be left alone with her thoughts. Her husband had been her rock, but her concern was inconsolable. Her pain at leaving Bryn was a very private one. Her youngest child was in danger and she couldn't explain how it made her feel ill. She felt physically sick and she couldn't discuss her feelings with him yet. The anxiousness was twisting her insides into knots. Conversation was out of the question; she didn't think that she could string a sentence together. 'I'm tired, Bob.' She sighed. 'I need to sleep, love.' She closed her eyes and put her head onto his shoulder knowing that she wouldn't sleep soundly but that she could doze and hide behind her eyelids where no one could ask her any stupid questions. Robert put his head back and closed his eyes too; mentally and physically exhausted. Although their minds were racing, sleep took them both within minutes.

'They're asleep,' Simon said to his brother. He nodded to the rear-view mirror. 'It's been a tough day for them. I thought Mum was going to keel over at one point.'

'I thought they both would.' Mark smiled. 'They're not getting any younger, are they?' Simon shook his head. 'Poor Bryn; Broke my heart when he got upset at the hospital.'

'I think he did well for a fourteen-year-old boy. I think I'd have been a jabbering wreck if it was me,' Simon said shaking his head. 'Imagine being attacked by a grown man at that age. He must have been scared, really scared.'

'He's a good kid. I can't believe he's killed someone, accident or not it will be eating him away inside.'

'What else could he have done?'

'Nothing. He tried to run away, which says it all to me. He didn't want the conflict; it was forced on him and he was given no choice. He hit the bloke once, just once was all it took.'

'A blow to the head like that is enough sometimes. The brain is fragile. On another day that blow could have just cut and bruised him but change the angle slightly, even just a fraction and it is a different story, it's not assault anymore, it's murder.' Simon shrugged. 'Just a fraction of an inch either way, Farrell would be alive.'

'So true.'

'Bryn is not bad, he's unlucky.'

'I wonder why Farrell attacked him in the first place?'

'You know what our Bryn is like with his mouth,' Simon smiled, his teeth white in the darkness. They were passing through Llanfairfechan, the beach on their right. In the distance, across the Menai Straits, the lights of Beaumaris flickered on Anglesey. 'It sounds to me like he's had a row with the fat bloke, and he got pissed off and brought his mate along to give him a good hiding. We know how the rest goes.'

'Makes you wonder what would have happened if the Staffie hadn't intervened,' Mark mused. 'If it wasn't for Alice, it could be Bryn in the mortuary. I think Alice is due a treat.'

'She's spoiled rotten; he loves that bloody dog. She'll be worried about him wondering where he is.' Mark paused. 'Listen, thanks for this. I wouldn't have known what to do if you hadn't turned up.'

'He's my brother,' Simon shrugged. 'Anyway, it's Jacob we need to thank the most. We'd still be waiting for a mechanic and four new tyres if it wasn't for him.'

'He reminds me of Gandalf the wizard but in a three-piece suit,' Mark joked. 'He's all grey and mysterious with a magical solution to everything. All he needs is a wooden staff.'

Simon laughed out loud. 'I'll tell him that. He'll be made up; he loves the hobbits!'

'He does remind me of him though.' Mark laughed with him.

'I can see it!' Simon nodded.

'Seriously though, what is your connection? Is he your solicitor?'

Simon shook his head. 'He started out as a criminal lawyer but retrained and became an investment lawyer. He worked abroad, New York, Hong Kong, Tokyo, moving from corporate investments to international funding.' Mark nodded but looked confused. 'He invested a lot of money for some very powerful people.'

'What is he doing hanging around with a snotty nosed accountant like you then?'

'How many times.' Simon shrugged. 'I'm not an accountant.'

'You look after people's money and add things up for a living,' Mark grinned. 'You're an accountant.'

'There's no point in me explaining this to someone who has chosen to be punched in the face as his career.'

'I chose it because I can't add up. Carry on about Gandalf.'

'He's retired now but he still dabbles in finance here and there. He was a big name in his day. Now he helps people out when he can. It's more of a hobby now. When I asked for his help with Bryn, he didn't hesitate.'

'How do you know him then?' Mark frowned. 'Did you work together?'

'Sort of,' Simon nodded. 'I moved some money for one of his clients a few years back,' Simon said, 'The deal went very well, and we've been friends ever since. He's a good man to know in my game. He's given me some good contacts and puts work my way.'

'More adding up?'

'Mostly factoring.'

'Factoring, I knew it. Obviously, that's what I thought, factoring,' Mark said sarcastically. 'I knew he would be into factoring. Factoring is the future.'

'You don't know what it is, do you?'

'No.'

'I've explained it at least once.'

'Yes, you did at Christmas and you bored me, so I've forgotten.'

'I don't know why I bother.'

'Don't sulk. Explain it again?'

'I help businesses with their cash flow especially when they're running out of money,' Simon explained, trying not to insult his brother's intelligence. Mark shrugged and waited for further enlightening. 'Let's say you own a shop and you need a thousand pounds to buy more stock, but you've got no money in the bank.'

'Okay. What am I selling?'

'That doesn't matter. Shut up and listen,' Simon smiled. 'You have no money in the bank, but someone owes you five-thousand pounds, but they haven't paid you yet. I would take your invoices as collateral and lend you the money then when your customers pay up, I would give you back the invoices and keep some of the money as my fee.'

'Sounds simple enough.'

'It is.' Simon nodded. 'Short term loans make the world go around.'

'Why wouldn't I ask the bank? I mean why come to you?'

'Because your credit rating may be crap or your business might be a little bit shady, maybe it is not what's perceived as a legitimate business.'

'That sounds dodgy,' Mark grinned. 'Are you doing dodgy deals, bro?'

'No,' Simon shook his head and smiled. 'But I can sort out money for people that no one else would touch.'

'So, you're like a walking talking Wonga bank?' Mark smiled.

Simon shrugged. 'I suppose so, except the interest rate is much higher.'

'Higher than Wonga?' Mark chuckled. 'If it is, you're a fucking bandit!' Mark watched the waves breaking on the shore; the lights of the dual carriageway glinting yellow from them. He thought about what Simon had said for a few minutes. 'What happens if these dodgy businesses don't pay you back?'

'It's not my money that I use. I just introduce the right people to the right people and take a percentage. If they don't pay on time, then the penalties are severe. They're late sometimes but they all pay eventually, one way or another.'

'Sounds like it's low risk?'

'That depends on how much money is involved. Some of Jacob's clients need a lot of money quickly. When that kind of money is involved, there's always a risk for anyone connected to the deal. The richest people tend to be the most dangerous.' Mark nodded that he understood. Simon's occupation had always been a bit of a mystery to him. 'Jacob was well respected. People trusted him, important people.'

'Like who?'

'He once arranged finance for Kenya.'

'The country?'

'Yes.'

'I bet Wonga have never lent money to Kenya,' Mark said impressed.

'Kenyans yes, Kenya no.'

'So, if I need a few quid, I can come to you and Gandalf.'

'You don't have any customers. You punch people in the head.'

'Fair point,' Mark grinned in the dull light. Simon smiled and turned up the radio. They sat in comfortable silence as they crossed the Britannia Bridge onto the island. The dual carriageway was quiet and twenty minutes later they were pulling onto the winding B roads that would take them to Trearddur Bay. A golf course went by, bungalows, old and new builds; a huge nursing home and then a steep hill down onto the bay itself. The satnav took them by the crescent shaped beach; a white hotel to their right was illuminated by spotlights. The tips of the waves glowed white in the darkness, reflecting the light for a few moments before they vanished. Breakers crashed onto the dark rocks across the bay, climbing up into the air and then disappearing. As they turned a long sweeping bend they saw a huge stone-built house on the left, perched on a rocky outcrop; it looked like it belonged in a ghost story. The sign at the bottom of the driveway said, Craig y Mor.

'That looks like it should be in *Scooby-Doo*,' Mark said. 'Don't tell me that's where we are going, Mum will have a heart attack.'

'I wonder who lives there,' Simon asked, bending to see it.

'Herman Munster.'

'Jacob said it was a cottage not a mansion.' Simon smiled 'His place is another mile down here on the right.'

'Good.' Mark yawned. 'I'm knackered.' The coast road was a series of s-bends that hugged the rocky coves and tiny beaches that were the signature of that part of the island.

'This is it,' Simon said indicating and steering the BMW across the road onto a gravel driveway. Thick hedges interspersed with tall conifers surrounded the property. Untrimmed for years their drooping branches formed a spiky canopy over the pavement. A For Sale sign was fixed to a stone gatepost; the gates wedged open with logs. The headlights illuminated an old garage with a door that didn't look wide enough to fit a modern saloon inside and a sloping roof that was made from asbestos panels; the type so toxic when broken that no council dumps would touch them. The walls and roof were covered in ivy a yard thick at its highest. An old grass roller stood rotting next to it. The sculptured wrought iron handle was rusted, brambles twisted through the pattern. As the headlights illuminated the dwelling itself, Simon whistled. 'Now that's what you think of when you hear the word cottage.'

'It isn't what Uncle John thinks of when he hears the word cottage.'

'Mum says that was all a misunderstanding.'

'That's not what the judge thought. Anyway, I can see what you mean.' The walls were built from drystone, rendered and painted white. The low roof was Welsh slate; a leaded window fitted either side of a studded wooden front door. Window boxes were planted with winter pansies and coloured cabbages. 'At least it's all one floor,' Mark said yawning again. 'I don't fancy pushing Mum and Dad up the stairs to bed.'

'We're old but we're not infirmed yet you know,' Robert Evans said; his voice groggy with sleep. 'And we're not deaf either.' Simon and Mark grinned at each other and opened the doors to climb out. 'We're here, Barbara,' Robert said shaking her shoulder gently. She roused slowly and yawned. 'We're here, love. It looks like a lovely place.'

'Where are we?' She yawned.

'Wales. You've slept most of the way.'

'I was just resting my eyes.'

'Of course, you were.'

'Have they heard from Bryn?' she asked. The back doors opened, and their sons helped them out. 'Have you heard from Bryn?' she repeated to Simon.

'Not yet, Mum,' he said holding her by her elbow. 'Once we're in and settled, I'll call Jacob.'

They walked to the front door, their feet crunching on the gravel. Simon unlocked the door and it creaked open. Mark went inside, put on the lights and then went into the kitchen and found the airing cupboard and switched on the central heating. The ceilings were low with oak beams supporting them, the doorframes were arched, the doors studded. A wood burning stove stood in a wide-open fireplace, and an antique animal trap hung above the oak mantelpiece. A pastel patterned three-piece suite furnished the living room and a narrow corridor ran off the kitchen to the bedrooms and bathroom beyond. Simon went to check the bedrooms while Robert began to explore a Welsh dresser for alcohol. Mark came in from the kitchen with a bundle of quilts and pillows.

'Give them to me,' Barbara said. 'I'll go and sort the beds out.' Mark raised his eyebrows, surprised that she hadn't just plonked down in an armchair and waited for his dad to fill up her glass.

'There are some more blankets if you need them.'

'Grab them, son,' she said heading down the corridor. 'The place has been stood empty for a while. It will be cold until the heating has been on a few hours. These old places are always the same. It's as if the walls suck the heat out of the air as it warms up.'

'There is a bottle of whisky and half a bottle of port here, Barbara,' Robert said happily. 'It will help us to sleep.'

'You can have one, Bob and no more. If anything happens to Bryn, I want to be able to get up and out with no messing about,' she gave him a stern look. Mark came back with an armful of blankets and Simon came back from checking the bedrooms. They grinned at the look of disappointment on their father's face. 'Don't sulk, Robert Evans. It doesn't suit you. Right then, where are we sleeping?'

'You and Dad take the first bedroom on your left. It's the closest to the toilet. Mark and I will take the bedrooms at the back. The beds are made up, but it is cold. Throw those quilts on as well and we'll be fine.'

'Can you phone your friend Jacob and see how Bryn is please?'

'Okay, Mum,' Simon said checking his watch. 'You sort the beds out and I'll call him.' He nodded to Mark and they walked into the kitchen. Simon leaned close, his voice low and concerned. 'Listen, I want you to walk around the house outside, check for any weak spots.' He handed Mark the car keys. 'Close the gates and move the car to this side of the house so that it can't be seen from the road.'

'Okay,' Mark said, enthusiastically. He headed for the back door, which was locked and bolted from the inside. Simon took out his mobile to call Jacob when another thought came to him, 'Mark.'

'What?'

'Pull the 'For Sale' sign down too.'

'Why? Are you thinking of buying the place?' Mark smiled.

'I don't want anything to stand out, that's all.'

'Tell Mum not to hang any of her big knickers on the line. That would be a big giveaway.'

'Just go, will you,' Simon smiled and shook his head. He knew it was all bravado with Mark. Yes, he was a very talented fighter, but he was also a very young man way out of his depth emotionally. He was stunned by what had happened to Bryn. Simon knew that they were very close, and Mark would be struggling internally. They all were to some degree. He dialled Jacob and held his breath as the phone rang, hoping for the best. He was about to give up when it answered.

'Simon,' Jacob said, his voice sounding tired. 'Are you at the cottage?'

'Yes, thanks to you. God knows where we would be if you hadn't helped. We can't thank you enough.'

'You're very welcome, my friend. It's been empty for some time, but it warms up quite quickly, I'm sure you'll be fine there for now.'

'We're fine. Mum and Dad are out of harm's way, that's the main thing. How is Bryn?'

'He was sleeping when I left him,' Jacob sounded disturbed. 'He was putting on a brave face before that. I have a funny feeling that they're going to move him sooner rather than later.'

'What about his cheekbone?'

'I get the distinct impression that there are much more pressing priorities than his fracture.'

'What makes you think that?'

'There've been some very secretive phone calls to the sergeant in charge here. He's not giving much away, but I heard him mention that the Chief Constable was very uncomfortable with the situation here. It would appear that his concern is for the safety of the hospital, the patients and the staff and he wants your brother out of here quickly. It is shift changeover at eight o'clock and I'm inclined to think that they'll move Bryn to Altcourse before that. There are armed officers all over the place; much more than earlier on.'

'Well, if they move him, he'll be safe there,' Simon tried to convince himself. Jacob remained quiet. 'Do you think so?'

'Look, Simon there were some developments after you left.'

'What developments?'

'Through the course of the night, over a dozen funeral wreaths have been delivered to reception, all from different florists, all from different areas of the city and all addressed to Bryn Evans.'

'Shit.' Simon sighed. 'He doesn't know does he?'

'Of course, not but it tells me that the Farrells have the sympathy of a lot of other people in the same business. Keeping Bryn and your family from harm is going to be more difficult than I first anticipated,' Jacob said, the concern in his voice clear. 'I've made some calls to some people who carry influence and their initial reaction was positive, however Eddie Farrell is not known for his sense of fairness or balanced point of view.'

'We need to get Bryn released and get him somewhere safe until Farrell calms down. In the meantime, I'll tell Mum that he's asleep and everything is fine for now. When will you see him again?'

'I'll see him tomorrow, wherever he is. If he's in Altcourse then I will arrange a visit as his brief, if he is still at the Royal then I'll see him there. Either way I will call you. You need to keep your parents there until we have no other choice but to move them.'

'Thanks again, Jacob. Get some sleep.'

'You too, my regards to your family.' The call ended with a beep and Simon kept the phone to his ear for a moment. He could sense his mother behind him.

'Was that Jacob?'

'Yes, Mum.' He turned to face her with a tired smile. 'He said that Bryn is sleeping, he's safe and there's no news on them moving him yet. There are more police officers there now, so he'll be fine.'

'I should think so after what they did to that wall,' she tutted. 'I mean who would paint something like that and in a hospital too,' she shook her head trying to make sense of everything but struggling. 'It was disgusting, he's a boy. They are the ones that should be locked up, not our Bryn.'

'The police will make sure he is safe, Mum.'

'They shouldn't have to,' she said, sadness creeping through her. 'What is wrong with these people? I mean who do they think they are threatening people like that?'

'You should go and get some sleep, Mum. Things might look better in the morning.'

Mark walked into the kitchen from outside. He pulled the door closed and bolted it before locking it with the key. 'All done out there,' he said clapping his hands against the cold. 'We need to turn some of these lights off. This place is lit up like a Christmas tree and it stands out from the road.'

'Surely you don't think anyone would bother following us all the way here?' Robert said with a huff. Barbara looked at her sons, her hands on her cheeks as if the thought had never crossed her mind.

'Nobody followed us, Dad,' Simon said reassuringly. 'And there is no way that they can find us either. Now let's go to bed and get some sleep.' The Evans family looked relieved by his words but tired. They nodded and headed for the bedrooms. As they undressed and climbed between the crisp cotton sheets, they had no idea that the first vehicle belonging to Eddie Farrell had already crossed the Menai Bridge.

CHAPTER 24

Braddick climbed into the Evoque and picked up the phone to call the MIT office. He wanted as much information as they had on the Tuckers and had called a briefing to include DI Cain and the Drug Squad. Bringing in the Tuckers would be difficult and dangerous. They had financial clout and access to quality legal representation and from what he had gleaned in a short space of time, they had influence and muscle across the city. He didn't want to panic them into responding with violence. Actually getting a warrant would be difficult enough. All Braddick had at the moment was the verbal identification of their voices from a heroin addict, who had specifically stated that he wouldn't testify against them. The crime scene wasn't yielding anything to identify them. DNA would prove that the Johnsons were there but not much more; the rest was supposition. He doubted if he would be granted an arrest warrant with what they had at that point. The thought of trying to convince Cookie to testify crossed his mind briefly but he could see how that would work out. As an ex-employee of the Tuckers with a grudge against them, twenty years of opiate abuse and sleeping rough, he wouldn't have much credibility with the CPS, let alone with a jury. He turned on the engine and switched on the lights. A movement to his left caught his eye but when he focused on it there was nothing there. He pushed the Evoque into gear and drove across the deserted car park towards the drive-thru and the main roads beyond.

Cookie watched the black detective go. As far as coppers went, he was a good one. When the headlights had moved off, Cookie slipped out of the shadows and ducked underneath a wooden hoarding into a narrow alleyway. He picked his way over the rubbish and debris, being careful not to trip. It was a route that he had taken dozens of times, but it was still laced with danger, especially at night. He was in a rush, excited about his purchase and keen to inject it. The detective had given him enough money to buy some really good brown. Not the crap they sold for ten quid a wrap in the shit-hole pubs around Rathbone Road but the good stuff, stuff that would make his entire body feel like one huge erogenous zone during a twenty minute orgasm; the stuff that he couldn't stop thinking about, ever. He had enough brown in his pocket to keep him high for days. It was an amazing feeling that he rarely had. Having enough money in his pocket to actually get high, not just take the craving away, was a rarity, one that had the power to make life feel like it was worth living. His monotonous existence, stealing and begging to feed the craving was soul destroying but for the next few days he could hide away and get high without worrying where the next hit was coming from; for a few days he didn't need to stress or worry. He had all he needed in his pocket. Life was good for the first time in a long time. His belly was full, he had class gear to enjoy and a safe dry place to relax while he drifted through the beautiful opium clouds, flying free of the world and its shit.

Cookie reached the end of the alleyway and waded through waist high nettles to a rusting skip. He stepped onto an upturned shopping trolley, climbing onto the skip before pulling an extractor vent cover off and sliding inside the building. The ducting inside had been salvaged for scrap years ago making the vent nothing more than a solid window. He pulled the vent back into place and checked that it wouldn't fall off. Cookie dropped down onto a stack of pallets before climbing down onto the floor. The carpet warehouse was one storey, a vast open space the size of a football pitch. Metal columns supported the vaulted ceiling, which was still intact, keeping the interior dry. Cookie walked quickly across the wide warehouse, heading for the far-right corner where he had built a makeshift tent from some rope and old carpet remnants that he had found in the skips. His bed comprised of an old mattress, that he had dragged from a house clearance over a mile away, covered with a rug and some underlay. The removal men didn't want it and turned a blind eye when he asked if he could take it. He couldn't wait to get to his space and cook up his first shot, the anticipation was mind bending; pure oblivion was within his grasp. The drugs in his pocket were the keys to a magical kingdom, a place that he could only visit for a while, where everything felt incredible but he wasn't allowed to stay for very long. Whenever he returned to reality he always left a piece of him behind; he was never quite the same as he was before. It was as if each visit had a price, a slice of his humanity, a piece of the person that he was died each time. This time he had a weekend pass for an all-inclusive visit. He didn't care what price he would have to pay when he came down, he just wanted to get there and stay as long as he possibly could.

When he reached his camp, he grabbed for his works and lit a candle, watching the flame flicker and dance. The orange glow seemed to fill him with warmth and joy, his brain associating the light with the drugs that would come. Every nerve ending was twitching, burning like white phosphorous in his brain, desperate for the soothing opiate to quell the pain. The brown would feed the craving, satisfy it and then propel him out into heroin heaven and beyond. The monster inside him needed feeding and it was hungry, so hungry. He lined up his works in a methodical way like a surgeon preparing his instruments, metal spoon, cotton wool, foil, syringe, bottle of mineral water and rubber tubing before reaching into his pocket for his heroin. He opened a wrap and mixed it with the water until all the powder had dissolved and then warmed it gently over the candle. Using the cotton wool as a sponge to absorb the brown liquid, he sucked the mixture into the syringe ready to inject. His mouth was watering, his hands shaking slightly; his heartbeat was elevated in anticipation of the hit. The only thing that mattered was flushing the contents of the syringe into a vein.

Cookie took off his hoodie and picked up the rubber tube, tying it tightly around his forearm. The blue veins in his hand stood up. He tapped the syringe and inverted it and pushed an air bubble out. Then he pricked the biggest vein with the needle sucking blood into the mixture to make sure that he was in properly. He paused for a millisecond before pressing the plunger, removing the needle and releasing the rubber tube allowing the drug to course up his arm and into his brain. Cookie felt the warmth, the rush, the overwhelming feeling of ecstasy spreading through every molecule of his being and he leaned backwards, his head resting on the carpets. As the drug took him and he closed his eyes, a voice spoiled the effect, tried to drag him back but he ignored it. He wouldn't listen, not now, not at the exact moment that his nerve endings were experiencing delight like never before. His eyes rolled backwards, and he flew upwards towards the bluest sky ever, the colours mind blowing.

'I see you're still a junkie, Cookie,' the voice said. 'You always were too weak to know what was good for you. I guess you couldn't leave it alone.' Cookie's eyes flickered for a moment; the voice triggering some memories from the far reaches of his mind, but he ignored them, soaring higher still. 'Fancy seeing you after all these years.' A flicker of his lids then his eyes closed tightly once more. 'Tucker sent me back to clean up the bowling alley and to my surprise, I see you getting out of a Range Rover skipping off into the night like a kid with a balloon. Do you know what I thought to myself?' Cookie couldn't hear him; he was away with the fairies now, floating, flying, feeling magical. 'I thought, bless my soul that is Cookie, and he looks happy and he's going somewhere in a hurry. Now when you see a happy junkie in a hurry it is because they have got money in their pocket. So, I think to myself, how has Cookie got money? So, I decided to wait a while and guess what? The place is swarming with police.' The man searched Cookie's pockets and he took out three wraps of heroin. He mixed the contents of all three wraps with water and warmed it over the flame, before sucking it into the syringe. 'I wondered how the police knew about the bowling alley and so I put two and two together and figured that you told them. Now, when I told Tucker that the police had beaten me to it, you can imagine how pissed off he was. You remember how angry he used to get. He said I needed to sort it out.' He wrapped the rubber tube around Cookie's arm and tapped the back of his hand until the veins stood out. 'Now you can go to wherever it is that you useless junkies go to. Enjoy yourself, Cookie, you fucking idiot; nice knowing you.' The needle slid into the vein and he sucked blood into the syringe before plunging the heroin into his arm. He took the rubber tube off allowing the drug to be pumped up his arm into his brain and sent Cookie further into the magic place than he had ever been before. This time, he was never coming back.

CHAPTER 25

Bryn Evans had hardly slept at all; his thoughts were full of the nightmare that his life had become. He wanted to go home, he wanted his family around him; he wanted the smoke-filled living room and the comforting drone of daytime television. He wanted the smell of bacon and fish and chips, the Staffie following him around like his shadow. He wanted his life back as it was, boring and normal. His mind was drifting when the door opened, and the sergeant walked in followed by the doctor. Behind them were three men wearing different uniforms to the policemen. He didn't recognise them, but he guessed that they were something to do with prison. They seemed a little embarrassed by the fact that the sergeant was arguing with the doctor. Bryn hadn't heard what he was saying before he walked into the room but whatever it was, he certainly wasn't happy with the policeman.

'I'm not signing him out under any circumstances,' the doctor stood at the bottom of the bed protectively, folding his arms defiantly. 'He's fourteen for heaven's sake and he may need an operation to weld that cheekbone.'

'He's under arrest. We don't need your permission to move him, doctor,' the sergeant said calmly. 'Don't make this any harder than it needs to be.'

'I'll make it as difficult as I possibly can.'

'Being awkward isn't going to change anything. My senior officers want him out of this hospital. We're moving him for his own safety and for the safety of your staff and your patients.'

'Oh, come on!' the doctor snorted. 'That is a gross exaggeration.'

'I don't think you understand the mentality of the people that we are protecting him from.'

'He is perfectly safe here.'

'They put a window through and breached our security to vandalise a wall. That means that they were in the hospital. Bryn, your staff and your patients are in danger.'

'Vandalise a wall?' Bryn asked confused. 'Has something else happened? I'm in a bit of a bubble here in this room so I don't know what has been happening.'

'It's nothing for you to worry about, Bryn,' the sergeant said. 'We can't watch all the entrances and exits in this building and guarantee the staff's safety, so my superiors want you moved to the vulnerable teenagers' unit at HMP Altcourse. We can be certain that you will be protected there. I'm sure your brief explained all this to you.'

'Yes.' Bryn nodded.

'This isn't right,' the doctor insisted.

'It is the best thing for Bryn right now, doctor,' the sergeant unfastened Bryn's cuff. 'Take my word for it that your patients and staff are in danger as long as Bryn remains here.'

'Is it that bad?' Bryn asked quietly.

The adults blushed and looked at each other. 'Look, Bryn,' the sergeant said looking him in the eyes. 'Anthony Farrell is from a big family and they're all very angry at you. They blame you for everything and are not prepared to see the possibility that you didn't mean to kill him. We can't protect you in here.'

'I understand,' Bryn said calmly.

'This is ridiculous,' the doctor snapped. 'He's a kid.'

'And that's exactly why we're moving him.'

'Don't worry, doctor. I'll be okay.'

'What if he needs that operation doing?' the doctor clutched at straws.

'We'll cross that bridge when we come to it,' the sergeant nodded to the G4s guards, who handled prisoners in transit. He handed Bryn a baseball cap and gestured towards a wheelchair that was being pushed by one of the guards. 'Put this on and sit in the chair and we will cover you with a blanket.' Bryn frowned, unconvinced by the disguise. 'I'm not just concerned about the Farrells, Bryn. It's to keep the press from slowing you down on the way out. We need to move quickly. It is only until we get you to the rear entrance. The ARU will be with you all the way and they'll escort the van to Altcourse.'

'Okay.' Bryn shrugged. His stomach was twisting in knots. The thought of being taken outside and locked in a van and taken to prison scared the living daylights out of him. All the prison documentaries that he had watched came spinning back across his mind; bare-chested gang members with tattooed faces, dead staring eyes, makeshift shivs in their hands. The ever-present fear of being attacked or raped, predators and prey locked in the same buildings. It all flooded back to him and he felt weak with fear. Fear of being incarcerated, fear of being alone away from his family, fear of being assaulted, fear of never getting out, fear of dying and the fear of fear itself. The anticipation of what could happen was crippling. He sat in the chair, put on the hat and covered his legs with the blanket, pulling the peak down to hide the tears in his eyes. He wanted his mum. He didn't want to be a murderer anymore.

Three guards, two armed officers and the sergeant flanked the wheelchair as they sped through the ward towards the lifts. The group were silent as they travelled down to the ground floor. When the doors opened, they shielded him as they stepped into the reception area, a large brightly lit area surrounded by shops and cafes. It was deserted now but for a few homeless people trying to steal an hour in the safe warmth before being tossed out by security. They headed through the quieter corridors towards the rear exit. The pack of paparazzi that had been there all day had grown tired of waiting and drifted home to bed one by one. Bryn stared into the newspaper shop and caught the headline of an early edition of the *Liverpool Echo*.

'Teenage Killer Arrested'

The words bounced around inside his mind. All he had done wrong was to be in the wrong place at the wrong time. He looked into the shop windows, books and newspapers, sweets and chocolates, football shirts and towels, all normal things in the right place, right time; his reflection was all wrong. It wasn't who he really was. A teenage killer surrounded by policemen and prison officers on his way to jail; that wasn't Bryn Evans. The swelling and bruising around his face made him ugly in the glass; the reflection of a monster, the distorted image of a killer. The convoy reached the rear exit and the sergeant moved to speak to the uniformed officer who was guarding it. He waved them through the doors and Bryn caught a glimpse of the prison van. It reminded him of a horse box, white with four blackened windows along the side. The thought of being on the inside trapped and restrained almost sent him into a panic. Leaving the warmth of the hospital was final. The harsh cold reality of where he was going hit him. He had lost his liberty; his family had been forced from him and now he was being dragged from the last tangible piece of normality that he had. His limbs began to tremble.

'You'll be okay, Bryn,' the sergeant said as they reached the van. He could sense Bryn's fear. One of the G4s guards unlocked the rear door and the others stood Bryn up and went through a series of welfare checks. Bryn felt like he was on the outside looking in. They helped him up the rear step and another door was opened. He was put inside a tiny compartment and sat on a ledge-like seat; the Perspex door was closed and locked. Holes allowed the air to flow but it was claustrophobic and distressing. Bryn felt like an animal in a box. 'Keep your head down, Bryn and you'll be okay,' the sergeant called from outside. The door was closed and two of the guards moved into the driver's cab. He felt the vehicle vibrating as the engine started.

'Are you okay in there?' the remaining guard asked. He smiled and checked the door.

'I'm as okay as I can be,' Bryn said quietly, grateful for his concern.

'Good,' the guard leaned closer to the holes in the door. 'I know the seats aren't very comfortable, but we'll be there soon,' the guard reassured him. 'Are you sure you're okay?'

'Yes, thanks, I'll be okay.'

'Good, I'm glad.' The guard leaned closer his voice almost a whisper now. 'Make the most of it because Eddie Farrell has told his lads on the inside that you're coming. They can't wait to meet you. I wouldn't start reading a new book if I was you.' He smiled coldly. 'I don't think you'll live long enough to finish it.' He banged hard on the door making Bryn jump and turned to join the others in the cab. The interior light went out and Bryn was left alone and frightened. He looked out of the tinted window as the city went by, his vision blurred with tears.

CHAPTER 26

Braddick was sitting at his desk when his detectives started to drift in for the day shift. The smell of aftershave, perfume and fresh coffee drifted to him. His body craved sleep, only adrenalin kept him ticking. He was hoping that their minds were fresher and sharper than his felt. Ade Burns was one of the first to arrive. He looked as dishevelled as he had the night before. Braddick noticed that he had changed his suit, but it still looked as if he had picked it up off the floor; he decided that was just his way.

'Brew, Guv?'

'Go on,' Braddick nodded. 'This one is stone cold.'

'Have you been home?'

'Not yet. Things were busy after I sent you lot home,' Braddick stretched his arms above his head. 'Typical, it's always the way, eh?'

'You could have bet on something happening,' Ade nodded. 'Anything new to report?'

'You heard about the bowling alley?'

'Yes, Guv,' Ade said shaking his head. 'I called in to take a look myself on the way in; how solid is the ID on the Tuckers?'

'A junkie called Danny Cook called in asking to meet up, you heard of him?'

'That doesn't ring any bells for me?'

'He goes by the nickname Cookie.'

'Still doesn't mean anything to me. Where is he from?'

'Apparently they were all from the Toxteth area. He hung around with the Tuckers when they were teenagers and when they went into business, he sold smack for them for a few years,' Braddick shrugged. 'They found out that he was using more of their gear than he was selling, and they beat him up, broke his arm and chucked him in the Mersey.'

'Dismissed for gross misconduct,' Ade said putting two mugs of coffee onto Braddick's desk, 'sounds fair enough in their world.' He took a mouthful of coffee. 'And this Cookie guy saw the Tuckers there?'

'No but he heard them.'

'Heard them,' Ade asked his eyebrows raised in question.

'He had been living in the bowling alley when they broke in and brought the Johnsons there. He recognised their voices,' Braddick said frowning. 'He saw the Johnsons tied to chairs and listened to the entire thing. I know it's not enough to prosecute but it is solid enough for me to believe him. I'm counting on Kathy Brooks being able to put them at the scene.'

'Fingers crossed, Guv.'

'Was she still there when you called in?'

'No. She'd left about a half hour before I got there. One of the techs said they'd recovered plenty of trace and that Kathy had sent them in as priority. She was going home for some sleep; said she won't be in until dinnertime.'

'Even on priority, it will still be a few days before we hear anything.'

'Are we going to lift the Tuckers anyway?'

'Yes, but I'm waiting the nod from upstairs.'

'That will be fun. From what I saw at the bowling alley they're nasty bastards, the Tuckers.'

'I'm looking at their PNC records now, trying to get to know them,' Braddick yawned. 'There isn't much that they haven't been dragged in for, but nothing seems to stick to the older brother, Joe. Tommy seems to get the brunt of any charges filed.'

'Taking the rap for his brother, no doubt?'

'It looks that way.'

'Either that or he's stupid.'

'I don't think either of them is stupid,' Braddick said staring at the computer. 'It will take more than we've got now to pin these murders on them. I can't see them cracking either. It is down to us to find something concrete.'

'Something will trip them up eventually, Guv, it always does,' Ade said optimistically. 'Have we got a name for the SIO yet or are you still at the helm?'

'It would seem that there's no rush to nominate a senior investigating officer or they can't find one stupid enough to step in and take over,' Braddick smiled and yawned again. 'Once we're in a position to make an arrest they'll be queuing up to take the credit. I think they're waiting to see just how shitty this one really is before they make a decision.'

'That sounds about right. What happened with Bryn Evans?'

'They moved him to Altcourse during the night.'

'That's odd,' Ade said slurping his brew.

'What do you mean?'

'I thought he was going into the Reynoldstown Unit.'

'He is.'

'One of my mates is a screw there,' Ade said shaking his head. 'Reynoldstown doesn't take anyone between lights out and seven in the morning under any circumstances. Apparently, they only have one screw overnight. The inmates are in lockdown, monitored by CCTV.' He checked his watch. 'Mind you it's gone seven anyway. I bet they locked him up last night and moved him this morning.'

'Do me a favour will you,' Braddick said worried. 'Find out where he is. I said that I would ring his brother this morning and give them an update.'

'I'll do that now,' Ade said standing up. He walked towards his desk and then came back for his forgotten coffee cup. 'Oops, looks like we have a visitor.' He said looking over Braddick's shoulder. Braddick looked around to see the uniformed figure of the Assistant Chief Constable, a short potbellied man with a whisky nose called Alan Parry. 'I'd have put my best suit on if I'd known he was coming.'

'Have you got a best suit?'

'No, they're all crap. The ACC has come to give you a bollocking, I can tell by the look on his face,' Ade joked as he walked away.

Braddick tried to wipe the smile from his face as he stood up to greet his superior. 'Morning, inspector,' the ACC said gesturing towards the empty Detective Superintendent's office. It still had Alec Ramsay's name on it. 'I need a word in the office if you have a minute. Sorry to come down unannounced but it won't take long.'

'It's no problem, sir.' Braddick walked towards the door, opened it and stood aside for the ACC to enter. He followed him inside and closed the door behind him. The uniformed officer walked to the window and looked at the view over the Albert Docks and the river, his hands folded behind his back. In the distance, where the river snaked by the airport, it looked black and wet like treacle but across the road near the docks the water was slate grey. Dawn had broken but it would be a few hours before the street lights went out.

'I've heard that you want to bring the Tuckers in for the Johnson murders, inspector,' he said without turning around. 'Bad men that need locking up, but we must get it right.'

'You sound like you're familiar with them, sir.'

'I haven't always been behind a desk, inspector,' the ACC turned his head a half smile on his face. 'The Tuckers have been bad for generations and I've had plenty of experience of their exploits.' He turned back to the river. 'As for the Johnsons, I was given responsibility for a spate of lorry thefts from the docks when I was a Chief Inspector. The Johnsons came up several times over the years. I'll be glad to see the back of the lot of them.'

'Did you ever lift them, sir?'

'I locked Joseph Tucker up for a GBH about ten years ago. He glassed some young kid in the Revolution Bar on Mathew Street. Right mess he was, over a hundred stitches in his face,' he explained; disappointment in his voice. 'We had him nailed, victim's statement, witness statements from inside the pub, landlord's statement corroborated by the barmaid; he was going down, no doubt about it.'

'What happened?'

'His brother Tommy is what happened.' The ACC snorted. 'Joseph was banged up on remand when Tommy started visiting our witnesses. The next thing was Tommy walked into Coppice Hill nick and claimed responsibility for the attack. Of course, when we re-interviewed our witnesses, they couldn't be certain which brother had done it. Some of them claimed that they'd completely forgotten what they saw. The landlord locked the doors, sent the keys to the brewery with his resignation and buggered off to Southern Ireland. The case fell to bits.'

'They walked?'

'They walked all right. It didn't even get to court.'

'There's not much you could have done, sir.'

'No, there wasn't. That was when I put in for a desk.' He shrugged, looking defeated. 'I'm telling you this because I need you to be belt and braces on this because these bastards will make sure that your witnesses are worth nothing.' Braddick nodded that he understood. 'You're sure that what you have is good enough to pick them up?'

'Yes, sir. We've found the murder scene and I have a positive ID on the Tuckers.' Braddick kept his answer short and guarded. He knew the ID was shaky at best.

'Your witness is familiar with them?'

'He's an ex-employee.'

'Good,' the ACC said turning around. 'Let me know what you need once you've done all the risk assessments. I'll let you have everything at my disposal.'

'We have the go ahead?'

'You do.'

'Thank you, sir.'

'Another thing, I'm not appointing an SIO, Braddick.'

'Sir?'

'Apparently your time with the NCA has impressed somebody,' the ACC said; an acidic tone touched his voice. 'As of now you're officially in charge of the Major Investigation Team on an 'acting up' basis. Once we know what's happening with DS Ramsay, we'll make a permanent decision.' Braddick nodded but didn't speak. He kept his face neutral so the ACC couldn't gauge his reaction. 'It is a lot of responsibility but I'm sure you'll be fine.'

'Sir.'

'I haven't had time to inform DI Cain yet,' the ACC lowered his tone. 'I would appreciate you keeping this under your hat for now.'

'Cain, Sir?'

'Yes, from DS. Do you know her?' he asked confused.

'Yes, sir, we've met.'

'It was indicated to her that she would be the next Chief Inspector,' he shook his head as if disappointed. 'She probably would have been if you had not come back. She'll be disappointed so it would be better if she hears it from me.'

'I see, sir.' Braddick remained impassive. He hadn't come back to the force seeking promotion. He had come back to lick his wounds. His silence had his senior baffled.

'You can use this office as your own for now, of course.'

'I'll wait until there's news about DS Ramsay, sir. I don't think we should take his name off the door just yet.'

'Ah, yes. Maybe not. Is there anything you need to ask me?'

'Not right now, sir.'

'Okay.' The ACC walked to the door and opened it. 'You will let me know what you need on the Tucker operation.'

'Within the hour, sir.' The ACC nodded; a half smile on his face before turning and heading towards the lifts. 'Tosser,' Braddick muttered under his breath as he returned to his desk. No congratulations, no 'nice to have you on board', no handshake, no fuck all. The ACC was the type of officer that Braddick dreaded becoming, the life crushed from him, all thirst for the job long gone.

'Ade,' he called over to his sergeant. 'I need all the risk assessments completed to pick up the Tuckers and let's get eyes on them as soon as possible. I want them under surveillance ASAP.'

'Have we got the go ahead?'

'We have. Let's make sure that we get it right.'

CHAPTER 27

Tucker waved his hand and the driver turned off the lorry tractor unit. The engine shuddered to a halt and the headlights went out. He was hoping beyond hope that the container was still attached to its trailer and that they could just hook it up to their lorry and drive it away. His men were parked up in various places nearby, armed and ready to go at his signal. They couldn't risk being pulled over by the police on a random stop and search and he needed to know if his shipment was intact and if so, how many of Farrell's men were guarding it, before they went rushing into a gunfight. He opened the door and climbed down onto the road; his brother climbed down after him.

'Keep your eyes peeled,' Tucker said to the driver.

'Will do, boss.'

The garage that Johnson had told him about was directly in front of them, completely in darkness. It was the ideal site for a chop shop, fronted by a genuine mechanic business, out of site with no neighbouring properties overlooking it. Vehicles could come and go without arousing suspicion. He could see an inky black stripe at one side of it; the blackness looked wet, dull light shimmering from the surface. The dark silhouettes of barges lined the far bank. Johnson had told the truth; it was the last building on the estate before the canal.

'There are no lights on,' Tommy whispered.

'Thanks for that, Einstein,' Tucker hissed. He bent low and covered the ground between them and the garage, stopping when he reached the wall. It was constructed from corrugated plastic sheets bolted to a framework of metal girders. The workshop frontage had four roller shutters that were high enough to allow an articulated lorry inside. Each shutter was closed and fastened to metal anchors in the concrete. Tucker waved his brother over and they crept around the building until they reached the customer entrance. The door was locked, half glass and half wood. There was a roller fitted above it, but it hadn't been pulled down. He put his hands above his eyes and looked through the glass, his breath causing condensation on the glass. The reception area was fitted out functionally but lay empty, no sign of life. The door into the service area was closed; he couldn't see if his container was in there. Tucker swore and banged on the door. He turned to his brother, 'Get this fucking thing open.'

'Should we call the lads first?'

'For what?' Tucker pointed to the empty reception. 'Do you think they're going to jump out and surprise us?'

'It could be a trap.'

'It could be, and you could be a brain surgeon but you're not,' Tucker said angrily, 'so open the fucking door!' Tommy prised a wrecking iron behind the lock and put his weight behind it. The frame cracked and the door creaked open. Tucker stepped inside and walked across the reception, stopping when he reached the service bay door. He grabbed the handle and twisted it, pulling the door open. Skylights in the roof allowed some watery light in, enough for him to see that the garage was empty apart from a dismantled shipping container in the furthest bay. He reached around the door and switched on the light. His heart sank as he stepped inside and walked across the empty bays to reach the container. The roof and sides had been peeled away, the hollow structure cut open with welding lances leaving the metal blackened and jagged. As he looked around, he could see that every cavity had been emptied. 'The double-crossing bastards have nicked our drugs,' he said to Tommy. Tommy noticed that the drugs had suddenly become 'ours' now they were missing. 'They've cleared this place out and taken the zombie with them. We're fucked.'

'What are we going to do, Joe?'

'We're going to find out where they have taken it and get it back.'

'How?'

'Get the others in here quickly and check the rest of the place over. Pull it to pieces, search every inch of it. There must be something that we can use to find them.'

'Okay,' Tommy frowned. 'But what are we looking for?'

'Look for anything that tells us where they might have relocated to. There's no way that they have closed down the operation completely.' Tucker waited while Tommy called their men.

'How do you know that they haven't just scarpered?'

'They have but it's temporary.'

'What do you mean?'

'When Johnson escaped, Karpov knew that someone would come here sooner or later. Could have been the police, could have been us or it could have been Johnson himself coming back for his brother. They're smart. They will have had a place lined up in case they had to move in a hurry. There was always an exit plan; we just need to find out what it was.'

The sound of engines grew louder. Tyres squealed and doors opened and slammed closed. Hushed voices chattered and a dozen heavies ambled in as they spoke. 'Search the place, lads. Pull it to pieces. We're looking for anything with an address on it, invoices, receipts, lists of suppliers or the like,' Tommy ordered. 'It's a big building so you start in the reception, the rest of you start at the back and work your way forward.'

As his men got to work, Tucker walked around the trailer again, desperate for some answers. He had been double-crossed by the people he had trusted for years. They'd supplied him since the early days, since the very beginning. His contacts in Amsterdam had always been true to their word. He had never had cause to doubt them, not once. Every deal that they'd made from the early days onwards had been honoured and run like clockwork, never a quibble or question. The price was always right, and the quality of the product was superb. They'd made a lot of money together and the only reason he could think of as to why they'd screwed him was that someone had come along with more money or more muscle, or both. Money and fear could turn best friends into a liability. The fact that they'd set him up to fall from a great height gutted him. They knew that this was the biggest shipment that he had handled and if it went wrong, he would be finished. Maybe that was why they turned on him. Maybe his greed was his weakness. Maybe he had stuck his neck out too far and they saw how vulnerable his position was. Or maybe they were just backstabbing arse bandits. The more he analysed things the angrier he became. He should have broken the shipment down into smaller loads, eggs in one basket theory. Words bounced around his head, perhaps, maybe, what if, could have, should have, hindsight is a great tool. It was easy to be smart after the event, but this was a mistake that he wouldn't recover from. Anger boiled inside him, anger and embarrassment together, a powerful combination. It wouldn't take long for word to leak out across the city that he had been ripped off. Not just normal ripped off but set up proper, shafted, made a fool of, bent over and done up the arse, ripped off. He would be the laughingstock of the city and all the credibility that he had earned over the years would be gone, wiped away in the blink of an eye. Eddie Farrell had sat down with the Karpovs and planned how they were going to fuck him over, actually had conversations about how to ruin him. They'd meticulously organised his demise. He imagined them scheming, plotting his destruction in detail and it made him sick with anger. Whatever happened next would be the end for someone, him or them. There was no way that they could coexist anymore. Most outfits in the city simply tolerated the others knowing that war was bad for business but after this, Nicolai Karpov and Eddie Farrell would die at his hands or he would die at theirs. This was the end of the world as he knew it, one way or the other.

Tucker thought about the shipment and what could have been. He would have made ten million at least, probably closer to fifteen, enough to retire and walk away. One big score and then life on a beach drinking ice-cold beer. Instead, he was looking at financial ruin and worse. His financiers would hear about the deal being scuppered and they would come for their money as soon as they did. The shipment was a big one. Now that it had been removed from the container it would be unlikely that the Karpovs would keep it intact. It would be broken up into smaller more manageable amounts. It would be impossible for him to recover the entire shipment. The more he thought about it the more desperate he felt. For the first time that he could remember he felt unfairly treated and helpless to do anything about it. He saw the irony that he was a hardened criminal who felt hard done to because other hardened criminals had targeted him. It was ironic yet he felt bitterly disappointed that they'd stolen his drugs. It was a 'why me' moment and he hated himself for feeling so weak. He was Joseph Tucker. Nobody fucked with Tucker. Nobody. Did the Karpovs and Farrell really think that they could rip him off with no come back? Obviously, they did. How could they disrespect him so much? They either overestimated their power or underestimated his, whichever it was they'd made a huge mistake.

Tucker spat on the floor and looked around. He noticed the mezzanine floor above. He climbed the stairs up to the office, noticing the shattered window as he did so. He envisioned Liam Johnson jumping through it, landing on the container, running for his life. The office door was closed and locked. He twisted the handle and rattled the door, but it didn't give. Turning his back to the door, he donkey kicked it twice. The second time, it splintered and flew open. A feeling of dread touched him as he stood looking into the unlit office. Something bad lurked in the shifting shadows. He could sense it. Then he smelled it too. Tucker reached inside and flicked on the light. Above the desk, the dead body of Ray Johnson was hanging from a metal stanchion, his face purple, the ears and lips blue; his tongue lolling from the corner of his open mouth. An electrical cord had cut deep into his neck, the wire barely visible, hidden by jagged flesh. A wet patch had spread from the groin downwards and the smell of urine, excrement and early decomposition drifted to him. The bulging eyes stared at him accusing him, blaming him, daring him to claim that it wasn't his fault. He watched fascinated for a few seconds before a red flashing light behind the desk caught his eye. It was attached to a box fitted to the wall. Realisation hit him in an instant. 'Tommy!' he shouted as he bolted down the stairs. 'Get the fuck out of here!'

'What is it?' Tommy came running from the rear bay.

'We've triggered a silent alarm or something,' Tucker bolted down the stairs, clearing the last three in one leap. He slipped on the stone floor and fell heavily onto his shoulder. Picking himself up, he sprinted across the service bays and stopped panting at the reception door. 'Get everyone out. The cops will be on the way!' Tommy ran by, followed by three of their men. He grabbed at the reception door and pulled the handle. It wouldn't move. He couldn't fathom what had happened. They'd forced the door to gain entry, but it wouldn't move. He tried again but it wouldn't budge then it occurred to him what had happened.

'Someone has pulled the roller shutter down!' Tommy lit a cigarette and inhaled deeply. 'We've been locked in from the outside.'

'Someone must have been watching us break in.'

'Yes, watching us and then locking us in so the cops find us here,' Tommy moaned. He kicked the desk. 'They are taking the piss out of us.'

'What?' Tucker said running to the door. He put his head against the glass and looked out. The metal shutter had been pulled down and fastened from the outside. He shook the door in frustration. They'd had him over again. Tucker was fuming. 'Open the door you bastards!' he kicked at the wood and bruised his foot. 'There must be another way out if here, find it!'

Tommy told the men what had happened, and they ran back into the service bays to look for another exit. Tommy turned to speak when Tucker got the first whiff of gas. He looked at Tommy's cigarette glowing as the air around them ignited and they were engulfed in a cloud of flames.

CHAPTER 28

When he reached HMP Altcourse, Bryn Evans was tired and sore. The meds were wearing off, the pain becoming unbearable. His face was bruised and puffy, his vision impaired by the swelling, leaving him feeling fragile and vulnerable. Just walking around was agony. The slightest bump or knock sent shockwaves of pain through his broken face. The G4s guard who threatened him stayed in the van while he was unloaded, watching, glaring. Bryn wondered if he was that scared he might make a complaint about him, but he didn't want to make enemies as soon as he arrived. There was no way Bryn could prove what he had said. He knew that the G4s guards were involved in the transportation of prisoners and their involvement ended at the gate. It all seemed surreal and he began to question whether he had said anything at all. His brain was such a muddle that it all blurred into one long nightmare.

He was surprised to find that he was processed very quickly and bundled into a cell. When he asked where he was, they told him that he was in something that the guards called the First Night Unit. The guards were rude and abrupt, but Bryn was in too much pain to protest. When he asked about the Reynoldstown Unit for vulnerable inmates, he was told that his induction would take three to five days and that 'they' would decide whether he was a vulnerable prisoner or not. When he tried to explain his situation for the third time and that his brief had assured him that he would be placed into the protective unit, he was slapped across the back of the head which sent shockwaves of pain through his face and skull. It was enough to convince him to remain silent. All the promises that had been made at the hospital carried no weight in prison. The prison had its own rules and regulations and when it came down to processing new inmates it respected no authority from beyond its walls. Bitterly disappointed but not overly surprised, Bryn resigned himself to the fact that he was caught up in the tide of judicial process and there was no way to swim against it. It was too powerful and relentless to resist. He would just have to bite his lip and see where it took him. No one could help him on the inside. He was given a grey tracksuit, a blanket and a cell. His cell was dark but warm and surprisingly comfortable and he slept for most of the night, although his sleep was haunted by the weirdest dreams.

The next morning, he was woken up at seven by a bang on the door and the sound of keys rattling in the lock. A guard opened it and poked his head around the door.

'Bryn Evans, I presume?' he asked chirpily.

'Yes,' Bryn said in a whisper, scared and in pain. He pulled the blanket up to his chin.

'The assessment team need to interview you before you go for breakfast, but they're tied up at the moment. Someone will be here to see you shortly, okay.'

'Okay.'

'My word.' he frowned. 'Your face is a right mess. Are you in pain, son?'

'Yes.'

'I can't give you any drugs; not even a paracetamol but I'll let the unit doctor know that you're in pain. He'll need to assess you before anything else can be arranged. He can prescribe you some pain meds.'

'Okay, thanks.'

'I might not be able to give you any drugs but I can send you a cup of tea if you want one while you wait?' he said smiling, concern in his eyes.

'Yes please.'

'Right you are,' the guard smiled again. 'I'll ask someone to bring you a brew. I'll see you around no doubt.'

'No doubt,' Bryn agreed. He didn't see how they couldn't. Guards or prisoners, he presumed that they spent their lives confined behind the same fence. 'Thanks.'

He tried to sit up but the pain in his head intensified so much that he lowered it back down quickly. The room spun for a second, so he closed his eyes and waited for the dizziness to pass. As his balance returned, he sat up and leaned forward, using his hands to keep him upright. He turned towards the door as he heard it opening again. Another guard looked in. He shook his head and whistled.

'You look like you've been in the wars,' he said. 'The assessment team are on their way. Sit tight for now.'

'Thanks,' Bryn said feeling like an exhibit in a freak show. The guard turned and almost bumped into an inmate who was standing behind him.

'What happened to him, sir?' the youngster asked, gawping at Bryn.

'He asked a stupid question,' the guard said with a smile. 'Go and get your breakfast and mind your own business.' The inmate took one last look at Bryn and then moved on. Bryn could hear multiple sets of footsteps passing the door. Blurred faces went by, black, white, yellow, and brown. Some looked older than their years, some looked much younger. 'Come on, move along,' the guard waved the youngsters on. 'Someone will be along to see you soon,' the guard said pulling the door towards him. A young inmate turned into the doorway, almost crashing into him.

'Sorry, sir,' he apologised to the guard. 'I was asked to bring a cup of tea for someone.'

'Carry on,' the guard said walking off down the corridor.

'Are you waiting for a cup of tea?' the teenage boy asked. He had red hair and freckles and stood in the doorway with a plastic cup in his hand. Bryn didn't answer, he just nodded weakly. 'Only, Mr Peters asked me to bring you one, you see. He must think that I look like a tea boy, eh?'

'He must do,' Bryn said weakly.

'I'm Gaz but everyone calls me Ginge.'

'I'm Bryn.'

'Hi, Bryn,' the kid nodded and smiled, 'here's your tea.'

'Thanks.' Bryn stood up on unsteady legs. He walked towards the boy, guessing that he was about his own age. Behind him he could see others passing the door, glancing in curiously, laughing at his injuries. Their voices echoed from the walls; the acoustics like an indoor swimming pool.

'Blimey, someone made a mess of you, didn't they?'

'Yes.'

'What does the other bloke look like,' he joked. Bryn didn't answer. 'Looking at your face I bet he's proper fucked up his hands eh?'

'Probably,' Bryn muttered.

'Does it hurt?'

'Yes.'

'Did it happen in here?' the kid asked gesturing to the door with his thumb, 'Because there are loads of fights in here. It goes off in here every day.'

'No, it didn't happen here.' Bryn didn't want to explain what had happened. He didn't see how he could without saying that he had killed his attacker with a brick.

'Not a big one for gossiping, are you?' H smiled. 'Never mind. Do you take sugar?' the boy frowned, taking the hint that Bryn wasn't in the mood to explain. 'Only he didn't say either way, so I went for one spoonful. Most people have one, don't they?'

'I don't usually take sugar, but it doesn't matter I'll have it as it is, thank you.' Bryn tried to smile but his face was too swollen. His left eye was virtually closed, the right a slit between swollen purple lids. 'My mouth is so dry.'

'Sorry about the sugar.' The kid held the cup out for him. Bryn reached for it. His fingers brushed the plastic when the kid pulled it back and threw the scalding hot liquid in his face. Bryn staggered backwards, blinded and shocked by the pain. He held his arms out trying to fend off any further attack, but he couldn't see anything. 'You're fucking dead,' the kid hissed as he punched Bryn on the nose. Bryn was knocked down onto his backside with a thump; his head struck the bed frame hard, blinding white pain flashed through his brain. The blow to the back of his skull stunned him. He tried to stand, blood pouring from his nose and he felt vomit rising in his gullet. Another teenager stopped in the doorway his mouth open in surprise.

'Hey, leave him alone.'

Ginge turned towards him. 'What the fuck has it got to do with you?' The attack stopped for a moment as he kicked the door closed. As it slammed shut, the metallic clunk sounded final, echoing from the thick walls. The kid pulled his foot back and aimed a kick at Bryn's upturned face.

CHAPTER 29

Tucker felt his long hair sizzling as the flames engulfed them. He could hear it crackling as it withered and burned. He covered his face with his arms trying to protect his exposed flesh from the fire as the flames swirled around him, blinding him, stealing his oxygen. Doubled over, he staggered blindly in a circle, desperate to escape the inferno but with no chance of doing so. There was simply nowhere to go. He could hear men screaming, calling for help, calling for their mothers, calling for the pain to stop. Tommy's voice was among them, close enough to recognise but too far to find him. His knees buckled and the air in his lungs burned to be released. He knew that if he exhaled, he would have to inhale burning gas, frazzling the delicate tissue in his lungs. He couldn't escape the flames and he knew that death was seconds away, a death that he had inflicted on others, the slow painful agony of burning alive. His skin had started to blister and burn when a deafening crash rocked the building.

CHAPTER 30

Bryn felt the kick land. It was like a sledgehammer hitting the side of his jaw. His top and bottom teeth impacted so violently that the molars and premolars cracked filling his mouth with enamel and blood. The exposed nerve endings felt like electricity was passing through the roots into his jawbone. He cried out and spat blood and teeth at his attacker, covering his head with his forearms. Another kick thumped into his arms, knocking them painfully against his bruised face. He tried to turn away from the attack, but he was wedged between the bed and the wall. Ginge used the wall to support him as he threw kick after kick. Bryn deflected some with his arms but some hit home. His strength was sapped by the pain. He had to stand up or he knew that he would die. His instincts and training kicked in as he struggled up, chin down behind the shoulder so that he couldn't be knocked unconscious, hands high protecting his head and face. He twisted his head at an angle so that he could see the kid coming through the slit in his eye. A wild punch was deflected from his forearm. Another skimmed the top of his head. Bryn ducked beneath a third shot, bent his knees and turned his hip; as he came back up, he blindly threw a left hook, catching the kid clean on the chin. The kid's mouth was open, magnifying the impact of the blow. His eyes rolled back into his head as his knees buckled; his brain switched off and he crumpled to floor. Bryn stepped back, his hands still raised when the cell door was flung open and three guards rushed in. They stopped dead in their tracks as they surveyed the scene. The skinny ginger kid was unconscious on the cell floor and their new inmate, a murderer, was standing over him poised to strike again.

CHAPTER 31

He parked up in the centre of Trearddur Bay village which consisted of a Spar shop and a Chinese restaurant called the Imperial Palace on one side of the road and a minimarket called Trearddur Stores, which had a small cafe attached to it on the opposite side. They were the only shops for miles and locals and tourists alike used them religiously. Unless a tourist was exceptionally organised and brought everything that they would need, they would have no choice but to visit them at some stage of their visit.

He was tasked with finding the Evans family. All he knew was that they were in the bay in a house which was for sale. He had toured around all night looking for properties that might fit the bill, but it was a pointless exercise. The recession had hit the bay as hard as anywhere and there were dozens of properties for sale at any one time.

If he was going to find where the Evans family were holed up, then all he needed to do was sit near the shops and wait. The search of the Evans house in Liverpool had shown that the recycling bin was crammed full of extra strength lager tins and vodka bottles. Someone had a drink problem and sooner or later they would come and buy it from the only place around. When they did, he would follow them back to where they were staying; all the little rats in one trap. When Eddie Farrell found out where they were staying, he would be very grateful to whoever found them; very grateful indeed. He flicked through Bryn Evans's Facebook pictures and waited.

CHAPTER 32

Tucker felt a bone shuddering impact rock the building and the vibrations ran through his bones. The deafening sound of carbon fibre splintering and glass shattering reverberated through the building. As the noise subsided the sound of a diesel engine roaring filled his head. Fresh air rushed into the garage and the flames seemed to dissipate upwards away from him. He felt strong hands grabbing at him, lifting him from the floor. He sucked clean cool air into his lungs and slapped at his smouldering clothes with his hands.

'Get up, boss!' the truck driver shouted as he dragged him towards the gaping hole in the wall. Debris littered the scene where the tractor unit had reversed through the garage wall. 'I saw someone locking you in, figured that you might need some help. Where is Tommy?'

'Over there somewhere,' Tucker croaked. He coughed and staggered towards the lorry cab. 'Grab him. I can hear sirens coming.'

The lorry driver picked his way through the rubble and stopped when he heard groaning. Beneath a sheet of corrugated plastic, he found the charred figure of Tommy Tucker, his face blackened, hair singed and clothes smouldering. Tommy coughed as he dragged him up. He put his arm over his shoulder and carried him towards the truck.

'Give me a hand. He weighs a ton. Pull him up,' he shouted to Tucker as he pushed him from below. They manhandled him into one of the passenger seats and slammed the door closed. The cool breeze soothed the burns on their skin. The driver ran around the cab and climbed into the driver's seat. He pushed the gear lever into first and pulled the truck forward out of the building, taking a large section of wall with it. Plastic panels clattered on the road outside. He looked behind him and stopped. Tucker's men staggered from the wrecked building through the jagged hole in the wall, some carrying others.

'The cops are on the way. Get away from here and regroup at the factory,' the driver shouted to them. Some looked like they would make it to their vehicles, and some didn't. He put his foot down, drove the truck towards the canal and steered it onto an access road behind the chop shop before heading in the opposite direction to where the police were coming from. He opened the windows to allow the smell of burning hair and clothes out. The Tuckers were slumped in the passenger seats, eyes closed, mouths open, skin reddened and blistered. Their hair frazzled and gone in places, weeping bald patches spotted their scalps. He shook his head as he picked up speed. Joseph Tucker had a very bad temper and he didn't fancy being in the firing line when he recovered. Whoever had set him up needed to make sure that they were a long way away when he came to.

CHAPTER 33

Eddie Farrell woke up with a thick head and a sore throat. On his arrival home he had given Eddie Junior specific instructions about finding the Evans family and then locked himself away in his study where he self-medicated himself with a bottle of bourbon. He checked his watch, glad that he hadn't missed much of the day. There was much to do. The smell of bacon cooking drifted to him and he could hear the sound of the blender whirring, Junior making his breakfast protein shake. He was always on his weights early, pouring protein down his throat and shoving nandrolone up his arse. Size and mass translated to power and respect on the streets and Junior was obsessed with power. Everything seemed quite normal except that his youngest son was dead, his head caved in with a brick. He picked up his phone and checked his messages. One in particular interested him and he pressed the call back button.

'Hello, Eddie,' the voice answered, sounding pleased to hear from him. 'I heard you were back. I'm so sorry to hear about Anthony. Such sad news.'

'Thanks, Harry,' Eddie replied with a yawn. There was going to be a lot of heartfelt words of sympathy to deal with. He couldn't cope with people trying to be nice, but he knew their intentions were good. 'I picked up your message about the Evans family. Have you had any joy?'

'Not yet,' Harry said as he watched the shops from his car. 'I had a drive around for a few hours last night. There are dozens of places for sale. I've decided to try a different tactic.'

'Such as?'

'I'm parked in the village watching the shops. There are only two and I can see both. They'll come along sooner or later and when they do, I'll let you know where they are.'

'Good work, Harry. What about the little bastard who killed my Anthony?'

'I had a word with big Barney. You remember him, did a twenty stretch for shooting Irish Tony.'

'Of course, I do,' Eddie half smiled. 'I haven't seen him for years.'

'Barney works for the probation service now. He passed all his exams inside. He's been straight for years,' Harry chuckled. 'Well, sort of straight if you know what I mean.'

'I know what you mean.'

'Well he has the lists of who is serving time, where they are and what they have done and guess what?'

'I'm not in the mood for guessing games, Harry,' Eddie said biting his thumb nail to the skin. 'Please just get to the point.'

'Sorry, Eddie, I know I go on a bit. The long and short of it is that Ginger Frank's son Gary and three of his mates are in Altcourse. I've had a word with one of the screws that we know, and they'll be on the lookout for our matey boy Evans. He won't be able to hide in there.'

'Nice one, Harry. I owe you one.' Eddie smiled. 'You let me know when you find the rest of them.'

'I will do, Eddie. You take care.'

The line went dead and Eddie felt better. At least things were in motion. Anthony was the intelligent son, well balanced with a good sense of humour. He was the one that would have taken over the businesses with Junior by his side as his enforcer. Losing him was like losing his purpose in life. Junior didn't have the brains to run things. Violence was his answer to everything and that would be his downfall in the end. The threat of violence was a powerful tool, but Junior couldn't tell where to draw the line. He would piss off the wrong person and wind up dead. The truth was that Eddie didn't think that Junior would be able to hold his own in a rumble. He confused size and strength with being able to fight but the two didn't always go hand in hand. Eddie had met men of less than ten stone who would destroy bigger men, no matter how much they could lift. Losing Anthony would change his long-term plans. He would need to rethink things but all that would come in good time. His mobile began to buzz, and he rubbed his eyes and looked at the screen. Victor Karpov. Victor rarely called him directly. He used his representatives to communicate. It made it harder for the law to listen in or to trace and also made it easier to filter the bullshit. Obviously, some things needed to be said directly to the person concerned. He never called directly unless he was pissed off about something. Eddie took a deep breath and answered.

'Victor,' he said with his voice full of sleep, 'nice to hear from you.'

'Eddie, how are you feeling?'

'I'm as well as can be expected.'

'You have my deepest condolences, Eddie. I cannot imagine what you're going through.'

'Thank you.'

'Are you home from your trip?'

'Yes,' Eddie nodded. 'I arrived last night.'

'Good, good. I'm glad that you arrived home safely. This will be a difficult time for you,' Victor sounded sincere, but his tone changed quickly. 'Tell me, Eddie have you heard from Yuri or Mikel?'

'Not since I left Ko Lanta, why?' Eddie asked feigning concern.

'Were they okay when you left them?'

'They were fine. What has happened?'

'Don't worry about it,' Victor said flatly. 'I have been trying to get hold of them but they're not answering their mobiles. They're probably in a black spot.'

'It was a nightmare getting a signal out there, even in the hotel.'

'I know, Mikel complained about it a few times.'

'They might be travelling between islands.'

'What makes you say that?'

'I'm just thinking aloud.'

'Did they mention moving on?'

'They're always talking about moving on, especially Yuri,' Eddie lied. 'That man can't sit still for five minutes before he wants to see what is around the corner. Have you checked with the hotel reception?'

'Of course.'

'Is their luggage still there?'

'Yes, but it has been packed up as if they're ready to leave.'

'Sounds like they're moving islands. They mentioned taking a fast boat and having the cases sent on after. Some of the fast boats don't have the room for luggage.'

'I see,' Victor said. 'Where did they say that they were going?'

'They didn't say specifically,' Eddie lied. 'We were always chatting about the other islands along the Andaman coast. They could have gone to any of them. They'll be in touch when they can get a signal. I wouldn't worry for now.'

'You're right. It is probably nothing to worry about,' Victor agreed reluctantly. 'Have you had chance to speak to Nikolai yet?'

'No.'

'You need to,' Victor said. He paused. 'There have been developments with our last acquisition. We have some problems.'

'Tucker's zombie shipment?'

'Yes. We have a situation, but it isn't for discussion on the telephone,' Victor said paranoid about phone taps. 'I think you should call Nikolai and get up to speed as soon as you can. We're going to need your help.'

'Okay, I'll call him before I leave but I'm going to be busy for the next few days at least.'

'Of course, you're going to be busy,' Victor remained calm. 'I understand that but please call Nikolai and speak to him.'

'I'll try him before I leave. I'm going to arrange things for my son this morning so I'm going to be tied up most of the day.'

'Yes, of course you will. Will the authorities release his body so soon?'

'Not until they're ready but as the case is clear cut it shouldn't be too long before they do. I can arrange for an undertaker to prepare things for when they do release him. I have a large family and I need to speak to them all.'

'Ah, that will be very difficult for you,' Victor sounded genuine. 'My thoughts will be with you. Family is important at times of sorrow.'

'Thank you.'

'I wonder, did Yuri have a chat with you before you left Thailand about your...' he paused, stuck for the word to use, 'response to Anthony's death?'

'Yes, we spoke.' Eddie had ice in his voice.

'I assume from your tone that it was a difficult conversation?'

'It wasn't difficult for me,' Eddie said calmly. 'Yuri asked me not to go after my son's killer and I told him to go and fuck himself.'

'I see,' Victor cleared his throat uncomfortably. There was a painful silence. 'Your reaction is only to be expected under the circumstances. I understand what you have to do.'

'Good,' Eddie said casually. 'Then we don't have a problem then, do we?'

'No, we don't but I do need your response to be low key, Eddie.' he paused but there was no response from Eddie. 'I'm sure that you can see where I'm coming from.' Another pause. 'I understand that you want to see this man dead but I would appreciate it if nobody knows that he is dead.' he waited a few seconds, 'be professional and make him disappear without too much fuss. You know what I'm saying.'

'I know what you're saying.'

'Good. Then I can count on you to do the right thing. I don't want any more attention from the police.'

'I will do my best, Victor.'

'Your best has always been good enough for me, Eddie.'

'That's all that I can promise right now,' Eddie said calmly. He didn't know if he would be able to keep his word. His gut instinct was to leave pieces of Evans and his family all across the city. He wanted their heads on spikes outside the town hall, but he also needed to keep Victor Karpov off his back. It was time to part with the Karpovs completely, but he needed to manage his exit cleverly. 'I will keep our business priorities top of mind.'

'Thank you. That's all I can ask.'

'As long as you realise that I will be pursuing him with everything that I have at hand.'

'Of course, you will. I understand. Speak to Nicolai, will you?'

'I will do. I'll call him when we get off the phone.'

'Thank you, Eddie and good luck later on. I do not envy your position at all. I'm very sorry for your loss.'

'Thanks, Victor.'

'And if you hear from Yuri or Mikel, you will let me know, won't you?'

'Of course.'

'Goodbye, Eddie, please let me know about the funeral arrangements.'

'I will. Thanks again.' Eddie hung up and swung his legs out of bed. He pulled on black tracksuit pants and a grey jumper and walked to the bedroom door. The handle felt cool to touch. He opened the door and padded barefoot down the stairs. The aroma of bacon grew more intense. He walked into the kitchen and headed for the coffee pot. Junior looked up from the frying pan and smiled thinly trying to gauge his father's mood.

'I've made you a bacon butty. Do you want sauce on it?'

'Brown please, son.'

'How are you feeling?'

'Shite to be honest,' Eddie grunted. 'I feel like I've been kicked in the guts. It doesn't feel real does it?'

'No. I can't believe it,' Junior said plating up. 'I've sent Harry after the Evans family. I thought he was the best for the job.'

'He is.' Eddie nodded. 'You've done well, son. I want them in boxes. Every fucking one of them.'

Eddie opened the cupboard to get the sweeteners. As he touched the handle his mobile buzzed again. He swore under his breath and looked at the screen. Nikolai Karpov. Junior put a bacon sandwich in front of him and Eddie took a big bite before he answered the call, angered that Victor had obviously told him to call immediately.

'Nikolai, what a surprise,' Eddie said sarcastically.

'How was your trip home?' Nikolai ignored the barb.

'My trip was fine. I'm back safe and sound and I'm eating my breakfast. What do you want, Nikolai?'

'Things have become a little complicated. We need to talk.'

'Things like what?'

'We've had to pull out of the garage temporarily,' Nikolai sounded irritated. 'We had a visit last night.'

'A visit from who?' Eddie was mildly interested. He took another mouthful of bacon.

'Tucker.'

'Tucker?' Eddie nearly choked. 'Was the shipment gone?'

'Of course.'

'It didn't take him long to work out who had it. How the fucking hell did Tucker find out about the garage?'

'One of the Johnsons escaped. He must have told him.'

'Escaped?'

'Yes.'

'The plan was that the Johnsons ripped off the container and you would make sure that they didn't have the chance to blab, so what happened?' Eddie said, chewing loudly.

'There was a hiccup.'

'Hiccup?' Eddie scoffed. 'You mean you fucked up and let one of them get away.'

'He jumped through the office window and climbed out of the roof,' Nikolai explained. 'No one could have seen that happening not even you, Eddie.'

'Fair play to him,' Eddie said sounding impressed. 'So, he escaped and then told Tucker where his container was.'

'Yes.'

'Has he surfaced yet?'

'No.'

'What happened to the other brother?'

'It's a long story. We'll talk about it later.'

'I'm going to be busy later. You'll have to sort it out yourself for a few days. You have my men at your disposal.'

'I'm not sure that's good enough, Eddie. We have a sensitive situation to deal with.'

'I don't see the urgency.'

'You don't?'

'No,' Eddie slurped his coffee. 'You have Tucker's shipment, don't you?'

'Yes.'

'And everything has been moved from the garage?'

'Yes.'

'Then what is the problem?'

'Tucker is the problem. We had him cornered at the garage, but he escaped.'

'You're not doing very well at keeping hold of people, are you?'

'They drove a truck through the wall,' Nikolai snapped. 'There was nothing we could do about it. We don't know if he is alive or dead but if he is alive, he will be coming for his drugs.'

'Then you had better get the shipment split up and moved on hadn't you.'

'I need your help for that.'

'Like I said, I'm going to be busy.'

'Victor called me earlier.'

'I know.'

'He said that you know where your priorities lie.'

'I do, Nikolai.' Eddie was beginning to lose it but he kept his voice calm.

'In which case we need to meet up and talk. There are some things that we cannot discuss on the telephone. I'm not offering you an alternative here, Eddie. I understand your dilemma, but we have a serious problem to deal with and it won't wait until you've finished your little vendetta. This Evans kid will still be there next week. We may not be.'

Eddie rubbed his hand over his forehead, rubbing his temples with finger and thumb. He squeezed his eyes closed and chewed another bite of sandwich. The urgency in Karpov's voice concerned him. He had never heard him sounding so vulnerable, almost frightened. He wasn't sure if frightened was the right word but there was something in his voice that was unusual. There was obviously more to the issue than either Nikolai or Victor had explained; something that couldn't be discussed on the telephone.

'Okay, Nikolai.' Eddie sighed, wiping his mouth with the back of his hand. 'Give me a time and a place and I'll be there.'

'Thank you, Eddie. Can you meet me at the mill at ten?'

'Okay,' Eddie agreed, finishing his breakfast. 'I'll see you there.'

CHAPTER 34

Bryn felt sick, his mouth full of blood and pieces of tooth. He looked down at the unconscious boy on the floor. His face looked angelic, asleep. Or was it blank, expressionless or dead? He looked down at the blood on his top and the world began to spin. The guards were shouting instructions that were beyond his comprehension. Their voices sounded like echoes in a train tunnel. They grabbed him and pushed him backwards onto the bed, more guards arriving; more shouting their voices deafening and incoherent. Everything was garbled and confusing. His vision began to fade as a subarachnoid haemorrhage began to cause pressure on his brain. The injury caused when his head hit the bed was at the back of his skull, the blood from the external scalp injury not instantly obvious to the guards; the injury to his brain completely invisible. Bryn felt himself falling away from reality, the noise fading, the pain gone and he suddenly realised that he couldn't breathe. His body went into spasm but as he drifted away, he didn't care anymore.

'This kid is fitting!' the guard holding him shouted. He was young and inexperienced and easily panicked.

'The doctor is on the way,' another guard called from outside.

'Tell him to run!'

'Doctor!' The call echoed up the hallway. 'We need you here now!'

'Something isn't right here,' the guard began to panic. 'He's turning blue!'

'Is he breathing?'

'Fuck knows!' the guard hissed putting his cheek next to Bryn's mouth. 'Where is the fucking doctor?'

'He's here,' someone shouted from the corridor.

'Move Ginge out of the way,' someone ordered. Two guards picked up the stunned boy, his faculties returning to him slowly. They dragged him from the cell to make way for the doctor who was followed by a male nurse pushing a trolley. 'Doctor,' the guard called. 'This kid is fitting, and I don't think he's breathing.'

'Let me get to him,' the doctor made his way to the bed. Bryn's body was still in spasm, his lips turning blue. Blood from his nose injury was beginning to crust around his mouth and chin. 'What the hell happened to him, he looks like he's been in a car crash?' the doctor leaned over Bryn and opened his mouth to check his airway.

'The bruising around his eyes is old, doctor. Most of the injuries were there when he arrived.'

'Most?' the doctor retorted. 'Does this blood look fresh to you?' the doctor snapped as he examined Bryn. 'He's not breathing. There's an obstruction in his airway,' the doctor said, urgency in his voice. He pushed his fingers inside Bryn's mouth, blood had pooled in his throat. Turning him onto his side he tried to clear the congealed fluid. Bryn didn't draw breath. 'He's stopped breathing!' the doctor slapped Bryn hard between the shoulder blades.

Nothing.

Another hard slap.

Nothing.

He looked inside his mouth again.

'His teeth are broken. I think he's got teeth and blood stuck in the trachea,' he looked over his shoulder at the guards. 'Is there an ambulance on the way?'

The guards looked at each other, faces blank. 'Jesus Christ has no one called an ambulance!' he snapped. 'Get one called now!'

'Go to the office and call one,' the senior guard ordered. 'And tell the governor what's going on,' he added. A guard ran off immediately.

The doctor was running out of options. Looking into Bryn's mouth again he shook his head and turned to the nurse. 'Give me a hand lifting him up.'

'Are you going to use the Heimlich manoeuvre?' the nurse asked panicked.

The doctor nodded. 'Three attempts and if he doesn't respond then we're going to have to perform a cricothyroidotomy.'

'What is that?' a guard asked. The doctor held Bryn like a rag doll, his head hanging on his chest, arms limp, face blue. He squeezed the boy hard. His body twitched but there was no sound from Bryn's chest, not even a gasp. He squeezed again. No reaction.

'I need to make an incision in his throat so that we can breathe for him,' the doctor said on his last attempt at the Heimlich. Bryn flinched but didn't respond. 'Put him down on the bed, quickly now,' he said to the nurse. 'How long are the paramedics going to be?'

'Fifteen minutes at best.'

'Okay, we have no choice now.' The doctor sighed. 'There's a blockage in his windpipe I need to bypass it, or he'll die. Does everyone understand and agree?' everyone nodded. 'I need a dressing, a scalpel and two drinking straws. Can you get me some from the dining room?' A guard ran off at full speed, his footsteps reverberating from the walls.

'How will we sterilise things?'

'We haven't got time. Infection is the least of his worries.'

'Okay. What do you need?' asked the nurse.

'It's been a while since I've studied this, but it is simple enough,' the doctor said nervously. He ran two fingers over Bryn's throat. 'We need to find the indentation between the Adam's apple and the cricoid cartilage,' he muttered to himself. 'Hand me the scalpel and a gauze swab.' A guard arrived in the cell door panting.

'Here are the straws,' he puffed handing them to the nurse. The nurse wiped them with a sterile pad, the best he could do under the circumstances. The doctor took the scalpel and made a half inch incision, an inch deep. He pinched the incision and inserted his index finger to open the wound.

'Pass me the straws,' the doctor said. He took them and inserted them into the incision. Then pushing them further, he blew into them with two sharp breaths. Bryn's chest rose slightly with each one. 'Two, three, four, five,' he whispered before doing it again. 'Two, three, four, five, he's not responding.'

'Keep going,' the nurse said. 'His face has changed colour.'

The doctor put his lips over the straws and breathed again. 'Two, three, four, five.' A hissing noise came from the incision. Bryn began to breathe for himself.

'You've done it,' The nurse sighed with relief.

'Well done, doctor,' the senior guard said relieved.

'Pass me the tape and a pad.' He stuck the pad around the straws and taped it into place. 'Find out where the paramedics are. He needs a hospital right away.' The doctor opened Bryn's eyes and shone his penlight at them. They didn't respond. He knew it was nothing to do with his breathing. Something was wrong with his brain.

CHAPTER 35

Braddick climbed out of the Evoque and shoved his hands deep into his coat pockets. He shivered and shifted his weight from one foot to the other as he waited for Ade Burns to catch up. The canal side industrial estate was quiet, some derelict units, some empty and up for rent. The wind blew off the canal cutting through his overcoat and the material of his trousers. He nodded a silent hello to the uniformed officers who manned the cordon and then they ducked beneath the crime scene tape and walked towards the garage. Debris was strewn across the road. He was about to speak to Ade when his phone rang. He fumbled for it from his inside pocket with cold fingers, muttering beneath his breath.

'Braddick.'

'DI Braddick?'

'Yes!' he snapped, wondering if there were many other Braddicks in the ranks. 'How can I help?'

'I'm calling from the admissions department at HMP Altcourse,' the woman explained. Her voice was local, almost guttural but she was doing her best to disguise it and failing miserably. 'I have a note on file to inform you of any incidents involving an inmate named Bryn Evans. The warden has asked me to call you immediately.'

'What has happened?' Braddick stiffened. He felt his muscles tense.

'Bryn was involved in an altercation this morning which resulted in a head injury. He's been taken to hospital by ambulance.'

'What condition is he in?'

'I don't have the details.'

'Do you know which hospital?'

'The warden wasn't sure if they would take him to the Royal or the Neuro-care Centre at Walton. Apparently, the paramedics were undecided.'

'Do you know what happened?'

'I don't have the details.'

'Was he attacked?'

'I don't know, Inspector. I don't have...'

'The details, I know,' Braddick quipped. 'Thank you for the call. You've been a great help.'

'You're welcome, Inspector. Bye.' The line went dead and Braddick shook his head and looked up at the sky. Bryn Evans was an unusual case and he felt responsible for him.

'Bad news, Guv?'

'That was Altcourse calling to tell me that Bryn Evans has been shipped to hospital with a head injury.' Braddick sighed. 'He's been in some kind of altercation, but the woman didn't have the details.'

'You've got to feel sorry for the poor kid. How bad is he?'

'I don't know but she said that the paramedics were considering taking him to the Neuro-care Centre at Walton.' The expression on Ade's face reinforced what he was thinking himself.

'That doesn't sound good does it?'

'No.' Braddick thought for a few seconds. 'There's nothing we can do about it from here. Once we're done, I'll call and find out where he is.' He walked on towards the industrial unit.

'There are no signs on the building, no business name anywhere.' Ade noticed.

'There's no CCTV anywhere either,' Braddick said looking up and down the road. 'This place is out of sight and out of mind. They could be up to anything down here and no one would know. Not a camera in sight.'

'That's suspicious itself.' Ade stopped and kicked at a piece of broken plastic. 'Nobody runs a business nowadays without surveillance. They can't get insurance without it.'

'Do you think this place is insured?' Braddick said with raised eyebrows.

'I'll be very disappointed if it isn't,' Ade answered sarcastically. 'Very disappointed indeed.'

'Prepare to be disappointed, Sergeant.' Braddick smiled. He pointed towards the canal. 'I met a DI in Staffordshire last year and he reckoned that most of the heroin and cocaine that's moved south from Manchester goes by barge.'

'It would be safer than putting them in a car I suppose,' Ade said thoughtfully. 'No chance of being pulled over and searched.'

'That was his theory. They had a three-month purge on known traffickers stopping them every time they saw them on the road and didn't find an ounce on them. He went to his DS with his suspicions that a large amount of the drugs were being brought south on the canals.'

'What happened?'

'Nothing.' Braddick shrugged. 'They didn't have the resources to investigate his theory and waterway laws are very different and difficult to enforce. He retired last Easter, but I think he might have had a point.'

'This place couldn't be much closer to a canal.'

'Makes you wonder doesn't it,' Braddick said looking at the colourful barges that lined the far bank.

'It does.'

'Did Google manage to dig up anything on the owners?' Braddick asked, already knowing the answer. Experience told him that this was a chop shop and the owners would be ghosts.

Ade shook his head, 'It's registered to an umbrella company in Bermuda. There are no directors listed here and no tax returns submitted for the address. Whatever was going on here, they made it untraceable.'

'I'm getting pissed off with dead ends,' Braddick moaned. He looked at the hole in the side of the building. The reception was in ruins, smashed and burnt. 'That's too big to be a car or a van. I'm guessing a lorry?'

'Smash and grab?'

'Grabbing what though?' Braddick shook his head. 'I'm going to talk to Kathy before I speculate.'

'That would make sense. I'll shut up, shall I?'

They walked towards one of the service bay doors that had been opened, white clad technicians were walking to and fro; triangular yellow evidence markers were spotted on the ground. A group of local police officers were huddled, talking in whispers, at the far end of the service area. Kathy Brooks waved at them from inside. 'Are we keeping you busy?' Braddick smiled.

'Well,' Kathy said, hands on hips. 'Your overtime bill for this month will be hefty. Come on inside. This will get your grey matter ticking.' Braddick and Ade exchanged glances. Braddick shrugged and rolled his eyes. He wasn't sure that he wanted his grey matter ticking any faster than it was already. The local SIO waved and walked towards them.

'DI Braddick?' he introduced himself. 'I'm DI Barns. I believe this might be related to a case you're on?'

'It sounds like it from what I've been told,' Braddick nodded. 'Thanks for the call. What have we got?'

'We've found two bodies. Raymond Johnson was found hanged in the office upstairs. I believe he's related to a victim you're investigating?'

'Yes, cousin I believe.'

'His hands are tied behind his back so he had help,' the DI explained matter of factly. 'There's a second victim at the rear of the garage, Kathy Brooks reckons he burned to death in a gas explosion. We have no ID on him yet. The gas main was still leaking when the fire brigade arrived but the fire had blown itself out. They think that whatever crashed through the wall caused a blowback and the fire blew out. Kathy can fill you in on the rest. If you need anything else, call me.'

'Cheers,' Braddick said with a quick handshake. He walked back to Kathy and Ade. 'I'm ready when you are. What have we got so far?'

'We'll start over here.' Kathy walked towards a trailer to their left. At first the shape confused Braddick but as they neared it he realised that it had a container on it. The red container had been dismantled, the sides and lid peeled back from the base. 'first, we have this container which has been dismantled to allow access to the hollow sections in the structure,' she said looking into one of the larger cavities. She turned around and gestured to the empty service bays. 'The oil and tyre marks on the concrete are fresh. This place was full of vehicles recently but this is the only thing that was left behind.'

'Why leave something that can be traced?' Braddick asked. 'These things have trackers don't they?'

'No, not GPS trackers,' Kathy said shaking her head. 'This one has a tracker plate. It's like a barcode but they're specific to individual shipping companies. We've run the tracker number on it but without knowing which shipping line it was on, the number is useless. We'll get there by a process of elimination but it may take a few days.'

'It was obviously used to smuggle something and then brought here to be dismantled.'

'It certainly looks that way,' Kathy agreed. 'We've swabbed the void spaces and one of them tested positive for Ketamine.'

'Ketamine?' Braddick asked concerned. 'Is it zombie?'

'I think so,' Kathy nodded. 'Whatever was used to wrap the drugs was punctured at some point, probably during the extraction.'

'I'm guessing that this is what the Johnsons stole,' Braddick said. 'This is what got them killed.'

'And we know the Tuckers killed the Johnsons.'

'So this is Joseph Tucker's container.'

Ade nodded.

'That would certainly fit with our next find,' she said walking up the stairs to the mezzanine floor. When they reached the office, the mortuary team were recovering Ray Johnson's body. 'Ray Johnson was hung above the desk, hands tied behind his back. From the lividity and body temperature, I would say he has been dead less than twenty-four hours.' She pointed to the black body bag. 'He still has his ID on him. Whoever killed him wanted us to know who he was.'

'That's not a mistake that even the most stupid killer would make so we have to take it as intentional,' Braddick shrugged. 'They left us a container that we can trace and a victim that we can identify, all pointing at Tucker.'

Ade looked at Braddick, 'Did Tucker do this or is he being stitched up?' he asked with a frown.

Braddick shrugged. 'It looks that way doesn't it? He killed the other Johnson brothers so it would make sense that he killed Ray and if that's his container, then what other conclusion would we come to?'

'I'm inclined to agree with you that there is a bit of jiggery pokery going on,' Kathy said straight faced.

'That's a technical phrase, right?' Ade smirked.

'She's a scientist,' Braddick shrugged.

Kathy ignored them, a half-smile on her lips. 'It may look like someone stripped the container, murdered Johnson and then evacuated the building taking everything with them, right?'

'Certainly, looks that way at first glance.'

'Look at this,' Kathy said as they walked back down the stairs and headed towards the reception area. The walls and ceiling were scorched. 'We found this male towards the rear of the building.' A large male in his fifties lay on his back, his eyes wide and staring, skin blistered and burned. 'Lividity and body temp put the time of death at between midnight and three.'

'So, it is unlikely he had anything to do with Ray Johnson.'

'Very unlikely.'

'What do we know about the fire,' Braddick asked. He found it difficult to take his eyes from the blistered skin. Karin's face drifted to him. The pangs of guilt squeezed his insides. He wondered how long the pain lasted before his heart gave out. 'Was he alive before he burned?'

'I've checked inside the mouth and nose.' Kathy nodded slowly as she spoke. 'There's significant tissue damage to the back of his throat and his nostrils.'

'He breathed in the flames.' Ade sighed. Nobody answered. Nobody needed to.

'Where did it start?' Braddick asked, changing the subject.

'Over here,' Kathy walked towards the back wall. 'There are burn patterns which originate from the gas main over here. It was capped off with a rubber plug but the plug was attached to the door that links the reception to the service bays. They used a wire filament to make a booby trap. When the reception door was opened, the cap was removed and gas began to fill the building. All it needed was a light to be switched on or a cigarette and boom.'

'So that caused the explosion and subsequent fire?'

'Yes.' She pointed to the dead man. 'He was closest to the main where the gas was concentrated.'

'A makeshift burglar alarm,' Ade commented with a crooked smile. 'They must have had an idea that someone was going to break in. You don't leave a trap like that on a whim. That was designed to kill whoever was coming.'

'And destroy any trace,' Kathy added. 'If that hole hadn't been punched in the wall the entire site would have continued to burn until the gas was cut off.'

'You're right,' Braddick agreed. 'If we find out who he is, we'll have a better idea what happened.'

'We'll take his prints and have them run through the system before he's moved.'

'I'll put money on him being in the system,' Ade mumbled.

'Let's hope so. If he is we'll have a result straight away.' Kathy walked away from the body. 'Here's where it gets interesting,' Kathy said pointing to the reception area. 'We entered the building through the hole in the wall of the reception area and then we walked through to the service bays and opened one of the doors. There are no exits to the rear and all the roller shutters were down and locked.'

'So he was locked in here?' Ade assumed.

'Someone definitely laid a trap,' Braddick nodded. Ade looked confused but kept quiet. 'You're saying that someone broke in through the reception, opened the door to the service area and triggered the gas leak and then someone outside locked them in.'

'Yes.'

'Then someone else drove something big through the wall to let whoever was trapped in here, out,' Braddick added.

'Exactly,' Kathy agreed.

'But we don't know who was trapped and we don't know who did the trapping,' Ade said looking at the dead man. 'I think he's one of Tucker's men.'

'I'll have his prints done now and let you know straight away. We've recovered some DNA trace near the trailer.'

'What?' Braddick asked.

'There's some blood on the container and phlegm and saliva on the floor near the trailer.'

'Someone spat on the floor?' Ade asked.

'Yes.' Kathy frowned at the thought. 'Disgusting habit but some people don't even realise they do it. Once I have the results back I'll be in touch but…'

'But it'll take a few days,' Braddick smiled. She nodded thin lipped. 'Thanks again, Kathy.'

'No problem.'

'Let's go and find the Tuckers shall we,' he said to Ade.

'I don't think they're going to be at home in bed do you?'

'No.' Braddick said shaking his head. He looked around at the scorched walls and ceilings. 'If they were in here they're going to be a little crispy around the edges.' They headed towards the service bay doors. The air became fresher with every step. Braddick couldn't wait to be free of the stench of burnt flesh. His mobile rang. 'Braddick.'

'Hello, Guv it's Google.'

'What's up, Google?' Braddick smiled.

'A body has been found in a warehouse near the bowling alley,' Google said with a sigh. 'It's our witness.'

'Cookie?' Braddick asked with a sinking feeling in his guts.

'Yes, Guv.'

'Is it an overdose?'

'Yes, Guv but I'm suspicious about something in the report.'

'I'm on my way back; we can talk when I get there.'

'Right, Guv. See you when you get back.'

The line went dead as they exited the unit. 'More good news?'

'Danny Cook has been found dead near the bowling alley,' Braddick replied sliding the mobile into his inside pocket. 'Overdose apparently.'

'That's not going to help us lock up the Tuckers.'

'No it isn't.'

'Did they get lucky or did they make their own luck?'

Braddick frowned and nodded, knowing the answer deep inside. 'The thing with luck is it can run out.' Braddick looked around and then looked back inside at the container. 'Let's say that you ran this business,' he turned to Ade. 'Why would you suddenly shut it down and set it ready to burn?'

'Maybe I thought that the police were on to me?'

'Would you rig a gas main if the police were coming?'

'No,' Ade said frowning, 'If I'm not running from the police then the only other reason would be another outfit was on to me.'

'In which case, you might rig the gas main.'

'Makes sense.'

'Okay, then you had to think about a large shipment of drugs that had just landed, a container full in fact,' Braddick looked at the canal. 'How would you move them?'

'That would be the safest option,' Ade nodded to the canal. 'No police cars, no rival gangsters to steal my drugs, ideal really.'

They walked across the road to the canal bank. Four barges were moored against the far bank, hatches battened down for the winter. Three of the moorings were empty. Braddick walked further along the bank to see what was around a curve in the canal. At least a dozen barges were moored, inactive until their owners deemed the weather warm enough to sail once more. A dog walker on the opposite bank nodded hello, a curious look on his face.

'Afternoon,' he shouted.

'Good afternoon,' Braddick called back. 'Do you walk your dog here every day?'

'I do,' he answered suspiciously, half walking and half stopped.

'Tell me, when do the barges start moving?'

'Depends on the weather really,' the dog walker shrugged, his Labrador threatening to drag him over. 'Nothing much happens until March, April.'

'Are there always mooring s available here?' he asked pointing to the empty berths.

'Are you thinking about buying a boat?'

'Something like that,' Braddick lied.

'It is always full here. All year round,' he looked towards the empty spots. 'They moved off the day before yesterday heading towards Chester. There's a boatyard there. Most owners get their repairs done this time of year, unusual to see three empty berths anytime here.'

'Thanks,' Braddick said with a wave. He looked at Ade. 'Coincidence?'

'I would be very surprised if it is.'

'Get onto Google and ask him to contact the Transport Police and ask them if they have had any of their boats on this stretch of the canal in the last few days. I would think that three barges moving towards Chester at the same time would stick in your memory when it is this quiet.'

'Will do, Guv. I'll get them to send us a layout of the waterways south of here as well.'

'We had better share this with DI Cain too,' Braddick added. He looked at the dull brown water and thought about going to see Bryn Evans briefly. If he did, it would have to be later on. He had promised his brother, Mark, that he would keep in touch and decided to give him a call when he got back to his vehicle.

CHAPTER 36

Simon walked into the kitchen and switched on the kettle. He opened three cupboards before he found the mugs and took four, placing them in a line on the granite worktop. Three glass jars held tea, coffee and sugar and then he realised that they had no milk. He swore beneath his breath and switched the kettle off remembering a couple of shops that they'd passed the night before. He decided to drive there and buy some breakfast supplies before his parents woke up. They were stressed enough without adding hunger to their list of woes. He patted his pockets for the car keys and then remembered that he had put them on the table near the front door. As he walked into the living room, his mobile began to ring.

'Hello, Jacob,' he answered, keen to speak to him and get the latest news on Bryn. 'How are things?'

'Things are not good, Simon,' Jacob sounded worried. 'They are not good at all. Are you all okay there?'

'We're fine. Everyone is sleeping. What's happened?' Simon stammered.

'I'm afraid Bryn has been rushed into hospital.'

'Is he okay?'

'No, Simon. He isn't.' Jacob paused to choose his words carefully. 'I'm afraid he was attacked in prison. He has a serious head injury and is being taken to hospital.'

'How did that happen?' Simon asked lost for words. 'He was supposed to be protected.'

'I don't know how it happened. I'm sure we can look into it at a later date but casting blame doesn't improve the situation now. I'm very concerned about him.'

'How bad is he?'

'He is critical, Simon.'

'Jesus, what is wrong with him?'

'All we know is that there was an altercation in his cell, and he was punched and kicked. He stopped breathing but a doctor at the prison performed an operation, a tracheotomy of some sort but although he is breathing, he's unconscious and unresponsive which is very concerning. That's why they think he has damaged his skull. It could be something that they missed at the hospital. Head injuries are so difficult to see.'

'I don't understand how this could happen, for God's sake,' Simon pushed his hair from his face and shook his head as he tried to make sense of the information. 'A tracheotomy, isn't that where they cut into the windpipe to stop you choking?'

'Exactly. The doctor working that day said that he thinks he was choking on his teeth,' Jacob said quietly.

'What?' Simon hissed. 'His teeth? Someone knocked his teeth out?'

'I'm afraid so.'

'How hard do you have to hit someone to knock their teeth out?' Simon asked aloud. 'No wonder they are concerned about his head. If he's unresponsive then that's very worrying. Where are they taking him to?'

'Walton Hospital. It specialises in neurology.' Jacob waited a few seconds while the news sank in. 'I'll be going there as soon as we're finished here. I have a driver coming for me now.'

'A driver?' Simon asked confused.

'You have my car.'

'Sorry, I forgot. I'm struggling to keep up with all this. We'll leave here immediately,' Simon said, shocked.

'I'm not sure that you should.'

'What?'

'Your parents are safe there. You'll be bringing them back to the lion's den.'

'They will want to be with Bryn.'

'Simon, they may not allow anyone but his legal representative in to see him.'

'That's ridiculous. Even though he is so sick?'

'He's on a murder charge, Simon. The law is the law and it applies to everyone no matter what the circumstances.'

'Shit! What the bloody hell are we supposed to do, just sit here and wait?'

'I think you should wait until we have a prognosis and then make a decision.'

'We can't stay here while Bryn is in hospital in a critical condition. Mum and Dad will run there if they have to. God help anyone who tried to stop her seeing him.'

'They will.'

'How could they stop a mother seeing her child?'

'How do you think things happen in Strangeways, Simon?'

'That's different.'

'It is not. He is a prisoner in the care of Her Majesty's Prisons, and they will treat him accordingly. Your mother won't be allowed in without permission. Once we have a prognosis, she may well be able to gain that permission, with my help of course, but until then he is a prisoner.'

'She will cause havoc if they don't let her in.'

'They will arrest her and lock her up, Simon.'

'That I would like to see.' Simon sighed. 'They would have to shoot her,'

'Under the circumstances maybe such a suggestion should be kept to one's self,' Jacob said thoughtfully. 'I do not see what good it would do sitting in a waiting room where you would be both useless and in danger. The result will be what it will be. Only Bryn and the doctors can influence proceedings now.'

'What do you think I should do?'

'Perhaps you should wait a while before you tell them what has happened?'

'I can't do that, Jacob!'

'I'm thinking about their safety.'

'I know but if he is that bad anything could happen.'

'And if they do not know how bad he is then they cannot worry about it. Ignorance is bliss in this situation.'

'Yes, but I'm not ignorant. I know the facts.'

'You know the bare facts and that's all you know.'

'Until the doctors examine him, none of us know what will happen.'

'I know that but if anything happens to him and I hadn't told them,' Simon felt a lump in his throat, 'I couldn't live with myself.'

'Okay, I understand. But my advice is to at least wait until the doctors at the hospital have assessed him.'

'We're two hours' drive away here; we could be too late.'

'It's your decision ultimately, but I don't see them letting you see him. I would be surprised.'

'What if he dies, Mum and Dad would never get over it and they would never forgive me if I hadn't told them.'

'He will probably already be at the hospital. Give me twenty minutes to get there and I'll call you. Then you can make a decision.'

'I can't not tell them, Jacob. Not even for five minutes'

'I understand.'

'We'll see you at the hospital.'

'Indeed. I fear that you will. Be careful.'

'Keep me posted.'

'Of course,' Jacob paused. 'Simon, about the calls that I said I would make to some of my more influential clients.'

'Yes.'

'I was assured that pressure would be applied to Eddie Farrell indirectly. My contacts seemed sure that they could persuade him to back off.'

'Thank you,' Simon said unconvinced. 'I'm not sure that Farrell is the type to be persuaded, are you?'

'Given some time, yes; money makes the world go around. It is the immediate future that concerns me the most. Be careful and I'll see you at the hospital.'

'Bye.'

Simon stared at the screen for long seconds after the call had ended. He fought a running battle in his mind over what to do. Should he tell them the full extent of Bryn's injuries or not? Did he have the right to lie to them in order to protect them from the truth? Would they thank him for it? He didn't think so but he didn't want to walk his parents into danger either. Jacob was right. They wouldn't let them sit around his bed as if nothing had happened. He was on remand for murder. He had to apply some clarity to things no matter how difficult it was. The Farrells had managed to get to Bryn despite all the assurances. His parents would be sitting ducks if he took them back to the city. They all would be.

'Are you all right?' Mark's voice made him jump. He looked sleepy and rubbed his eyes. He had a black vest and blue boxer shorts on. 'I thought I heard voices.'

'You did. I was on the phone,' Simon said walking past him. He closed the door that led to the bedrooms and spoke quietly. 'Let's go into the kitchen. We need to talk.' They stepped into the kitchen and Simon closed that door too. Despite being half asleep, Mark looked worried.

'What has happened?'

'Bryn has been attacked in prison.'

'Fucking hell!' Mark growled. 'They said he would be in isolation.'

'Obviously something went wrong.'

'Is he all right?'

'No. They think he has a head injury. A bad one.'

'What do you mean they think he has?'

'He's unconscious and unresponsive.'

'Where is he?'

'They have taken him to Walton.'

'Is he going to die?' Mark asked.

'They don't know yet,' Simon shrugged. 'Jacob is going to ring as soon as the doctors have assessed him.'

'Are you going to tell Mum and Dad?'

'Of course.' Simon frowned.

'I don't think we should, not yet,' Mark shook his head as he spoke. 'I don't think Mum could handle it. I think we should wait. They won't let us see him, will they?'

'No. They won't let us just walk in and visit him.'

'Then there's no point in going there, is there?'

'I know what you're saying but I'm not sure that we should keep it from them, Mark. What if something happens to him and we didn't give them chance to get there.'

'They will be in danger. We all will.'

'I think they have to weigh up the pros and cons themselves.'

'They can't, Simon, because they're parents. They can't make a rational decision while our Bryn is lying in a hospital bed. We have to think straight.'

'What if he dies, Mark? Can you imagine what they would think if we hadn't told them that he was critical?'

'Do you think being there at the hospital if he dies is going to do them good?'

'No but...'

'But what?' Mark pressed his point, his temper strained but under control. 'The last time they saw him he looked like he had done twelve rounds with Tyson. That was bad enough.'

'I know but what can we do?'

'If we rush them all the way back to Liverpool and they do let them see our Bryn, he'll be in a coma with tubes coming out of every hole.' Mark leaned on the worktop and filled a glass with water. He sipped it and shook his head. 'They can't take that. It will see them off.'

'What a bloody mess,' Simon said, inhaling loudly. He knew that Mark had a point.

'They don't need to see him in that state again.'

'I know what you're saying but you can't make that decision for them.'

'If you tell them now, they will be in that car before you have finished your sentence.'

'I know.' Simon sighed. 'What about Bryn? He'll be alone and frightened. What if we don't tell them and he doesn't get the chance to have his mother there with him at the end?'

'What would you do if it was you in that bed?'

'I wouldn't want her to see me like that, but Bryn is a boy. He will want his mum there, no doubt about it.'

'Look at what they have done so far.' Mark held up his hands and counted off on his fingers. 'The funeral wreaths, the graffiti at the hospital, slashing your tyres, a brick through the window and they burned down the gym!'

'We don't know that they burned down your gym.' Simon switched the kettle back on and reached for the coffee jar. He twisted the top off and put two spoonfuls of granules into a mug.

'You can kid yourself if you like,' Mark said pointing his finger. 'I know who set fire to the gym and so does everybody else. They got to Bryn in a prison. Just how hard do you think it would be to get to Mum and Dad in a hospital?'

'Once they hear about Bryn, we won't have an option.' The kettle boiled and Simon poured the steaming liquid into his cup. Black coffee wasn't his first choice, but he needed something, anything that might settle his nerves. The smell drifted to him making his mouth water.

'You could narrow down their options by taking the car.'

'What?' Simon asked confused.

'You could go to the hospital now. Gandalf could get you in to see Bryn.'

'I don't know about that, Mark.'

'It makes sense. Take the car and go and see how he is. I'll tell Mum and Dad what happened when they wake up. They might not wake up for hours anyway.'

'What if they do and I'm halfway there?'

'I'll tell them that you left in the middle of the night and that you'll let us know what has happened when you get there. They'll understand when I explain that there are no guarantees that we'd be allowed to see him anyway.'

'What if he dies, Mark, and I'm in Liverpool?'

'He won't.'

'What if he does?'

'He won't.'

'You have to consider the alternatives.'

'No, I don't.'

'Then I do.'

'If he dies at least they didn't have to sit there and wait for the door to open and a doctor to come in and say how fucking sorry he is.'

'I don't think Mum would agree.'

'They're better off here,' Mark hissed, tears in his eyes. 'Fucking hell! I don't know what to do for the best.'

'None of us knows what to do for the best.' Simon put his hand on his shoulder. 'If it makes you feel any better, Jacob said the same as you.'

'There you go, if Gandalf says don't tell them then I must be right.'

'What a fucking mess,' Simon said shaking his head.

'What are we going to do?'

'We're going to drive to the shops and buy some breakfast supplies, milk, bacon, bread, butter and when we come back, I'll call Jacob, we'll eat and make a decision what to do. Deal?'

'Deal. Let's go.'

'You need to go and put some pants on.' Simon gestured to Mark's lower half. Mark looked down and shrugged.

'smart-arse.' He half smiled and punched his brother on the arm. They laughed but their eyes showed the sadness inside.

CHAPTER 37

Eddie Farrell stepped out of the shower and grabbed a towel. It was the little things that reminded him of her death. Every day something hit him like a steel dart through the head. The towelling material felt flat and stiff, not soft and fluffy the way they used to before cancer called on their home. It didn't matter what conditioner the cleaner used, they weren't the same, one of life's subtle reminders that his loss was permanent. First his wife and now Anthony; both snatched from him with little to no warning. He blamed that fat fuck Paulie, he blamed Bryn Evans, he blamed the Karpovs, but mostly he blamed himself. Anthony's death had served as the catalyst to change. It was a wakeup call that he couldn't ignore. It was time to downsize and move on. He was going to move along to the next chapter of his life without the Karpovs. They were a huge outfit but that was their biggest problem. The organisation was too big, too slow and spread too thin. Victor Karpov was a dinosaur but he was getting old and his successors were not as focused as he was. To Victor, the Karpov dynasty had been carved from flesh and fed on the blood of the men who had died to protect it. It was a legacy that those who bore the name Karpov would carry with them for generations to come. The Karpovs' ancestry was born in the salt mines of the east, a poor family blighted by cold, starvation and disease. Now the Karpov name struck fear into its enemies from the decorated chambers of the State Duma to the back alleys of Europe's cities and beyond.

All that said, the sum total of the Karpovs' investment in his city was Nikolai Karpov. He was the token Karpov participant, backed up with the threat of the Karpov name and the reputation of its members. It wasn't deemed necessary to send dozens of its brotherhood to the city when making an alliance with a recognised outfit such as the Farrells was easier to manage. Their men stood out in the UK and their visibility became a liability. Taking on an established outfit and offering them a 'franchise' to use the Karpov name amounted to the same thing. It added up to higher profits and minimal risk. If things became violent, it wasn't their men that died, if the police raided, it wasn't their men who went to jail and if things were going along swimmingly they had no men to pay from their cut. Having the most soldiers stationed in a city was no longer necessary. Their network of assassins was the key to maintaining power. Anyone who stood in their way, threatened the organisation or became an informer was disappeared quickly and without fuss.

Eddie knew how they operated. He had been partners with them for years, but he was beginning to resent their presence. It was his operations that generated their income and his men that put their lives on the line week in and week out, yet the Karpovs took thirty per cent. Granted they had direct access to some very useful smuggling outfits on the continent but that didn't outweigh the negatives. They only sent their men in numbers when someone pressed the panic button. If Nikolai cried for help then a small army of Karpov men would be sent to the city and they wouldn't leave until order was restored. There were over fifty Karpov men in Manchester, where they had no affiliations with local outfits; twenty in Leeds, fifteen in Preston, fifty in Newcastle, and over one hundred south of Birmingham. They were only a few hours away. No one could match them for power or strength. He wanted shut of them but he would have to be clever. If he made an enemy of Victor Karpov then he would die very soon after. It was that simple. He wanted Nikolai gone, then he would be able to convince Victor that replacing him was unnecessary and inadvertently he had given him the ideal opportunity to do just that.

He towelled himself dry and sprayed deodorant under his arms. His tan was dark, his white bits milky and unhealthy looking. He looked in the mirror, breathed in and opened the door, padding along the corridor to his bedroom. Bob Marley was singing 'Exodus' on the radio and he hummed along to it as he opened his double wardrobe and picked out a dark blue Armani suit, white Versace shirt and dark tie to match. He wanted to look smart, professional and intelligent while he made arrangements for Anthony. Nobody was going to take him for a mug while he organised his funeral. Then he would have to do the rounds of meeting family members, close and distant and old friends, some in the business and some not. Meeting with Nikolai had not been on his agenda but he was curious what had gone wrong. Apart from that, the zombie shipment would net him a fortune once it was distributed. Of course he would make sure the Karpovs got their full share this time. It would be the last. He dressed and checked himself in the mirror, happy with what he saw. A splash of Armani Code made his skin sting for a second and he grimaced as he walked out of the bedroom door.

Eddie walked down the stairs and slipped his feet into polished, black brogues. He felt a draft on his neck and noticed that the front door was ajar. It creaked and opened slightly as a breeze moved it. Eddie walked over and opened it, looking around the garden quickly before closing it once more. Junior was forever leaving the bloody thing open when he went for a run around the grounds. He had lost count of how many times he had scolded his son for it. He picked up his wallet and keys from a marble coffee table and then headed into the kitchen for his mobile.

'Eddie Farrell!' a voice called out jovially. He turned around to see Eddie Junior sitting on a kitchen chair, his mouth gagged with duct tape, hands tied behind his back and a sawn-off shotgun to his head. His eyes were wide open; fear sparkled in the black pupils. 'You work for the cunt who stole my drugs and I want them back,' Tucker smiled evilly, his face was red and blistered in patches. The weeping bald patches on his scalp and tufts of frazzled hair gave him the appearance of a character from a Hollywood horror movie. He rammed the shotgun hard against Junior's ear. The jagged edge of the barrel ripped into the top of Junior's lobe; blood trickled down his neck. Eddie sensed people behind him blocking any escape and he heard a pump action shotgun being chambered. 'Now you need to answer two questions for me or Junior's brains will be sliding down your fridge, understand?'

'What do you want to know?'

'Simple, Eddie. Where are my drugs and where will I find Nikolai Karpov.'

CHAPTER 38

Braddick walked over to Google's desk which was next to the windows on the north side of Canning Place, overlooking the Pier Head. A giant white cruise ship was docked behind the Three Graces and a tidal wave of passengers was heading into the city centre. He sat on the edge of the desk opposite his sergeant and folded his arms.

'Look at all those tourists heading into town. The shops on Mathew Street will be booming today.'

'It is a good day to have a stall full of Beatles T-shirts.'

'Some of them will be wearing Beatles T-shirts for the rest of the voyage.'

Braddick chuckled. 'I wonder how many relatives get a T-shirt. Red one for Mum, white one for Dad, suitcases full of Beatles memorabilia sailing across the Atlantic.'

'I would rather have a fridge magnet.'

'Any day,' Braddick agreed. 'What is bothering you about Danny Cook, Google?'

Google picked up two photographs and handed them to Braddick. One showed an injection point on the left arm, the second a point on the right. 'How long did you say Danny Cook was using heroin?'

'From his teens he said.'

'So, we could assume that he would know what he was doing with the stuff.'

'I would say he was an expert.'

'Both of these injection marks were fresh. You can see where they bled here and here.' Red stains marked where blood had trickled down his forearm. 'I haven't met any users who would be able to inject and then be clear enough to inject a second time shortly afterwards.'

'You're right. That wouldn't happen.' Braddick looked at the photos again thoughtfully. 'What if he injected but missed a vein in one arm and then tried again in the other?'

'That's possible but then I looked at the number of empty wraps near the body.'

'Go on.'

'He couldn't have loaded that much heroin into one shot. That means that he injected and then gathered himself together and prepared a second hit.'

'I can't see how it could be done without help.'

'They were my thoughts exactly. If he wasn't our witness I wouldn't be questioning this but I find it difficult to ignore. What do you think?'

Braddick shrugged and looked at both pictures. 'I think that you're right. What does the tox-screen show?'

'Nobody asked for one.'

'Have one ordered.'

'Thanks, Guv. Do you think it is a coincidence?'

'Not a chance but proving it is anything but an accidental overdose will be difficult.'

'Well maybe there is a way.'

'How?' he frowned. 'What have you found?'

'I checked the list of items found at the scene and there are two syringes listed, one of them is used, one clean.'

'If someone else injected him then there may be prints?' Braddick nodded. He rubbed the stubble on his chin thoughtfully. 'Have you sent them to forensics?'

'I needed you to sign off the cost. It isn't strictly our case.'

'Get them sent off. Any problems come to me.'

'That's what I thought you would say but I wanted to check with you.'

'Even if we find a print we couldn't prove much but at least we'll know what happened to him. Good work,' Braddick patted his shoulder as he walked away.

DI Steff Cain stepped out of the lift. Her face lit up when she saw him. 'Hey,' she said walking towards him. 'I've just heard about your witness. That's a shitty break.'

'It helps Tucker but we'll nail the bastard,' Braddick said without stopping. He didn't have time to chat. 'I'll talk to you later.'

His thoughts were on Joseph Tucker. He had a lot to answer for. The more Braddick found out about him the more he despised him. He despised him and people like him. They were bullies. He would get what was coming to him. They always did eventually. The last few days he had become reckless and that would be his downfall. He had crossed too many lines and put himself and his organisation under the spotlight. People feared him but when he was locked up behind bars no one on the outside would fear him anymore. After a while, even his friends and family would stop defending him; most of them would stop visiting completely, their own busy lives the priority. They always did. Braddick had seen it a dozen times. Tucker was a brutal killer, nothing more and nothing less yet people looked at him in awe. Reputation and wealth counted for a lot in criminal circles, no matter how it was acquired. It seemed that the world loved outlaws and gangsters from Robin Hood to the Krays.

Braddick hated the films that glorified gangsters. He had lost count of how many versions of the Kray twins' story had been made, each one more graphic with better actors and a bigger budget than the last and yet people flocked to see them. He couldn't see the attraction. Most people knew the story, had read a book about them, seen at least one documentary about them and probably one film of their life and yet they would watch the newest version without question. He didn't see the fascination with the life of violent criminals. Did people wish they could be like that in another life or did they think the outcome would be different in the latest version where everybody lives happily ever after? Gangsters made a living bullying the weak and killed those who wouldn't be bullied; all for their personal wealth. To Braddick they were murderers and nothing more and he was an advocate for the death penalty. Murder was murder in the eyes of the law but not all killing was murder to Braddick. Shooting the enemy during a war wasn't murder. Executing a child killer or murder rapist in a Texas jail wasn't murder. He applauded it. Dropping a drone on a car full of terrorists in Iraq wasn't murder, in fact it was something to celebrate but murder for greed he couldn't abide. Tucker, Eddie Farrell and the Karpovs were greedy men prepared to kill for money. That was murder. Killing for sex or just for kicks, that was murder. Killing Karin and Cookie because they were witnesses, that was murder. He knew that they would find Tucker sooner rather than later and he knew that they would have enough to put him away for good; the problem was that he seemed to be on a mission to self-destruct and he didn't care who he took with him along the way. He thought about Cookie and his final list of belongings. His syringes were his valuables, more precious than jewels in his world. He thought about that list and ran his fingers over his stubble. Karin Range had a short list of items found at the scene too; he knew because he had asked for it. He had asked for it and looked at it and then put it away somewhere, its contents of no consequence to him back then. He thought that maybe he should have looked harder.

CHAPTER 39

Harry Bedford watched a steady stream of people come and go. The Spar shop attracted the tourists, the smaller independent Trearddur Stores was patronised by the locals. He could tell the difference by the regional identifiers on their number plates. The locals mostly had plates with 'C' for Cymru. Older cars sold on Anglesey had plates ending in 'EY'. Anything marked 'M' denoted Manchester and Merseyside. He was focusing on those. The other obvious difference was that most of the tourists donned sunglasses despite the gloomy weather and the vast majority of holidaying males wore cargo shorts even though the wind threatened to tear the flesh from their shins. The locals were dressed appropriately for the weather being well aware that they lived on an exposed rock in the Irish Sea.

His attention was drawn to a dark BMW as it drove by him. It indicated left and stopped outside the Spar shop, his theory about tourists gaining more credibility. The number plate was marked Merseyside. Two young males climbed out of the vehicle and headed into the shop. Ten minutes later they reappeared and piled four carrier bags into the boot. Harry could see that one of the bags was full of beer. He checked Bryn's Facebook page and scrolled through the photos. The younger man was there pictured in a boxing ring, a gym and at home with family and friends.

'Gotcha,' Harry said as he started the engine. He checked both ways and then turned his Volvo around to face in the direction that the Evans brothers had come from. A Range Rover driver hooted his horn in protest at his manoeuvre. The driver opened his window and leaned out to flick the V-sign. Harry felt a flush of anger and opened his window. 'What the fuck is your problem?' he shouted across the road.

'You're my problem,' the driver shouted back pointing his finger. 'I don't know where you're from but in Wales we use our indicators to let other drivers know where we are going. It's a simple concept. You should give it a try to take it with you when you fuck off home.'

'Fuck you!' Harry flicked the finger unable to think of an intelligent answer. He leaned his head out of the window, his face red with anger. He had never been good at holding his tongue. The Range Rover drove off in the opposite direction, its driver chuckling to himself as he flicked the V-sign again. Harry wanted to follow him and knock him on his arse but he didn't have the time. As he looked over his shoulder, the dark BMW pulled alongside to allow another car to pass. The passenger looked at him, their eyes meeting for a second. Harry found it hard to break eye contact despite the need to be discreet. The vehicle moved on and indicated left to follow the coast road. Harry had driven that way the night before but it had been dark then. He put the Volvo into first gear and pulled out to follow them.

A deafening blast came from behind him as another horn made him jump. 'For fuck's sake!' he moaned to himself. He hadn't indicated again. Looking in the rear-view mirror he saw the grill of a dark Mercedes. Harry replied to the horn with a blast on his own and flicked the finger in the mirror. As the Evans brothers turned left, the noise attracted the attention of the passenger and he looked back to see what was happening. Their eyes met for the second time. Harry drove on and followed the BMW allowing another car to pull in between them. They drove slowly by the crescent shaped beach, dog walkers and crazy windsurfers enjoying the bracing wind. Harry slowed down as they approached the hotel, the car in front of him indicating to turn right into the access road. He kept his eye on the BMW as it navigated the cliff bends at a casual pace. Waves crashed against the rocks, showering the road with white foam. He began to think that the men were taking a sightseeing drive when it indicated to turn left into a walled cottage. He thumped the steering wheel in delight and put his foot on the accelerator, speeding up as he drove past the driveway. He looked straight ahead showing no interest in them.

Mark Evans looked over his shoulder as the Volvo pulled away. He had an uneasy feeling about it.

'Did you see the Volvo behind us?' he asked Simon.

'The bloke with road rage?'

'Yes.'

'What about him?'

'I don't know. There was something about him that made me nervous.'

'Like what?'

'I don't know, just something in his eyes.'

'No one could know that we are here. Only Jacob and the detective know where we are.'

'All the same he made me nervous. I think I'm just on edge. I might take a run along the rocks while you cook breakfast. It might clear my head.'

'I'm hoping that Mum and Dad aren't up,' Simon said checking his phone. He shook his head and sighed.

'Nothing from Jacob yet?'

'Not yet.'

'I suppose no news is good news,' Mark said. Simon nodded and smiled but didn't believe a word of it.

CHAPTER 40

Bryn was taken from the ambulance into the Walton neurology department. The paramedics and a prison warden stood by his trolley as a surgical team gathered for his initial assessment following a CT scan. Jacob Graff had arrived shortly after he had come back from his scan and was invited into the room as his brief and to represent his family.

'This is Bryn Evans, he was sent for a CT scan,' the consultant began. 'He has facial trauma, some of which is historic. He was treated at the Royal yesterday after an assault and released into custody late last night. We have requested that their records are sent over immediately.'

'They have arrived,' a male nurse said from the back of the huddle.

'Thank you. He was attacked again this morning in his cell. He has a fractured cheekbone, broken teeth in the right upper and lower jaw, a broken ethmoid and bruising to the nose. Most concerning is a laceration to the back of the skull and there are clear signs of a subarachnoid haemorrhage. He is unresponsive and has been unconscious for nearly three hours. There are symptoms of secondary cerebral ischaemia and we've administered nimodipine for the bleeding and phenytoin for the fits. Neither of which is having any effect, the bleed is worsening so we need to go in and clip it and we need to do it now.' The surgeon turned to Jacob. 'We need to gain permission from his parents or guardian and we need it quickly or he will die.'

'Okay,' Jacob said concerned. The consultant starred at Jacob's bruised face and nose with interest. 'Pardon me for my ignorance but what do you need permission to do exactly?'

'We need to carry out a craniotomy. I need to cut a small flap in the back of his skull and clip the damaged blood vessel in the brain to stop it from bleeding. Without the procedure his brain could be damaged irreparably at best and he will probably die.'

'Thank you, doctor,' Jacob said taking his mobile from his pocket. 'I will make the call for you now.'

'We need adrenalin!' a female doctor called. 'We have asystole!'

Jacob looked at the consultant, confused and concerned. 'What does that mean?'

'The heart monitor has flat lined,' the consultant said moving away quickly. 'His heart has stopped beating…'

CHAPTER 41

Eddie Farrell looked over his shoulder. Tommy Tucker was aiming a pump action shotgun at the back of his head. Tucker's face was blistered, one ear blackened and burnt. Behind him stood three bruisers who looked like they'd been under the grill too long.

'Seeing as though you're pointing a shotgun at my son's head,' Eddie said, pulling out a chair from under the table. He sat down and steepled his hands together, elbows on the table. 'I'll forgo the introductions. You know who we are so I'm assuming that you're the Tucker brothers?'

'Correct,' Joe sneered.

'We've never met but I've heard a lot about you.' Eddie looked into his son's eyes and tried to remain calm. He could see fear in Junior's expression; beads of sweat formed at his temple and ran down his face.

'I'm not here to have you blow smoke up my arse or to swap war stories, Farrell,' Tucker said with a shrug. 'You and the Russian cunt that you work for stole my shipment.'

'That isn't true,' Eddie said calmly.

'Oh, it is true.'

'I had nothing to do with it.'

'You must think I'm a fucking mug?' he pushed the barrels into the flesh of Junior's ear causing more blood to trickle down his neck. Junior grimaced in pain.

'I was at your chop shop last night. My container is there but my drugs aren't.'

'Let's get things straight right from the get go,' Eddie said calmly despite his heart trying to punch a hole in his ribcage. 'Number one, that unit belongs to a company owned by a fictitious company set up by the Karpovs. I have moved a few Mercedes a week from there as a front for them,' Eddie paused and counted on his fingers. 'Number two, I've been in Thailand for six weeks,' Eddie said, leaning back. 'I had no idea what the Karpovs had planned. I wouldn't have gone along with it if I had. I don't fuck over my own kind.'

'Bollocks!' Tucker snarled. 'You've been up their arse for years. Since when does the great Eddie Farrell give a flying fuck about knocking over a shipment of drugs?'

'I don't give a fuck about taking someone's drugs, you're right. As long as it belongs to the Turks or the Albanians or better still, those Latvian jokers who think that they can walk into the country and set up business wherever they like. When have I ever given you or any of the local outfits any mither?'

'Oh, thanks for leaving us alone you're a local legend aren't you, Eddie?' Tucker snorted. 'Do you think any of us locals like you? You're about as popular as a hot poker up the arse. We put up with you being around because of those Russian cunts that you pander to. If it wasn't for them, you would have been buried years ago. You're past your sell-by date, Eddie and this little shit hasn't got the backbone to take over. I can smell the piss from here.' Tucker looked over Junior's shoulder and snorted. 'Have you pissed your pants, young Farrell?' Junior closed his eyes, embarrassed and frightened. Anger rose purple from his neck to his hairline. 'Enough talking bollocks, Eddie, you tried to shaft me, and I caught you out. Where are my drugs?'

Eddie Farrell looked down at his hands and bit his bottom lip as he thought about the situation. He shrugged and smiled.

'Have you lot bought a sunbed business and overdone the sessions?' he asked sarcastically.

Tucker frowned and put his arm around Junior's neck. He dragged him backwards, the chair scraping loudly on the tiles. A choking noise came from his Junior's throat. Tommy stepped forward and rammed the butt of his shotgun into Eddie's shoulder, winding him.

'Okay, okay, okay,' he gasped. Eddie half stood, palms down against the table. 'It was meant as a joke. Don't hurt him.'

'Don't hurt him?' Tucker said angrily. He was furious. 'Do you think that you can take the piss out of me?'

'No,' Eddie shook his head, his hands still raised. 'I was trying to lighten the mood, that's all. This is all very tense and uncomfortable. Seeing my son with a gun to his head is making me very nervous. He doesn't know anything about the shipment.'

'Maybe not but his head will explode when I pull this trigger. Where are my drugs?'

'I don't know,' Eddie said with a shake of his head. 'I don't know where Karpov has moved the drugs and that's the truth. I didn't land back in the country until yesterday. How could I know?'

'Bullshit!'

'Check my passport,' Eddie shrugged. 'It is in the drawer behind you. Check when I left the country and when I landed, and you will see that I couldn't have been involved in stealing your shipment. The Karpovs set this up without my knowledge.'

Tucker nodded to his brother and he walked over to the kitchen units and opened the drawer. He took the passport out and flicked through the pages. He passed it to Joe and aimed his shotgun at Junior while he checked the dates. 'He's telling the truth.'

'I told you,' Eddie shrugged and sat back. He folded his arms and tried to look relaxed. 'Now you know that I'm telling the truth can we talk business?'

'Are you taking the piss?' Tucker laughed sourly. He glared at Eddie with hate filled eyes. 'I would rather stick wasps up my arse than do business with you!'

'I have something that you want,' Eddie shrugged. 'And you could do something that would help me out of a tricky situation. We could both walk out of here better off than we are now.'

The Tuckers looked at each other for a moment. 'What are you talking about?'

'Do you know that my son Anthony was murdered?'

'I heard a rumour.' Tucker shrugged. 'Something to do with that fat fucker Paulie Williams I heard?'

'He was there.'

'Are you looking for a sympathy vote?'

'No.'

'Then what has that got to do with anything?'

'I intend to crucify the scumbag who killed my son and I intend to kill his family,' Eddie said folding his arms again. 'The Karpovs have made it clear to me that they won't be happy if I do?'

'Why not?' Tucker was suddenly curious.

'They like stability and they think that I might attract unwanted attention from the police and the press. Whatever their reasoning, we're going to sever ties one way or the other.' Eddie shrugged and sat forward, looking into Tucker's eyes. 'Now one way is that I cut ties myself and do as I please, in which case I'll be seen as an enemy by

Victor Karpov. That's a quick way into a box. The other way is somebody takes out Nikolai Karpov and I'm left in the clear, blameless and free to avenge my son.' Tucker licked his lips. 'I don't know where your drugs are, but I do know where Nikolai is and you can bet your life that he knows where they are.'

'How many men has he got with him?'

'His closest men are in Manchester.' Eddie shrugged. 'The only people protecting him right now are my men. I can give him to you, and he can give you your drugs. We all walk away with what we want.'

'Why would I trust you?'

'Because I've lost one son this week and you have a sawn-off shotgun to my other son's head' Eddie shrugged. 'It is in my interest to tell you the truth and help you to get your shipment back intact.'

'Don't trust him, Joe,' Tommy spoke. 'Give me half an hour with him and I'll make him squawk.'

'How can you make me tell you what I don't know?' Eddie half smiled. 'Karpov knows where they are, and he will be splitting up the shipment into smaller loads as we speak.'

'How do we know that he hasn't already moved it?' Tommy sneered.

'He needs my network in the city to distribute it and they don't do anything without my say so.'

'Don't listen to him,' Tommy growled.

'Will you shut up!' Tucker snapped. 'We don't have a lot of choice here. We need those drugs back.'

'You know this makes sense,' Eddie said looking at Tommy. 'I give you Nikolai Karpov. He gives you your drugs. I get the Karpovs off my back while I deal with business and Junior keeps his brains inside his head.'

'I think your father has just saved your life, young Farrell,' Tucker said into Junior's ear. 'Go and change your trousers. You stink of piss. Take him upstairs,' he ordered one of his men. 'You have a deal, Farrell but if you cross me, you and your son are dog meat.'

CHAPTER 42

Ade Burns looked at his computer. A map of the Shropshire Union Canal filled his screen. Steff Cain looked over his shoulder her perfume filling his nostrils. Ade couldn't remember her wearing perfume for work and his detective's brain computed that the perfume arrived just after Marcus Braddick did.

'Where is he then?' Cain moaned. 'I appreciate being kept in the loop but I want to hear it from the monkey not the organ grinder.'

Ade raised his eyebrows at Google, who turned away smiling. 'Organ grinder?' he repeated. 'That's not a phrase I would use in front of everyone in this building. Some people might be offended.'

'Especially that little brunette DC in Vice,' Google added. 'What's her name again?'

'Belinda,' Ade grinned.

'Now there is an organ grinder,' Google said taking off his glasses. 'Do you know that I heard she can...'

'I don't want to hear it!' Cain said sticking her fingers in her ears. 'Please just tell me what I need to know and let me get back to my own misogynists. You bloody men are all the same.'

Ade shrugged and pointed to the screen looking a little disappointed. 'The chop shop is here on this section of canal. South from here they could access the Bridgewater Canal here or the Trent and Mersey Canal here. If they stay on this route then they could be anywhere on the Cheshire Ring which is here.' He looked up at her blank face. She looked back at him and shrugged.

'So you're telling me that there could be a shipment of drugs on a canal boat, which could be on that canal or it could be on that canal or it could even be on this canal, which is basically a big circle around Cheshire?' she frowned. 'How much canal is that?'

'That stretch is sixty miles and that stretch is about ninety,' Ade smiled sarcastically.

'So there could be some drugs somewhere on these one hundred and fifty miles of waterways which just happen to run through some of the most unpopulated areas of Britain, none of which are in my jurisdiction?'

'In a nutshell.'

'Tell Braddick thanks very much,' Cain said, walking off in a huff.

'Will do,' Ade called after her. 'Thanks for your time!'

'Fuck you, Ade,' she said flicking him her middle finger.

'In my dreams,' Ade muttered beneath his breath.

'I think she wanted something more specific,' Google said dryly.

'The DI told me to keep her in the loop,' he said looking at the map and scribbling some notes. 'She can consider herself 'looped'.' He picked up the telephone and dialled the switchboard asking to be put through to the Transport Police at Ellesmere Port. There might be one hundred and fifty miles of canal to look at but what Cain hadn't waited for him to say was that they knew three boats had sailed south on the same day. That very important point narrowed down the search area to forty miles. The area helicopter could cover a detailed search of an area like that in no time at all. All he needed to know was if there were any places where you could hide a barge along the way, boatyards, mills and the like. If she hadn't been such a bitch, preoccupied with where Braddick was, he might have told her.

CHAPTER 43

Eddie Farrell watched as Tommy Tucker bundled Junior down the stairs. He had been dressed in grey tracksuit pants. Three stairs from the bottom, Tommy kicked him in the small of the back. With his hands tied behind him Junior lost his balance and tumbled head over heels landing heavily on his back. He struggled violently against his bindings, his face turning red with anger. Tommy grabbed his clothes and pulled him up by the scruff of the neck.

'I'm warning you now that if your brother lays another hand on my son, the deal is off and you can whistle for your drugs,' Eddie pointed his index finger angrily. 'I don't think you would be so brave if he was untied.' Tommy glared at him. 'Go ahead and untie him and see what you're made of, Tommy.'

'Fuck you, Farrell,' Tommy grunted, slapping Junior across the face. 'We're in charge here!' Junior struggled harder. Tears of frustration ran from his eyes. 'If I had my way you would both be dead.'

'Calm down, Junior,' he said to his son. 'He's as thick as pig shit but he knows that you would break him in half. Struggling will turn him on.'

'Shut up, both of you!' Tucker shouted. 'Let's get this done then we can go our separate ways.'

'That suits me fine,' Eddie said locking eyes with Tommy.

'How do you propose we do this?' Tucker asked turning to Eddie.

'I need to call Nikolai,' Eddie said staring hard into Tommy's eyes. He decided right there that he was going to slit his throat. 'I need to know where he is and arrange to meet him.'

'Do it.' Tucker snapped.

'What if he warns him?' Tommy said angrily. 'I don't know why you're trusting this tosser!'

'I've told you to shut up,' Tucker warned.

'Yes, like you did at the chop shop when I said it might be a trap,' Tommy sniped. 'Who is the brain surgeon now, eh?'

'Shut up!' Tucker said banging his fist on the kitchen table. 'I've heard enough of your bitching.' He looked at Eddie and nodded. 'Make the call and if I get a sniff that you're tipping him off then Junior loses his bollocks before I blow his head off.' Eddie took his mobile from his pocket. 'Put it on speaker.'

Eddie switched it onto speaker and speed dialled Nikolai. The call was answered but nobody spoke. 'Bpar,' Eddie said quickly.

'Bpar,' Nikolai replied. 'How are you, Eddie?' the Tuckers looked at him suspiciously. 'I'm so sorry to hear about your son. Victor sends his condolences.'

'Please thank Victor on my behalf,' Eddie said genuinely. 'I need to talk to you in person,' he paused. 'Today if possible.'

'No problem,' Nikolai sounded affable. 'I'll be at the mill about three o'clock this afternoon?'

'Perfect,' Eddie nodded at Tucker. 'I'll see you later.'

'Okay, Eddie. See you later.'

The call clicked off and Eddie put the phone back into his inside pocket. 'I'll take your phone,' Tucker said beckoning with his index finger. 'Where is this mill he was talking about?'

'Oh, come on, Tucker.' Eddie tilted his head to one side and frowned. 'Do you think that I'm stupid?' he shook his head. 'If I give you the mill then you don't need me anymore. We play this my way now or not at all.'

'Fuck that!' Tommy snarled.

'I'll tell you how we're going to do this, Farrell.' Tucker wagged his finger. 'first, slide that phone over here.' Eddie did as he was asked. Tucker picked it up and checked the last number dialled. It was listed as Bpar. The number didn't show in the call history but there were only a few records stored. Eddie deleted his history every day. 'Okay, Junior stays here with Grunt.' Tucker gestured to a mountain who looked like he ate six-inch nails for breakfast. Eddie and Junior exchanged glances. Neither looked happy at the proposal. 'How far away is this mill?'

'Forty minutes.' Eddie shrugged.

'We'll leave here at two o'clock. The meeting is at three. If you do not hear from me by half three you shoot Junior in the bollocks, leave him for half an hour and then shoot him twice in the chest and twice in the head, understand?' Grunt nodded. Tommy pushed Junior across the kitchen to Grunt. Grunt pushed him down into the chair that he had been sat in earlier. Junior looked pale, exhausted from the fear and the adrenalin. 'You think that sounds fair enough, Eddie?'

'Not really,' he said, shaking his head.

'What is the problem?'

'I leave here in my car and you follow me in your vehicles with Junior,' Eddie sounded confident although he didn't feel it. 'Some of my men will be at the mill. Nikolai likes to have a few of them around. When we get there I will go in and order my men to take Nikolai captive. When it is done, I will exchange him for Junior, you take Nikolai. Junior, my men and I drive away and leave you to find out where your shipment is.'

'Junior stays here,' Tommy snapped.

'No chance,' Eddie shook his head. He made eye contact with Tucker. 'Either we swap Nikolai for Junior at the mill or this doesn't work.'

'Do you think the drugs will be at this mill?'

'Your guess is as good as mine but one thing is for sure and that is that Nikolai knows where they are.'

'How many men do you have at the mill?'

'I'm not sure but Nikolai usually has two or three with him. He may have more there if the shipment is there, to protect it.'

'What about the rest of our men?' Tommy asked. He was sceptical at best. 'We should tell them to meet us there.'

'We don't know where there is yet, brain box!' Tucker thought about it for a moment. 'Numbers won't matter while we have Junior and when we haven't got Junior then we'll have a Karpov, which is even better. We'll tell the men to stay at the factory.'

'It is simplicity itself and we all get what we want.' Eddie agreed.

'He's right,' Tucker nodded reluctantly. 'Okay. You have your plan. Deviate from it for one second and Junior...'

'I get the message,' Eddie interrupted. 'There is no reason to repeat it.'

CHAPTER 44

Mark Evans walked out of the back door of the cottage and waded through knee high grass across the back garden to an arched gateway in the wall. The stone wall had been rendered and painted white decades ago but the elements had taken their toll. The latch was rusty and the two bolts were stiff when he tried to slide them back but they gave way eventually. He opened the gate, hinges squealing and stepped through onto a rocky headland behind the cottage. The sound of the waves became louder, reassuring and soothing. There was an edge in the air different to the city. It was fresh and exhilarating. To the left he could see the *Scooby-Doo* house in the distance and to the right the headland gave way to a series of rocky coves and small beaches before it climbed upwards to The Range where the cliffs were high and steep. He chose to run to his right, away from civilisation as sparse as it was. The grass was spongy beneath his feet, the exposed rocks slippy with moss. He couldn't run at full pace but that wasn't the point anyway. He wasn't trying to improve his fitness; he was searching for the peace and tranquillity that the sound of the waves crashing on the rocks could bring. Something that could take the worries away, make them vanish for a while. He could taste the salt in the air as he ran, the sound of the gulls calling echoed above him. The path was narrow but well-worn by tourists and it followed the coastline just metres from the edge. As he made progress along the jagged coves, he could see the road that hugged the coastline to his right.

Less than five minutes on he spotted the shape of a Volvo parked; two wheels on the narrow kerb, two wheels on the road. Between him and the road a field of waist high grasses, red fescue and reeds moved with the wind. As he neared the crest of a hill he saw the figure of man standing in the grass. He seemed to be watching the cottage through binoculars. The man was less than one hundred yards away from the path, yet he didn't flinch as Mark approached. Mark stopped and looked at him unsure what to do. Was he watching the cottage or was he innocently looking in that direction? Mark looked back to see which direction he was looking. There was no doubt that he was looking at the cottage. He didn't want to be paranoid, but the events of the previous day had unsettled him. The coastline was a Mecca for birdwatchers and wave watchers alike; he could be watching them, or he could be an innocent tourist enjoying the views. The watcher lowered his binoculars and spotted Mark. He raised them again and pointed them directly at him. Mark frowned and shook his head in disbelief, still unsure what he was up to. The watcher raised his right hand and waved at him.

'What the fucking hell is that all about?' Mark mumbled to himself. The watcher smiled and turned away, walking towards his car. Mark didn't know what to do or what to think. Half of him thought the man was stalking them the other half thought that he was inventing ghosts in his mind. No one could know where they were could they? *But what if they do?*

Mark watched as the man waded through the grasses and reached the Volvo. He opened the door, took one last look in the direction of the cottage and then he looked at Mark and smiled. Mark didn't react; his expression was confused and impassive. The watcher climbed into the Volvo and started the engine. As he drove away up the hill towards The Range he beeped the horn as the vehicle disappeared behind the low hawthorn hedges that lined the road. Mark took out his mobile and checked for messages from Simon. The screen was blank and he didn't have a signal. He felt tense and anxious as he pulled up his hood and began to run. The sound of the waves soothed him as he jogged along the coast and he picked up a narrow pathway that took him along the tops of the rocky outcrops, zigzagging up and down just metres above the waves. After five minutes he reached a stile in a dry stone wall. He climbed over it, the grass much longer on the other side and he put his head down and followed the path which was no more than a foot wide. His breathing had become faster but steady and the muscles in his legs were beginning to burn. Long grass grew from both sides of the path, threatening to claim it back for Mother Nature. It made it difficult to see where to tread but he picked his footing carefully and pushed on. He put his head down against the wind and ran as fast as he dared. The headland became hillier and the path weaved up the incline leading up to the wide grassy fields that made up The Range. His lungs were feeling the burn and he felt the sweat running down his back as he took on the long sloping climb.

Something in the field caught his eye but his brain didn't calculate the image at first. It was a subtle movement that drew his attention from the path in front of him. He thought he had seen a man with binoculars; thought he saw him smiling then wave. His brain wasn't focused on his footing as his shin hit a length of rusty barbed wire that had been laid across the path, hidden by the long grass. The wire caught around his right leg, cutting and ripping the skin. The force of the impact catapulted the wire and it whipped around the left leg too. The barbs dug deep into his flesh as he stumbled from the path. He heard the wire whistle through the air as it whipped around his limbs. Mark couldn't stop himself as he fell headlong onto the exposed mossy rock. He toppled headlong, carried onwards by his momentum, his bodyweight propelling him forward. He clawed at the slippery rocks but found no purchase as he began to slip towards the edge. Mark turned onto his front and clawed at the rocks but it didn't halt the slide. He heard the waves below him as his legs went over the edge and then he had the sense of flying, falling and spinning in the air as he plummeted towards the rocks below.

CHAPTER 45

Eddie checked that the people carrier was behind him as he indicated left into a narrow tree-lined lane that led to the canal and the mill. The mill had once been a dry dock for barge repairs but the boatyard that owned it had gone bust in the nineties. The main structure was hidden by the tree canopy and the brick wharf where barges were once loaded and unloaded was only visible from the canal itself. Built from sandstone it blended into the canal bank, the perfect bolthole with access from the roads and the waterways. Opening a series of heavy wooden-lock gates allowed barges to sail inside where they could shelter from the elements while repairs were made; or since the Karpovs acquired it, shipments of drugs could be unloaded and transferred to the roads.

Eddie slowed down as the lane weaved through the woods which were mostly coniferous. He spotted the reddish bricks of the mill and counted two vehicles parked outside. Tucker's people carrier pulled over and stopped as arranged. Tucker had given Eddie ten minutes to get inside and secure Nikolai Karpov. Junior's life depended on him hitting that deadline. Eddie trundled into the clearing which acted as a car park and parked next to a black Shogun. He knew that the Karpovs favoured the Mitsubishi. Turning off the engine, he climbed out and headed to the entrance. The door was unlocked and unguarded, which was odd. He lifted a large iron latch and pushed the door open. Dead leaves were piled behind it making it difficult to open fully. He slipped inside and walked down four stone steps into the main body of the building. The roof was a series of vaulted chambers supported by sandstone columns. Five arched doorways allowed access for barges from the canal; each was closed with huge oak doors. The interior was lit by powerful portable tripod lights which cast shadows at the corners of the building. He stopped and listened. Only the sound of water dripping from the roof reached him.

'Nikolai!' he called out. His voice echoed from the cavernous ceilings. No one replied. He walked further into the building, the air colder and damper the further he went. 'Nikolai!' Again there was no reply. He had a bad feeling about what was going on. He was on a deadline, Junior at the end of a shotgun.

'Eddie,' Nikolai stepped from behind one of the columns. He looked towards the entrance behind him to see if anyone was following him. 'What is going on?'

'Thank God you played along when I called you.' Eddie sighed. 'I used the Bpar number like you said to if there was ever trouble, but it was so long ago when we discussed it that I didn't know if you would remember.'

'Planning for trouble is the first thing you should do, Eddie. Bpar means 'enemy' in Russian,' Nikolai nodded thoughtfully. 'When you dialled that number, I knew that you were in trouble immediately.'

'Thank you, anyway. I had a shotgun pointed at my head,' Eddie said as he approached him.

'Okay, what is the situation?'

'The Tuckers have my son in a people carrier outside. If I don't turn you over, they will kill him. I have ten minutes to go to the door and wave them in. Where are my men?'

'It is clear!' Nikolai called. Eddie's men made themselves visible. He nodded at them individually. 'Apologies for my caution but we didn't know who was going to walk through the door first.'

'I understand,' Eddie said looking at his men.

'We were sorry to hear about Anthony,' one of them said.

'Thanks,' Eddie said shaking his hand. 'But we don't have time for this, or I'll be burying both my sons.'

'What do you need me to do?' Nikolai asked. He didn't seem flustered by the situation.

'I need you to pretend that my men are holding you. I'll call the Tuckers in and we will exchange you for Junior. Once we have Junior, we'll shoot them.'

'How many of them are there?' Nikolai asked frowning.

'The Tuckers and three of their men,' Eddie shrugged. 'One of their men is huge. They call him Grunt. When I shoot him, you dive onto the floor and we'll kill them all.'

'Okay,' Nikolai nodded. 'I trust you, Eddie. Let's get your son back.' He paused to think. 'Break my nose.'

'What?'

'Punch me in the nose,' Nikolai said. 'The blood will make it look much more realistic.' Eddie nodded to his lieutenant and he jabbed the Russian with a straight punch snapping his head back. Blood began to flow from one nostril. 'Okay, that's better.'

'Give me a weapon.' Eddie tuned to his men. They handed him a nine-millimetre Glock 17. He checked that the magazine was full and chambered it. 'Right. We all know what to do?' They nodded that they did. 'Make sure that you're between the Tuckers and the door. When Nikolai hits the floor don't stop shooting until they have stopped breathing, got it?'

'Got it.'

Eddie stuffed the Glock into his belt behind his back and climbed the stairs. He slipped through the door and walked towards the people carrier. The overhanging trees cast shadows on the windscreen, and he couldn't see inside. The lane was lined with thick bushes and he couldn't see if anyone was hiding behind them. Eddie edged closer to the vehicle and he cursed beneath his breath when he saw that it was empty. Tucker was smarter than he had given him credit for.

CHAPTER 46

Mark hit a rocky protrusion on the cliff face and bounced off it. It sent him spinning in the air before he landed flat on his back on the rocks below. The wind was knocked from his lungs and his left leg felt broken. He tried to move but a bolt of pain ripped through his abdomen, even breathing was difficult. The sound of a wave crashing on the rock filled his senses and he was hit by a wall of sea water. It engulfed him, filling his ears and nose with stinging saltwater, choking him as it ran down his throat. The cold snatched his breath away and numbed his limbs and its awesome power lifted him up and then dumped him like a twig as it ebbed. As the water receded, Mark sucked air deep into his lungs. He scrambled with his fingers trying to find a handhold to pull himself up away from the next wave. His nails were ripped and cracked against the rocks and sharp limpets. The next wave hit him and he held his breath as it tossed him against the rocks like a piece of driftwood. His muscles cramped with the cold as the wave tried to drag him back beneath the surface. It took all his strength to cling to a rock with both hands and as the water receded again, he began to scream for help.

'Help me! Help!' he called and then another wall of water engulfed him.

CHAPTER 47

Eddie turned and ran back to the entrance, turning sideways to slip through the door. He scraped his shin on the doorframe and cursed loudly as he reached the steps. His feet slipped as he reached the top step and he had to stop dead to prevent himself from falling flat on his face. He gathered himself and ran down them quickly. When he reached the bottom he saw the Tuckers fronting up his men. The Tuckers had their weapons trained on Junior and his men had their guns trained on them. It seemed that no one wanted to aim at Nikolai.

'What the fuck are you doing?' Eddie shouted at the Tuckers. 'We had a deal!'

'I thought that I would make sure that you were sticking to your side of the bargain,' Tucker smiled coldly. He stared at Nikolai and grinned. 'Did that hurt?' he said gesturing to his bloody nose. Nikolai stared at the floor, looking frightened and dejected. He was playing his part well. 'You had better get used to the pain because you're going to wish that you had never been born when I get hold of you.'

'Let's get this done!' Eddie said, standing beside Nikolai. He shoved him forward a few steps. 'Junior for Karpov as we agreed.'

Tucker nodded and pushed Junior forward harder than was necessary. He fell to his knees. Eddie bit his lip and pushed Nikolai again. 'Walk forward,' he ordered him. The Russian glanced in his direction unsure but he did as he was told. Eddie grabbed Junior up to his feet and dragged him back to where his men were standing. 'Cut him loose!' His men removed the gag and Junior gasped in air like he had never tasted it before.

'I'm going to fucking kill them!' he gasped. He rubbed his wrists and turned to face the Tuckers. They stepped forward and grabbed Nikolai roughly.

'At last,' Tucker said driving the butt of his sawn-off into Nikolai's midriff. Nikolai fell doubled over, choking for breath. He looked up and waited for Eddie to start shooting but he didn't. 'Piss off, Farrell!' he said pointing the shotgun at Eddie. 'You've got what you want now leave us to it. I'm sick of looking at your smug face.'

'We're going,' Eddie said gesturing to his men to move towards the entrance. They looked confused but did as they were told. He looked at Nikolai and shrugged. 'Sorry Nikolai but as you once told me, business is business.' The Russian sneered and looked at the floor. He shook his head and spat at Eddie's feet. Tucker kicked him in the ribs and he fell onto his side gasping for air.

'We're done for now but I'm sure we'll cross paths again,' Tucker said with a crazy grin on his face. 'I'm going to cut bits off this piece of shit until he tells me where my drugs are.' Tucker began to shake violently, his eyes wide, mouth open and hanging loose. A croaking noise came from his throat. And the crackle of electricity filled the air. Eddie heard the unrecognisable spitting sound of a muzzled nine-millimetre. Then a second joined the cacophony of death. His men began to fall around him, clutching at bullet wounds, screaming and dying. Blood and brains splattered his cheek as his lieutenant's head exploded. He turned, startled and confused. Darts hit his chest, piercing his skin and fifty thousand volts flowed through his nervous system stopping him in his tracks. He remembered hearing Junior cry out and he watched in awe as three of Tucker's men were shot within seconds of each other. The silenced weapons continued to spit death as his consciousness slipped away and darkness took him.

CHAPTER 48

Simon Evans looked at his watch and thought about calling Jacob but decided against it. He would call when there was something to say. His parents were snoring gently, exhausted by the events of the last few hours. He opened the back door and looked outside. He could hear the waves crashing on the rocks beyond the garden gate. A gull cried overhead, and he looked up and watched it soar above him, hovering on a thermal unable to make progress against the wind. It seemed to hang in one position, squawking in protest. He walked across the unkempt lawn and looked at the gate. The paint was blistered and peeling, its hinges crusted with rust. Mark must have left it open. He stepped out onto the headland and enjoyed the views. Trearddur Bay was to the left, *Scooby-Doo* house dominating the left side of the vista. To his right was the beach, Ravenspoint rocks across the bay and the mountainous silhouettes of Snowdon in the distance. It was picture postcard beautiful. He looked to the right and heard a gull cry again. Looking up, he couldn't see the bird that called. Another cry carried on the wind, from further away this time. It sounded almost human, desperate and urgent. When the wind blew again the sound was gone, just a trick of the sea on the rocks making the acoustics warp. He shivered and turned back to the gate. A wave crashed below, louder than before. The tide was turning and coming in. He was about to close the gate behind him when he heard the cry on the wind once more. Something inside him tightened, making him ultra-aware. He held his breath and listened again. The wind blew and he heard it again, a cry for help carried on the breeze.

CHAPTER 49

When Eddie came around his limbs were numb. His mouth was dry and his head was aching. He remembered the last few minutes before he lost consciousness but couldn't make sense of it all. His chest felt tight and he tried to move but he was bound. He looked around and realised that he was strapped to an engine block. Junior was next to him on his left. He was on the adjacent side of the engine at a right angle to him. Looking over his other shoulder he saw Tucker, also strapped to the engine. They were sitting on the floor of the wharf, backs against the engine, feet sticking out in front of them. Tucker and Junior were gagged. He was about to call to Junior when a familiar voice spoke to him.

'Eddie, Eddie, Eddie,' the voice said tutting. Victor Karpov was standing at the edge of the canal, his back to him, his hands shoved inside his pockets against the cold. 'I'm so very disappointed.'

'Victor,' Eddie felt his mouth dry up completely. He licked his lips. 'I can explain. This isn't what it looks like.'

'Isn't it?' Victor turned and frowned. 'I think it is exactly what it looks like.'

'I can explain everything, Victor.'

'Perhaps you should explain to them,' Victor gestured with his head.

'This I have to hear,' a voice said from behind him.

'Me too,' another voice agreed.

'What?' Eddie whispered as Mikel and Yuri Karpov stepped into view. 'Mikel, Yuri!' he tried to sound excited while fighting the urge to vomit. 'It's great to see you! Victor was worried about you weren't you, Victor.' Victor stared at Eddie, disgust in his eyes. 'It is great to see you.'

'It is not great for you, Eddie. It is a huge surprise for you to see us,' Yuri said smiling coldly. 'You thought that we were at the bottom of the Andaman Sea being picked clean by sharks, didn't you?'

Eddie opened his mouth to speak but Victor raised his hand to silence him. He shook his head in disgust. 'Don't try to deny it, Eddie,' he said sternly. 'Luckily, a long tail boat carrying tourists heard them calling for help. Your Thai flunky couldn't keep his big mouth shut. He was easy to find and he spilled the truth before they'd laid a finger on him. You can't buy loyalty at any price, Eddie. You're living proof of that.'

'Your friend Rut did succumb to the sharks. I've seen the video. They cut his hands and feet off before they threw him in. That's how to do it,' Mikel said smiling.

'I don't know what you're talking about. Whatever the Thai said, he's lying,' Eddie shook his head vehemently. He was about to protest further when Yuri stepped closer and kicked him in the face. Eddie's head was rocked backwards hard against the engine block.

'You arranged for us to be left at sea surrounded by sharks,' Yuri said shaking his head. He pulled out his gun and aimed at Junior's left knee. 'I never did like you, Eddie,' he said as he pulled the trigger. Junior's body jerked violently and Eddie could hear his muffled screams, high-pitched and agonising. 'How does that feel, Eddie?'

'Don't, Yuri!' Eddie begged as he aimed the gun at Junior's other leg. Yuri fired and Junior jerked again. 'No, no, no, please don't!'

'That's what I thought as I watched your pet rat sailing off into the distance,' Mikel said. 'Nobody listened to me either.' Yuri fired another two bullets into Junior's shins. Junior began to shake, his right foot at right angles to his leg. 'It's not a very nice feeling is it?'

'Victor, please stop this!' Eddie gasped. He spat blood onto the floor. 'You have to believe me that I wouldn't turn on you like that!'

'I did believe you,' Victor nodded. 'We gave you the chance to prove yourself when we went along with the exchange. We have been here waiting to see what you would do. Nikolai went along with it because he convinced me that you wouldn't double-cross us but you did.'

'I never would have believed it until I saw it with my own eyes.' Nikolai said from behind him. He stepped into view. 'We thought that the Thai might have been acting for someone else and maybe lying to protect them. When Tucker took your boy we had the perfect opportunity to see for ourselves.'

'You didn't let me down, Eddie,' Yuri said. He kicked him in the face again. Eddie's nose split down the middle. His front teeth punctured his top lip, protruding through the skin. 'I told them that you were a fucking snake. Lift it up!' Yuri ordered someone behind them. A hoist rattled into life and the sound of heavy chains being pulled across stone drowned out everything else. The hoist lifted the engine block two metres into the air, four men, the Farrells and the Tuckers one each side dangled from it. Eddie looked at Junior. He was twitching and struggling against the straps, blood pouring from his ruined legs. Eddie could hear him fighting, his voice muffled by a gag and duct tape. The hoist rattled again and carried them over the edge of the wharf above the dirty brown water of the Shropshire Union Canal.

'Victor!' Eddie shouted as his legs kicked at fresh air. He knew what was coming. 'Let my son go!' he cried to the Russian. Victor shook his head.

'That's the worst part for you, Eddie,' the old man smiled. His thin lips were almost snakelike. 'Knowing that your treachery has robbed you of burying either of your sons will fill your last miserable minutes. When you take your last breath and your lungs fill with filthy water you will know that your son is dying next to you and that it is your fault.' He shook his head. Victor waved his hand to the operator. 'Drop it!'

The hoist released the block and it hurtled the few metres into the water. There was a whooshing sound as the water closed above it, ever expanding circles rippled out from the epicentre. The surface was disturbed by four sets of bubbles, fast and furious at first but they soon dwindled to just a few before they stopped altogether. Beneath the surface, Eddie Farrell cursed Bryn Evans, the cause of all his woes and he let go of his last breath. He thought about his empire, wiped from the face of the earth in a moment, his sons dead, his legacy gone with them and as he involuntarily inhaled the Shropshire Union Canal he hoped that he would see him again in hell.

CHAPTER 50

Simon jogged along the path his eyes fixed on the waves as they dashed the rocks below. His mind was focused on the intermittent cry that drifted on the wind. He kept going despite becoming breathless, the haunting sound driving him on. When he reached the stile he climbed over it, pausing on top of the wall to listen again. He could distinctly hear the word 'help' now. Jumping down into the long grass, Simon jogged along the narrow path which led up the hill. He could see that the rocks had risen steeply from the sea. The call came once again, nearer now but it was difficult to tell which direction it came from. Simon stepped off the path and saw drops of blood on the rocks and he followed them towards the edge. The wind was stronger at the edge and he felt unsteady on his feet as he leaned over and looked down.

Mark was perched on a ledge just above the waves, clinging on for his life. He called out again as another wave crashed over him, threatening to drag him beneath the swirling foam. Simon spotted him as the water ebbed.

'Mark!' he shouted. Mark looked up but daren't let go of the rock. 'Hold on!'

Simon looked around, desperate to find help. A hundred yards away on the tip of the rocky outcrop a red life ring stood attached to a metal cross. He remembered reading about them years before. 'The ring of confidence' they'd been called. Thirty-eight life rings positioned around the island. Simon sprinted as fast as he could, the wind numbing his face. He grabbed the ring and ran back, wrapping the rope around his waist. Mark pointed to the rocks. Simon followed his direction. He could see a ledge that ran at an angle down the rocks and headed for it. Sitting down, he began to edge along the ledge towards the waves. Mark clung on as the waves swamped him time after time. Each one took more of his strength, his body temperature dropping all the time.

Simon took the ring and threw it but the wind took it and it landed thirty metres from his brother. Mark shook his head, realising that there was no way that he could climb up the ledge even with help. His leg just couldn't support any weight at all.

'I can't climb,' Mark shouted. 'My leg is broken.'

'Shit!' Simon said pulling the life ring back up the rocks. He took out his mobile and checked the signal. He had one bar. Dialling the emergency services, the call connected and then clicked off. When he looked again his signal had gone. 'Shit, shit, shit!' He put his mobile against a loose stone and tied the life ring around a jagged spike of rock. He pointed to the sea behind Mark. Mark looked at where he was pointing, a confused look on his face. 'When I get to there, jump!' Mark frowned as Simon stood up and threw the ring into the sea. He waited for a wave to come, the swell making it deeper below him and then he jumped.

CHAPTER 51

The Karpovs stood and watched the bubbles until they stopped completely. Victor shook his head and turned to the others. 'I want more men brought into the city. Have them secure the services of Eddie's contacts and distribution network. If you meet any resistance, remove it immediately. If we do not get a grip on his part of the business quickly then someone else will. We move fast and we move hard, no mercy.'

'It won't take long, uncle. It should take a week or so,' Nikolai said nodding. 'The transition will be a smooth one. I'm familiar with all his contacts.'

'Good,' Victor smiled thinly. 'Where is the shipment of zombie?'

'It is hidden inside the petrol tanks of the Mercedes that we moved from the chop shop. They're on a car transporter heading for London as you requested.'

'London?' Yuri asked.

'We can get three times the money for it in the capital,' Victor said rubbing his hands together. 'If this drug is as good as they say it is then we will move it quickly and then we can decide if we want to conduct more business with our friends in Amsterdam.'

'Makes sense,' Mikel agreed. 'You're not sure about them, are you?'

'They did business with Tucker for years, but they stabbed him in the back for money,' Victor shrugged. 'If they turned on him then they would turn on anyone for the right price. I'm not sure that we need to take those kind of risks are you?'

'It depends how quickly the zombie sells and what mark-up we achieve,' Yuri said thoughtfully. 'It may well be worth the risk.'

'You're always reckless, Yuri.' Victor sighed. 'Risk is a young man's game. A certain amount of risk is acceptable when you're young and starting out trying to establish yourself in the business. We are more than established. This is the end of an era,' Victor said solemnly. 'Have your men clear up in here and then we'll meet up later on.' He hugged each one of his nephews in turn. 'Good work. Another dead fool who underestimated the Karpov family. Still, he is not the first and I fear that he won't be the last.'

CHAPTER 52

Simon and Mark clung to the ring as they doggy-paddled with the tide along the coast. The prevailing wind kept them close to the rocks and blew them along while they kicked and paddled to reach the sandy coves behind the cottage. Untying the life ring and swimming away from the rocks had taken fifteen minutes of freezing cold struggle but once they were away from the breakers, their progress was steady. They picked a direct line towards the shore where the rocks were much lower and easier to climb. After half an hour of frantic paddling, they reached the rocky shallows which led to the sand.

'What happened?' Simon asked panting. Mark looked tired, as if he could sleep in the water. He knew that he had to keep him talking. 'How did you fall off the path?'

'There was barbed wire across the path,' Mark stammered. His voice was hoarse, thick with phlegm and exhaustion.

'You always were clumsy.'

'Twat in the Volvo,' Mark stammered.

'What?'

'Twat in the Volvo.'

'What do you mean?'

'The twat in the Volvo put the barbed wire across the path,' he struggled to get his words out. He wasn't sure that the man had put the wire there but he felt that he had. It made sense in his mind. 'I'm fucking sure he did.'

'What makes you think that?'

'I saw him,' Mark grunted. 'Twat.'

'Keep kicking,' Simon said smiling inside. Mark was still strong enough to abuse someone. It meant that they could reach the shore. The wind and the tide took them swiftly along the coastline and they steered their float into the first cove that was shallow enough for them to climb out of.

'We'll be all right now,' Simon said as his feet touched the bottom. Mark looked grey with exposure. Simon put Mark's arm over his shoulder and took his weight. They stumbled up the sand and scrambled across the rocks onto the grassy headland behind the cottage. Simon wanted to get his mobile from the headland, but it would have to wait until Mark was safely in an ambulance and he had warmed up. His fingers and thumbs were numb with the cold. The wind blew making him colder still and then he noticed the black smoke and orange flames that were coming from behind the wall. The cottage was ablaze.

CHAPTER 53

Jacob Graff couldn't get an answer, but Bryn didn't have any time to spare. He watched as the doctors struggled to restart his heart. A female doctor was applying chest compressions while another pumped air into his lungs. A third doctor injected adrenalin as a fourth prepared to zap him. He called for everyone to stand clear and applied the paddles to his chest. Bryn bucked, his back leaving the bed but there was no response. After being hit three times with the defibrillator paddles, he finally responded but his condition was still critical.

'Have you got permission?' the consultant called over to him. His face was stern and demanding. There was only one answer.

'They want you to do whatever you need to do to save his life,' Jacob said with confidence in his lie. He was certain that was what his parents would have said had he managed to ask them. Simon had been desperate for information on Bryn's condition, yet he hadn't answered his calls. He couldn't help but wonder if the Farrells had found out where they were.

* * * *

Mark and Simon stumbled through the grass towards the back gate of the cottage. Black smoke spiralled skywards and the air was acrid with fumes. They looked in horror as the back door burned furiously. Orange flames licked at the roof tiles, jumping and flickering, setting alight the soffits and guttering. The bedroom window cracked loudly and then shattered into a hundred pieces.

'We can't get through there!' Simon shouted, pulling Mark with him. 'We'll have to go around.' Mark hobbled alongside him as they half ran half stumbled around the garden wall to the front of the cottage. They reached the gate and stopped. The front door was open, thick smoke billowed out of it. The curtains in the front room were ablaze and glowing embers floated skyward on the wind.

'I've called the fire brigade!' a man's voice came from behind them. They turned around to speak to him.

'How long will they be?' Simon asked in a panic.

'That's the twat in the Volvo!' Mark said astounded. Simon looked again but didn't hear what Mark had said.

'Wait here,' he shouted to Mark as he turned and ran towards the house. Mark glared at the Volvo driver and then tried to run after Simon, but his leg gave way beneath him and he fell to the floor scraping his hands on the pavement. He could only watch as Simon disappeared into the smoke-filled doorway.

'I hope your mum and dad are okay,' the Volvo driver, Harry Bedford, called as he drove away. Mark felt his blood boiling with frustration. He felt like screaming but he didn't have the energy. The sound of the front window splintering beneath the heat made him flinch. He had just about managed to get to his feet as the first fire engine arrived.

EPILOGUE

A month later

Barbara and Robert Evans were sitting in the visiting room at HMP Altcourse in the Reynoldstown unit. Bryn was still fragile but on the mend. His parents were beginning to relax after their traumatic experiences. Being pulled from their bed by Simon had saved their lives. The three of them had made it as far as the hallway before being overcome by the choking fumes. Firemen with breathing apparatus had finally pulled them out of the inferno. As each day without incident came and went, the family became less afraid. There had been no further contact or threats from the Farrell family since the fire. Detective Braddick had indicated that Farrell may have gone abroad to live following a disagreement with a Russian mob. It gave them some satisfaction to find out that their persecutor had been so frightened that he had left the country. When he found out, Robert had lifted a glass to karma. In fact, he had lifted a few when no one was watching.

'Jacob reckons that you'll be out by the end of the week!' Barbara said smiling. 'The CPS have decided not to press charges.'

'They don't do anything quickly do they?' his dad said.

'It will be so good to have you home although your bedroom has been tidier than it ever has.'

'Thanks, Mum, I'm glad you've missed me! I'm looking forward to seeing Alice,' Bryn said without thinking.

'The bloody dog is the first thing that you mention. Well thank you very much!' Robert joked. 'You do know that when they drilled a hole into your head all they found was sawdust.'

'Sorry. I didn't mean it like that.' Bryn laughed. 'Is Mark still staying at ours?'

'Yes, and he's a pain in the arse,' Robert said lowering his voice. 'Six weeks he has to keep the weight off that leg. Six bloody weeks! I'm glad there's only two weeks left,' he shook his head and winked. 'I've told Simon that the next time he falls into the sea he needs to throw him something that doesn't float.' He winked again. 'Like a brick, eh?'

'Robert Evans!' Barbara elbowed him in the ribs.

'What?' Robert said genuinely unaware of what he had said. 'What did I say?'

'If you don't know then you're stupider than I thought,' she frowned and shook her head. 'Silly man.'

'What did I say?' he complained to Bryn.

'Don't worry about it, Dad.' Bryn smiled, although the slip had not been lost on him. They couldn't spend the rest of their lives never saying the word, 'brick'. Things would get back to normal eventually although he knew that he would always be the kid who killed someone with a brick. Maybe in time people would forget. He would take one day at a time.

* * * *

Ade Burns was sitting in a pub on the dock road. The Navigation was one of his favourite haunts. He checked his watch and took a long drink from his third pint of bitter. His contact was over an hour late. He thought about leaving but didn't want to miss him. This was vitally important. He looked out of the window and saw a Volvo parking across the road. The side door opened, and Harry Bedford peered around it. He caught sight of Ade and waved as he made his way to the bar. Ade signalled that he didn't want another pint just yet. Harry made his way through the busy bar and sat down opposite him slipping his car keys into his jacket pocket.

'Sergeant Burns,' he said sarcastically. 'How are things, still fighting the forces of evil?'

'Daily, Harry.'

'You're fighting a losing battle.'

'It feels like that sometimes, I can tell you.'

'Well I might have some news that will cheer you up.'

'Come on,' Ade felt butterflies in his stomach. 'Don't fuck me about. What have you heard?'

'The Karpovs have moved onto Eddie's turf, lock, stock, and fucking barrels. They have taken over the lot. No one has seen or heard a whisper from him or Junior,' Harry leaned closer and whispered. 'Word has it that the Karpovs did the lot of them in, the Tuckers and the Farrells.'

'And who started this rumour?' Ade asked calmly. He didn't want to get excited just yet.

'This isn't just any rumour. From what I've heard, the Karpovs have cemented all Eddie's assets into their operation. Anyone that kicked up a fuss isn't around anymore. You remember Aussie Dave, don't you?'

'Of course, I do. I sent him down for a five stretch.'

'He's disappeared off the face of the planet. Apparently, he told Nikolai Karpov that he could go and fuck himself. He said that he wasn't working for them on the door at the Revolution Bar and that if he wasn't working for Eddie Farrell anymore then he was taking control of the door himself. He didn't turn up for work the next night and three fucking big Russians are controlling Revolution and two other bars next to it. They are quite openly admitting that they work for the Karpovs. No one has seen him since, just the same as Eddie Farrell.' He nudged Ade and leaned closer again. 'Word has it that the Russians are not denying taking Farrell and the Tuckers out of the game. One of their men told me that they were fish food.'

'He told you himself?'

'Scout's honour he did.'

'What do you think?'

'I think that if he was alive then we would have heard from the cunt.'

'That's what I'm thinking.'

'Not a week went by without him calling me to sort out one mess or another. I was getting sick of doing his dirty work. I'm glad the Karpovs have killed the cunt. I can get on with my life now and so can you.' Harry Bedford stood and finished his beer. 'I don't know what he had on you and I don't care, sergeant but I'll bet you'll join me for a pint to celebrate.'

'I don't mind if I do,' Ade said with a wry smile. His ten-year-old gambling debt was finally paid off. The Karpovs had done what he had wanted to do for years. He felt as if a massive weight had been lifted from his shoulders. Detective Sergeant Adrian Burns was enjoying work once more, the monkey on his back gone for good.

****

Marcus Braddick followed Boris Petrov from the City Gate bar and stayed behind him as he walked through an unlit car park and climbed the Roman Walls at the Eastgate entrance. Chester Cathedral towered in the darkness; its silhouette gigantic against the glowing street lights behind it. Petrov turned right towards Phoenix Tower and looked over his shoulder. Braddick ducked behind the stone steps and waited for him to walk on. Petrov was drunk, staggering from one side of the parapet to the other. Braddick had watched him drink himself into a stupor, patiently waiting for the opportunity to talk to him alone. When Cookie had died, it sparked an idea in his mind. He had traced the evidence box found with Karin and sure enough there had been a syringe in her belongings. It wasn't the one that they found in her arm; that had been destroyed in the fire. He had the syringe sent to him and signed off a forensic inspection under the guise of a case that they were working. Sure enough, a partial print was found, and a name had come back. Boris Petrov. He may have befriended her, and they may have used drugs together, but he intended to find out.

When he looked into Petrov, he found that he had a record and had served time for manslaughter. His records showed that during his time inside, he acquired a tattoo, a knife inside a pair of shackles. It was a badge of honour for someone who had killed while in prison on the order of their organisation. It marked Petrov as an assassin. That information, along with his print on the syringe found near Karin Range, told Braddick all he needed to know. Karin Range was a witness against a firm connected to the Karpovs. The fact that a known Russian assassin had left a print at her home couldn't be a coincidence in any way. He was a murderer and Karin had been murdered.

Braddick tiptoed up the steps and walked quietly behind Petrov. He was fifty metres behind him when Petrov entered an unlit stretch of wall before Phoenix Tower. Braddick began to jog, picking up the pace as he neared him. Petrov continued to stagger onwards unaware that he was being stalked. The wall was at its highest point when Braddick ran behind him; the canal and towpath some fifty feet below. Petrov heard him and turned to face him. He staggered backwards as Braddick approached him at speed. Petrov didn't know what the black man wanted but he didn't want to hang around to find out either. He steadied himself on the wall and then turned and ran as fast as his legs would carry him. Braddick was surprised by his turn of pace and he tripped and fell, ripping his jeans at the knee.

'Petrov!' Braddick shouted after him but he was away, his footsteps fading into the distance. He was much faster than he looked. Braddick got to his feet and ran after him. The Russian was drunk, weaving left and right but he made it to the Northgate steps which led down to the main road. He took the steps three at a time and reached the road as Braddick reached the top. Petrov looked up at his pursuer and grinned and then bolted across the road beneath the Northgate arch that led into the walled city. The driver of the Scania truck that hit him had no chance of stopping. Petrov's head burst open as it impacted the front of the truck, spraying the windscreen with pinkish grey goo. His body dropped beneath the wheels being further damaged beneath the crushing weight of the articulated lorry. His abdomen split spilling his intestines in the gutter. Braddick watched as the brake lights came on and the truck squealed to a stop. He looked at the Russian, a thin smile on his lips and then turned and walked back into the night.

A note from the author

I hope you have enjoyed Brick. If you have, please tell your friends! Third party endorsement is the key to the success of any author and makes a huge impact on awareness. Many thanks to my readers who share links and plug my series on various groups. Brick is the first in this series, which runs in tandem with The Anglesey Murders series and linked to the Detective Alec Ramsay series. You can download the rest of the series here;

https://www.amazon.co.uk/dp/B07X11C27N

If you have a second, please leave a few words on Amazon reviews. It would help me immensely;

https://www.amazon.co.uk/dp/B01J413O6M

Special thanks to avid crime reviewers, Sarah Hardy at;
https://bytheletterbookreviews.com
And Noelle Holten at;
http://crimebookjunkie.co.uk/
Their time and passion for books is incredible. Your reviews have been professional, exciting and inspirational, thank you.

On Facebook, a massive thanks to; Tracy Fenton and Sharon Bairden, and all the other admins at The Book Club. David Gilchrist at the UK Crime Book Club. Shell Baker at the Crime Book Club.

Thank you for your help. Your commitment to your groups is amazing and you bring much joy to your members, and introduce so many, to authors that they would otherwise never discover. The help that you give authors with promotions and book launches is much appreciated. Thank you.

Printed in Great Britain
by Amazon